The Temple Deliverance

(The Temple - Book 4)

Set in the present day, this fourth novel in The Temple series finds young church minister Helen Johnson and archaeologist Sam Cameron facing danger once more. In the grip of winter their struggle to ensure good triumphs over evil moves towards its dramatic conclusion.

Also by D.C. Macey

The Temple Legacy - published August 2015
The Temple Scroll - published August 2016
The Temple Covenant - published April 2018

.

The Temple Deliverance

(The Temple - Book 4)

Butcher & Cameron

D C MACEY

Published by Butcher & Cameron

ISBN-13: 978-0-9933458-9-0

Chapter 1

SATURDAY JANUARY 4TH

As a senior priest and the personal assistant to Bishop Ignatius, the patriarch's right hand, Iskinder Anibesa had a clear and comfortable vision of his life and role. He normally felt good about himself and the progress he had made from quite humble beginnings into the higher echelons of the Ethiopian Orthodox Tewahedo Church; it was not so today. Sitting in the front passenger seat of an ageing saloon car, he found himself in unfamiliar circumstances and he was unhappy. He cast nervously about as the car rattled along.

Iskinder glanced towards the driver, his Church's representative in Malta. The young deacon was clearly delighted to be playing host to such an important man. The deacon's lean frame hinted at a man who enjoyed sports, perhaps running. His close-cut hair, smooth, clean-shaven features and open demeanour allowed Iskinder to read the junior priest's attitude, which was at once puzzlement about the reason for this unexpected visit and awe at having to host such an important countryman. Iskinder could offer the young man no plausible explanation so opted to give none, other than it being important Church business.

Returning his attention to the road, he shivered again as the windscreen wipers started sweeping back and forth, clearing spots of rain that were now falling from the overcast sky. He drew his jacket tighter against what he experienced as winter cold. The deacon noticed the movement from the corner of his eye and leant forwards to fumble with buttons on the dashboard.

'I've put the heater on, but I'm not sure it works too well. Maybe not at all. Sorry.' He threw a slightly sheepish glance towards his passenger.

Iskinder managed to nod his head in acknowledgement while still keeping his chin tucked down against his chest.

'How long does it take to reach Marsaxlokk?'

'Not long. Ten minutes more. Especially today – see, there's no traffic; it hasn't picked up since the New Year yet. Come Monday, it will be busier.'

'Come Monday, I expect to be back in Africa. No, come Monday, I *pray* to be back in Africa.'

The deacon looked suddenly anxious. 'But you will be here for tomorrow's service? The congregation is excited at your being here. I am hoping you will take part in the service. We are all hoping—'

'Yes, yes, I will be pleased to participate in the service. Though, please turn the heating on in the church tonight, otherwise you will have to explain to Bishop Ignatius why his assistant has died of hypothermia while in your care.'

The deacon was placated. They lapsed into silence as the car rushed through the short stretch of countryside that separated the Maltese capital Valletta from their destination. The country road was flanked on either side by nearly continuous runs of shoulder-high yellow-white stone walls. They limited Iskinder's view to gateway flashes of the winter-green land beyond, where potato crops were taking advantage of the seasonal rainfall. Here and there, thick clusters of prickly pear trees spilled over the boundary walls.

The car crossed a ridge and instantly their restricted outlook vanished and the scenery opened as the land beyond the ridge sloped gently down towards the sea and the fishing village of Marsaxlokk, its honey-coloured stone buildings clustered against the coastline, ageless and unmoved by sun or sea.

The deacon slowed as they entered the village. The car bumped and rocked its way along an over-patched and worn road that ran between the tightly packed low-rise houses and stores lining the route to the seafront. He drove the car directly onto the broad quayside and there, disregarding the traffic signs, steered an exaggerated arc across the near empty car park to bring the car to a halt outside the tourist information office.

The quayside was devoid of people. Half a dozen cars were parked, scattered at random along its length: perhaps owned by skippers or crew of some of the fishing boats currently moored in the harbour. The only movement came from gulls swooping low to shriek outrage at the car's arrival, and the fishing boats bobbing as they tugged gently against their ropes. The drops of rain increased to a steady drizzle.

'We're here,' said the deacon, turning expectantly to look his passenger in the eye. 'What would you like now?'

'Can you wait here for me?'

'Yes, of course. There are parking restrictions, but nobody is here to enforce them today.' The deacon looked about and shrugged. Then he stretched back into the rear seats and rummaged on the floor, retrieving an umbrella. 'You'll need this.' He handed it to Iskinder. 'Would you like me to come with you?'

'Thank you and no. Please just wait here. I have no idea how long I'll be.' Iskinder got out of the car, clutching his briefcase. He struggled for a moment to unfurl the umbrella then hurried to the entrance of the tourist information office. There, he stopped to shelter and raise the umbrella before glancing about.

From the comfort of the car, the deacon continued to watch, puzzled and slightly worried at the senior churchman's furtive behaviour. Then, for the first time since he had collected Father Iskinder Anibesa from Valletta airport, he saw the worry lines ease from his charge's face. He saw the briefcase-holding hand rise, struggling to greet somebody.

Looking in the direction of Iskinder's wave, the deacon's eyes traced across the car park, over the quayside road and came to a halt where a solitary man sat at a café table. An awning stretched out over the pavement to cover a cluster of tables – today, protecting them from rain, though on any other three hundred days of the year, the awning would be fending off the sun.

***

Placing her lunch plate into the dishwasher, Helen straightened up, took her coffee and crossed to the kitchen window. She wondered how Sam was getting on and half envied him the warmth of Malta.

It had been freezing when she saw him off from Edinburgh Airport the day before. Almost as soon as his flight left, the wind started to get up. It kept building, growing through the night into what Elaine told her was the fiercest winter storm she could remember.

During the morning, the wind had begun to ease back. The trees and bushes that shielded the view of the stone wall at the bottom of the manse garden had stopped their frantic bending and straining. Now, just the top boughs waved back and forth in harmony with the easing of the wind. Above, the sky was filled with dark glowering clouds that had rolled in from the east. A movement in the garden caught her eye. A snowflake. Then another and another. Then, as if some big net in the sky had been opened to release its haul, the snow came.

Helen hurried to the kitchen door and opened it. The cold air washed past her, and she stood still, listening, watching. Her first Edinburgh snow. The distant sounds of the city were gone. For the first time since she had moved to Edinburgh, everything was truly silent – muted by the great muffler of falling snow. She looked up and could see nothing but falling flakes. In front of her, they were already settling on the lawn. She loved the snow and smiled broadly. Stepping back into the kitchen, she appreciated again the building's solidity and the tranquil refuge it now offered after the months of fear and horror that had followed her arrival in a new country, a new home.

It had all started on a high when her father had arranged an assistant minister's post for her with his old friend, John Dearly, the minister of St Bernard's. It hadn't been plain sailing. Elaine, the parish's senior elder had not taken to her at first, but subsequent events had drawn them close together, as they had with Elaine's daughter Grace – now a student but still very much part of life at the manse.

Sam, Helen's archaeologist boyfriend – former soldier, brilliant linguist and all-round catch – had also come into her life. But in just a matter of weeks over the past summer, her idyllic life had begun to shatter. The brutal murder of old Archie Buchan, the long-retired former minister of St Bernard's, had coincided with the discovery of ancient Templar artefacts. More violent deaths had followed, coming ever closer to home, even to this very kitchen, where her mentor, John Dearly, had been savagely dispatched – the catalyst for her to assume the leadership role within the parish.

Her new position had brought with it a signet ring, a symbol of her position and responsibilities, and unexpected revelations of a secret inheritance in the form of a trust fund, even a Swiss bank account in which her predecessors – John Dearly, Archie Buchan and others before them –

had hidden their secrets. Much knowledge but, for Helen, little understanding.

With unexpected wealth had come unabating violence – the relentless pursuit by the mysterious Cassiter and his followers who seemed to know more than even Sam about the Templar artefacts now in her possession. No matter where she and Sam went, the Templar legacy followed them doggedly, even to the heart of Africa, the grinding heat and dust of which were a world away from the Scottish winter now insistently making its presence felt in the manse garden.

The phone rang. Helen was jolted out of her thoughts and hurried through to the study. She didn't recognise the displayed number.

'Hello, Helen Johnson speaking.'

'Ah, good. Miss Johnson, hello. It's Alan Ralston here.'

'Yes, how can I help you?' The name was vaguely familiar, but Helen couldn't quite place it.

'Miss Johnson, we've not met. I'm phoning for my father, Billy Ralston, your tenant out at Temple.'

'Oh yes, of course. I'm sorry, Alan; I knew I should know the name but couldn't place it. I've just not had the chance to come out and visit your father at the farm since I inherited it.'

'Don't you worry about that. The land will be here whenever you're ready, and I'm thinking summer is the time to see it at its best.'

'Okay, though I was just as keen to have a look around the woodland, next to the farm, that you look after for St Bernard's. How is your father? What can I do for you?'

'Well, that's the problem, Miss Johnson. Yon storm, it was a wild one, brought down some trees in the wood during the night. Half a dozen at least. Big old boys.'

'Wouldn't you expect to lose the odd tree in a storm?'

'Aye, but this is a cluster, came down together. My father went up to have a look this morning just to make sure, and he didn't come back for his lunch.'

'I see. What's happened?'

'I went up myself a wee while back, to try to find him. It's odd, very odd; I've never seen anything like it.'

'Well, Alan, what's happened?'

'The downed trees have cut a swathe through the wood as they fell, opened a great jumbled clearing right in the middle of it. Like a bombsite. Their roots have come up and weakened the ground. My father must have stepped on some turf and gone right through, nothing underneath.'

'Oh, no! How is he?'

'Oh, he'll live. Broken arm, maybe a twisted ankle too. I've got him out and back here to the farm. He's sitting quietly, just waiting for the ambulance to get here.'

'Well, thank God.'

'Aye, for sure. I thought he'd maybe fallen into some old mine workings opened by the tree fall. Half the county is riddled with old tunnels, some of them can run out a good distance from the original shaft. Up to a mile and more. Many of the tunnels were never reported by the miners; they just burrowed where they wanted. Above ground, nobody could see what they were up to.'

'Sounds as though he was lucky. Is there anything I can do?'

'The thing is, it was no mine workings, Miss Johnson. It looks like an old chamber. I mean very, very old. You know, it's odd. My family has worked the land for umpteen generations and nobody has ever talked of old buildings there. I've always thought it was pristine ancient woodland – that's why we always worked so hard to preserve it. You know our tenancy agreement requires that.'

Helen knew. She knew too that the woodland was exactly where she and Sam wanted to investigate; they were both certain it was somehow linked to her Templar inheritance. To date, they had been thwarted by government regulations, unable to hunt around the area because it had protected status as a site of special scientific interest.

'Miss Johnson, I'm thinking you'll want to come out and see, but my father's worried. The trees coming down was an act of God, you know. We've always looked after the woodland; you can't think this was a breach of our tenancy terms—'

'Alan, stop worrying and put your father's mind at rest. I understand; the storm was blowing hard here too. I've seen the tenancy reports. Year after year, he, your whole family, have always done a good job. Tell him if anyone knows all about acts of God, it's me! Now get Billy off to hospital. Phone me later to let me know how he is and if there is anything I can do to help. Then we can arrange a time for me to visit sometime tomorrow. And, Alan …'

'Yes, Miss Johnson?'

'From now on, please just call me Helen, okay?'

'Yes Miss … Helen.'

Helen hung up the phone and paced back to the kitchen. She stopped at the window and looked out at the snow that now completely covered the lawn and continued to fall, even heavier than before. She cast an eye up into the snow-filled sky.

'Thank you. Thank you.' Unable to stop herself, she punched the air. 'Yes! Yes, yes, yes!'

***

The grand dining room fell into silence, and thirty-one seated men watched an electric-powered wheelchair hum its occupant through the open doorway and make its way to the vacant place at the head of the table. Eugene Parsol had arrived.

He paused for a moment then lifted a glass from the table and took a slow sip. His eyes closed and his cheeks drew in slightly as he savoured the vintage. He didn't need to look to know what was before him; it was an image he had seen repeated every year since he had succeeded his father, an image his father would have seen every year before that, and had been witnessed by his antecedents far back into earlier, and now long forgotten, generations. Fifteen affluent but soberly dressed men sat in line on either side of the table and, at the foot, was his son, his depute and heir, Eugene Parsol Jr. Occupying the chair immediately to his right was Cassiter. There was no sound; they were all still, waiting for his address.

'Gentlemen, thank you all for coming. I appreciate that bringing our annual gathering forward has disrupted many of your plans for the New Year's celebrations, and I thank you and your partners for attending at such short notice.' Parsol paused, allowing time for a dutiful murmuring of acknowledgement to run round the table.

He banged his glass down on the table and, instantly, silence returned.

'I have weighed all your words and thought long on what to do ...' His gaze travelled down one side of the table and back up the other – contact, nod, proceed; contact, nod, proceed ... Everyone was acknowledged. 'To be clear, last year was a disaster.' He looked down at his wheelchair and slapped his hands on the armrests. 'I have suffered personally, we had to lose good men, our enemies have prospered and the Templar treasury was found and snatched from our grasp.' His calm voice did not betray anything of the scale of loss incurred.

'And yet ... and yet, none of those setbacks will matter when we take the real hoard. The coin and gold bars found on Crete are as nothing to the Templars' greatest secret. We know we are a single step from it, and we will

9

have it. Now!' His voice rose in an assertive crescendo as he banged a fist on the table. The guests rose and cheered, shaking clenched fists in the air.

The moment passed, and as the men settled down again, waiting staff hurried round and refreshed glasses. When the staff retired, Parsol raised his hand to command silence. Again, all present waited for his words.

'The things we don't know, we will act now to discover. What were Johnson and her friend Cameron really doing in Africa? Why were they so friendly with the Ethiopian bishop? Why haven't they moved to retrieve the hoard? Perhaps, they still do not know they hold the key, the knowledge. No matter, we will stand ready, and as they unpick the puzzle, we will move to collect what is rightfully ours.'

He looked sharply to Eugene Jr, who looked back along the table towards his father; the young man was upright, proud and strong – just as he himself had been, forty years before when regarding his own father. 'Eugene, I want you to go directly to Scotland, take personal charge of our people there. Nothing must slip through our grasp.'

Parsol reached out a hand and rested it briefly on Cassiter's arm. 'And you must go to Malta at once. Follow Cameron. Whatever links were made with those priests in Africa must be important. One is even now in Malta, it appears on a simple ecumenical trip, but there is no other obvious reason for Cameron to be there right now. There are no coincidences in this game. Have your team monitor both of their movements. If the two meet, find out why. Use whatever methods you deem appropriate – just be sure to get the answers. We must know what the Ethiopians know. Once you have the facts, tie up the loose ends – permanently.'

Parsol turned his attention back to the group sat around the table. 'Everyone else, return to your homes and wait. We do not yet know to whose region the chase will take us. So you must all remain vigilant and be ready to respond to any call for assistance we may issue. This is the endgame. There can be no mistakes.'

He raised his glass. Taking his cue, all those around the table stood and raised their glasses towards him.

'Gentlemen,' said Parsol, 'this is the year when we finally claim what is ours. Our birthright will come home. Our enemies will be destroyed. Santé!'

***

A little breathless, Iskinder hurried into the sanctuary afforded by the café's canopy. Stepping beneath it, he lowered the umbrella and wiped from his face the streaks of rain that had been driven against him in his dash to the café.

Rising, Sam reached out a hand in welcome. 'Good to see you, Iskinder.'

As they greeted one another, a waiter stepped through the doorway and retreated moments later with an order for coffees.

Sam could tell Iskinder was not acclimatised to the mild Mediterranean winter. While he found it comfortably warm compared to Scotland and the cold grip of a northern winter, it clearly represented a drop from the temperatures of Ethiopia. 'Are you okay sitting out here? Would you rather go inside?'

Iskinder promptly sat and waved Sam back into his seat. 'Outside is cold but better. I don't think we want to risk anyone overhearing our conversation.'

'There are no customers inside,' said Sam; 'the café's empty.'

'Outside is better.'

'Fine by me.' Although the threat of the past year seemed to have gone now, taking precautions did nobody any harm and Sam approved. He sat back into his seat and looked across at the priest. Here, far from his bishop and the dictates of Church protocols, he did not seem so confident. In fact, he seemed quite anxious. Sam gave a little laugh to himself, realising this was the first time he had ever addressed Iskinder by his name; he had always been simply 'the bishop's assistant'. 'So, Iskinder, how are you? How's the bishop? And what's the big mystery that's brought us both a long way from home in such secrecy?'

Iskinder settled more comfortably into his seat, watching the waiter return and place cups of coffee on their table. 'I'm fine, thank you, as is Bishop Ignatius who sends his regards to you and, of course, to Helen …' He paused and remained silent, until the waiter retired back inside the building.

'Glad to hear it and please pass on Helen's regards to him. But Iskinder, this is an out-of-the-way spot. What's going on?'

The priest scanned the quayside, which looked abandoned in the falling rain. 'The box that Bishop Ignatius gave to Helen, she had its twin. Have you managed to open them yet?'

Sam had guessed the boxes would be at the root of this visit – they had remained a mystery ever since the bishop had handed his over to Helen at the tail end of their African adventures. Both boxes were about the size of a child's first jewellery box, four inches high, five deep and six wide. Every side highly polished wood, patterned with intricate inlays to create flowing seemingly abstract images of great beauty. A pair so wonderfully crafted that it was impossible to find their lids or any other openings, and they came with the explicit warning that forcing the boxes open would destroy their contents. They were a puzzle, the equal of all the other Templar concealments Sam and Helen had encountered.

'No. I've tried umpteen ways, and they've defied me so far. But now Christmas is behind us, I'm planning to focus on opening them. We are convinced they are a clue to something, but what that is, we don't know. What we do know is every previous clue has been hard to unpick but high in value. Perhaps this will be the same.'

'A word of warning. It seems that somebody in Addis Ababa has been asking questions about why the bishop and I met with you and Helen in Tanzania before Christmas. They also asked about the meeting in Nairobi when Bishop Ignatius gave her the box. They knew all about the box.'

Sam leant forwards. 'Who? When?'

'I don't know who. The questioning has just come to light in the past few days, but it seems to have started three or four weeks ago. Somebody must have been there watching us. But were they watching Helen or the bishop?'

Sam drew his lips tight as he processed the news. Then he took a sip of coffee. 'Iskinder, you and the bishop must be careful. If this is the same group that took an interest in Helen previously, they are very dangerous people; but we thought they had been wiped out in Crete last summer. Could it be something different? The bishop had a heavy security detail with him when he gave Helen the box in Nairobi. Could there be a leak there?'

'No, they are members of the Ethiopian military and the Church's most trusted men. They would die for our Church without hesitation. They cannot be the source of this worry.'

'Okay, well forewarned is forearmed. Let's hope it's just a journalist snooping for a story, but you both must be careful, very careful, until we know for sure.' Sam fixed Iskinder with an earnest stare. 'Seriously, Iskinder, you must be careful.' He paused and waited for the priest's acknowledgement. 'Good. Now, you said that was a warning, but it's not why we are here; what exactly brings us together?'

'The Ethiopian Orthodox Tewahedo Church looked after Helen's box for more than seven hundred years. We knew exactly how it had come into the hands of our Church and what our duties and responsibilities were. We fulfilled those to the letter. Keeping it safe and hidden from all comers, until Helen returned to reclaim it with her ring, the true sign of its ownership.'

'Yes, you did your duty. If only others in our world had such integrity, this would be a happier and safer place for everyone.'

Iskinder smiled at Sam's compliment to his Church. 'But what we have never known is how to open the box and what its purpose is.'

'Helen and I are in the same boat. That is the puzzle we need to solve now.'

'Just so. However, I may have something to help you.' Iskinder began to rummage inside his briefcase. 'Since people have been asking questions in Addis, and knowing your caution over using electronic communication, the bishop instructed I hand this to you in person, at a place where nobody would think to look for us.'

'That's why we're here?'

'No, not quite. This is inconspicuous, but I have another reason for meeting you here. First, let me show you this.' Iskinder pulled a neatly folded sheet of paper from the briefcase; his voice dropped to little more than a whisper. 'This is a copy of an old document held in the Church archive. A very old document.'

Sam reached out a hand and spun the paper round so he could see it more clearly.

'The bishop and I have always accepted the received wisdom and knowledge of our predecessors. Once we had returned the box to Helen and honoured the covenant made so many generations ago, I was prompted to go back through the Church archive to see if I could find something, anything, that might shed more light on things.'

'I thought the bishop had told Helen everything you knew.'

'Yes, he did. But this piece of writing has probably not been read since the time the covenant was made. Look at the script.' The Ethiopian priest slid the sheet still closer to Sam, who scanned it with a professional eye. As a highly skilled linguist and archaeologist, he loved to explore ancient scripts and unpick their meanings.

'This looks impressive,' said Sam, 'but I don't know the script.'

'No, you wouldn't. It's an old variation of Coptic writing that has not been written in many hundreds of years.'

'You can read it?'

'No, but we have one or two old priest scholars who can make out parts.'

'Well?' said Sam, without taking his eyes off the text in front of him. 'What can you tell me?'

'It is a letter that came with the bishop who carried Helen's box into Ethiopia. Not part of the official package, a private note written to the bishop in Addis Ababa by the Coptic pope, John IX of Alexandria. It refers to a conversation overheard between the Templar knight who delivered the box to Alexandria from Scotland and his sergeant.'

'Overheard?'

Iskinder suddenly looked a little embarrassed. 'That is how it seems.' He stretched out his hand and touched the sheet. 'See, there is no pope's seal, just writing – a private note, nothing more. But I have seen that signature on other documents, and I had our old scholars double-check'— his finger shifted to the bottom of the text and tapped—'and that is the same signature. It's genuine. It is the pope's signature.'

'I believe you, but what is important about this?'

'It starts with a little preamble. It is written not long after Pope John IX became the patriarch in Alexandria. It tells of events relating to the end of his predecessor's time, his own early days, and a secret visit by a Templar knight. Then it mentions the Temple of Jupiter—'

'Jupiter? That's Rome. Centuries before the Templars' time. Can it be relevant?'

'Yes, but it was not written in Roman times. This is written in the fourteenth century by the pope who sent Helen's box for safekeeping with the Ethiopian Church.'

'And he's written about the Temple of Jupiter? Are you sure your people have translated it as they should?' Sam was interested, very interested. Even so, this seemed an anachronism – just completely the wrong period. Why Jupiter? There should be a Christian-era link.

'Yes. I am sure. They could only make out a few parts, and I told then no speculation, only facts. But it is hard for them, this script drifted out of use shortly after the text was written.'

'I'm not convinced by Jupiter though; it just seems wrong.'

Iskinder's finger continued over the sheet. 'This part they don't know. We think it is simply explaining that this might prove useful in solving the mystery of the boxes. I wonder if the Coptic pope anticipated the Templar would not return to claim the box. We can never know.' His finger tapped again. 'But here is interesting. It definitely says the Temple of Jupiter.'

'Perhaps we should have met in Rome then,' said Sam.

'No. No, no. Not in Rome. The Temple of Jupiter in Leptis Magna.'

'In Libya? How can that be? Why Libya?'

'The reference to Leptis Magna is clear.'

'Well, okay, I'll take that as given for now. I know Leptis Magna was a thriving coastal city during the Roman era and then abandoned.'

'Look, within the run of text are tiny cartouches; can you see?'

'I'm not sure … they look like little smudges.' Sam pulled out his pocket magnifying glass, flipped it open and studied carefully. 'Yes, I see.' He glanced up. 'What does it mean?' His voice was calm as ever, but a spark in his eye showed his interest was fired up.

'It refers to the approach to the temple. My people disagree on this too. It means either a road or a row, as in a lined road or walkway or steps. Then it gets even muddier. One of my scholars thinks it mentions a sequence, one thinks a key. They won't agree.'

'A key?'

'Yes, a key. That's something you need for your boxes.'

'It is, isn't it? What else does it say?'

'In summary, the key or the sequence, depending which scholar you choose, was formed or placed on the approach to the Temple of Jupiter.'

'May I photograph this please?' said Sam, lifting his phone. 'I'm going to need to do my own homework before getting too invested in this. I really can't see how a road or steps can be a key to our boxes.'

'Please, just keep the paper. I have another, and of course, the original is safe in our archive in Addis Ababa.'

'I still don't understand what our boxes have to do with a Roman city,' said Sam while folding the paper and pocketing it.

'The bishop thought the only way to find out was to go there.'

'Go to Leptis Magna? To Libya? That's madness. Who would we arrange access with? It's effectively a war zone with power and authority just jumbled up – impossible.'

'I think the bishop had in mind that you and I make a discreet visit. Organised by somebody in the know.'

'Really? He thinks that will work? It's the most patrolled part of the North African coast. There's a constant watch to stop boats coming and going. And don't forget, you and I are Christians. If we fall into the wrong hands over there, it could end very badly.'

'Yes, I know. But with the right local connections and enough money, it should be possible to organise a trip.'

'Just where would we find such a connection?'

Iskinder shot a tight little smile at Sam then looked beyond him, staring through the drizzle that still fell onto the quayside.

Sam followed Iskinder's gaze to where the row of boats tugged at their moorings in the gusty breeze. 'A fishing boat?'

'One particular and very big boat. With a captain who has good friends and contacts on the Libyan coast. See the big blue boat?'

'To have live connections in Libya today, he must, almost certainly, be linked to people smuggling, and God knows what else. Are you sure about this?' At the far end of the line of boats was an old and large fishing boat. Built for deep-sea work, it dwarfed most of the other boats, its hull and superstructure all painted a pale bluish grey that was streaked with harsh lines of orange rust. A little gangway ran down from the stern of the boat to the quay.

Iskinder continued talking. 'I know. It's not ideal but needs must. We have a duty to help you, and this is the only way you will get to Leptis Magna. One of the Church's intermediaries has made an arrangement for us. We are to go and speak with the captain. According to our man, this captain is a frequent visitor to Libya. Oh, and I have been specifically instructed not to ask about his business – he is just a legitimate fisherman. And by the way, I understand he is a Christian too, so it would seem profit trumps doctrine over there.'

Sam was unconvinced. 'Well, I suppose it can't do any harm to speak with the man.' He leant back, rapped his hand on the café window and made a sign through the glass for the check. He pulled out some euros to settle the bill.

The two men walked quickly across the road to the quayside. As they passed the parked car, Sam noticed a young priest watching them with interest from the dry comfort of the driver's seat. The deacon averted his gaze at Iskinder's slightly irritated hand gesture. Then they were past, moving along the quayside to the big fishing boat.

At the foot of the gangway, they stopped. Sam could tell that Iskinder was nervous; this was as far removed from his natural environment as might be imagined.

'Best let me lead,' said Sam. He put a hand on the guide rail, but before he could step up, a scruffy deckhand appeared and blocked access at the top.

'Who're you?' said the deckhand. 'What do you want?'

Sam paused; he could feel Iskinder backing up behind him.

'I have a meeting arranged with your captain,' said Iskinder. 'Please let him know his visitor from Ethiopia is here, as he was notified.'

'Captain's not here. He's gone.'

'But we have a meeting.'

'Captain's gone. Come back tomorrow.'

'The priest said he's got a meeting with your captain,' said Sam.

The deckhand shrugged then lifted and swung over a little hinged bar that clanged on top of the handrail to close the top of the gangway. 'Come back tomorrow, eleven o'clock. He'll be here.'

'Come on, we're wasting our time, let's go,' said Sam.

'Agreed. Though it's not very professional.'

'I'm thinking professional is not a word I'd use to describe the captain of a boat like this.'

'Yes. Sam, will you come back to Valletta with me? We could have an early dinner at my hotel then arrange to meet in the morning. I'll attend my deacon's service, then we will return here by taxi – the deacon will have duties all morning, so I can't call on him for transport.'

'Yes, that all sounds good. Though it would be best for me if we travelled back here separately tomorrow. I really want to consider your text, and I might want to look around a bit in the morning. Malta is not an island I know well. We could meet here for an update at half past ten. Then we can go and meet your fisherman friend at eleven.'

'I have never met the fisherman; he's certainly not a friend. Just a contact, that's all. But I agree with your plan.'

As the rain renewed its downpour, they hurried towards the car. The deacon had been watching their approach in his car mirror and fired up his vehicle's engine when they pulled open the passenger doors.

Chapter 2

SUNDAY JANUARY 5TH

From his position of advantage, standing in a dark corner, Cassiter watched with interest. Sat in the middle of the barn was his subject – a man with questions to answer. Stood beside the subject were two men, sourced by Parsol's local connection. Burly men who Cassiter hoped he could rely on in a crisis. He wished he had his own team with him but losses in the past year had been high, and they were stretched very thin.

He had hurried to the island the evening before, arriving in time to watch from a discreet distance as his subject dined with Sam Cameron. Then he'd trailed them on their gentle evening stroll. Finally, Cameron had left to go into his hotel, and the subject had made to head back to his own hotel in the quiet of the Valletta night.

That quiet had been broken by the screech of tyres and the sound of hurrying footsteps. His subject had turned to see the source of the disturbance only to be enveloped in a scuffle of feet and shadowy shapes.

Now, in the pre-dawn darkness, Cassiter raised his hand, signalling to his men to begin. At once, one of the men ripped away the hood that had been covering his subject's head. Cassiter gave a little smile to himself when he saw the harsh light flood into Iskinder's eyes. The priest blinked frantically and glanced about, trying to get his bearings. His wrists had been bound tightly to the armrests of an old metal-framed chair that had been dragged from a corner where it had provided years of break-time comfort to hardworking farmhands. He was disoriented; the gag, tight around his mouth, prevented any protest.

Iskinder blinked again. An unshaded electric bulb swung gently somewhere above him. The reach of its harsh light failed to fill the whole space, leaving pools of darkness beyond the circle of light.

Cassiter stepped forwards. He leant on a stick. It made him angry that his previous clash with Cameron and that church minister girl, Johnson, had left him disabled. Yet, he was better off than Parsol. When the pair had been dragged from the rubble of the tunnel collapse on Crete, Cassiter had found himself nursing a crushed knee; Parsol would never walk again.

'Welcome to my workshop,' said Cassiter.

Iskinder shook his head from side to side while shrieking a muffled objection through the gag.

'Didn't quite catch that, I'm afraid. Still, not to worry, you'll have an opportunity to talk in a minute.'

Standing close to Iskinder, Cassiter leant his weight on his stick while stretching out his free hand to stroke Iskinder's hair. 'I've got some questions. But first, I'm going to make it easier for you by letting you know how badly things go for people who don't answer me quickly.'

Cassiter manoeuvred round the chair until his right hand touched Iskinder's left wrist. His fingers explored the binding, and he nodded appreciatively towards the man who had tied it. 'Good work. That won't come undone in a hurry.' The guard acknowledged his praise with a curt nod. 'Now, shall we begin?'

The priest shook his head, while leaning it away from Cassiter.

Cassiter caressed Iskinder's hand, stroking it gently. 'I need to know what's been happening. Why they visited you in Tanzania, and what was the box Bishop Ignatius gave to Helen Johnson in Nairobi? I need to know it all, do you understand?

'Most of all, I want to know what you've been discussing with Cameron and what your plans are.' Cassiter leant down close to Iskinder's ear and continued in a theatrical whisper. 'Everything. I need to know everything.' He reached up and freed the gag.

The priest gasped in air then let out a shout of rage. 'Never. I will not betray my bishop's confidence. Never! Let me go!'

'You don't have a choice. You will tell me.' Cassiter's voice was calm, almost comforting, but inside, the old thrill was returning. It had been a while since he had a person completely at his mercy. Now, here he was, and his victim was connected to Helen Johnson and Cameron. It couldn't be better. He could harvest knowledge, enjoy the task and take some proxy revenge to assuage his appetite until he finally caught up with the minister and her mate.

'I am an emissary of the Ethiopian Orthodox Tewahedo Church. Release me; you have no right to hold me.'

Cassiter looked down at his captive and laughed. He looked into the priest's eyes and saw the man flinch. 'Tell me what I want to know, and I will be merciful. You can die quickly.'

Cassiter's fist slammed into the side of Iskinder's head.

'Tell me everything,' said Cassiter. His voice and face betrayed no emotion.

Iskinder shook his head groggily.

'As you wish, but now you will tell me on my terms.'

Cassiter forced his fingers beneath Iskinder's tied hand, wriggled his hand to secure the best position then began interweaving their fingers, slotting each of his strong digits between the milk soft fingers of the priest. Ready, Cassiter caught his breath, closed his eyes for a moment. 'It's time to talk now, priest.'

'Go to hell.'

'Very well, then I must commence, and you will come to hell with me. We'll talk again when I've finished here.' Cassiter applied pressure, bending back the priest's fingers. He felt the resistance of muscle and tendon bracing against the pressure he applied and gave a little smile as he ramped up the load. He heard Iskinder's little gasps of pain as the priest's hands tried to resist his. It was futile; wrists bound to the chair-arms meant there was no defensive leverage.

'Stop. Stop! In the name of God, please stop.'

'Not yet, I'm afraid. Just let me finish what I'm doing.' Cassiter stepped up the pressure again, increasing the torque applied to the priest's fingers. Experience told him that he was almost there. He could feel the tension mounting. Then, with a sudden snap, one of the fingers gave. The sound was lost beneath Iskinder's scream which renewed again and again as more fingers distorted and snapped.

Done, Cassiter released Iskinder's hand and stepped back. Leaning his weight on his walking stick, he watched the priest. Saw how the broken hand, tied to the chair's arm, was held still to minimise any further pain while the other strained against its bonds in a desperate and unfulfilled bid to reach across and comfort its twin. Minutes slipped by, and the screams and groans subsided into muttering as the first wave of pain subsided a little. Cassiter did not understand what Iskinder was saying. In his pain and distress, the priest had reverted to Amharic, his mother tongue.

Reaching out, Cassiter took one of the broken fingers and twisted it hard. 'English. Speak only English. Do you understand me?'

Iskinder howled in distress. Unable to form any words in the depths of his pain, he could only nod a desperate acknowledgement. With a final vigorous twist, Cassiter let the finger go and stepped back. Now he was content to wait a while, allowing his victim's pain to subside sufficiently for him to converse. Meanwhile, he pointed into the shadows at the far end of the barn and waved one of his men away to fetch one of the large potato crates that were piled up ready for the gathering of the next harvest.

Cassiter sat on the upturned crate and leant close to Iskinder's tear-streaked face. The priest's frightened and pained eyes glanced at Cassiter then darted away, scared of what any further eye contact might bring.

'We'll speak in English now,' said Cassiter.

Iskinder nodded then gave a little groan as he arched his back as far as his bonds would permit, trying without success to find some way to ease the pain in his broken hand.

'You look uncomfortable, priest. I can help with that but only once you've answered my questions. Do you understand?'

Iskinder kept his eyes gazing down.

'I said, do you understand? Answer me when I ask questions, or I will shake your hand again.' Cassiter reached out towards the broken hand.

'Yes! Yes! English. Only English! I swear. Please, please ...'

Cassiter let his hand drop and commenced his questioning. He could tell the man was holding nothing back. Broken by the pain, all the priest wanted was the end, which would come only when Cassiter was content.

'Inside my briefcase, there's a paper. You can have it ...'

Cassiter listened carefully to his victim's gasped account then opened the man's briefcase. Inside was a folded sheet of paper; he withdrew the copy of the text. A quick glance confirmed what Iskinder had explained, it was old and unintelligible. He'd get it to Parsol as soon as possible. The Frenchman had historical experts who might confirm its meaning.

The questioning was over. He had no idea of the significance of the little box that had been given to Helen Johnson and would need to think through the implications of Cameron's proposed trip to Libya. One thing he was sure of, the priest had nothing more to tell. Standing up, he limped to the other side of his victim's chair and allowed his hand to stroke Iskinder's unbroken one. The priest let out a cry of fear as Cassiter's fingers interwove with his. The sound merged into a deeper shriek of pain as pressure built on his joints, and his feet drummed in despair on the concrete floor while Cassiter exerted yet more pressure, absorbing the raw human energy that poured from the broken man.

One guard averted his gaze. He had heard all about Cassiter's party piece, but seeing it for real, he didn't have the stomach for it, and there was a deadness in Cassiter's eyes that frightened even him.

Stepping back, Cassiter let the broken digits be and took a moment to survey the crumpled, moaning form that had so recently been a proud human being. He pointed at the potato crate. 'Put him in that.' Then he waved for the guards to follow him, and he set off towards the barn doors, his stick tap-tapping on the floor. The guards came behind, dragging the crate and Iskinder out into the night.

'Dig a hole, a deep hole. Bury him.'

'He's still alive, sir.'

'Bury him.' Cassiter moved away to his car, got in and instructed his driver to return to Valletta. The local men Parsol had organised to support his actions were a disappointment. They lacked the backbone of his own men. He felt the losses he had incurred and once again promised himself that Cameron and the Johnson girl would suffer an eternity of pain for the harm they had caused him, an eternity.

As the tail lights of Cassiter's car receded into the distance, his men took an executive decision. They stowed their shovels and lifted the crate onto the back of their pickup truck. With a groan, Iskinder lifted his head. His eyes peered out through the slats, unfocused, unseeing. The pickup headed for the coast.

***

Sam sat at the same outside table he had occupied the previous day. His coffee finished and the clock ticking, he wondered where Iskinder had got to. As it approached eleven, the appointed time for their meeting with the captain of the blue boat, he decided to make a move.

Putting some euros inside the folded bill, he slipped it onto the plate that the waiter had delivered shortly before. Then he stood, tapped on the window and was gone long before the waiter arrived to clear the table.

Over on the quayside, Sam took a final glance around. There was no sign of the priest so he resolved to go it alone. As he approached the gangway, his access was blocked by the same deckhand who had barred their way the previous day.

'What's up, man?' said the hand.

'You told me to call back at eleven this morning. Here I am. Is the captain available?'

The deckhand gave a shrug, raised his hand to stop Sam at the foot of the gangway then turned, disappearing into the bowels of the boat.

The vessel was old and the paintwork was in desperate need of a refresh, but Sam knew that neither age nor appearance counted for much. In the final analysis, what really mattered were: was it watertight, and were its engines and equipment well-maintained and functional? Seaworthiness was all – everything else was just window dressing.

He stepped a little to the side, looked along the length of the hull and suddenly recognised that beneath the tired paintwork was a vessel with a very trim line. He guessed it could deliver a fair turn of speed if called on.

'What do you want?' The captain's voice pulled him back to the moment.

Sam smiled at the man, received nothing in response.

'I'm looking for you. We understand yours might be the boat we should charter for a few days, if we want to take a quiet trip.'

'We?' said the captain looking about.

'Yes, we. My companion couldn't make it. He's a priest, so I'm guessing his morning service lasted longer than he'd expected. He'll be along shortly, I'm sure.'

'Carlos said there was a priest. That's good, I've been expecting him. Not so good that he hasn't turned up.'

'You were expecting him?'

'Yes, a business friend tipped me off that some African church has been looking for a boat to charter. They were given my name. So I've been expecting a visit. But you're not African.' A note of suspicion suddenly hung in the air.

'No, I'm not, but we're together. Your man spoke to us both yesterday.'

'I know, but your priest friend is the man with the introduction. Go find him and come back, then we'll talk.'

'I'll do that, but I really don't know what time he'll turn up. In the meantime, can you confirm, are you available for charter?'

A dry laugh reached down to him from the deck. 'Come back with your priest friend later, and we can talk. Then I'll check my availability.'

'I'll be back, don't worry. But to be clear, are you available right now?'

'As I said, we can talk with your friend when he gets here. I know his credentials, I know nothing about you.'

'Okay, but just tell me, are you available for charter right now?'

'No, the boat's on another charter, starting tomorrow morning, and that's going to keep me busy until the middle of the week.'

'Have you got an agent we can contact if you've already sailed when my colleague turns up?'

'No, only me.' After a moment's thought, he pointed towards the tourist information kiosk set further along the quayside.

'If you do need to contact me, go in there, ask for the manager, tell him you need to get a message to Captain Blue; he'll manage it.'

'Captain Blue? Really?'

The captain slapped his hand against the dirty blue bulkhead. 'It's the colour of the boat. That's all he needs to know, all you need to know. All anyone needs to know.' He fell silent, pulled a packet of cigarettes from his pocket. Putting one between his lips, he flicked on a lighter, brought the flame to the tip and drew deeply. Eyes closed, he held the smoke in his lungs for a moment while turning away from Sam. He leant his elbows on the ship's rail and slowly exhaled.

Realising the interview was over, Sam turned without a word and walked away along the quayside. It was quite clear that Blue had not seen Iskinder this morning, so the priest was missing. First job would be to find him. Sam didn't fancy a trip to Libya, but if that was where the answer to opening the two boxes lay, he'd go.

***

Helen carefully followed the hand signals that guided her off the road and into the natural layby formed at the gateway into the field. The snow had stopped falling now, but a thick white blanket had settled over everything to merge roadside, verge and ditch into one even white surface. She had to trust completely in Alan Ralston's intimate knowledge of his land and continued to edge forwards, responding to his beckoning fingers. She stopped in immediate reaction to his signal.

Alan strode to the driver's door and pulled it open. 'Helen, good to meet you. Thanks for coming out. It's rotten weather.'

Helen reached out a hand. 'Nice to meet you, Alan, and it's my pleasure to be here.' She placed her rubber boots in the snow beside the car door. Kicking off her shoes, she swung her feet out and round to slip them into the boots. 'Never mind the weather, more to the point, how's your father? I'm so sorry he's had this accident.'

'He'll live. It can't be helped. Now watch your step here, the snow's deep, and it gets worse as we cross the field. There's been some drifting. Do you want my arm?'

'Thanks, but I'll manage. I love the snow, don't you?' she said, while fastening her coat against the cold and swinging her bag across her shoulder.

'Well, I expect it's alright if you don't need to go out in it. On the farm, I mostly do. So I'm not so keen.' He touched his hand on the bonnet of Helen's car. 'That's a nice 4x4 you've got there. It's just what you need to come out here today.'

'It's my boyfriend's. I borrowed it. I didn't think my little car would make it out here in this weather.'

'Good thinking. The council are struggling to keep the main roads clear just now. You'd never have got here today in a wee city car. I'd have had to come and get you out with a tractor.'

Alan stepped through the open gate into the field and she followed. Once he'd swung the gate shut, he pointed past his Land Rover which was parked just inside the field. 'It's in that part of the wood over there.' Alan delved into the back of his vehicle and pulled out a roughhewn stave. 'Here, you'll find this useful as a walking stick for crossing the field and in the wood too.'

Taking the wooden pole, she looked up the gentle slope to a treeline perhaps a hundred paces off. 'Right, let's go.'

The wood was much thicker and deeper than it had appeared from the road. Even though the ancient deciduous trees had shed their leaves for winter, the thick overhead latticework of interwoven branches contrived to cast everything into shadowy shades of grey.

At ground level, filling much of the space between the gnarled old tree trunks, were the shrubs and bushes that spent all summer jostling one another for any flashes of sunlight that might break through the overhead canopy. Today, they were still, wet-black branches and twigs linked and woven like three-dimensional spiders' webs, spreading to fill the available space and cut visibility for anyone trying to get through the wood.

'This is thick,' said Helen.

'It is that. We don't encourage visitors. It's a protected habitat.'

'I know, and I'm thinking you could get lost in this quite easily.'

'Well, I don't know ...'

The interwoven tree branches, together with all the undergrowth and bushes, were like a blanket that raised the ground temperature just enough to discourage what snow that reached the ground from settling.

It took only a few minutes of effort, pressing through and weaving around the wooded undergrowth, before Alan led them into a clearing. For the first time since they had entered the woods, Helen got a clear sight of the afternoon sky, before her gaze dropped to appreciate the carnage before her.

Two of the ancient trees whose boughs had devoted centuries of growth to weaving their canopies together had pulled each other over in the storm. They had died as one. Not content with that, the wind had ensured the weight of the falling trunks had toppled the next two in line and two more beyond. All six trees now lay, stretching away, black and lifeless.

A deeper black lay between the nearest two fallen trunks. Alan grabbed

Helen's arm to stop her getting any closer. 'Careful, that's the hole.'

As soon as it was pointed out, she could see it. A black hole set against the wet, black earth. Alan swung his rucksack down and opened it. He pulled out a lightweight rope ladder, secured one end to the spreading root limbs that now reached out lifeless to the sky then threw the other end down into the shadows.

'There's probably some rule against this, but I think you'll want to see – it's fascinating. But let's get down now, while the best of the daylight is still available, then I think you should aim to be back on the main roads as soon as you can.'

Alan handed her a torch and, sticking a second torch in his pocket, grabbed the ladder and started down. His voice reached up to Helen from the hole. 'It's only about twelve feet to the bottom. A straightforward climb. I'm down now.' Helen saw his light flash on, the beam cutting a swathe through the shade below. She gripped the ladder and followed him down.

Reaching the bottom, Helen got her feet steady and looked about. From her vantage point at one end, where the sides were little more than three feet apart, the trench quickly widened to where, she guessed, her outstretched arms would not be able to touch both sides at once. Ahead of her, she could see Alan who had stepped several paces into the trench, his torch beam shining through the gloom to highlight the far end, around twenty feet ahead.

'What is this place?' she said.

'I don't know. It's not a natural feature, and it's certainly not old mine workings. See, the sides are set with clean, cut stone. At best, miners would have used wooden pit props. And watch your feet as you follow me in, the bottom is littered with stone. I'm thinking it's from a stone roof that the roots of the trees ripped apart as they fell.'

'I think you're right,' said Helen, carefully following Alan into the heart of what she now recognised as a chamber. She shone her torch on the ground. In gaps beneath the rubble of fallen stone, she saw more slabs set flush to the ground. 'Look, there are proper flagstones on the floor too.'

Kneeling, she slid her hand down the stone-built wall and traced the line of flagstones to where the ceiling rubble covered it.

The stone had sharp edges, unworn, as though just cut yesterday by a mason. But she guessed that over the centuries, tree roots had slowly forced their way in, opening the way for water, and she could see the resultant staining and algae growth that told of its real age. The hairs on the back of her neck stood up. Helen knew exactly who had made this place, but she had no idea why.

Rising, she followed Alan deeper into the chamber. 'Alan, this is fascinating. I'm so pleased you let me see it, but perhaps, we'd be better waiting until Sam gets back, and he can look at it properly. This is right up his street; he's an archaeologist.' She needed to know what the chamber's purpose was but knew from bitter experience it was best to keep others out of their business as much as possible. She had a duty to protect Alan by ensuring he didn't get involved.

'I think you're right. This needs a professional inspection. Who'd have ever thought this would be here? And I wonder what it's for.'

'I don't know, but I'm sure Sam will shed some light on it for us. It's such a tragedy that the whole roof has fallen in.'

'Yes, though it must have become unstable. It was an accident waiting to happen.'

Helen knelt again. 'Look at these ornate pieces of stonework. All shattered and broken. The ceiling must have looked fabulous.'

'Yes. It's all crushed now though, just chips and splinters.'

'Here's a bit, look.' Helen knelt in the middle of the floor. Reaching among the shattered stones, she pulled out a piece, cube-shaped, about the size of a tennis ball. Five sides were ornately worked, the sixth a sheer break. 'Look, the carving on this is gorgeous; I'm going to take it for Sam to look at. Can you see any more?'

She stood and stuffed the stone into her shoulder bag as Alan cast about for more.

'None that I can see. Lots of splinters and chips, but it's all rubble. I think that might be the only one to have survived intact.'

She had to agree with Alan. It was disappointing, but her pulse was racing nonetheless. She and Sam had wanted to investigate their Templar wood, had been blocked by the environmental laws, and now, ironically, nature itself had opened it up for them. She needed to let Sam know about the find. He needed to see it. With a last glance about, she headed back for the ladder.

***

Sam paused at the door and listened. He could make out the murmur of voices, three or four people. He tapped gently and waited. The speaking stopped and a chair scraped as someone stood up. The sound of new shoes squeaking across a marble floor heralded someone's hurried move towards the door. A moment later, it opened, and a worry-faced African man, middle-aged and dressed in his Sunday best, looked out at him. The glimpse of hope on the man's face instantly switched to disappointment when he registered the visitor was only a stranger.

'Can I help you?' he said as Sam looked over the man's shoulder towards the two other men who still sat at the table.

The furthest away man was making to stand now. It was the deacon who had acted as Iskinder's driver the previous day. Focusing on the third man who had now started to stand too, he was disappointed to register that it was not Iskinder. Where could he be?

'Welcome, Sam. Welcome,' said the deacon. 'Let him in, he is Father Anibesa's friend.'

With a nod towards the doorman, Sam entered and met the deacon halfway across the room. They shook hands.

'Do you know where Father Anibesa is?' said the deacon.

'I'd hoped you would tell me that. He missed our meeting at the quayside in Marsaxlokk this morning. What's going on? When did you last see him?'

'Yesterday. He had agreed to lead the church service this morning before going on to meet you. There has been no sign of him. I sent somebody to his hotel earlier'—the deacon waved a hand towards the man who had let Sam in—'but he wasn't there. The receptionist said Father Anibesa did not return last night.'

Sam felt a twitch of concern. Iskinder was a stickler for process and procedure. The man would never have switched hotels in the night and certainly would not have missed a commitment to preside at a church service. He hoped it was something innocent, but he couldn't think what.

'Have you tried his phone?'

'Twenty times, more. There's no answer. He's vanished, gone completely.' The deacon's voice rose very slightly.

'He and I went for a stroll after dinner last night. We parted at my hotel, and he intended to walk back to his. Have you informed the police? Checked the hospitals?'

The deacon shook his head, slumping down into one of the chairs. 'No, there's been no time. When he didn't show up before the service, I had to conduct it. Everyone was disappointed he did not appear. Once it was over, I sent out to his hotel and since them we have been discussing what to do.'

'Well, I think we need to stop thinking and start acting. You need to phone the hospital and the police too. Perhaps he's had an accident. Let's get going. Can you call them?'

The deacon nodded and reached for his mobile phone.

Sam took a seat beside the deacon and listened as the calls established that Iskinder was not in any known difficulty.

The deacon gave a forlorn shake of the head.

'Come on,' said Sam, standing. 'Let's go and report him missing, officially. We need to find him, and we need help.'

The deacon stood too. 'You don't think anything bad has happened?'

'Probably not but he's missing. You need him, I need him, and Bishop Ignatius certainly needs him back in Addis.' Sam noted the deacon's expression of anxiety deepen at the bishop's name. The young man clearly did not relish delivering this piece of news. 'If it helps, I can tell the bishop. We'll call him as soon as we've reported Iskinder as missing. I need to speak with Ignatius anyway.'

***

The snow had almost filled in their outward tracks by the time Helen and Alan finally made it back across the field. On the other side of the gate, Sam's car was now covered in snow.

'I'll help you clear that lot,' said Alan as he opened the gate, pulling hard against the weight of snow that had built up since he'd pushed it shut earlier.

'That's kind of you, thanks.' Helen paused and looked back at the field, the wood beyond was now obscured by the falling snow. For just a moment, she thought she could make out a third set of tracks leading away towards the wood. But no one other than her would be mad enough to cross the field in this weather. It must just be the afternoon light casting shadows.

'Get in and get your engine started. I'll clear the windows.'

Helen was happy to follow Alan's instruction. Until that moment, she had not realised just how cold she felt.

Snow vanished from the side windows as Alan swept it all away with a series of broad swipes. She loosed her coat and pulled off her gloves, giving Alan a thumbs up through the windscreen. He grinned back at her and pointed at the side window.

Reaching for the window controls, she opened the window a couple of inches.

Alan leant in against the opening. 'It's heavy here, but you'll be fine once you reach the main road. Go slowly, and I'll follow you down to the junction.'

'There's no need, Alan. I can manage fine.'

'That's as maybe. But believe me, my father would have a fit if he thought I hadn't seen you safely off. I'll follow behind you once I've got my vehicle out of the field and the gate shut. I'll catch you up in no time.'

'Okay,' said Helen. She loved driving and was confident in the snow, but Alan was clearly not going to allow her to drive off alone on his watch.

'Right, now follow my signals; I'll guide you while you turn around.' Alan stepped out into the lane, and she followed his lead as she carefully turned the vehicle around. He waved her off and headed for his Land Rover while she gingerly began the journey back down the lane. There were several half-filled snow ruts that had been formed by the wheels of passing vehicles, and she was happy to follow in them, though a little surprised that anyone else would have been driving here today.

It took only a few minutes for Helen to work her way back down the narrow lane. Her headlights cut through the falling snow but did little to extend her range of vision. Ahead, they picked out a road sign, and she knew the T-junction was near. She slowed, allowing the vehicle a gentle approach. Alan's Land Rover headlights were now visible in her rear-view mirror – he would catch up soon.

Reaching the junction, she paused and checked carefully in both directions; there were no headlights visible on the main road. She checked in both directions again and began to edge out.

She had driven Sam's vehicle almost across the junction and was straightening up in the city-bound lane when, out of nowhere, a shadowy blur suddenly appeared. Its lights off and engine revving, a big 4x4 slammed into the side of hers.

The sound of grinding metal and a roaring engine filled her world. Her head cracked against the side window. The blast of a discharging air bag then saved her from banging into the steering wheel. She only vaguely sensed the motion as the vehicle spun twice around and, before it could settle, was hit again.

Screaming tyres struggled for grip as the bull bars of her assailant's big 4x4 once again banged into the side of Helen's, forcing her vehicle off the road. Her vehicle tilted over at a crazy angle as the nearside tyres settled into a ditch.

The attacking 4x4 pulled back to deliver a fourth hit and topple Helen's vehicle into the ditch's ice covered water that, today, lay concealed beneath a layer of snow. Even as she sat stunned and helpless, she looked across at her assailant but could see little in the afternoon's winter shadows, her vision now failing as her eyes began to close. Then, as quickly as it had begun, the attack was over; the big 4x4 straightened onto the road and rushed away just as Alan's Land Rover pulled up, horn blaring and lights flashing.

Helen gradually came round, still belted into the driver's seat. Alan had already clawed away the air bag and begun a preliminary first-aid check.

'Helen! Helen, can you hear me? You're going to be okay. I've called the emergency services; they'll be here soon. Just stay still, work with me now, let's make sure there's nothing broken. Can you answer my questions?'

Helen muttered a confused response while he did a thorough check. Held up by the bad weather, it took the emergency services nearly twenty minutes to arrive.

***

Sam implored Elaine to take care and hung up his phone. He slipped it into his pocket and looked across the corridor to where the deacon stood watching him.

'You're leaving, aren't you?'

'I'm sorry. I have to.'

'But what about him?' The shaken young deacon jabbed a finger towards the frosted glass doors of the mortuary. 'What about us?'

Sam crossed the corridor and put his arm around the deacon. 'You're going to be alright. The police are all over this; they'll manage everything.' He hoped he sounded more convincing than he felt. 'I have to go now, but I'll be back as soon as I can.' Guiding the deacon with his arm, Sam gently propelled him towards the exit.

It had not taken the police long to provide some answers. A body had been found, and he and the deacon had agreed to identify it. An easy job, unmistakably Iskinder. The local police had been quite open. What they said and what Sam saw were enough to trigger every one of Sam's alarm bells.

It appeared cause of death had been easy to establish. Iskinder had been nailed into a potato crate that had then been thrown over a cliff to the rocky coast below. The pathologist was sure he had been alive when the crate was launched. The broken fingers were a mystery; the damage had nothing to do with the fall. Sam knew exactly what had caused the damage to Iskinder's hands. He knew it meant their worst nightmare was back.

Cassiter must have survived the tunnel collapse in Crete last year. Now he was back and once again on their case. And Helen had been targeted too. It couldn't be coincidence; the two incidents had to be linked, somehow.

They stopped outside the building, and Sam tilted his face up, allowing the relative warmth of the island's winter sun to wash across his face. Certain this would be the last quiet moment for a while, he tried to hold onto it but couldn't.

'Look, I'm going out to the airport right now. You stay with your congregation. I'm sure you'll be alright. There's something I must do in Edinburgh immediately. But I'll be back as soon as possible.'

Sam thrust out a hand to hail a passing cab. He pulled open its rear door, paused and turned back to the deacon. 'Try not to think about what you've just seen. Once I've got to the airport and sorted a flight, I'll call Bishop Ignatius and tell him what's happened.'

The deacon nodded numbly.

'What you just saw was horrible. I'm sure you are going to be okay but to be safe don't be alone for now.' Sam watched the deacon's face and saw the horror replaced by concern. 'Everything will be fine. Once I've done what I need to at home, I'll be back. For now, just be aware.' He closed the cab door, and it pulled away before the deacon could ask any further questions.

***

In silence, Elaine and her daughter, Grace, worked to take down and pack away the manse's Christmas decorations. They had promised to help Helen with the traditional take down. Since she was being kept in hospital overnight as a precaution, it fell to them to ensure bad luck wasn't attracted by leaving the decorations up.

'Well, if all of this comes from complying with tradition, I wonder what ignoring it would have brought,' said Grace, standing at the top of a stepladder from where she was handing down tree decorations to her mother.

Elaine took them one by one and absently placed them into the packaging, exactly as she had done over so many Christmases past for Helen's predecessor, John Dearly. They continued in silence for a little while.

Elaine gave her daughter's calf a nudge. 'I'm thinking we can both go to collect Sam from the airport; he's arriving on the last Heathrow shuttle this evening. What do you think?'

'I'm up for that.'

Chapter 3

MONDAY JANUARY 6TH

The snowstorms of recent days had eased off. While the sky overhead was still full of grey cloud, it was at a higher altitude now and the atmosphere was lighter. A taxi turned into the manse's driveway and stopped just a few steps from the front door. Sam got out. Turning and leaning back into the cab, he offered Helen his arm; she took it and stepped out to join him in the morning cold.

Grace had just cleared the snow away from the footpath and steps leading up to the front door, and now she and Elaine hurried down towards the taxi.

'Helen, how are you feeling?' said Grace.

'Come on into the warm,' said Elaine. Mother and daughter bustled Sam to the side as each linked an arm with Helen to support and guide her back into the manse. Sam didn't bother resisting; he paid the driver and followed behind as the noise of the retreating taxi faded.

'Come in, come in. Back home, this is where you need to be,' said Elaine, guiding Helen along the hall towards the kitchen.

'Your mum and dad want you to phone as soon as you're settled,' said Grace.

Helen nodded. Sam had contacted them as soon as he had arrived back from Malta the previous evening. 'I'll call them in a while.'

Grace placed a cushion on the kitchen chair as Helen sat then slipped another between the chair back and her spine. 'How's that?'

'Great, thanks. I'm fine. Nothing's broken; I'm just shaken up.'

'More than that, I think,' said Sam, sitting opposite her.

Elaine placed a pot of coffee on the table and sat too. 'So what exactly happened?'

'I'm not sure. There was a crash. I don't know whether the other driver lost control in the snow. One moment I was pulling out into the main road, the next he'd come from nowhere and hit me. Then it must have turned into some sort of road-rage attack; the driver seemed to snap and drove at me again. I'm not sure what happened after that. I think Alan Ralston arrived – he'd been following me – and scared the other driver away.'

'The driver must have been a total nutjob,' said Grace, as she slid mugs of coffee across the table. 'Did anyone manage to get his vehicle registration number?'

'I certainly didn't; perhaps Alan did. I was too shocked to notice, then I think I blacked out when he smashed into the car the third time.' Helen reached out her hand and clasped Sam's. 'Oh Sam, I am sorry about your car. Have you heard if it's badly damaged?'

He squeezed her hand back. 'I've no idea. I'll find out what happened to it later. It's insured, so don't worry about that. The car can be replaced – it's what's happened to you that matters.'

'Well, I'll be okay. I hope the police catch the driver, but I think I was just in the wrong place at the wrong time.' She saw a change in Sam's expression. 'What?'

Sam glanced around the table then took a breath before starting. 'It might have been an accident, but I'm not so sure.' He had played through in his mind how he should break the news that Cassiter was still around. In the event, it was easier just to recount what he knew of events in Malta.

Elaine had suffered at Cassiter's hand, and though her stoic features betrayed no emotion, Sam spotted her complexion pale as he broke the news. Grace looked angry and Helen remained expressionless.

'It's not over then?' said Helen.

'It's not over,' he replied.

'Poor Iskinder. I will have to telephone Ignatius in Addis; he will be devastated at the loss.'

'We're going to need to be careful again. Very careful,' said Sam.

'I thought it was all resolved before,' said Grace.

'Well, we certainly found the Templar treasury, but there must be something else.'

'What?' said Elaine.

'I don't know yet. But I'm beginning to think it's to do with what's inside the boxes. It seems they saw Ignatius give Helen the box in Nairobi. I'm thinking they wanted to know more, which is why they tracked Iskinder and tried to get information from him.'

'Do you think they did?' said Grace.

'No more than I got. Iskinder told me everything he knew about the boxes. Yet that little amount seems to have been enough to brutalise and kill for.'

'Cassiter doesn't need much excuse to be violent. What are you thinking, Sam?' said Helen.

'I think that from what I've heard of your encounter it was no accident or road-rage incident. You were targeted. Why? I don't know. Let's make sure nobody goes out alone for now. In fact, why don't you all stay here in the manse together for a few days?'

The three women all nodded agreement.

'What about you? How do we challenge this?'

'Well, let's start by telling the police everything we know – get them on board. Recent history will certainly give them reason to provide some protection, even though DCI Wallace has retired. What was his sergeant called?'

'DS Brogan. I'll call him in a little while,' said Elaine.

'Great. If you do that, Elaine, I'll go with Grace to collect some things for you both from your house.'

'You didn't say what our next step should be,' said Helen.

'Iskinder wanted us to go to Libya, to a place called Leptis Magna.'

'To Libya?' Helen looked shocked.

'I know. I didn't fancy the idea, but he was certain it was the only way.'

'I wonder what's inside the boxes,' said Grace. 'It's another one of those Templar secret puzzles isn't it?'

'Yes, so it seems. I'm thinking … you recall there was lots of bullion and coin found in Crete? That was the Templars' banking assets, their treasury, but that may have been only half of their possessions. What wasn't there were the Order's arts and treasures that they were known to have collected. Those are still out there somewhere. Cassiter and his people must know it too, and they are tracking us again – presumably to stop us finding it first.'

'Again, Sam, what's the plan?'

'Simple. We have to get ahead and make sure we find whatever it is first.'

'Here we go again,' said Elaine. 'Shouldn't we just let the police deal with the whole thing?'

'Yes, we need the police for protection, but I don't think we can rely on them to solve the puzzle. The police will never recognise the clues. Crikey! We know what's behind it all, and we can't spot the solution.'

'Why not just break the boxes open and see what's inside?' said Grace.

Sam shook his head. 'These are historical artefacts; we can't just break them open like looters. More important, Ignatius and Iskinder have both told us that breaking the boxes open will break the message, losing it forever. No, we need to solve this.'

'Sam, I really need to phone my folks now. Tell me what you propose.'

'I need to look into how we can find whatever is hidden in Leptis Magna without actually going there. It seems to have something to do with slabs or some such, set on the way up to the Temple of Jupiter. If we can find that, then we have a head start.'

***

Helen had slept much of the day. Feeling better, she entered the study, walked behind the desk and drew the curtains shut, closing out the fast encroaching twilight. She leant on Sam's shoulder, peering over it to see what he was doing.

'Well?' she asked.

Sam pointed at the screen. 'I'm just checking seat availability for flights to Orkney.'

'Orkney?'

'A stroke of luck. Turns out Colonel Gaddafi allowed a German University to do some archaeological work there a few years back. I've been in touch with the university's administration department, but the academic staff aren't back to work until next week. What they did tell me was one of their senior staff working on those Libyan fieldtrips was British – Professor

Miles Bertram. He's retired now, but it was easy enough to find his contact details. Seems he's living in a sheltered retirement complex in Morecambe.'

'Great. Where's that?'

'North-west England, on the coast. One-time popular holiday destination, now a little less so.'

'If your man is in England, why are we going to the Northern Isles?'

'I spoke with the warden of his accommodation. Turns out our Professor Bertram is not so retired. He goes up to Orkney each New Year to do some digging and research around the Tomb of the Eagles. The owners give him unfettered access while it's shut to the public at this time of year, and in turn, they get to use anything he unearths in their exhibition for the following tourist season.'

'Can't you just phone him?'

'No, it would appear our professor is very old-school. No mobile phone, and no email, now he's retired. The warden has no idea of his address in Orkney. I just need to go up and find him at the tomb.'

'We,' said Helen.

Sam glanced at her. 'Are you sure you're up to a flight?'

'I'll be okay; we're both going to Orkney tomorrow.'

Sam recognised the tone in her voice and didn't bother arguing. He turned to the computer screen and confirmed there were plenty of seats available on the flight.

'We'll be fine, lots of empty seats, as you'd expect at this time of year. I won't book the flights; I don't want anyone to be able to work out where we're going. We can just buy seats when we get to the airport tomorrow, if we get there well ahead of take-off time. Then it's just a matter of hoping Professor Bertram can shed some light on what's at Leptis Magna that might be so important.'

'Yeah, let's hope he can. I'm not keen on the thought of a trip to Libya right now,' she said.

Sam nodded. 'I spoke with Ignatius again while you were sleeping, passed on your condolences over Iskinder. The bishop's pretty cut up. I'm guessing he was fonder of his assistant than he ever let on. He wants you to phone him.'

'I will. They probably depended on one another more than he realised.'

'Agreed, poor old man. Poor old Iskinder too. Oh, Elaine phoned Xavier and told him what had happened to you. He's coming over next Monday.'

'There's no need for him to do that,' said Helen, though inside she was pleased. The old Catholic priest from Sardinia had been a confidant of her mentor, John Dearly. Now that John was dead, Xavier represented a rare link with the past and the secrets John had taken to the grave with him.

'Well, I'm pleased he's coming. If anyone can help throw some light on the boxes, it's him.'

The front doorbell rang and was immediately followed by the sound of Grace's light step hurrying down the hall then a warm brogue of a voice rolling in through the opened door.

'Come on, it's Francis,' said Helen, leading Sam towards the study door. Francis, the local Catholic parish priest had been John Dearly's loyal friend and had transferred that loyalty to her when she took over John's church and duties. She suddenly felt the need to be in the company of all her group.

Chapter 4

TUESDAY JANUARY 7ᵀᴴ

Eugene Jr scowled at his assistant. 'What do you mean, we can't follow them? Why not?' Walking round the table that was doubling as his desk, he jabbed a finger into the man's chest. 'It's not good enough. You messed up the car crash business. Now you can't even follow them in a public place. What happened?'

'They took a taxi to the airport and bought tickets at the ticket office.'

'Where? Where did they go?'

'It was with a local airline. They fly out to the islands. I couldn't get close enough to hear what they were doing, but I watched, then I lost them when they went through security.'

'Dolt! Is there nothing you can do right?' Eugene Jr slapped the man's face. 'My father will eat you alive for this incompetence. For God's sake, he'll eat me alive. How could you lose them? How?'

'I know where they went, sir. Only two Loganair flights departed after they went through the security gate; they must have gone on one of those. One went south, to Jersey. The other went north, to the Northern Isles, Orkney and the Shetlands. They must have gone on one of those routes.'

For a long moment, Eugene Jr glared at his man. 'Why didn't you start by telling me this?' He waved his hand in dismissal and pulled a phone from his pocket. Cassiter's electronic surveillance team were based in Paris now, but they would be able to crack the airline's system and find which flight Cameron and Johnson had taken. Then he could find out what was going on. He didn't think his father had a man on the islands, north or south; he would need to get somebody out there quickly.

***

A little before four in the afternoon, the small passenger plane landed at Kirkwall Airport. It was just half past four when Helen and Sam collected their bags, cleared the passenger exit channel and hired a car.

They stepped out of the little airport building and into the cold air of an already blackened night. Helen shivered and pulled her jacket closed. Ahead of them, flakes of snow danced and flurried around in the tugging breeze before dropping to melt on the salt-strewn walkways.

The path ahead fed into a neat, if modest-sized, car park. It was evenly lit by golden glowing floodlights. Sam carried the bags and Helen pressed the car's security fob. Her action quickly triggered a flashing of yellow hazard warning lights. 'Over there,' she said, pointing before hurrying off towards a little car.

'It's dark so early,' said Helen as Sam threw in their luggage and slipped into the driver's seat.

'Yes, we're a good way north here. And it feels very cold. The sea's all around which actually keeps the temperature up compared to the mainland, but the wind chill's the killer. Right. Let's go.'

Helen rubbed her cold hands against her still colder cheeks. 'My face is frozen.' Reaching out a hand she redirected one of the air vents towards her, enjoying the blast of warming air. 'What now? It's dark, and you deliberately didn't book a hotel.'

'We can't be too careful. Now we know Cassiter and his friends are back, every move must stay under the radar, as far as possible.'

'So?'

'There are plenty of farms that do bed and breakfast, and I reckon there are very few tourists at this time of year. We'll have no problem finding a room available for cash, almost untraceable.'

'What about our flights and the hire car?'

'If they're looking, which previous experience says they will be, what we've done with no pre-bookings and over-the-counter cash payments will only have slowed down their finding us. It won't prevent it ...'

The lights of the terminal and car park spilled into the surrounding dark to light up a junction, a street sign and a strip of main road that stretched away a hundred paces or so in either direction. Beyond that, the road vanished into the blackness. Only a little glow of light from the windows of a distant croft broke the broad sweep of the dark.

'Which way?'

'We'll go left.'

'The road sign said Kirkwall was to the right.'

'Yes, we don't need to go there at all. Where we're going is the southmost of the islands, South Ronaldsay.'

'Another island? Do we take a ferry too?'

'Nothing as exciting, I'm afraid.' The car's headlights picked out the road ahead but their brightness did little to dispel a sense of isolation; the emptiness beyond the beams was almost palpable. 'I doubt you'll see much in the dark, but the road we want runs directly to the destination. It hops between a couple of islands in the process using a series of causeways.'

'Oh, that's clever.'

'Well, it wasn't done for the islanders benefit. Do you remember a British politician called Churchill? Winston Churchill?'

'Of course, who doesn't? He was your leader in the Second World War.'

'Well, he ordered the causeways built during the war to protect the British Navy based at Scappa Flow. They were to stop Nazi submarines from slipping between the islands and attacking the fleet at anchor. You'll see in a minute ... or you would, if it weren't so dark. Scappa Flow is an enormous natural harbour, one of the biggest in the world. Handy if you have a big navy ... pretty well empty now, of course.'

Sam lapsed into silence as the snow fell a little harder, big flakes now driven by a rising wind. The windscreen wipers managed easily enough, and the fall turned to slush and water almost as soon as it hit the road. He brought the car to a halt at a little junction and pointed directly ahead. The headlights shone through the falling snow to reflect off black water that rolled and shifted unceasingly beneath the winter wind.

'That's Scappa Flow,' he said.

'It's close,' said Helen.

'Yes, we're right at the water's edge now.' Sam drove the car forwards and turned to the left. 'Here's the first causeway, right now.'

The dark was suddenly lonelier still. As Sam hurried them across the causeway, their world shrunk to only headlight beams, falling snow and the metallic crash barriers lining either side of the narrow road. Silently, they both absorbed the atmosphere. An isolated and lonely road bound on either side by deep, dark waters.

Once across, the headlights seemed to expand their reach to include passing verges and occasional signs.

'Sam, that said, Italian Chapel. What is that?'

'It's a bit of a tourist destination, though I've never been. If there's time tomorrow, we could pop in and see. No promises though, it depends how we get on. The Italian prisoners of war built the chapel; I believe it's very beautiful. There were lots of them kept up here during the war. They were the ones who helped build the causeways.' He drove on through the snow.

Reaching South Ronaldsay, they followed the road to the island's south end. Sam reasoned they may as well get as near to their final destination as possible. He eased back on his speed so they could check out signs for roadside bed-and-breakfast offers as they passed. Several of the farms, their presence signalled by the occasional lit window, displayed B&B signs. He kept going south.

Close to a turning signed as the way to the Burwick Ferry, Helen pointed out a B&B sign. Set just a little back from the roadside sign was a light marking the farmhouse.

'That'll do nicely,' said Sam. 'Let's get an early night and be ready to find Professor Bertram in the morning.'

Chapter 5

WEDNESDAY JANUARY 8TH

The late northern dawn was lightening the horizon while Helen and Sam enjoyed a cooked breakfast and their host tried her best to answer Sam's questions.

'Aye, we often have tourists stay here but not at this time of year. We're handy for the Tomb of the Eagles, right enough, but it's shut up for the winter. I don't think you can get in at all.'

'We're looking for somebody who's working there,' said Sam.

Shaking her head, the farmer's wife moved forwards to refill coffee cups. 'No, there's nobody working there just now. I'm friends with the visitor centre manager, and she was only saying the other day that she wished she hadn't let her seasonal staff go so early before the winter. There's more work they want to do on access paths, but it'll have to wait until the spring now.'

'No, not an employee. An archaeologist working for himself.'

'Oh, right enough. That'll be Professor Bertram. Why didn't you say?

He comes up each year and stays through January.'

'Miles Bertram, yes. That's the man.'

Putting the pot down on the table, she delved into the broad pocket at the front of her apron and pulled out a handset. 'When he comes to the islands, he always stays in the next farm up, it's closer to the tomb. I'll call Mrs Gould now. If you're lucky, he'll not have set off for the tomb yet.'

She sat at the table and smiled at them both. 'Let's see if you're in luck.'

Helen was closest to her and could just hear the phone's tone. The ringtone stopped as the call was answered by the sound of a distant voice, but Helen struggled to understand it.

'Hello, Jeanie, it's me, Isa. How are you this morning?' Isa half turned away as though part of a conspiracy. 'That's good. That's very good. I'm pleased to hear it. Everyone's fine here too, thank you.' She turned her body back towards the table and caught Sam's eye. 'Tell me, Jeanie, do you have your Professor Bertram there? Or is he away to the tomb already?'

Isa paused and listened for a few moments. Then, still keeping eye contact with Sam, she frowned and shook her head. 'Oh well, it was worth a try. I've got a young couple here who were hoping to link up with him. What do you think?'

Isa listened to the reply, pursed her lips and nodded. 'Okay, if you think so, I'll tell them.' She smiled then half turned away again as her conversation ran on to things Sam and Helen knew nothing of. Two or three minutes later, the call ended and Isa slipped the phone back into her apron pocket as she turned back to face her guests.

'Well, that was my friend Jeanie. Her family work the land up the road, not far from the tomb. Professor Bertram has already set off; he likes a walk. You'll need to go direct to the tomb if you want to see him. She says you'll be fine to go there. Drive right up to the visitor centre. It's all closed up but you can park and then walk on to the tomb; just follow the signs.'

***

Sam had insisted they purchase rubber boots to replace those Helen had lost in the car crash. Going on any rural car journey in winter without was asking for trouble. All of a sudden, Helen saw the merit in his forethought. From a wet and deserted car park, a slippy, puddle-strewn path led towards their destination, and all the while, flurries of snowflakes flew past them on the wind. The generally flat farmland continued its gentle rise ahead of them to where it formed a near horizon, beyond that it plunged away unseen to the wild sea below. Above the horizon was a mass of dark clouds, low and heavy, driven in from the wild North Atlantic by the unswerving wind that continually buffeted them and tugged at their jackets and trouser legs.

They stopped and turned, looked back to where the island sloped and spread gently away. Farmland green everywhere, broken by occasional outcrops of weathered grey rock and a scattering of farm steadings, grey like the bedrock. Cold as it felt in the wind, the snow mostly didn't lie under the relative warming influence of the nearby seas.

'No trees,' said Helen.

'It's the wind – nothing natural stands much above waist height unless it's given some shelter, but the land's fertile, excellent for farming. In fact, humans have lived off it for thousands of years. It has been farmed since before the pyramids were built, when almost all the British mainland was just ancient woodland.'

'How did the people get here before there were proper boats?'

'I'm not sure. There was a time before the last ice age ended when Britain and the islands would have been joined to the European landmass. Maybe they were already here and got cut off when the Doggerland flooding occurred. Maybe stone-age man had better boating skills than we give them credit for.' Helen had moved close to Sam, finding some shelter from the wind in his frame. He raised a hand to her shoulder and squeezed gently. 'Come on, let's keep moving.' They turned and continued along the track.

'Doggerland? I've never heard of that,' said Helen.

'It doesn't exist anymore, other than as the name of a meteorological sea area.' He waved a hand towards the east. 'Out there, in the North Sea. Doggerland was the land bridge that linked Europe to the British Isles. Towards the end of the last ice age, it's believed it was hit by a double whammy. There was a general and steady rise in sea level, drowning out much of the lowland plains. On top of that came what we call the Storegga Tsunami. A giant underwater landslide launched a wall of water twenty-five metres high. It swept over the islands and the eastern coastal lands – it was a true monster, one of the biggest ever. All part of the process that permanently cut Britain off from Europe.'

'Wow, but everything seems so ageless here.'

'Ageless, but nothing is ever truly permanent.'

They kept walking. The track underfoot was wet, though easily passable, and it took only a few minutes to reach their destination. Close to the cliff edge, the still green ground rose more sharply, exposing yet another stony outcrop, however, closer inspection showed this one was slightly different. Not all raw stone here. The line of exposed bedrock was broken in the middle section by a series of laid stones, perfectly colour-matched and weathered with their surroundings; only on closer inspection was it clear that human hands had been at work.

'Here we are,' said Sam.

'Let's hope your professor's here, and I hope there's some shelter.'

'I can't see him. If he's here, he must be under cover. See how what looks like bedrock is actually laid slabs? There's a darker patch down low in the centre; I think that might be an entrance to a passageway. The professor's probably inside the tomb. We'll find out soon enough. Come on!'

Even before they reached the outcrop, it was clear Sam was right. The dark patch resolved into a small opening, formed thousands of years before by skilful hands that had carefully constructed the entrance passage. The lintel slab above the opening had been selected and exactly positioned to support the weight of rock above it for an eternity.

There was no sign of Professor Bertram. They crouched down to get a better look at the entrance. A thick blue nylon rope had been fixed above the opening and looped down and round to disappear into the passageway. The floor of the passageway was covered with wooden planking. Getting onto his hands and knees, Sam peered in.

'It goes back a good bit then I can see light. Electric light – the professor must already be here.'

'How do we get inside?'

'We can crawl on the boards,' said Sam, still peering into the passageway. Then he noticed another much slimmer rope that trailed across the boards. 'Hold on, what's this?' He gently pulled on the rope and felt something move at the far end. He pulled again, and realising what it was, he continued to pull, steadily drawing the cargo along the passageway towards them.

'What is it?'

'I think it's a trolley. Yes, here it comes. See, it's like a big skateboard.' He kept pulling and the trolley appeared. 'You can lie on your back and pull on this thicker blue rope to propel yourself along the passageway on the trolley. Fancy a go?'

'What do you think?' said Helen, twisting and settling her back onto the trolley.

'Perhaps I should go first?' said Sam.

Helen looked up at him. 'Next time. I'll see you inside.' She pulled on the blue rope, and the trolley slowly rolled back into the passage. The low walls were solidly constructed of neatly set stones, topped by a series of tightly fitting lintels that sealed and protected the passage.

The passage was only nine or ten feet in length, and it took just a few seconds for Helen to propel herself through. She emerged into the heart of the cairn and blinked in the harsh electric lights that shone down from roof fixtures to illuminate the whole inside of the chamber. She rolled off the trolley, and it immediately vanished as Sam pulled it back to him.

Helen rose to her knees and rubbed her eyes while they adjusted to the bright light. She blinked a little and glanced about her. For just a moment, she froze, then jumped to her feet. In front of her stood a short man, apparently stout, but she guessed, under the several layers of clothing, he was far slimmer.

His neatly trimmed grey beard complimented the short-cut silvered hair that bristled thickly across his whole head.

'Can I help you?' he said.

'I hope so,' said Helen. 'You are Professor Bertram?'

'That's me, and who exactly are you? I don't ever have visitors here.'

'I trust we haven't disturbed you too much. It's just there are some questions my friend needs to ask you.'

Sam emerged from the dark passageway into the lit chamber, and even as his eyes struggled to adjust, he stood up. After taking a moment to regain his composure, he stepped forwards and reached out a hand. 'Sam Cameron, sir. I'm an archaeologist at Edinburgh. And this is Helen Johnson, a church minister and my ... err ... my associate.'

'Edinburgh, eh? Been to a few workshops there over the years. Not for a while though. Cameron ... Sam Cameron?' He looked quizzically at

Sam as he took the proffered hand. 'Your name is familiar; I'm sure I've read two or three papers you've published. They were impressive.'

'Thank you, sir. And I have to say you have built up an enviable reputation over the years. If my publications ever get remotely close to yours, I'll be doing something right.'

Miles waved away the compliment. 'That's in the past now. I've been retired going on ten years, and before that, I was in Hamburg for nearer two decades. All my published work was focused on the classical period. Now I'm retired, I can do what I want.'

'Yes, I'd heard you were in Hamburg. In fact, it's your old university that put me in touch with you. They thought you'd be the man to help me out.'

'Oh, how's that? What do you want? It must be quite something to bring you all the way up here from Edinburgh in this weather.' Miles turned and stepped along the chamber towards a little trestle table that had been set up to one side, a folding chair beside it. He sat. 'Though, I'm not sure I can help. I keep to myself these days. I like to do a little work at my own pace now, on things that interest me.' He glanced back along the chamber towards Sam and Helen and beckoned them towards him before sweeping some papers from an adjacent knee-height stone slab that he had been using as a table extension.

Sam and Helen joined him at the table and sat, side by side, on the stone slab.

Professor Bertram fixed Sam with a steady gaze. 'Sam, you say? And Helen? Well, why don't you both call me Miles and tell me why I'm being disturbed in a place where I've come to expect perfect solitude.'

They chatted for a few minutes. In conversation, Sam confirmed the name of the woman at Hamburg who had made the recommendation. Helen noted a wistful smile cross the old man's face at the mention of her name then it passed, and the conversation continued.

'So tell me, Sam. What's your speciality? Why are you actually here?'

'In the past year or so, I've found myself focusing more on the Middle Ages, the twelfth, thirteenth, fourteenth centuries. Particularly the Scottish Wars of Independence.'

Miles looked puzzled. 'I don't understand why you're here then. You are working several thousand years after all this.' He let his hands arc up to indicate the cairn. 'What's here for you?'

'It's you, I think,' said Helen with a smile.

Miles' eyebrows contorted slightly as he tried to make sense of what she'd said. 'Me?'

'Yes. Look, Miles, by accident, my studies have become focused on the Middle Ages, but a chance discovery is taking me back to the Roman era.'

Miles nodded. 'Archaeology can overlap. But Rome to the medieval? It seems far too broad a time period.'

'Yes. Yet I understand when you retired you took up an interest in Scottish Neolithic island life, and I have no idea what prompted you to make that leap; before you retired, your work at Hamburg specialised in the Roman Empire – that's what I'm interested in.'

Miles suddenly laughed. 'I can't argue with that. When I retired, I wanted to keep involved, but with something where I set the pace'—he glanced about—'and this was perfect. Nobody ever bothered me. Until now.' He laughed again and reached out a hand to shake Helen's forearm. She smiled.

'So, our interests converge, and I have an urgent question about Leptis Magna,' said Sam.

'Leptis Magna?' Miles' voice was bright with surprise.

'Yes. You were there on a dig some years ago.'

'Leptis, yes, of course I remember it. But it's not a name I would have expected to hear spoken here. What can I do for you? Leptis was meant to be my swansong.' There was a sudden sparkle in the old man's voice. 'I don't know what I can do or tell you. But if I can help you, I will.'

'Thank you,' said Sam, pulling out his copy of the Coptic pope's letter to the bishop in Addis Ababa. Keeping it inside its clear plastic pouch, he laid it on the trestle table in front of Miles and told a little of the story, explaining the reference to roads or steps or a key at the Temple of Jupiter.

A series of quick-fire questions and answers followed. Miles seemed to get younger with each exchange. Finally, he jumped up and paced the length of the chamber. Pausing at the far end, he muttered to himself for a few moments. He tweaked and shuffled a little cache of eagle claws and skulls he had recently discovered. Then he hurried back and resumed his seat.

'This is very interesting, and I can see why Hamburg sent you to me. You see, back then it was the Gaddafi era in Libya. We were very lucky to get in at all. There was always politics, of course, and that dictated to some extent what we worked on at Leptis Magna.

'Much of it had already been excavated by the Italians before the Second World War but then, of course, abandoned, and what with one problem or another, we were pretty well the first modern archaeological team to go there.'

'It must have been a great experience,' said Sam.

'Unbelievable, quite incredible. Have either of you ever been to Africa?'

'Oh yes, we've been to Africa, but never Libya,' said Helen.

'Well, trust me; it's an archaeologist's paradise. Or at least, it was before the post-Gaddafi breakdown in law and order. Committed as I am, I'm not sure I would go back at the moment.'

'So can you help? The Temple of Jupiter?'

'Yes, yes. The Temple of Jupiter, the road, you said, or steps or keys? Hmm, as I said, I can understand why Hamburg referred you to me if you'd mentioned the Temple of Jupiter.'

'Go on,' said Sam.

'Well, the expedition had a brief that, after a general sweep of the site, it was to focus on specific areas that interested the Libyan Government. The Temple of Jupiter was not included. I think we were about day two or three in when there must have been one of those periodic spats between the British and Libyan governments. Gaddafi's men realised I was British, not German, and they decided I was not allowed to work on the dig. But due credit to the Germans, they said, if I was expelled they would all go too.

'Gaddafi's men let me stay so long as I was not directly involved in the excavation. The rest of the team focused on the prescribed work in the main part of the city to the west of the Wadi Lebda. I was left to my own devices on the east side of the wadi. A handful of ruined buildings and temples, the ancient quayside and not much else.

'I think the Libyans allowed me there because they thought it was less interesting; maybe they hoped I might even up sticks and leave the expedition in a huff. Believe me, that didn't happen. I spent a very happy month focusing on two or three spots away from the action, and they included the Temple of Jupiter.'

'That sounds like fun. Did the officials leave you alone then?'

'I think, eventually, the Libyan supervisors put me down as a bit of an eccentric, harmless, so they basically ignored me. When we came to leave, the university did not want my work anywhere near the official records – they were worried about not being invited back. So all my notes, pictures and findings travelled out with me as personal possessions, and they've stayed that way ever since.'

Miles glanced from Helen to Sam and back, his eyes glinting triumph in the electric light.

'The Temple of Jupiter?' said Sam.

'Ah, yes. To the point, of course. The Temple of Jupiter. I think I know exactly what you are referring to.'

'Really? That easy? You know?' said Helen.

'Well, we can never be absolutely certain. But if that letter you are carrying has a meaning as you describe, it can be only one thing. And let me tell you, even if you were at the temple it would not be immediately obvious to you, not at all.'

'This is great news for me, Miles. What is it?'

'Unless I've gone right off track, which is unlikely, it's all stone after all, not much moveable material … There is a route, an ancient walkway leading from the Temple of Jupiter down to the then new docks.

'They were built by the Emperor Septimius Severus – in my opinion, a complete waste of money. I believe they contributed to the silting up of the Wadi Lebda. It's quite amazing how, throughout history, governments have continued to squander money on poorly planned public works, don't you think?'

Sam gave a humouring smile. 'Absolutely, but Miles, the temple.'

'The temple. Yes, the temple. There is only one thing that could possibly represent what the author of your letter meant. I don't think it's the walkway you're interested in. The stairway is stone; of course, nobody's walked on it since the Saracens took Leptis from the Byzantines. The city was of no use to the new Muslim rulers, and gradually, over the following centuries, it was simply lost to the desert sands. I would imagine just a small resident population remained into the medieval era, maybe a little later, but by the time of the Barbary corsairs, it had completely vanished under the sand.'

'Byzantine? I thought we were talking Roman,' said Helen.

'By that time, control of Leptis Magna had passed from Rome and the Western Roman Empire to Byzantium and the Eastern Roman Empire. Thence, eventually, to the Muslim Saracens,' said Miles, his chest inflating slightly as he prepared to launch into automatic and give a well-practised and oft-delivered briefing.

Sam pressed his hand against Helen's forearm, discreetly checking her before she could ask another question. This was clearly Miles' hobbyhorse; allowed the time, it seemed he might expand all day without actually answering Sam's question.

'My key?' said Sam.

'Yes, yes, of course.' Miles returned to the topic. 'It's the stairway, very straightforward when you know to look. It took me a while, but I finally linked it all up. mind you, I spent a month there with little else to do.

'To either side of the stairway, starting from the top and on every alternate step down, pairs of tiles were set. Not immediately obvious to somebody strolling along. The stair is too wide to see the detail of both decorated tiles at the same time, but as soon as you know to look, there they are.

'You see, unlike much Roman fresco and artwork, the individual tiles in isolation seemed to make no sense, had no pattern. Each tile seemed similar to its partner on the opposite side of the stairway but not an exact copy, and the thing missing from the whole sequence was always a pattern. It's what you would expect to find, and there wasn't one, just random.'

'What does that mean?' asked Sam.

'I thought about it a lot. The absence of a pattern in the tile sequence was a real puzzle, especially for artwork on such a prestigious building.' Pausing for a moment, Miles fixed Sam with his gaze. 'Of course, in the end, it came to me. The absence of the pattern is the pattern.'

'I'm sorry, you've lost me.'

'I think they are a sequence, a code sequence, perhaps that's your key – hidden in plain view for nobody to ever notice. It's the only possible purpose for the tiles I can come up with. I can't prove my theory – after two thousand years, I never stood a chance of finding the message to decode. It will have been lost to time, long ago. They invested a lot of effort in keeping secrets secret – loved their codes and ciphers.'

Sam shifted on the stone. It was hard and becoming uncomfortable, but he moved, because instinctively, he wanted to be just a little closer to Miles. 'What do you mean a code sequence? Can you remember the tiles?'

Miles laughed. 'There were a dozen of them, and it was a long time ago. But of course, two thousand years ago there were no toughened steel vaults, no electric alarms. If you wanted to keep something secret, you did it by guile, by cunning. The use of codes and concealment was very common.'

'Yes,' said Sam. 'Yes, it was.'

'So, to see these tiles and how they're laid out, we would need to go to Leptis?' said Helen.

'I wouldn't go there these days. You'd be very lucky to come out with your life. But no, you don't need to go to Leptis Magna to see the tiles. I have a full set of photographs at home in Morecambe.'

'You do? May we see them?' Sam's voice was as steady as ever, but inside, his heart was pounding. Had they found what he needed, here, in the most remote and unlikely of places? Had they?

The conversation continued a little longer and reached an impasse due to Miles' plan to stay on Orkney for another two weeks and Sam's desperation to see the photographs as soon as possible. Finally, Miles promised when he got back to his farmhouse lodgings that afternoon, he would borrow the telephone to call his daughter. He'd warn her to expect a call from Sam and make sure she was ready to give him access to the photographs as soon as possible. He'd call the warden at his housing complex too, just to make sure they got access okay.

Miles chatted a little more, until finally, he made it clear he needed to return to his work. They moved back to the little passageway entrance. Helen gave Miles a brief hug, refastened her jacket and crouched down. Twisting and settling her back flat on the trolley, she looked up as Miles jotted down his daughter's phone number for Sam.

'Goodbye, Miles, I hope we meet again,' she said and reached up to grab hold of the blue pull rope.

'Oh, hold on one moment, please.'

Helen paused as Miles turned his attention back to Sam. 'While you're up here, there's something interesting just a bit further along the coast, close to the cliff's edge. I think it's medieval, more your time than mine. An engraved stone marker. It must have fallen centuries ago, been overgrown and finally buried beneath the turf. I unearthed it a couple of winters back. I think it may be right up your street.'

'Great, we'll have a look right now.'

'You won't be able to, I'm afraid. I covered it up again to preserve the site. Always meant to get in touch with somebody with an interest in the era, just never quite got round to it.'

'Oh well, another time maybe.'

'Yes, another time. But I'll ask my daughter to look out the photographs of that too. I think you'll find it an interesting artefact. I'm no expert on the period, but I think the markings may have some Templar significance. That's not surprising as the Earl of Orkney was apparently involved with the Templars.'

Involuntarily, Helen's hand gripped the blue rope tighter.

'That does sound interesting,' said Sam, reaching out his hand to shake Miles' as Helen finally pulled on the blue rope and disappeared from view, heading back out into the winter's cold.

***

Sam returned the keys to the car-hire kiosk and joined Helen in the cafeteria where she had bought them hot soup and rolls. She gave him a smile as he sat.

'It seems like we've had a successful trip.'

'Yes. Anything that ensures I don't have to go to Libya is positive.'

'I? Knowing who's involved, you don't think I'd let you go alone?' said Helen.

Sam shook his head. 'I knew you'd think that, but if I'd gone, you couldn't have come.'

'How so?'

'You're a Christian minister, a woman and an American. That would single you out for every sort of special attention from the extremist elements. You'd be a prize many would sacrifice anything to capture. It's just not safe for you.'

Helen was about to argue when she stopped herself, thought and nodded; Sam was right. They finished their soup and made for the departure gate, eager to get home.

Even as Helen and Sam lined up to board the plane, passengers newly arrived from Edinburgh, including two burly men on very private business, funnelled through the arrivals channel.

Chapter 6

THURSDAY JANUARY 9TH

Helen gave the slightest of shivers as Sam drove his hire car past the place where she had so recently been rammed and forced off the road.

'That's where it happened,' she said.

Sam glanced sideways to where Helen indicated then returned his focus to the road ahead. He was taking no chances, even though the council had, at last, got to grips with recent snowfalls, and the main road was glistening wet-black. The verges were stacked with brown, grit-stained snow, ploughed aside by the road crews. The black leaf-free hedgerows were topped with a thick slab of snow, and beyond, the fields were buried in an unbroken layer of white.

'Turn in here,' said Helen.

Sam flicked on the indicator and turned off the main road.

Helen looked over her shoulder into the back seat. 'This is it guys.' In the back sat Davy and Julie – students from Sam's tutor group. Following their unintended involvement in previous incidents around Helen's Templar inheritance, they had become enthusiastic and trusted aides. Today, they were on hand to help Sam undertake a brief appraisal of what had been found in the woods.

Ten minutes later, they had parked up, grabbed their gear and walked up the field to the treeline, where they paused and looked back down and across the field to the hire car by the gate.

'There are more sets of footprints running back and forth across the field than I would have expected,' said Sam.

Helen had to agree. She recalled the set of tracks she thought she had seen amid the falling snow on her first visit. Perhaps she had been right after all.

A movement caught their attention. In the distance, they could just make out a tractor cab slowly making its way between the hedgerows that defined the lane.

'That will be Alan clearing the road,' said Helen.

'It'll certainly make access easier,' said Julie.

'I'm not sure we want that,' said Sam, glancing again at the footprints.

He turned and headed into the woods; Davy and Julie followed. Helen paused to raise an arm and wave towards the tractor. She smiled to herself as the driver acknowledged her with a bright flash of the floodlights that were ranked along the top of the tractor's cab. She turned and followed the others.

***

'Who's there?' Miles Bertram called along the low passageway. There was no answer. He stooped and peered into it. From the gloom within the passage, he could see only bright daylight. He was sure he had heard voices. Muttering to himself, he turned back to his work. He must have been mistaken – probably just the wind. He'd had visitors the day before. In all his years of winter research, he'd never had a visitor; it couldn't happen twice in successive days.

Miles thought about waiting for a bus and two coming at once then shook his head, laughed quietly and made his way to the far end of the cairn. As he ducked away into the side chamber, he did not see the trolley roll away into the passage. Nor did he see the blue pull rope tense. Moments later, a new visitor began to pull himself through the passageway and into the cairn.

***

'It's quite a site, bigger than I'd envisaged,' said Sam. Having pegged and taped off the immediate area, they had rigged a rope ladder and clambered down into the trench. Standing on what had once been the vaulted ceiling of the buried chamber, Sam had carefully worked his way along the length of the trench, checking the walls as he went.

His initial inspection over, he turned his attention back to the team who were spread out along the trench's length.

'It seems to be a single space. I can see no signs of side chambers or doorways.' He let his hand drift across the clean lines of the cut-stone walls. 'This is old. Much older than you would think from the state of the stone but being buried has protected it from weathering. Fine craftsmanship too. The best of masons worked on this.'

'Do you think it was our lot?' said Helen, crossing the chamber to join him.

'The Templars?' Sam shrugged. 'I've seen nothing to support that yet. Perhaps once we clear the fallen roof stones, we'll find clear evidence of who built it. But for now? Yes, my money's on your Templars. After all, they must have left this wood in trust for a reason. I can't think of any better reason to do that than to pass on a secret chamber. Whatever its purpose is.'

***

Miles Bertram didn't understand what was happening; he only knew he'd had enough.

Things had happened in a flurry. A strong hand had propelled him against the neatly stacked stones that formed the inside walls of the cairn. A second hand had quickly followed, forcing his face into the stone. His nose had broken at once. As the blood started to flow, he had pulled his head away from the stones only for it to be driven back again with added vigour. A split in his forehead had opened and a second stream of blood flowed down to fill his eyes and blind him. Then he was dragged back and thrown face down on to the stone floor.

'What's going on? Stop this. Who are you?' Miles rolled onto his side and tried to lever himself up on his arms. Age had weakened his body, but he had always been game.

'You have no right to be here. This is private land, and there's nothing of value. Just go. I'm going to report this to the authorities.'

There was a second assailant, a man whose presence Miles had not initially registered. He raised his boot and brought his heel down against the locked arm that supported Miles' weight as he started to rise. The elbow joint snapped, and Miles collapsed back to the ground with a scream of pain and fear. He tried to reach his good arm round to tend the snapped elbow – he never reached it.

The boot returned and met his face, scattering teeth that he had spent a lifetime preserving and protecting. Then the boot settled on his good arm, pinning it to the floor. As his pained cries finally subsided into laboured moans, strong hands reached down and gripped his shoulders to drag him up to his knees. The interrogation began.

The men inflicting the pain didn't really understand the questions that were being asked. Certainly, they could make little sense of the answers that

Miles Bertram directed towards the screen of the mobile phone they held open.

They did understand the clear instructions that reached them in French-accented English through the phone's speaker each time their victim failed to answer a question satisfactorily. And each time, they obliged Eugene Jr by inflicting more pain. They didn't bother holding back, knowing the man on the receiving end would never need to recover. Eventually, the beating seemed to elicit the required responses, and the remote inquisitor declared himself content.

From his place on the ground, Miles Bertram was scarcely aware of the men clearing up their mess. He was so dazed he hardly noticed when he was tied to the trolley and pulled through the passageway into the daylight. Outside, his broken and swollen face did not register the cold; his eyes, almost completely closed, did see the slightest squint of blue. The clouds of yesterday had cleared to leave a perfect pale blue winter sky, resting sharp against the shimmering silver of the sea.

He was aware of the quite unbearable pain in his broken elbow as the two men took an arm each and dragged him beyond the cairn to the cliff edge. There was no pause there. He simply left them, was aware of falling. Time for just one spin, blue sky to silver sea, then to black and nothing more.

***

Sam had rolled down the blind to block out the winter night. He returned to the kitchen table and sat beside Helen, resting a comforting hand on hers. He could see that, in spite of the kitchen's warmth, she was shivering.

Helen smiled at him through tear-filled eyes as she continued her telephone conversation. 'I'm so sorry, Ignatius. I want to come to the service, if it's at all possible. Promise you'll let me know the date of the funeral as soon as arrangements are made. If I can come, I will. Let's speak again soon. Now, I know you really need to speak with Sam; he's right here. I'll pass you over.'

Wiping away tears from her eyes, she passed the telephone handset to Sam and sat quietly as the long-distance conversation played through. Finally, the call ended, and Sam put down the handset.

Helen looked at him expectantly. 'Well?' she said.

'Strikes me there's a lot of Old Testament in Ignatius' perspective.'

'Oh?'

'Eye for an eye.'

'Oh, right. How did you handle that?'

'I didn't. It's not for me to influence Ignatius.'

'We know who we're up against. I certainly don't want him to go rushing in and getting himself hurt.'

'Me too. I've said all that I could. I told him that it was best to leave things to the experts. Though, I couldn't tell him who those experts were. Anyway, he was still up for me to go on the fishing boat to Leptis Magna to finish what we started, if only as a way to vindicate the sacrifice Iskinder has made.'

'You're not still thinking of going, surely?'

'No, I explained that I think I've found the solution to the message in his ancient letter right here in the UK.'

'How did he take that?'

'I'm not sure. To be blunt, I think his mind is focused more on repatriating Iskinder's body.'

'Poor man, poor both. All this killing has to end one day, Sam.'

'Yes, it does. But I think it will only end when the solution is found. Whatever these people want must be incredibly valuable.'

'What do you think it is?' said Helen.

'Well, it's got to be Templar artefacts, hasn't it? Treasures, something or some things they gathered. And it would seem to be something more valuable to the hunters than all the gold we unearthed before. And somehow, the answer is in the boxes, which we can't force open. We simply have to solve the puzzle. I'll be interested to ask Xavier what he thinks when he gets here on Monday, that's for sure.'

'Hmm, you're right. He may have a better idea than any of us.'

'Now, what about an early night? It's a fair drive to Morecambe and we want to be there for midday.'

'Okay, when will we need to set off?'

'I'm thinking eight o'clock. That will allow us a little time to spare.'

Chapter 7

FRIDAY JANUARY 10TH

Miles Bertram's neat retirement home was set three or four streets back from Marine Road, the main thoroughfare that carries traffic to and fro along Morecambe's seafront. One of a cluster of similar little bungalows, it provided comfortable living for the independent elderly, together with an alarm link to a warden's office should that independence ever falter.

Miles' daughter Patricia met them at his door and welcomed them inside while giving a cheery wave towards the nearby warden's office door. The warden waved back. Professor Bertram's daughter was a frequent visitor who occasionally popped into the office for a chat. Content, the warden pulled her office door shut behind her and started her daily stroll around the complex. A stroll that would end as it normally did with a visit to her sister's nearby home for lunch.

Once Helen and Sam were inside, they happily accepted Patricia's offer of refreshments. Then Helen engaged in polite conversation as Sam moved from his seat on the sofa to sit at the dining table. There, he tuned out the conversation in the room and focused on the two packets of photographs that Patricia had laid out for him.

The first was just a slim envelope. Inside, he found a dozen or so photographs. He instantly recognised the green but treeless features of South Ronaldsay and began flicking through. Three or four in, he found the pictures Miles had flagged. The turf had been cut away from a protruding stone edge to uncover a long slender slab that might once have stood several feet tall. Miles had not placed a scale measure beside the stone, so it was hard to be certain. What Sam could see were symbols engraved into the stone.

He flipped on to the next picture. This wider shot put the fallen stone in context. It would once have stood proud, set back a few paces from the cliff edge. Exactly at the point where, far below, the winter wilds of the North Sea merged with the oft raging North Atlantic. Sam wondered about the remoteness of the stone and its purpose at just that spot.

He flipped to another picture and suddenly leant forwards. Here was a close-up of the engravings. The stone had stood weathering for a long time before it eventually dropped towards the unwitting protection of the earth. Nonetheless, he immediately recognised the Templar seal. The unmistakable outline of two knights on a single horse was perfectly captured. There was more beneath, perhaps a boat, maybe a box? Sam pulled out his magnifying glass to see better.

Now he saw clearly. Carved in the middle were the two Templar knights on their horse riding away from a sunrise and towards what may have been a tree or plant topped with a few dotted holes … stars? The object beneath the knights came into focus, a ship carrying a box. It too sailed away from the sunrise … west?

Sam thought for a few minutes while flicking back and forth between the images. Then he put the pictures to one side. They were interesting, but he needed context. This was a stone that should be visited when all of this was over. Right now, he needed to focus on Leptis Magna and the Temple of Jupiter.

He drew the second envelope towards him. This was thicker, heavier. Opening it, he began to turn through the pictures – a visual record of Miles' unauthorised Leptis Magna dig. There were the predictable team pictures, the general interest shots featuring the western half of what was a quite stunning and undisturbed classical city. Then there were the pictures Sam wanted, the careworn and less glamorous eastern side of the city.

In particular, the Temple of Jupiter. But there was no imposing temple – that was long gone. The stone, all taken, perhaps by locals to build homes and boundary walls, perhaps by British or French officials who had made many trips to loot columns, statues and whole buildings for their own needs. The temple's proximity to the ancient harbour would have made it a prime target. All that remained were the foundations of the temple and an imposing stair leading up the slope from the port.

It was clear Miles had enlisted the unauthorised assistance of a young German student. She appeared in a series of the shots, her arms outstretched, each hand holding a scale pole – Sam guessed to help establish the scale and length of the stone stair.

He looked back and forth and suddenly realised she was not holding the posts up to fix scale, though they did serve that purpose. All the photos were taken from the same spot. In each successive image the young woman was another pace further down the stairway. She was marking the positions of things set in the ground.

Turning the pictures, Sam felt a tightening in his chest. He stopped, closed his eyes and took a deep breath, holding it in. The image remained fixed in his mind. Exhaling, he opened his eyes, the image was still there.

He flipped to the next picture and the next and again. A series of photographs – close-ups, capturing the detail of the walkway tiles whose positions were singled out by the young German assistant in the first set of pictures.

Sam knew the tiles, knew them exactly. He had looked and looked at them hundreds, perhaps thousands, of times. The tiles were perfect representations of the various faces of Helen's boxes.

***

It was a little after one when Helen and Sam drove off. With Patricia's blessing, Sam had two envelopes of photographs in his jacket pocket. 'Daddy was quite clear on the phone,' Patricia had told him. 'He said you were to take whatever you needed. He wants them back, of course, for sentimental reasons, but you just take what you want.'

There was a long drive back to Edinburgh ahead of them, but at last, they had something that linked to the boxes. The link was from the wrong period, but he'd worry about that later. They had something tangible to work with.

Sam rapidly explained to Helen what he had found, keeping up a flow of information as he turned the car into Marine Road. The road followed the coastline, running parallel to the wide-open expanse of the Morecambe Bay sands. Now they were driving east, and further ahead, they could just make out where the road began its turn north to follow the shape of the great bay.

'They're vast,' said Helen, looking out across the sands. Turning her head, she look back, westwards, to where the Irish Sea was nothing more than a far off silver line that underscored the sky. Everything for miles around was flat, all shades of yellow and grey. To the north, a barely discernable grey-black smudge lowered beneath the winter clouds to mark the northern side of Morecambe Bay where the hills and peaks of the Lake

District National Park closed in on the coast.

'Yes, the sands seem never-ending, a very impressive sight, but it's all tidal so don't be fooled – walkers frequently get caught out. Every year, people are lost, drowned on the sands.' Sam chanced a quick glance out across the sands and briefly stretched out a flat hand towards them. 'For miles and miles, the sands are flat so only a little shift in the tide will have them covered by water in a flash. And you can't see from here, but the sands are riddled with natural dips and gullies. The incoming waters can rush in unseen ahead of walkers who suddenly find they're cut off with water closing on them from all sides. It's not a good place to be when the tide's on the flood. What's dry now might be under a dozen feet of water or more before you realise—'

Sam stopped speaking. Helen looked at him and saw he was watching in his rear-view mirror.

'What's up, Sam?'

'I think we've got company.'

'Oh, are you sure?'

'Big silver car. It turned onto Marine Road behind us, and I'm sure it was parked just along from the sheltered housing complex too.'

He sped up a little. The silver car behind matched his speed. He pushed the speed up above the local limit, the car behind did the same.

'Yes, they're on us.'

Helen had shifted her head to watch the other car in the wing mirror. 'What now?'

'We have to lose them. I'm not sure how; this is a fairly straight road.' Sam allowed his speed to drop to the speed limit and saw their tail do the same.

A little ahead was a tour coach that had paused at the kerbside to allow its passengers a chance to admire the spectacle of the sands. The coach's offside amber signal lights started flashing to indicate its intention to pull away. It began nudging forwards and out, trying to force a break in the traffic flow that would allow it to get underway. Sam's natural instinct was to give way and let the coach out ahead of him; he slowed a little, and the coach continued to manoeuvre out into the flow.

At the last moment, Sam accelerated the car hard and veered out into the oncoming traffic lane, driving the car as fast as he could to force a way past the bus as it continued to pull out and build up speed. The bus's horn sounded in fury while, directly ahead, the first in a line of oncoming vehicles flashed its lights and braked desperately. Sam registered more distant horn tones as the subsequent vehicles applied brakes and expressed their exasperation.

Their car powered ahead of the bus just as the driver brought it to a lurching halt, filling the eastbound lane and jutting over into the westbound lane, bringing all the traffic to a stop. The first of the line of westbound vehicles was stationary directly adjacent to the coach, almost cab to cab. The two drivers exchanged looks, shook their heads and prepared to get underway again. Stuck behind the coach, the driver of the silver car was blasting the horn in frustration. The coach driver shrugged to himself and took his time to restart. The first idiot car driver had got away, this next one could wait a while, and he knew exactly how to slow a car down. With another wry shake of his head, the coach driver selected gear.

'That was close,' said Helen. Her hands still gripped the seatbelt, white-knuckled.

'Needs must,' said Sam, glancing in the driver's mirror. The bus was just starting to move. He gunned the engine harder and lost sight of the bus for a few moments as the road ahead turned to follow the line of the coast.

'But they'll catch us again, soon enough; this is a long road.'

'What can we do?'

'Hold tight again.' Sam braked suddenly and spun the wheel to the right. The car shot across the westbound carriageway, up a slight incline and into a car park. In the few moments it took Sam to steer the car into the car park, he had got the speed down and they appeared to be just another couple come for dog walking or to enjoy the view. Sam stopped the car in an empty parking bay located amid a line of parked cars. They all faced out across the road and towards the beach on the other side.

'Keep down,' said Sam as he switched off the engine ignition and slid back a little.

Helen eased back in her seat too, then mirrored Sam to peer out across the lip of the dashboard as the bus drove slowly past. Its angry driver could be clearly seen muttering to himself and obstructing the pushy silver car behind.

Then the vehicles were past and Helen let out a long sigh.

'Close thing there. Let's not do that again.' Helen looked across at Sam. 'That was a truly lunatic piece of driving, Mr Cameron. Lunatic!'

'Yes, but it got us away for now, bought a little time.' For a long, silent moment, Sam gazed out across the sands. Then he stretched an arm through to the back seats and grabbed their rubber boots. 'Get these on.'

'Why do we need these? Where are we going now?' Helen opened the passenger door, swung her legs out and changed into the boots while Sam did the same thing on his side.

'I think we need to change our mode of travel. They'll be back soon enough. It will only take a couple of minutes for them to get past the coach and realise we've already left the main road. Then they'll double back. We need to be out of sight by then.'

They got out, pulled on their winter jackets, and Sam put their shoes in his rucksack.

Helen looked about. There was no hiding place. In one direction, the road stretched open and unbroken back into Morecambe; the silver car would soon be returning from the other.

Sam pointed towards the beach. 'Come on.'

They hurried out of the car park and dodged traffic to get across the road where a pedestrian path allowed them over the breakwater and down onto the beach.

'Over there,' said Sam. Perhaps a hundred paces out on the sands was a long line of people, each spaced several feet apart and carrying what looked like a large bag. All had their backs to Sam and Helen and were walking slowly away from them while moving parallel to the shoreline. The pair broke into a slow jog, hampered by their rubber boots and the slight give in the surface sand.

'What are they doing? Beachcombers?' said Helen.

'My guess is they're picking up rubbish. It's getting everywhere now.'

'How's this going to help us?'

'Let's just blend in. Hopefully, we'll give our pursuers the slip, and in a while, we can phone for a taxi to get us back into Morecambe. We can pick up another hire car there.'

'What about ours?'

'It'll be fine in that car park. We'll just have to pay a recovery fee to the hire company.'

They stopped talking and focused on closing the distance on the line of people.

'Hello there!' Sam hailed. At about the mid-point of the line, someone turned and waved. The woman paused for Helen and Sam to reach her as the line slowly moved ahead.

'Can I help you?' she asked.

'Yes, what are you up to?' said Sam.

'Plastic picking,' she replied. A woollen hat was pulled down firmly over her hair, loose trails of which wafted and jerked in a wind that seemed to have got up in the time it had taken them to run across the beach. Her hearty voice, heavy with a Lancastrian accent, was accompanied by an open smile. 'I've got my environment students out here. They're contributing to a national pollution survey and doing some good in the process. And how can I help you?'

'Well, we thought we might help you,' said Helen.

'Great, the more the merrier.' She pulled some sturdy black plastic refuse sacks from a roll and handed them across. 'Here, take these.' She laughed as they took them. 'I know it's ironic that we're using plastic bags, but what can you do? Any bags you don't use by the end, please give them back; we're on a tight budget.'

She pointed away towards the end of the line. 'If you want to join up at the end out there, just walk in line to the next person and pick up any plastic you see. Sorry, I don't have any spare picker sticks, so it will mean a little bending.'

'That's no problem.' Sam took the bags, stuffed two into his pocket and fluffed two open, handing one to Helen.

'Okay, thanks for your help; though we don't have much time left, I'm afraid. The tide's already turned, and this onshore wind will bring the sea back in quicker than normal. Have fun, but please, listen for my whistle. We have a strict rule to make sure nobody gets into difficulty with the water. When the time comes, we all leave at once. When you hear the whistle, turn to the shoreline and walk straight towards it. It'll be like a long crocodile, just keep close to the person next in line. That way, I know everybody gets well clear before the water returns.'

'Fine,' said Sam. They hurried further out into the sands to join the far end of the line, and the lecturer returned to her spot in the middle.

As the line moved on, Helen and Sam bobbed up and down, picking up a wide range of plastic waste. All the while, they scanned the road looking out for the pursuer's car.

'There it is,' said Helen.

They both watched as it drove slowly back along the road.

'Well, they worked that out pretty quick,' she said.

'Right, it's whether they spot our parked car that matters now. Let's hope not.'

Both breathed a sigh as the silver car passed the car park and kept heading into the town centre. The moment of relief was short-lived. Somebody in the car must have belatedly thought to check the car park, and the car executed a rapid U-turn.

The silver car entered the car park, cruised slowly along the line of parked cars and stopped abruptly beside their abandoned hire car. Two men got out; they were clearly big and burley even when seen from a distance. They looked closely at the car, tried the doors, found them locked and began to scan the area.

Sam saw one man's hands rise up to his face.

'Hell,' he said.

'What is it?'

'Binoculars, and he's looking at the line of people.'

'Will he know what we look like? Surely, he won't recognise us from that distance?'

'These are pros. To have known they were following the right people, they must have pictures from somewhere. They'll know us if they get a good look. Pull your hat down,' said Sam as he hunched up the collar of his jacket. 'Drift out a little further; see if there's a gully we could drop into.'

As they moved further out, a shrill whistle cut through the crisp salty air to call them all back to shore. As one, the parallel line of students dutifully turned hard right and started to walk in a single column back to shore, each watching for the one directly in front. Unnoticed by the receding line of students, but clear as day to any distant observer, the furthest two in the line suddenly stood out, separated and heading away from the shore.

The men in the car park saw it at once, checked with the binoculars then hurried across the road and down onto the beach. They sprinted towards the spot where they had last seen Helen and Sam. Ignoring the lecturer's cautionary calls and whistle blasts, they ran on, out into the sands. The lecturer gave up and continued to marshal her wards safely off the sands.

Sam led Helen down into a little gully not much deeper than his height. Taking Helen's hand, he ran away from the shore. The going was not so easy in the gully. The sand was wetter and every step sank an inch or so beneath the surface. Struggling on, they met a side channel and turned into it.

'What will we do Sam?'

'Keep moving until we find another gully running in towards the shore. We can follow it to get back to dry land unseen, I hope.'

They hurried on, and as the gully curved, it forked in two, one channel leading off towards the beachfront.

'This is our turning,' said Sam.

'Sam, look.' Helen pointed along the main gully and felt a little shiver run down her spine. Water, only three or four inches deep but like a mini tidal wave, was flowing inexorably towards them.

'Come on. We have to hurry. Run, quick.' Sam pointed Helen into the side channel that forked off towards the shore and followed her.

'Shouldn't we get out of this channel?' called Helen, over her shoulder.

'Yes, but if we break cover we'll be spotted by the men, for certain. Just keep going.'

Now they could hear the shouts of the two chasing men who were frantically running back and forth across the sands, peering into channels, scouring the gullies, desperate to complete their task, to close on their prey.

Helen struggled forwards, and Sam followed right behind. The hunting voices were closer now, loud, angry with frustration. Sam felt his feet sink just a little more into the sand. He looked down; the sand was softening because the water had now caught up with them. In his heart, he had known it would be hard to outrun it.

Helen sensed the change underfoot, looked down then back at Sam.

'I'm struggling to lift my feet, Sam.'

'I know; it's not good.' In only moments, the water had risen to ankle height. It was impossible to move.

A cry of triumph sounded behind them and Sam turned his head to see a man standing twenty paces off and looking down towards them from above the gully.

'Stop!' A pistol appeared from beneath the man's jacket and pointed directly at Sam. 'Stop, or you're dead.'

Sam raised his hands; Helen raised hers too.

A movement close beside Sam's head distracted him for a moment. The second man was standing right above them.

'This is all a mistake,' said Sam. 'I don't know what you think you're looking for; whatever it is, you've got the wrong people. We've been out picking plastic litter.'

'Yeah, right. How come we've just followed you from the sheltered housing complex? And how come our buddies who went in there after you left called to tell me the woman there gave you a bunch of pictures?'

'So, give us the pictures, and you can go free. That's all we want. I'm thinking you'd better hurry, or you'll be having to swim out of here,' said the second man.

Sam didn't move. The man fired a shot, and a little spurt of water kicked up beside Helen's boot.

'The next one goes in her head. She'll not get out after that, swimming or otherwise. Give my partner the pictures!' He shifted his pistol's aim, and Helen felt the malicious intent behind his attention.

'I'm counting to three, then she's gone. One ...'

Sam reached into his pocket and pulled out the packets of photographs. Stretching up, he passed them to the man who now knelt at the channel's edge.

'Good.' The gunman relaxed slightly. 'Now, let's have a look-see. Bring them over.' His partner hurried across the sand to hand over the prize.

'Sam, I'm completely stuck. I can't shift my feet at all.'

'Me too. We just need to hold on for a moment. There's nothing we can do until they go.'

'They've got the pictures; what can we do?'

'You two, stop chattering,' shouted the gunman. They watched as he swapped the gun for the photographs. The second man swung round to cover them as the first took out his phone and made a call.

Stuck in the bottom of the channel, it was impossible to make out the conversation, but it was clear the gunman was making a report while he pinned his phone between shoulder and chin and used his hands to flick through the pictures.

The water was up to Sam and Helen's calves; it would soon be lapping over the top of their boots.

'Keep your legs and boots still, Helen, but work your feet so your heels are up inside your boots and you're standing on tiptoes.'

'Like being a couple of inches taller is going to save us.'

'Keep your legs still. Trying to get out will just work you deeper into the sand. Right now, we are both stuck. Slowly, work your heels up. When the time comes, you can just push up and, I hope, rise up and leave your boots stuck to the bottom. Please, just do it.'

The silence told Sam that Helen was complying, while he too tried to work his heels up and free from the sole of the boots.

The gunman finished his call and reached out to take his gun back and return the sheaf of photos to his accomplice. Then he passed his phone over too. Sam and Helen saw him point towards them and saw the accomplice train the phone on them, presumably making a video record.

'There's good news and there's bad news.' He gave a little laugh and nudged his partner before bringing the pistol to bear. 'The good news is our boss is very pleased with us, and he's asked me to thank you for finding these pictures.' He squinted across the pistol to his partner. 'The bad news is I'm to shoot your lady friend so you can watch her bleed. And my boss says to tell the bitch he's watching too. The only thing that could make this better is if he could pull the trigger. But at least he can enjoy the movie.'

'No wait, let's talk about it, please,' said Sam.

'No time for talking now. We want off the sands before our feet get wet too.'

He looked down into the channel where the water had now risen over Sam and Helen's knees. 'Pity we can't stay to the very end, I'm thinking a drowning would have made a good ending to the video.'

Sam tried to sway his body in front of Helen but the gunman swayed too. His aim was careful. 'Here it comes, baby. Get ready to cry.'

Sam waved his hands as a distraction; Helen knew what was coming and stared straight back at the gunman.

The pistol spat out a round and before they heard the report, the bullet had ploughed into Helen's thigh just above the waterline. She cried out in pain, Sam roared in rage and the two men cheered as the phone captured the event.

Helen bent at the waist as her blood flowed out to redden the water around her.

All Sam could do was reach out a hand to steady and comfort her. He turned his head back to shout at the gunmen who continued to record the event.

'You're going live to the boss now; we'll get one hell of a bonus for this job.' Their elation was clear, their enjoyment palpable and their timing rubbish. Standing on the gully's edge, their combined weight was a challenge too far for the sand supporting them. The inflowing tide had steadily softened the channel walls at the waterline.

The laughter stopped, replaced by cries of shock as the gully's wall crumbled and the two men plunged into the channel, disappearing from view. Moments later, they resurfaced, waving arms and gasping. The phone was gone, the pistol was gone and the photographs quickly spread out and dispersed across the water before soddening and sinking.

Sam let go of Helen and delved into his pocket to pull out the empty plastic bags. He fluffed up the first one; flicked and rolled it to capture air them tied the open end tight, making an ungainly float. He repeated the process with the second bag.

The water was already above Helen's waist, her face at water level as she bent down and used her hands to apply pressure to her leg wound.

'Helen, can you hear me? Are your heels free? Get your heels free.'

She looked up and nodded. 'They're free, but Sam this hurts, I can't stand up for much longer.'

'You don't need to. It'll be hard, but just let go of your wound and lie back in the water. Kick your feet out of your boots then take these floats; you'll be fine.'

'My leg—'

'I'll deal with that as soon as you're afloat. Just stay floating on your back. You'll be fine. Trust me, Helen; do it now.'

Helen nodded, took a deep breath and straightened up, letting go of her wound. She leant backwards into the water and wriggled her feet free of her boots. One leg came up to the surface, the wounded one trailed beneath. She reached out her arms and felt Sam's hands reach hers, forcing the black-bag floats into her grip. Pressing her arms down into the water, she felt the buoyancy pressing back in support.

'Keep flat against the surface and you'll be fine,' said Sam. He pulled her closer while fighting against the steady drag of the inrushing water. Then he propelled her past his stuck body, allowing his hand to stroke her cheek as she passed. 'This is going to hurt a little, I'm afraid,' he said.

Helen gritted her teeth. 'What's not hurting anyway? Get yourself free now, Sam.'

'Not just yet,' he said. The water was at chest level now. 'Hold on to me I need both my hands.' Struggling to keep a grip on the black bags in her hands, Helen used three fingers to catch into the collar of Sam's jacket to keep them from drifting apart.

'I can't hold on for long, Sam; my fingers are starting to slip.'

Hands beneath the water, Sam unfastened his belt and desperately dragged it out of the restraining trouser loops. He brought his hands up and grasped her arm for a moment, taking the load off Helen's struggling finger grip. Once she had reset her grip firmly, he let her go and focused on fastening the belt round her wounded thigh. He pulled it tight, cutting off the blood supply above her bullet wound and drawing a cry of pain.

They both became aware that the cries of the men behind them had changed. Shock had given way to fear, and now to panic. Before kicking his feet free, Sam chanced a glance over his shoulder towards them. There was nothing he could do to help. They were further down the channel, and with their boots firmly stuck in the channel's bed, the water was already washing over their heads. They were lost.

He filled his lungs, kicked his feet free from his boots, slipped onto his back, and brought his legs up to float on the surface. Then he shifted his grip on Helen so they were side by side and floating along the channel towards the beach, propelled by the inrushing tide. With every moment, the water level rose and suddenly there was no channel, just one vast expanse of inrushing water. They took a few moments to ensure the buoyancy bags were stable as the waters carried and pushed them.

Satisfied, Sam looked about and realised the swirl of the tide had carried them to less than fifty paces from the steps where they had first entered the beach. A good way further along he could see a little crowd gathered. The lecturer and her students were staring away out to the spot where Helen and Sam had last been seen. Sam stopped floating and started swimming. If he was quick, they might get out and away without being seen.

Chapter 8

SATURDAY JANUARY 11TH

The manse's main bedroom was on the first floor directly above the study. Its windows faced to the front. There, Helen was lying in bed, and for the first time since the shooting, she was feeling just a little hungry. She wanted to eat before telephoning her parents to report on the gunshot wound. Sam had already informed them, so at least she would not have to deal with the emotion inherent in breaking the news. Still, eating first seemed a good idea.

Elaine and Grace had already visited and were now down in the kitchen preparing food. Whatever it was, she hoped there wouldn't be long to wait.

She heard a car draw to a halt in the driveway. Doors clicked open then banged shut.

The sound of the doorbell ringing carried up the stairs. More visitors.

Sam rose from the chair beside her bed and hurried down the stairs. There he answered the front door to a man and woman, both smartly dressed. The woman expressionless, the man smiling.

'Sergeant Brogan,' said Sam. 'How are you? Good to see you. Thank you for coming, I know Elaine left a message for you the other day.' He reached out a hand to greet the policeman.

'It's Detective Inspector Brogan, sir,' said the woman, 'and I'm Detective Sergeant Price.'

'Wow, congratulations, inspector,' said Sam, extending the shake with added vigour. Then he stepped to one side and waved Brogan past. Price followed close behind.

'Thank you, though to be fair, DCI Wallace had me pretty well pigeonholed for the post before he retired. I think I would have had to perform really badly at the selection panel to have blown the promotion.'

'I'm sure you got the job on merit alone. Helen will be delighted to learn your news.'

'Well, I'm afraid it's Helen I've come to see.'

'What about? She's upstairs in bed.'

Brogan looked almost embarrassed. 'I'm sure there's an explanation, but there are some questions I must ask her.'

'Now isn't really a good time.'

'Now is the time we've got, sir,' said Price. 'Miss Johnson was treated for a gunshot wound yesterday afternoon at the Cumberland Infirmary, Carlisle. Gunshot wounds are automatically reported to the police by hospital accident and emergency departments. We'd like to speak with her.'

The sergeant's sharp tone had brought Elaine and Grace to the kitchen door.

'Who are these people?' said Price.

'It's alright, sergeant; I know their names.' Brogan acknowledged

Elaine and Grace. Grace responded with a welcoming smile, Elaine with a curt nod. Brogan knew that was as good as anyone could ever hope for from the stern church elder.

'Yes, sir, I know. But we must do what is required.'

'And we will, sergeant, I'm sure.'

Sam thought he heard the sergeant tut to herself as she took a half step back, pursed her lips and folded her arms.

Price was aware her boss knew these people. Although she had been away on a training course the previous summer, she had heard all about how events had got so wildly out of control and knew too that DI Brogan and DCI Wallace, his then boss, had been in the thick of it.

After a few pleasantries, Sam led the police up the stairs to Helen's bedroom where she greeted Brogan and his sergeant warmly.

'Tell me, inspector … oh, that sounds very right, doesn't it, Sam? Tell me, inspector, how's my good friend DCI Wallace doing now he's retired? Or will that be plain Mr Wallace now?'

'To some, maybe, but he'll always be my DCI, and he's doing fine. In fact, I visited him between Christmas and New Year, and he was asking how things were with you all. I had nothing to report which he seemed pretty happy about. But here we are, and it seems you're all back in the wars again. I'm hoping there's a simple explanation?'

'Yes, here we are.' Helen smiled at Brogan and turned her attention to Price. 'I heard you ask a question. What exactly do you want to know?'

'All gunshot wounds are notifiable, Miss Johns—'

'Call me Helen, please.'

Price nodded acknowledgement. 'Yes, okay. Now, you've been shot; can you tell us what happened?'

'It all happened so fast. I'm not sure I can tell you much.'

'Well, let me help you. Yesterday afternoon you attended a hospital in

England with a gunshot wound'—Sergeant Price glanced at her notebook—'at 15.20 hours. Twenty past three.' She looked directly at Helen who was now sitting up in bed. 'The Cumbria Police have asked us to make some enquiries on their behalf. So, how were you wounded? Who shot you and why?'

Helen lay back on the bed. 'I'm feeling a bit faint now. Can we do this another day?'

Brogan rested a hand on his sergeant's forearm just as she leant forwards to repeat her questions with more vigour.

'I'm sure we can work something out. Sergeant, this lady is clearly not able to answer questions at present.'

Price frowned slightly but remained silent.

'Perhaps, I can answer for Helen?' said Sam. 'After all, I was there when it happened.'

'Were you?' Price turned her attention on Sam. 'What happened?'

'There's not much to say. We were on the sands at Morecambe doing some environmental volunteering, picking up plastic from the beach. Suddenly, two men appeared, they were a little distance off. We had never seen them before that day, have no idea of their names. One of the men produced a pistol and shot Helen.'

'Just like that? Out of the blue?'

'Well, they must have had a motivation, but they didn't share the details with us. They appeared on the beach and shot Helen. The tide was on the flood, so all of our concentration was focused on getting back to shore. We didn't see the gunmen again.'

'Really? They shot you and just vanished.'

'I didn't say vanished, just that we didn't see them again.'

'And why was that, sir?'

'Do you know Morecambe, sergeant? The tide there comes in very fast. We were almost caught out by it. There was a gun fired, a racing tide and we needed to get to shore. Happily, in the chaos we were separated from the shooter. Perhaps they didn't make it to shore. Who can know for certain? I'll tell you though, if they weren't strong swimmers, they were in trouble.'

'Okay, sir. But tell me, if this shooting took place in Morecambe, why didn't you go to hospital there? Why make over an hour's drive north to Carlisle before seeking medical treatment?'

'A gunman had just shot at us. I wanted to get Helen away from the area. Once we were in the car, I just drove away.'

'Why didn't you report it to the police? Even when you got to Carlisle. I don't understand.'

'Shock, I guess. It's scary to be shot at. Yes, shock.'

Brogan gave Sam a wry look. People could suffer shock after a shooting, but he knew enough about Sam's background and character to know shock was not a likely response. He stepped towards the bedroom door. 'Thank you for your time, Sam, you've given us answers to what the Cumbria Police asked. Thank you too, Helen. I hope you pick up soon.'

'But, sir,' Price protested.

Brogan waved her out of the room. 'That's fine, sergeant. We have what we need. You can feed back to Cumbria when we get back to the station. And you, Helen, you're clearly not in a fit state to talk. We'll come back in a few days to follow up again. In the meantime, take care of yourselves.'

Having seen Brogan and his sergeant off, Sam returned and sat on the bed beside Helen.

'That was tricky,' she said.

'It was, but at least Inspector Brogan knows you … us. Knows we are on the right side.'

'He's nice. I'm glad he got Wallace's job; he deserved it. But where are we now, Sam?'

'In a bit of a mess, I'm afraid. We lost the photographs that Miles Bertram passed to us, so we are no further forwards in cracking the code to open the boxes.

'There's something else, Helen. It's just as we feared; I think things went badly for Miles' daughter. There was something on the news about a woman's body being found in a burnt-out retirement bungalow in Morecambe.'

'Patricia?'

'Has to be.'

'Oh no! Sam, it's getting out of hand, all over again. We need to do something. What can we ever say to Miles?'

'That's going to be hard, poor old boy. Then we've the problem of the lost photographs. There's only one option open to me now. I have to go to Libya.'

'No. Out of the question. Absolutely not.'

Chapter 9

SUNDAY JANUARY 12TH

Confined to bed, Helen devoted her time to thinking through how Sam's proposed trip to Libya could be rendered unnecessary. He had taken responsibility for preparing Sunday lunch and had divided his time between the kitchen and popping in and out of her bedroom, checking she had everything she wanted and determinedly avoiding discussing anything to do with Libya.

Her own doctor had visited the previous day and had diplomatically not made too many enquires as to the source of her bullet wound. He did pronounce himself happy with the treatment she had received at the Cumberland Infirmary, and he had promised to organise some physiotherapy.

Now with lunch almost ready, Helen summoned Sam. She wanted to be downstairs and sitting at the dinner table before the lunch guests arrived. Elaine and Grace would be coming direct from church and were due very soon. Francis would arrive a little later. As the local Roman Catholic priest, he always held back after the morning service to ensure any parishioners with problems received his immediate support.

***

The remnants of lunch had been cleared from the table by Elaine and Sam, and coffees served by Grace. Everyone was again sat at the table and looking expectantly at Sam as he thought carefully before answering Helen's question.

'I don't yet know what the true significance of the photographs was. They were taken at Leptis Magna and definitely showed a series of tiles that represented the same imagery as on the sides of our boxes. The chances of that being a coincidence are so low as to be incalculable. But why they are the same, I don't know.'

'Tell me, Sam,' said Francis, 'Helen's box is an artefact she inherited from John Dearly as part of his Templar paraphernalia. What does it have to do with a Roman city? It makes no sense to me.'

'I agree there is no obvious connection between the two. Their respective eras are so far apart there can be no logical link. And there's another puzzle consequent to that. If Helen's box, and its twin that was hidden in Ethiopia, are in fact from the Roman era, what can be inside that is so special to the Templars who didn't come into existence until centuries later? Beats me. I'm truly baffled.'

'The tiles must represent something, but what?' said Grace.

'Perhaps Xavier will be able to help,' said Helen. 'What time is he due to arrive?'

'He and Angelo will be landing this evening, quite late. Not sure when exactly. They will be going straight to the seminary tonight and plan to come round in the morning,' said Elaine, while checking her phone for messages. 'No, no change; they haven't left Sardinia yet.'

'I wish he'd stay here at the manse with us,' said Helen.

'He's always had his own ways of doing things, and he's not going to change now,' said Francis with a chuckle. 'But seriously, I agree with you, Helen, if anyone will have an insight into this, it will be Xavier. He and John did share things that I was not privy too.' Francis' voice showed no sense of exclusion or envy.

John Dearly, as minister of St Bernard's, had inherited a secret ring and role, and he'd died for it in the end. Xavier was a ring bearer too and had been subject to a brutal attack in his own church. That Francis had no secret ring or duties had made no difference to their longstanding friendships.

Francis gave a little involuntary shiver as he thought back to how his old friend had died. In fact, not being in the know may have helped to keep him safe more than once.

Chapter 10

MONDAY JANUARY 13TH

Xavier stepped forwards and embraced Helen. He kissed both her cheeks then leant back an arm's length while keeping his hands clamped tight to her shoulders. His expression altered from a smile of pleasure at their meeting to one of concern over her wound. Pursing his lips, he tutted and looked down towards the supporting walking stick and then Helen's legs, currently covered by a loose-fitting skirt. 'How are you? How are you? What have they done to you?' He turned to look at Angelo who stood a pace behind. 'What have they done to her?'

'I'm fine, Xavier. Well, I will be soon enough. It's just a flesh wound, the bullet went straight through. I guess you might say, I was lucky. See, I'm up walking already, a little.' She smiled a greeting over Xavier's shoulder towards Angelo. 'It's good to see you both, that's for sure. Come on into the kitchen, it's warmer.' She turned, linking her arm through Xavier's and they made a slow walk along the hall towards the kitchen; Grace closed the front door and followed behind.

In the kitchen, there was a flurry of movement as Francis rushed to welcome the visitors, and Elaine directed a nod of her head towards the new arrivals from her spot beside the window. Once he had exchanged an embrace with Francis, Xavier crossed the room to Elaine. He knew her well, knew she would never show her feelings, but that wasn't going to stop him showing his.

'Elaine, my friend, we meet again. It's always so good to see you.' He threw his hands up. 'But why must you live in this awful climate? Cold, wet …' He laughed, took Elaine's hands, and raised them to his lips, kissing them gently. She didn't resist. He allowed his fingers to rub across the scar marking where her finger had been amputated following Cassiter's attempt to extract information from her the previous summer. He touched his lips against the scar. 'You must be careful, Elaine. We have only one of you.'

Elaine nodded an acknowledgement of Xavier's concern and eased her hands free to reach for the kettle. 'You'll both want a hot drink, I'm thinking.'

'Yes, let's all have coffee,' said Helen, lowering herself onto a chair at the kitchen table while Francis fussed behind her. 'Come and sit next to me, Xavier'—Helen beckoned—'and you too Francis, here, on this side. Let's see if we can make any sense of all this. Sam will be back in a while. He's gone to the university to speak with a colleague in the history department, to see if there's a link between the Romans and the Templars that we've overlooked. And he agrees with me that going to Libya is not a good idea. Instead, he's going to use a scanner to find out what's inside the boxes; he's done that sort of thing before.'

Francis nodded agreement with the plan. 'Anything is better than going to Libya; that's just asking for trouble, and we certainly don't need more trouble.'

'Tell me about it,' said Helen.

Nearly an hour passed as they speculated on what progress Sam was making.

'Are we sure it's not safe just to prise them open?' said Francis.

'Yes, we're sure. I already told you what Bishop Ignatius said. When the Ethiopian Church was first entrusted with care of that box, they were explicitly warned that forcing open the box would destroy the contents. Sam said, in antiquity, it was actually a common way of guarding the most important of secrets.'

'I have heard this too,' said Xavier. He leant forwards a little and turned his head to catch Francis' attention. 'In past times, the only way to keep a secret was in your head or to write it down. Keep it in your head, and it dies with you. Write it down, and you have to protect it, very carefully.' His hands waved, and he gave a shrug.

'But why did they have to be so ingenious when devising it?' said Francis, thinking hard and tapping his fingers on the table.

After a few moments, Helen reached out her hand and pressed it lightly over his. The drumming stopped, and she smiled at him. 'Thank you.'

Their musings were interrupted by the sound of the front door opening and closing. It was followed by stamping feet and the rustling of a coat being shaken vigorously. Sam appeared at the kitchen doorway in his stocking feet.

'The snow's back on harder than ever. I'm glad I walked, the traffic's logjammed in the city centre.' He smiled towards Xavier and Angelo, and they exchanged warm greetings while Grace hurried to get Sam a hot drink. He soon settled into a place at the table.

'So where are we?' said Helen. 'Did you make any progress?'

'Not much further forwards, I'm afraid. I spoke with a couple of people in the history department. There is no obvious linkage between the

Romans and the Templars, other than their militaristic traditions of course, but that's not a natural link.'

'What about your scanner? Any joy with that? It must have been able to see inside,' said Helen.

'Yes and no. I was lucky that the scanner was not in use. It was booked today, but the team using it had been unable to get in due to the snow, so there was a slot free for us.'

'And?'

'Not much luck, I'm afraid. Oh, and we'll be getting a bill for the scan. The lab boys will prepare the results properly, and I'll pick them up tomorrow – no emails, just in case somebody is tracking us again'—he looked towards Helen—'and your leg wound says they are.'

'I thought your scanners could see through anything,' said Francis.

'Well, they're pretty good. We got to see what's inside the boxes, but I'm afraid it doesn't really help us.'

'How so?' said Helen.

'The boxes look a pair on the outside, and the scan confirmed they have the same construction inside.'

'And?'

'It's an unusual construction. A fine wooden surface decorated with inlays to form wonderful swirling patterns. All six faces of each box are similar yet they vary enough so each one is unique – that much we can all see. The external wood-patterned surface layer is lined inside with thin sheets of gold that form the shell of the boxes.'

Sam opened his bag and placed the two boxes in the middle of the table.

'Ah,' said Xavier, 'I have never seen such boxes before. They are pretty, but what do the patterns mean?'

'I'd hoped the photographs we lost at Morecambe Sands would help shed some light on it. But that's not to be.'

Xavier nodded while giving a sympathetic shrug of his shoulders. 'That was bad luck, but praise God, at least you both got out alive.' He squeezed Helen's forearm affectionately, and she leant her shoulder against his in response.

'Hmmm,' said Sam. 'We were certainly lucky.'

'Sometimes, even the unconvinced might be moved to see God's hand at work?' said Francis.

'I'll grant you this – there was a moment on the sands when I thought it was all over. Yet here we are,' said Sam.

'God's hand,' said Francis with conviction as he turned his head to look at Xavier.

'Amen,' said Xavier. He was quickly echoed by the others around the table.

'Okay, okay, we're all on the same side,' said Sam. 'Now back to the boxes. It gets yet more confusing, and based on what we've seen, I don't know what it means.'

They looked at him attentively.

'As I say, each box is of identical construction. A highly patterned wooden surface is secured onto a layer of gold sheet that forms the shape and structure of the box. Today, a designer might describe it as laminated. Then there appears to be an inner layer, again gold, that lines the inside of the box. Fixed between those two layers of gold sheeting are a range of little oblong iron bars, which seem to be coated in something, probably gold leaf. I have no idea what they are for at present. Finally, fixed to just one of the inner gold surfaces of each box is what seems to be a fine sheet of glass or crystal. Then nothing else.'

'Nothing?'

'Nothing. Well, the boxes do have an internal locking mechanism on one of the sides but no sign of how it can be unlocked. And the boxes are both completely empty.'

They sat in silence for a moment, all eyes on the boxes where they rested on the kitchen table. An enigma. A wonderfully crafted enigma – loaded with meaning, yet empty.

'So what does that mean?' said Helen.

'It means the boxes have a purpose when opened, beyond any contents, and there is no way of telling what the purpose of the boxes is without opening them.'

'And so?'

'We still need to open them. It seems a bit like a mission impossible. I think the glass inside is the vulnerability. Somehow, forcing the boxes open will break the glass.'

Xavier reached out his hands to draw the boxes closer. He turned them, looked carefully, then pushed them away again, raising his hands in apparent despair.

'Maybe,' said Xavier, his elbows resting on the table while his hands rose to show open palms towards Sam, 'maybe our Templars have been the cuckoos.'

'Cuckoos?' said Sam. 'What do you mean?'

'The cuckoos, you know, yes? The bird, it puts its egg in another bird's nest. A cuckoo.'

'Go on,' said Sam.

'Could it be, the Templars needed to hide something, and they knew the code to open the Roman box. We know the Templars gathered up many things, so that's possible, no?'

'Yes, that's possible,' said Sam cautiously. He leaned back, looked up to the ceiling. 'It is possible. The Templars were renowned for gathering artefacts. It's quite possible they collected these boxes.'

'Together with the code to open them,' said Helen as Xavier nodded agreement and encouragement.

'Well, that would certainly explain the overlap from classical to medieval periods. But you said the scan shows the boxes are empty,' said Elaine.

'And we don't have the code either, if that's even what's required to open them,' said Helen.

'Yes, yes, to both of you. I think we have to accept that the Templars have gone to a lot of trouble to keep the boxes safe, so they must contain something of value, even if we can't see it. I have no idea in what way, but the insides must be valuable. Yet we have no code to get inside, if code it is.' He paused for a long moment. 'But we do know where the original code is …'

'No!' said Helen. 'That's a bad idea. No way are you going to Libya, Sam, just no.'

'Well people are hunting us; we need to resolve this before they get to us. We know these people will stop at nothing to reach their goal.'

'I wonder what that goal is,' said Grace.

There was a sudden silence. 'It's gold, isn't it?' said Francis.

'Certainly, there was a lot of gold in the Templar hoard they were after before. But this feels different. If that was the Templar treasury we found back in the autumn, and it showed every sign of being so, what can this be? I know the Templars were cautious and seem to have covered every angle twice. But two treasuries? That is a stretch I don't buy, I'm afraid,' said Sam.

'You did say at the time that the find seemed to be all coin and bullion. No artefacts, no ornate jewellery – the sort of things a treasure hoard might be expected to contain,' said Francis.

'And no religious artefacts. None.' Xavier leant forwards, rested his elbows on the table and allowed his hands to describe a little globe in front of him. 'The Templar world was religion. Where are their artefacts? The icons? Those would have been valued more highly than money.' As he finished speaking, Xavier's lips pursed, his shoulders shrugged theatrically and his hands opened to reveal his palms. He looked around the table, shrugged again. 'Where are they?'

'You may be onto something there. For two hundred years, the Templars had an almost free hand to scour the classical world for religious artefacts. You'd think there would have been some things they would have valued highly enough to keep,' said Sam.

'And they might have stored them separately from the treasury as a kind of insurance policy,' said Helen.

'I think you could be right,' said Sam. 'Every experience we've had says the Templars have been very careful to compartmentalise all the clues. If they split up the knowledge, it's logical to think they may have split up what they were storing too.'

'But that implies that Cassiter and these other people are being driven by some knowledge we are unaware of. They must know what is out there,' said Francis.

'Remember that older silver-haired man in the Cretan tunnels? He seemed to be Cassiter's boss, and he certainly knew a lot; he even had his own dagger,' said Helen.

'Hmm, the aristocratic one. Yes, he did have a dagger, which may have made him, or at least his predecessors, a task bearer. He would have received some knowledge, just as John Dearly did, and you too, Xavier,' said Sam.

All eyes turned to Xavier. He shrugged and raised his hands. 'I know what I know. Remember, I knew nothing of the location of the hoard, so how could I know of another treasure. But I say again, it's odd there were no artefacts. None.'

'There are all sorts of Christian treasures that have an almost mythical presence, but nobody knows where they are or if they even still exist,' said Francis.

'Such as?' said Grace.

'Oh, all sorts. You know the sort of thing, I'm sure. Wood from the cross, Jesus' crown of thorns, drops of the holy blood. Though, I'm not sure things such as those could have survived so long, could they?' Francis glanced in Sam's direction.

'Given the right conditions, anything is possible, but organic matter is always most vulnerable.'

'There are plenty of other things to include,' said Francis, warming to the subject. 'The nails from the cross, the spear that is said to have pierced the side of Jesus. And of course, the big ones: the Holy Grail and the Ark of the Covenant. You know, I've read the Templars spent a lot of time searching. If such artefacts were to be found, it would surely have been the Templars who found them?'

'Probably,' said Sam, 'if those things existed to be found. But that doesn't really explain how Cassiter's people know what to look for now. Nor even that there was ever more than just the one treasury. After all, Xavier does not know of such a thing. Yet, whatever *more* is, it's perfectly clear they are desperate to find it. I'm guessing most folk would have been very happy with the coin and bullion.'

'Except, in the end, they didn't get the treasury,' said Elaine.

'Yes,' Helen continued, 'and we know by his ownership of a dagger and all his background knowledge, that silver-haired man was, or is, a task bearer, like Xavier, John Dearly and now me. So he knows something. What can it be?'

All eyes turned again to Xavier.

Xavier shrugged his shoulders and tutted quietly. 'I do not have an answer. All I can say is his predecessors must have had a piece of information about the Templar treasures that none of the other task bearers had.'

'With everything kept so secret, how could they?' said Francis.

Helen leaned forwards. 'I remember when you first told me about the Templars' flight from France. Those men involved in hiding the treasure would have been known to the other knights. Perhaps, one of the task bearers sought out information at that time, for his own purposes. Information he should never have had.'

'Yes, and perhaps that is how they know so much today …' The old priest's voice trailed away as he considered the implications – treachery, from the outset.

'So, what is it they are really hunting? And let's face it, these people are better resourced than even Helen and her fat trust fund.' Francis glanced anxiously around the company. 'What is it they really want?'

'I was watching a programme on the telly a while back,' said Grace, a little tentatively. 'It was about the Templars in Jerusalem. Just as Francis said, apparently, they were always searching for the Holy Grail.'

'They may well have been, though I'm not sure how tangible the Grail actually is.' Sam sensed the clerics gathered around the table bristle slightly, but he continued. 'On the other hand, we do know the Ark of the Covenant did exist, once. I believe that was much sought after too. If there was a real top-drawer prize among the Templar treasures, perhaps that was it.'

'Do you really think it could be that?' said Helen. 'I thought it was supposed to have disappeared long before the Templars came into being.'

'Long, long before,' said Francis.

'So, maybe that's a long shot too,' said Sam. 'But whether it's the Ark, the Grail or something we haven't considered at all, the people we're up against keep killing to get to it. Let's not worry about what it is; let's focus on where it is. And let's be very careful – you all mean a lot to me.'

Helen leant over to squeeze Sam's hand. 'And you are important to all of us, so you take care too.' She looked around her friends, thought of the deaths and brutality that had gone before, thought about the other meetings they had held around this very table … it seemed like they had suffered a lifetime of conflict, but it had scarcely been half a year. 'And being careful means no trips to Libya, that's for sure.'

A murmured round of assent supported her.

'One line that is open to us is the discovery at the Templar wood. I think I need to go and spend some time looking at it more carefully. For all their secrecy, until now, it seems the Templars were sensible enough to always provide a failsafe, more than one route to their hidden goals. Perhaps we can find something there.'

'Well, that's something we can do, and it's easily within our power. Now, please everyone, get some lunch,' said Helen.

***

It was mid-afternoon; Xavier, Angelo and Francis had gone with Elaine to see how the project to convert St Bernard's into a community centre was progressing. Grace had gone to meet friends from college, leaving Sam and Helen alone in the manse.

Sitting together at the desk in the study, they looked intently at the two boxes, the opening of which seemed so crucial, in spite of Sam's scan showing no significant contents.

'What do you think, Sam? They must open somehow, or perhaps, it's some sort of blind alley. You know, there's nothing to find inside, but we keep looking because that's what we're meant to do.'

'Could be, but if it's a bluff, where are we really meant to look? Never mind still not knowing what we're ultimately meant to find, I think we have to accept the boxes are the real deal. I know you're not going to like it, Helen, but I think I need to go to Leptis—'

'There is no way you are going to Libya, Sam.'

'It's the only place left we know has a clue to opening the boxes.'

'You'll find another clue. You said yourself, the Templars would leave more than one route to a solution – insurance in case of accidents. Libya's off the table.'

'Well, I think …' His voice trailed off when he saw a figure pass the study window, making for the front door. 'We've got a visitor. It's DS Price.'

A moment later, the doorbell sounded and Sam stood. 'I'll go.'

Helen sat behind the desk, the fingers of her right hand drumming lightly on the desk's edge. She knew Sam wanted to go to Libya, but she didn't agree with him. Price's arrival had prevented a conclusion being reached.

Sam guided the police sergeant into the room, and Helen smiled a welcome while waving towards the seat Sam had just vacated. 'DS Price, we weren't expecting to see you. Please take a seat and tell me how we can help? No Inspector Brogan this afternoon?'

Sam moved another chair towards the desk and all sat in silence for a moment as the sergeant rummaged in her shoulder bag. They watched her pull out a couple of pages of printed text and scan them briefly before looking up.

'DI Brogan's having to attend court today, and he asked me to drop in on you for a quiet word.' Her smile was not reassuring. 'You two have been getting about quite a lot in the past few days. I know DI Brogan seems disinclined to ask too many questions about the shooting incident. Though I'd certainly like to ask you a little more about Morecambe.'

'Oh?' said Helen. 'Why's that?'

'If you don't mind, I'll be asking the questions. I'll come back to Morecambe in a bit. First, that wasn't the only trip you've been on recently. Can you tell me what you were doing in Orkney?'

Helen's eyes flicked towards Sam, who gently cleared his throat. 'Why would you be interested in that?' he said.

'As I said, sir, I'd like to ask the questions, please. Orkney?'

'I needed to speak urgently with an archaeologist who was working up there. Needed some detail on another piece of academic research I'm doing.'

'I see, and if it was so urgent, why couldn't you just phone him?'

Sam gave a dry laugh. 'Professor Bertram, Miles Bertram, is a bit old-school, I'm afraid. No mobile phone. If you want to speak with him, it's got to be face-to-face.'

'So, it was definitely Miles Bertram who you went to visit in Orkney?'

'I've just said so, sergeant.'

'That's right, you did. The problem I have is I can't speak with Professor Bertram to confirm what you're telling me.'

'What do you mean?' said Helen. A familiar tightness was gripping her stomach. She sensed bad news coming.

'I mean, he's dead.'

'What? How? Sergeant, you cannot think for a moment we are involved,' said Sam.

Price fixed Sam with a deadpan gaze. 'We know you didn't kill him, sir. You left the island on the Edinburgh flight at around 16.30 on Wednesday the 8th. Professor Bertram stayed at his bed and breakfast lodgings that night. It was the next day he died. Or at least we think he did.'

'Think?' said Helen.

'He didn't return to his lodgings the next night and was reported missing. His body was found only yesterday.'

'Found where? How did he die?' said Sam.

'His body was found in the sea, washed up along the coast from where he had been working.'

'Well, I don't know why he would be on the cliff edge, but immediately behind where he was working, it's a fair drop to the water. He knew that, but there are some strong gusts of wind along that stretch of coast. Perhaps, he was just buffeted off,' said Sam.

'Perhaps, sir. We don't know how he died yet. He'd been in the water for a while, and I'm told, in among the rocks at the shoreline, it can be a very violent place.'

Helen felt the tension ease, just a little. Maybe it had been an accident after all.

'Well, there you are sergeant, an accident,' said Sam.

'I think the police in Orkney were originally tending towards that as a preliminary conclusion, though now we're not so sure.'

'Why so?' said Sam.

'Coincidence, sir. One unexpected death might be a random accident, but more, with connections, I'm afraid that certainly demands closer scrutiny.'

'More?' said Helen.

'Yes, which takes us neatly back to Morecambe.'

'If it's the two men who were chasing us, they must have been caught by the tide and drowned,' said Helen.

'Yes, that's clear enough. Though, it's still not clear what they were doing on the sands. They were certainly not dressed as environmentalists.'

'Well then—'

'However, *their* deaths are not what I'm interested in at present.'

Helen and Sam exchanged glances.

'What do you mean, sergeant?' said Sam. He realised where this was leading and could see Helen did too.

'I understand you visited a sheltered housing complex in Morecambe on the day the two men died on the beach.'

'We did. What of it?' he said.

'Why were you there?'

'To visit Professor Bertram's home. We had arranged to meet his daughter there to review some of his research. All above board, the professor had arranged it in advance. I understand he'd used the telephone at his bed and breakfast accommodation to telephone his daughter and the warden. Check with them.'

'Well, the warden has confirmed that arrangement. She also confirmed that you were seen to arrive and leave the complex.'

'So there's nothing to talk about, is there?'

'I wish it were so, sir. Only, immediately after you both left, what was described as "a big flashy car" arrived, and some men got out to visit your Professor Bertram's home. Shortly after that, they left, then the professor's home went up in flames.'

'Oh no,' said Helen. She already knew Patricia Bertram was dead but learning the sequence of events was still disturbing. The tension was back with a vengeance; she knew exactly what was coming.

'I'm afraid so, the house was gutted by the blaze. Sadly, once the fire brigade extinguished the fire, they found a woman's body inside – the professor's daughter, and it seems she didn't die easy.'

Helen closed her eyes, and it was Sam who responded.

'You said this happened after we had left. Clearly we were not involved,' he said.

'Clearly, you didn't do it. But clearly, you were not involved? I'm not so sure. Four deaths in quick succession, yes, at opposite ends of the country, but a father and daughter, and you visited both just before they died. And two heavies who'd first tried to gun you down? Now to me, that stretches coincidence beyond reasonable limits.'

The verbal jousting continued a little longer until Price recognised that she would learn nothing. Frustrated, she stood to take her leave. 'I don't understand why the inspector wants to tread lightly. This was an informal fact-finding discussion. Believe me, if I have my way, next time, you'll be down at the station, and there will be nothing informal then.'

Sam stood and guided Price towards the door, delivering any assurance he could with every step. She left as unconvinced as when she had arrived.

Shutting the front door, he turned to find Helen standing close beside him. Her face was worried, and she leant heavily on her walking stick.

'It's never going to end, is it?' she said.

Sam put his arms round her waist, lifting very slightly to take the weight off her wounded leg. 'We have to get in the driving seat.'

'How many more people have to die first though?'

'I don't know. What I do know is, to survive, we have to end it. Not sit back and wait.'

He felt Helen's head nod agreement against his shoulder.

'Come on,' he said. 'We need to take some action.' Helen leant on Sam's arm as they made their way back to the study.

'What do you mean?' she said.

'We think opening your boxes will provide the clue to finding whatever else the Templars hid. These people are after it too. We need to solve the puzzle first.'

'But the photographs that you thought would provide the answers were lost in the sea at Morecambe,' said Helen as she eased herself down into the chair behind the desk.

'They were.'

Helen was silent for a long moment. She looked out of the window;

snow was again falling from the dark and sullen clouds that had rolled in to fill the sky once more.

'You need to go the Libya, don't you?'

'Yes, I do, and I need to phone Bishop Ignatius.'

***

'You are my son; this is our birthright! Get these fools under control. Cassiter is in Malta. Must I come to Edinburgh myself to ensure there are no more blunders? Fix it, fix it now. I need information. If your team kill everyone we want to interrogate, we will never get the answers we want.

'Find out what is so interesting in that wood. Do not allow anything else to happen to that church girl or Cameron, until we know what they know. Then you can snatch them, and I will have Cassiter show you how we make an opponent suffer – we can both enjoy the spectacle. For now, retrace all your men's steps; make sure there are no loose ends that can link back to you.'

Shaking with frustration, Parsol hurled the telephone handset across his study. '*Merde, merde, merde!*' He lapsed into silence, scowling at the handset where it had come to rest behind the study door. Raising a hand, he swept his tousled silver hair back into the carefully groomed style he normally sported. The phone rang, and his face betrayed another flash of irritation as he powered his wheelchair out from behind his desk and made to retrieve it.

'Parsol speaking,' he said, his voice restored to its normal tone of controlled authority. He listened as he drove his wheelchair back behind the desk.

'That's good to know. Very good. Have you alerted Cassiter yet?' He reached out his free hand to open the email account on his computer screen. 'I see your message, good. Leave me to speak with Cassiter.' He hung up and instantly keyed in another call. It was answered as soon as the ringer sounded.

'Hello, Cassiter, good news. Cameron is flying back to Malta. Check your email for details of his flight. This is important. I know I don't need to tell you to be careful, but I think this may be our last chance. Whatever his interest in Malta, we need to know. I … We are all depending on you to find out what he is doing and what he knows. Keep me informed.'

Chapter 11

WEDNESDAY JANUARY 15TH

Looking along the quay, Sam was delighted to see the blue fishing boat was berthed where he had seen it before, back from whatever works the skipper had alluded to during their last meeting. Better still, he could see Captain Blue leaning on the rail, watching the world go by as he puffed on a cigarette.

The skipper watched him approach. When Sam came to a halt at the foot of the gangway, Blue exhaled a long stream of smoke in his direction.

'You're back then,' said Blue.

'I'm back.' Sam held the skipper's gaze. 'I'm thinking about our charter. Where do we stand on that?'

'I've been waiting for you. It's all sorted.'

'Good. You're happy with the job?'

'Yep,' he said and drew again on his cigarette. 'Charter fee's all paid and we're ready to go.'

'You know where we're going?'

'Naturally. Though why you want to go to Leptis Magna I don't know. It's a dead place. But hey'—Blue shrugged—'the money is paid, so you get to choose.'

'What about local militias and radicals?'

'No problem. I've got friends on that stretch of the coast. It's arranged; they know to give you a wide berth.'

Sam didn't bother asking who Blue's friends were. He guessed Blue would be channelling luxury consumables south into Libya and ferrying illegal immigrants north on the return journey.

'When can we go?'

'Come back here tomorrow, an hour before dawn. We'll sail with the smaller local fishing boats.'

Sam confirmed that Blue was able to wait off the Libyan coast for him while he was ashore at Leptis Magna then let things rest. There would be time to ask any other questions once they were at sea. This was his only ticket to Leptis Magna, so for now, nothing else mattered. He turned and headed away, scanning the quayside street for a taxi.

Blue continued to lean on the rail and watched Sam go. He saw the man sat at the café table across the street pull out his phone and make a call. Blue smiled. The café man had become conspicuous by his constant presence at the outside tables of the restaurant over the past days. What's next? he wondered.

***

Helen shuffled along the hall from the front door. Beside her walked Davy and Julie. She waved her stick ahead in the direction of the kitchen.

'Let's go in there; it's the warmest room right now.'

Julie offered Helen her arm as Davy moved ahead. 'Okay,' said Davy, 'but let me make the drinks. You just sit down at the table, Helen.'

Grace was already in the kitchen. 'I'll get your drinks; you all just sit,' she said, moving towards the hob.

'What exactly happened to you?' said Julie, pulling a chair away from the table for Helen.

'Oh, you know, it was just one of those things. Something and nothing,' said Helen, easing herself into the chair.

'It looks like something to me,' said Julie.

Helen waved her hand dismissively. 'It's nothing, really.'

Davy helped Grace carry coffees to the table, and Grace resumed her seat at the end while Davy and Julie sat opposite Helen.

'It's really exciting to think you have an ancient chamber on your land. Did you have any idea it was there?'

'None whatsoever. Yes, it's exciting, and Sam and I are grateful you are both prepared to help out.'

'No problem. Some others in the class have volunteered to help too; we're going to set up a rota. We all really hate nighthawks,' he said.

'What are nighthawks?' said Grace, raising her mug and sipping.

'Looters. They raid archaeological sites, mostly at night when nobody else is around, and metal detect for treasures. Sometimes local opportunists, sometimes organised gangs,' said Julie.

'It's not just the treasures they steal; they wreck the environment their finds are made in and destroy all the archaeological evidence and context. They do untold damage,' said Davy.

'Alan Ralston phoned this morning to say he's been up at the site in the woods, and there are a number of unexpected boot tracks in the snow leading from the road up to the wood and back. He's not sure how many; he thinks some might have been covered by recent snowfalls. And it seems somebody has been digging around at the chamber,' said Helen.

'I see. Can't the police help?' said Grace.

'I did speak to the police, but there's not much they can do, unless the looters are caught in the act. They are so short staffed that it's not a high priority right now. I've spoken to a local security firm. What with all the snow and some illness, they have staff shortages too, so they can't start any new sites right now. But they can provide cover on the site from Friday morning.'

'That's where we come in,' said Davy. 'We're going to mount a watch in the woods until Friday to scare off the nighthawks.'

'Isn't that dangerous?' said Grace.

'They're fly-by-nights. As soon as they realise the site has a human presence, they'll be off. Nothing to worry about,' he said.

'Okay.' Grace did not sound convinced.

'You *think* there's nothing to worry about, Davy,' said Helen. 'Please, just remember what I said on the phone earlier; if these people turn up again, call it in, retire and wait for the police to arrive. No heroics!'

'Don't worry; I learnt my lesson last summer. I'm not taking any chances,' said Davy.

'That's right, and I won't let him,' said Julie.

Helen noted the involuntary shiver that rippled across Julie's shoulders when she spoke. It immediately brought back memories of how Davy had been beaten to within an inch of his life by one of Cassiter's gang. Julie had been distraught, and for a little while, they had all feared the worst. 'Good. See he doesn't do anything stupid.'

Grace looked out of the window at the snow falling thickly across the garden. 'Rather you than me. I think it's going to be a cold one tonight.'

'Alan said he's put down some plastic sheeting and manoeuvred some bales of hay up into the wood to make a little windbreak for you. He's going to meet you at the field gate this afternoon; we just have to phone before you set off.'

'Luxury. Sure you won't join us, Grace?' said Davy.

'No, I'll be fine here, thanks.' She nodded her head towards the window. 'Good luck to you in that weather.'

Chapter 12

THURSDAY JANUARY 16TH

Sam hunched his rucksack high onto his shoulders, reached out to the handrail and walked quietly up the gangway onto the fishing boat's poop deck where he paused. The sturdy thrum of the vessel's diesel engine indicated preparations for departure were underway; otherwise, the boat seemed deserted.

'Hello, on board,' shouted Sam. 'Anyone home?'

He heard footsteps hurrying along the narrow covered walkway that reached from the open working foredeck towards where he stood at the stern of the vessel. The crewman who had blocked his and Iskinder's access just a week or so before appeared.

'You're late,' said the crewman.

Sam smiled at him. 'I don't think so. I'm the charterer; it's my time. Is the skipper available?'

'No. Come inside, I'll show you your cabin. You must stay in it for now. Keep out of sight, until we are away from the port. Then the captain will see you.'

'I want to speak with him before we sail.'

The crewman paused for a moment. An irritated look flashed across his face. 'Okay, come now. I'll tell him.' He turned and stepped through a doorway. Its outer steel watertight door was hinged outwards and hooked open; the heavy wooden inner door hinged inwards and was also wedged open. Sam guessed the arrangement was to allow for a cooling airflow through the heart of the accommodation, which probably meant the air-conditioning was kept off in port. He hoped it wasn't broken.

Following the crewman into the passageway, Sam counted off the internal doors. The crewman pointed through the first, also wedged open. 'That's the galley and mess. We all eat in there.' They passed two further doors, one was metal, and the increased vibration coming from beyond it told Sam it was the engine room's access door.

Then two further doors, one to either side, and finally, at the end was a steep, short stair, going down to the crew quarters and up to what Sam assumed was the wheelhouse.

The crewman stopped and opened one of the doors, waving Sam in. 'Wait here, this is your cabin.'

'The skipper?'

The crewman jerked his thumb towards the door on the other side of the gangway. 'That's his cabin. He's busy now. Wait here.'

The cabin door was pulled shut on Sam before he could ask another question. The click of a lock had Sam reaching for the door handle. Muttering a curse to himself, he turned to the porthole, only to discover it was welded shut. He was trapped.

It took only moments to survey the cabin. Behind him was the locked door, ahead was the outer bulkhead with its welded porthole. The forward bulkhead was filled by a pair of grubby bunks, fitted tightly between two wardrobes. The aft side of the cabin contained a built-in table with fixed benches to either side; the upholstery might once have offered comfort, but today, it was as tired and uninviting as the bunks. Into the gap between the furthest away bench and the outer bulkhead was squeezed a desk, the chair in front of it secured to the deck by a short length of chain.

Sam eased off his rucksack, letting it drop down on the deck. Then he inspected the desk and swiped gingerly at the fixed chair before settling down to wait. He could do nothing else.

Once or twice, he heard muffled voices and footsteps in the passageway. While straining to hear what was being said, he didn't bother trying to attract attention; it seemed clear that Captain Blue would have the door unlocked when he was ready and not before.

***

It had still been dark when the boat cast off and left harbour, setting off amid a little flotilla of other fishing boats. These were mostly smaller craft, and Sam had guessed they were committed to daytrip fishing while Captain Blue's vessel was designed for longer voyages. From the vessel's movement relative to the shore lights, Sam established they were heading east – not south, as he had anticipated.

Moving out from the lee of the island, the vessel began to catch the motion of the sea and developed a steady rhythmic roll from side to side as it pushed on through the water. One by one, the flotilla dispersed as each boat headed off towards its skipper's favoured spot. Finally, as the sun came up, the last of the smaller boats peeled away, leaving Sam with a view of an empty grey-blue sea and the thrum of the diesel engine below.

It was after nine when Sam was finally released from the cabin. The crewman unlocked the cabin door and beckoned him out.

'The skipper wants you now. Follow me.' He turned and took the three paces to the little stair at the end of the passageway and began to climb.

Sam followed, slowly climbing the stair while checking out the surroundings. The wheelhouse was about five metres wide, reaching across the whole width of the vessel but was only three metres deep. The forward-facing bulkhead was fitted with windows that spanned the whole width to provide an uninterrupted view. The run of glass continued along the port and starboard sides. Sam glanced behind to confirm the windows continued along the aft end of the wheelhouse; they did, broken only by a door that fed out onto a little upper aft deck.

A huge, black, leather swivel chair was fitted on the centre line of the boat. It was positioned within a waist-high U-shaped console that sprouted from the bulkhead beneath the forward-facing windows. Seated here, the skipper had an uninterrupted view of the seascape, and could reach all the key controls and access all the information needed without ever getting out of the seat.

Directly in front of the chair was a small wheel. Set on the console's flat top, immediately forward of the wheel was a gyroscopic compass display and, beside that, an autopilot unit. Mounted in the port side arc of the console were the engine controls, a VHF radio, and closest to the chair was a radar display. The starboard side of the arc included a regular echo sounder, a fish finder display, a computer screen and keyboard, and a second radar that bookended the whole console.

The crewman moved to the port side, beyond the console, and made himself busy scanning the horizon. There was a larger wheel there, currently unused. As Sam reached the top of the stair, the captain swung his chair round to face him and gave a dry smile.

'There you are. Welcome aboard. Enjoying the trip?' said Captain Blue.

Sam stepped across the wheelhouse deck, and steadied himself with a hand on a radar housing. 'Captain, I don't appreciate being locked up.

Don't forget, I'm the customer here. What were you playing at?'

The skipper gave Sam an innocent smile and shrugged his shoulders. 'What could I do? It was best you were not seen. I could not risk one of the other skippers seeing you wandering around as we all left port. Where would our secret be then?'

'You just needed to explain.'

'My friend, I was busy. The harbour master often likes to stop by for a little drink in my cabin before we sail. He could not see you. You understand this, yes?'

Sam gave a grudging nod. Captain Blue's reasoning was sound enough, but Sam felt it didn't ring quite true.

'You'll have a coffee with me now? Come, we have things to arrange.' He issued instructions to the crewman who headed for the galley while Blue waved Sam forward then switched his attention away, briefly looking in turn at each of the radar screens.

Sam leaned his hip against the forward bulkhead while looking down onto the foredeck. To the port side was stowed the fishing gear. To the starboard side were two powerful-looking RIBs, one modest in size the other larger; they were absolutely not fishing boat standard issue.

Sam was impressed at the range of navigation equipment. There was far more, and all of it much more modern, than might be expected for a boat of this age and apparent condition.

'You like my ship?' said Blue. 'Great kit, yes?' He swept his arm around the wheelhouse.

'Yes, very good and more impressive than I'd anticipated,' said Sam, eyeing one of the radars with its automatic traffic plotting display.

'You think this is good, you should see the engines. I've had a lot of work done on them. We're doing eight knots here. Slow and steady, nobody asks questions.' He broke off to give a hearty laugh and reached his hand out to rest it on the engine controls. 'When we need it, there is all the power you could want to outrun patrol boats anytime.'

Sam feigned being impressed. 'But what about NATO warships? You won't outrun them.'

Blue managed to both scowl and smile at the same time. 'NATO? Why are they even here? But look, why would I want to outrun them? I'm just a fisherman.' He waved a hand out towards the open deck ahead of the bridge where the fishing equipment was stowed. Sam judged it had never been used.

'What about the RIBs?'

'Humanitarian equipment, my friend. God willing, we will never need to rescue migrants. But we must be ready, yes? My soul could not live on if I were unable to help poor people in distress.'

Sam smiled and returned his attention to the immediate surroundings where the gyrocompass displayed a heading of ninety degrees – they were still heading east.

'So, captain, seems to me, if you keep this course, you are heading for Crete, and we'll never get to Libya. What's going on?'

Blue stood and leant across the console to slap Sam on the shoulder. 'Ha, my friend. It seems you know more about boats than I thought. You can read a compass heading. Good, good. I like a man who knows things. It can make life easier for me.

'We go east all day, maybe a bit of evening too. Then tonight, we turn and head southwest for Libya. We will be ready to drop you safely ashore before dawn.'

'You said you had friends there and could make arrangements. What can you tell me about the situation at Leptis Magna?'

'It is all arranged for you. My friends have influence along that part of the coast. There will be no patrols at Leptis Magna tomorrow ...' Breaking off, he beckoned to his crewman who had appeared at the top of the stair with two huge mugs of coffee gripped in one hand. Taking one mug, he waved his man towards Sam. 'And tomorrow is Friday; people will go to the mosque – a quiet day for your visit. As long as you don't do anything stupid, you will be left undisturbed.'

'These must be good friends of yours to be so helpful.'

'Rich friends, richer still now. They demanded a lot of money for your visit. A lot of money.' Captain Blue shrugged and lifted his mug towards Sam in salute. 'But it seems your African church friends have enough to pay and more. So everyone wins.'

'Everyone wins,' echoed Sam, wondering what slice Captain Blue had added to the bill for his own benefit. He took a welcome drink of the surprisingly good coffee.

'You will have all day Friday to do whatever it is you want, and we will pick you up one hour after dark from the same spot where we drop you. Be careful though, my friends have the power locally not to discover you for a little while. If you attract attention from the extremists or miss the boat, they cannot help you, and I cannot wait. You will be on your own.'

'Okay. Thanks for the coffee. I think I'll get something to eat now then spend some time focusing on what's ahead. Perhaps we can cover the detail later?'

'Of course, go, eat. The food is yours.'

***

Davy and Julie had settled inside the little three-sided shelter of straw bales. A sheet of plastic beneath kept them clear of the wet ground. Another was secured tight across the top to keep out the worst of the weather. A free front flap was fixed down with the stout stick Julie had used as a walking staff to help cross the snowfield to the wood. They snuggled together in a sleeping bag, keeping warm while alert to any sounds or disturbance at the site.

In the morning, classmates would arrive to relieve them, but the night had begun to seem very long.

'I doubt anyone would be mad enough to come out in this weather,' Julie said into Davy's ear, as she cuddled in just a little closer.

'I know. This is probably a waste of time tonight. The weather's just awful, but we made a promise.'

Julie gave a little laugh. 'Yes, we promised. And every cloud has a silver lining.' She snuggled closer still.

'Yes, it does, doesn't it?' Davy wrapped his arms around her, and they were quickly oblivious to the bad weather and sounds of the night. A little while later, they dozed off.

***

'Psst. Psst,' Julie hissed quietly into Davy's ear, gently shaking his arm. 'Wake up, Davy. Wake up.'

Davy pulled himself from sleep. 'What's up?'

'Listen, can you hear anything?'

'What?'

'I don't know, listen.'

Davy forced his arm up, gripped the sleeping bag zipper and pulled it down just enough to release his arm. His loosed hand swept the hood back so he could hear more clearly.

'What is it, Davy?'

'You're right there is something out there. I don't know what.' He pulled the zipper down further and slipped out of the sleeping bag. Once clear, he pulled on his boots, fastened his clothes and turned up his collar. 'It's cold, that much I do know.'

Clamping a woollen hat on his head, he slipped quietly out into the night. The wind had dropped away while they had dozed, and now everything was still. Whatever they had heard was not wind driven. In the dark woods, only black and silence prevailed.

Julie's head emerged through the flap. 'It's quiet, perhaps I imagined it.'

They both listened for a moment. 'Perhaps you did,' said Davy. He was just starting the weary slide back under cover when he froze and sensed Julie tensing beside him. The sound they had just heard was not natural. He placed his hand on Julie's shoulder. 'Get back under cover. I'm going to take a look. Get your phone ready, in case we need the police.'

Before Julie could object, he vanished into the night. She shivered a little and felt in her pocket for the phone, all the while listening out for sounds and praying Davy would be alright.

It seemed only moments later that she jumped at a figure suddenly looming into view over their hide. Then she relaxed a little; it was Davy.

'Call the police. There's definitely somebody in the trench. I can see a light bobbing, and they're digging about. You call it in; I'm going to challenge them.'

'Davy, just wait …' Julie's voice faded as she realised she was speaking to herself. Davy had gone again.

After a moment of exasperation, she scrabbled to put in the phone call. Her whispered conversation with the emergency call handler was difficult, but eventually, she ended it, satisfied that help had been summoned. Crawling out of the hide, she set off into the darkness, gingerly probing the unseen ground ahead with her makeshift walking staff. Where was Davy? She paused a moment to listen.

Julie knew the trench should only be a few paces off but had become disoriented in the dark. Now she didn't know where the trench was, was not even sure she could make it back to their bale hide. A sudden shiver ran down her spine; she was lost in the night.

Cautiously, without advancing or retreating any distance, she shuffled her feet to describe a circle, scanning into the darkness as she turned. Davy was gone; there were no telltale torchlights, nothing. Only blackness and the deeper black that she knew were tree trunks.

Then, just as the fear of the night tightened its grip, she heard a noise and spun round. Some paces distant, she could see a figure, silhouetted by the faintest of lights that now emerged from the ground beyond the silhouette. Davy was beside the trench, and he was right – somebody was in there.

As she started to move towards Davy, a second silhouette appeared close beside him. It had a hand raised and was holding what appeared to be a cosh or club. Julie forgot the dark and rushed towards Davy.

'Davy. Look out!' Her warning got Davy turning in her direction just as the club swept down towards him. It reached the point where, just a moment before, his head had been. Instead of breaking his skull, a heavy wooden bar crunched into his shoulder. Instantly, Davy slumped, his only functioning arm reaching out to grip his assailant's clothing. On his knees, he could do nothing as the attacker's arm rose again, ready to sweep the club down and dispatch him forever.

Even as the club commenced its descent, the attacker's head turned to weigh up the threat of Julie as she arrived out of the darkness. With a fierce shriek, Julie jabbed her walking staff forwards, aiming directly for the prowler's face. All her fear, her anxiety and her care for Davy were focused through the thrusting staff; it passed the attacker's flailing hand and met him square in the face. Letting out a cry of shocked pain, the man fell backwards into the trench. Even as he dropped, he locked a firm handgrip on her staff.

Puzzled, a second man stood at the foot of the trench. He swung his torch beam up towards the commotion, just in time to see a large object falling towards him. The butt of the staff caught him on the side of the head, felling him. Unconscious, he never felt the deadweight of his associate landing on top of him. Nor did he feel the subsequent thud as Julie landed on top of his companion.

Still mad, Julie leapt up and, in the angled light of the torch, wrenched her staff from the groggy man's hand. Taking no risks, she swung it up above her head and brought it down on his. The man sighed and slumped into unconsciousness.

Davy, still on his knees, had been peering over the edge, trying to make out what was happening below.

'Julie, are you okay? Hold on, I'm coming down.'

'Stay up there, Davy; I'm fine.' She gave both the men exploratory prods with her staff. They didn't move. 'I'm coming back up.'

Throwing her stick up like a javelin, she took the men's torch to light her way. At the top of the trench, she went to hug Davy then stopped herself. 'You're hurt.'

He nodded. 'I think my collar bone's broken.'

Julie shone the torch on Davy's body and looked anxiously at his slumped shoulder. 'Oh hell, that looks bad.'

Davy mumbled agreement.

'Look, I've called the police. We just need to keep these two trapped down there until they arrive. Can you hold on?'

'I don't know, perhaps we should get away while we can.'

'And let these two escape? No way. Look what they've done to you.'

'But Julie, I'm in no shape to help you. I can't move my arm.'

Julie paced along the edge of the trench. 'They're both out cold. If they do come round, I can manage them easily enough with this.' She gave her staff a wave. 'There's only one place they can come up, and I'll just prod them back down again.'

'Okay, but I still think we should get away. If they manage to get out, you won't stand a chance.'

'Well, let's make sure they don't get out.' Julie headed back to the access point and pulled up their climbing aid. Then she returned to Davy. 'Now, we'd better get a shoulder sling on you.'

She located the hide with her torch and pulled a spare jumper from her rucksack to improvise a sling.

'Who do you think those two are?' she said.

'I don't know. I know some nighthawks have a bad reputation but trying to club my head is more than you'd expect from them. I'm thinking they must be part of the gang that caused Helen and Sam trouble.'

'The ones that attacked you last summer?'

'Yes.'

'Well then, they're going nowhere, that's for sure.' Julie straightened up, gripped her staff more securely and peered back over the edge. 'No one's moving down there.'

'Let's hope it stays that way until the police arrive. Perhaps you'd better phone the emergency services again and ask for an ambulance too.'

'Okay, I'll do that,' said Julie, feeling in her pocket for her phone. 'Maybe I should ask for the fire brigade as well. Someone's going to have to lift them out of there.'

Chapter 13

FRIDAY JANUARY 17TH - a.m.

Sam left his cabin and entered the passageway. Very faint lights were fixed along its length and stopped at the stair to the wheelhouse. Moving through the half-light, he took the stair and carefully slipped behind the blackout curtain that hung at the top. He paused beyond the curtain. Everything was black, other than a few dimmed green and amber console display lights.

Standing quietly at the back, he allowed his eyes time to adjust. Slowly, he began to notice things. The skipper was sat in his seat, and Sam stepped forwards.

'We'll be there soon,' said Blue.

'What's the plan?'

'A couple of hours, and we'll put you ashore.'

'How? Will you go alongside?'

'No, there's nowhere safe for that. There's an old harbour at Leptis Magna, but it's no use. It's been silted up for hundreds of years. Nobody has a reason to dredge a channel; I doubt it has been used fully in generations.

'We'll take you to the beach in a RIB. Remember, Mr Cameron, Leptis Magna is uninhabited, so as long as you are discreet, you will have a day undisturbed.'

'Don't worry; I have no intention of drawing attention to myself.'

'Good, then you will be fine.'

With the sweep of an arm, Captain Blue described an arc ahead of them. Sam looked out through the wheelhouse windows to where a black sea and black sky met at a mostly imagined dark horizon; its presence picked out here and there by the occasional faint glow of electric light – shining halos of distant towns, breaking over the sea horizon to mark their presence. Land was near but not yet in sight.

'See, far off to starboard, that strong glow is Tripoli, dead ahead is Khoms and way off, on the port side, that's Misrata. We'll just keep on this heading for now. In an hour or so, we'll shift course and run parallel to the coast. Leptis is just to the east of Khoms. We'll launch the RIB and put you ashore as we continue slowly along the coast.'

'You have a routine then,' said Sam. He heard a throaty laugh.

'Yes, we have a routine. Now, look over there in the direction of Misrata. Can you see something?'

Sam looked carefully. Far away, he could just pick out the navigation lights of a vessel. Distant pinpricks. Red and green sidelights, two brighter white steaming lights between and above them. 'A ship. It's coming towards us.'

'Yes. Libyan coastguard.'

Sam tensed. 'We're not inside territorial waters yet, are we? Will they intercept us?'

'No, we're in international waters still. But by the time we meet them, we'll be in Libyan waters. They'll certainly intercept us then.'

Sam spun his gaze from the wheelhouse windows to where the silhouette of Captain Blue occupied the navigator's chair. 'What can you do?'

'Nothing.' Captain Blue gave a further laugh. 'Don't worry, she's expecting us.'

Sam felt sudden confusion. Was he betrayed?

The laugh continued for a moment longer. 'Don't worry, Mr Cameron. You are safe. We have an understanding, the captain of the patrol boat and I. Life is rubbish for him and his crew. Poor pay, when they get it. Some people like them, some people hate the job they do – disrupting the people smuggling operations. Life is not always so nice for them and their families. So I bring the luxuries that make life bearable. Nice things for their wives, sweets for their children. Whisky for the captain and his men.'

'Drink? Isn't that against their religious rules?'

'Yes,' said Blue. 'Now, I think it would be best if you stay in your cabin until this is done.'

Sam nodded. On reflection, he wasn't surprised at Blue's modus operandi. To be everyone's friend was probably the only way to conduct business on this coast. He retired towards his cabin to give his equipment one final check. While descending the stair, he heard the captain summoning a crewman to prepare a gift package for the approaching boarding party.

***

Sam pulled his cap down hard, fastened his jacket and lifted his rucksack. With a final glance around the cabin, he swung the bag onto one shoulder and followed a crewman along the passageway out onto the deck. He had already sensed the vessel was moving slowly, now it seemed the fishing boat had slowed almost to a stop. Just enough propulsion to keep it heading parallel to the coast, no more. They made their way forward, and as his eyes adjusted to the last darkness before the dawn, he became aware of shadowy movements on the deck ahead.

Three of the crew were busy preparing to launch the smaller RIB. A man stood in the sturdy RIB, steadying himself by holding one of its cable stays that were currently looped up on the winch cable's hook. Another man worked the winch, and a third crewman stood at the rail directing activity. Sam watched as the winch lifted the RIB clear of the deck, saw it swing out across the ship's rail and vanish from view over the side, down into the water.

On the deck ahead of him, he saw a hawser suddenly tighten against the little bollard it had been secured to. He knew that the other end would be secured to the bow of the RIB, taking the strain as the weight of the RIB dragged through the water beside the slow-moving fishing boat.

A shout from the third crewman had the winch operator wind up the cable with its now disconnected hook then hurry to the rail to help roll a scramble net over the side. The third crewman hopped over the rail and started to climb down. Sam noted the Kalashnikov slung across his back. Captain Blue may not be anticipating any trouble, but it seemed he was still taking precautions.

Taking a final glance about, Sam noted the coast, much closer now, a blacker darkness against the night sky, clearly uninhabited. Yet both further astern and ahead of their position, shore lights were shining, highlighting the location of Khoms and a network of coastal villages. The black in between marked his destination: the still and silent Leptis Magna. The RIB's engine spluttered, roared, then settled into a quieter mode as it powered ahead just enough to take the weight off the hawser. Sam swung his leg over the rail and scrambled down into the RIB.

It took only a few minutes to reach the shore, but in that time, dawn had started to break. The RIB pulled round a little promontory featuring the crumbled remains of a ruined building, suddenly highlighted in the breaking morning light. Sam guessed it must once have been a lighthouse signing the entrance into Leptis Magna's harbour.

Moments later, the RIB slowed and gently nudged up against the beach. One crewman jumped out. His Kalashnikov was still slung across his back. The man clearly did not anticipate trouble as he pulled on a short bow line, staying focused only on holding the RIB steady against the beach.

Sam tensed. Twenty or thirty paces ahead, emerging from the quickly receding twilight gloom were men. Three men, one held his automatic weapon unslung and at the ready. Sam urgently pointed them out to the crewmen who looked then laughed. One crewman lifted a length of sacking and told Sam to sit still as he made to throw it over Sam's head.

'I don't think so,' said Sam, swiping it aside and making ready to dive into the water.

'Yes, yes,' said the crewman, gripping Sam's arm. 'Everything is fine. Sit. Sit, please.' He pointed down to the bench Sam had just vacated.

Sam looked back at the beach. The three armed men were standing in a line, watching. They looked nervous and now all had their weapons at the ready. Knowing he could not outswim automatic fire, Sam scowled and sat down.

'Good, good. Do not move,' said the crewman, throwing the sacking over Sam's head.

Unsighted, Sam sat, furious with himself for having been so trusting. He began to frantically work out how he could overcome such odds while listening as best he could to the Arabic greetings. It quickly became clear the crewmen and the armed guards knew one another well.

Sam was puzzled; he was not seized, not shot, nobody was questioning his presence, just the sounds of chatter and boxes being moved. Then the sounds stopped. A crewman pulled the sacking off Sam's head, and he relaxed. Heading off up the beach were the three men, weapons slung across their backs and arms filled with boxes. This must have been some regular business that Captain Blue was conducting.

'Wait a minute,' said a crewman as Sam started to rise. 'Wait for them to go.'

'Who were they?'

'Friends.'

'And the sacking?' said Sam.

'Necessary. You don't see them; they don't see you. Nobody knows anything.'

'But they saw me.'

'I don't think so, or they would have arrested you.' The crewman grinned at Sam, tobacco-stained teeth suddenly visible in the growing light.

Biting his tongue, he watched the three armed men disappear from sight.

'We will be back exactly here, one hour after sunset. You can wait just over there, by the eastern quayside. But be here; we will not wait. The guards will not come back until then. You will be safe, whatever you are doing.' The crewman gave a shrug and looked at Sam as though he were mad.

Sam stepped off the RIB onto the beach, and the crewman on the shore immediately began pushing off. The RIB's engine sounded, and it began to back off into the sea. Then with a roar, it powered off towards the now more distant fishing boat.

Suddenly alone and exposed on the beach, Sam took a careful look about. He decided this was not a trap. There was no need for the armed men to have mounted such a charade. If they had intended to take him, they could have already done so with ease. It seemed Blue really had delivered. On impulse, he hurried across the beach to the little promontory from where he could take his bearings and see where the RIB was heading. Once he had done that, he'd be ready to start his search.

***

The sun was up now and well clear of the horizon. Comfortably concealed, Sam sat amid the jumble of great stone blocks that had once been the lighthouse at the end of the promontory. It provided shelter to the harbour against winds from the north and west. Another hundred paces to the southeast of his present spot, across the mouth of the now silted harbour was the eastern breakwater. A little beyond that rose a stretch of imposing wall, which he guessed would have been part of the city's defensive walls.

Together, the promontory and breakwater stretched out protective arms, providing a perfect shelter for ships in the harbour. Too perfect, in fact. As well as protecting ships, the features also helped to slow the seasonal water flow of the wadi that fed into the harbour from the hinterland. The slowing floodwater deposited its silt and sand into the harbour before flowing on out into the Mediterranean. Without a motivated empire to support dredging, the harbour had slowly silted up.

Now, what had once been a harbour was a neatly contained area that centuries of wadi-borne silt had filled and levelled. Subsequent plant growth created a wild garden of grasses, reeds, shrubs and bushes, bounded on three sides by weathered and dried out quays, and to the fourth side, where he had landed, a neat white beach had formed to border the sea's edge.

Gaddafi's men had banished Professor Bertram to the eastern side of Wadi Lebda, to Leptis Magna's port district; they had sent him away across the wadi, specifically to bar him from all the excitement of the main dig in the western half of the city. Placing him on the eastern bank of the Wadi Lebda, in the visually less inspiring eastern half of the city, had been a punishment for his nationality. A ruined lighthouse, the silted harbour, its quaysides and remnants of warehousing were less enticing than the grand architecture of the western side of Leptis. Even the three temples that had once stood around the harbour were largely gone or reduced to rubble.

Glancing down at his plan then back to reality, Sam fixed on his destination – the Temple of Jupiter. He smiled to himself; just for once, it seemed geography and events had combined to make his job easier, providing ready access to the spot that most interested him.

Sam looked south, beyond the quay, searching for the Temple of Jupiter. Where the temple had once stood, he could see nothing. The building had vanished completely. He was unconcerned; Professor Bertram had been clear enough.

Raising his binoculars, he focused on the southern edge of the quay and slowly tilted his glasses up. Beyond some initial thickets, nature offered mainly long green grasses spreading up and around the occasional white rocky outcrops of stone where the land rose up from the quayside. In just a moment, he found what he wanted – a grand stone staircase. It had once routed devotees from the port directly to the Temple of Jupiter. Two thousand years of sun and rain had bleached the honeyed white stone and conspired with countless leather-sandaled footfalls to round off the once sharp-edged blocks. The staircase's patina had weathered back into the landscape, natural camouflage, but nonetheless, the stair remained, just as Professor Bertram had promised.

Sam took his time to scan the surroundings one more time. It seemed safe. The sound of the pristine blue sea gently washing against the promontory was occasionally augmented by a screeching gull, otherwise all was calm. He could see the shrubs and plants that filled the silted-up floor of the harbour waving in the gentle breeze. He knew when he got there, he would hear their breeze-driven rustle and the hum of insects already out, busy under the warm winter sun. Off to the right of the temple steps, the green deepened and thickened to mark the course of the wadi. Beyond that lay the western side of the city. Even from a distance, it impressed. Abandoned to the desert for centuries, it had remained unchanged, an impressive monument to its time and its builders' intentions. Sam wished he could explore that side, but there was a job to do.

Scrambling down from the promontory onto the beach, he paced quickly south across the silted harbour. The sun warmed him now, and he paused to take off his jacket and shove it into his rucksack before pushing on.

Leaving the beach behind, he moved into progressively more dense undergrowth that flourished in the fertile silt. He felt the gentle touch of the grasses and shrubs. As he brushed past, their subtle liquorice scent began to rise in the morning's warmth, offsetting the clear, salty aroma of an unpolluted sea.

Amid the burgeoning green, he chanced on a footpath that led in the general direction he wanted. Tracks in the sandy path told of regular visitors or patrols, marks possibly left by the men he had seen on the beach that morning. There were certainly no print marks to suggest the presence of foraging goats or sheep who would have found the wadi-watered growth irresistible. The guards must be keeping local shepherds out.

The going was easy across the almost level silt-filled harbour. After about two hundred paces, there was a slight ridge that marked the southern edge of the harbour.

Beyond, the ground rose steadily. As Sam left the quayside, he was confronted by a defiant thicket that reached the height of a full-grown man. Looking around, he found a track that wound round and through it. Leaving behind the fertile earth of the silted harbour, the dense growth quickly thinned and shrank away to a bed of calf-high grasses, all suddenly grown vibrant green in the coast's winter rain showers. After only a minute's steady walk, Sam paused. Directly ahead were the steps to the

Temple of Jupiter.

He made a beeline for them and quickly covered the remaining distance. There, he stopped and looked about again. Still, nobody was in sight, though for the first time, he had a tingling sensation that kept him alert. He had no evidence to support it, but he just did not feel alone.

Standing at the foot of the steps, he almost laughed at the apparent absurdity of the construction. An imperial stair, twenty and more paces wide, row upon row of carefully cut and fitted stones leading from the port, up, up to what was now little more than a flat foundation where once a mighty temple had stood. He wondered what had become of the temple itself.

Had its thick stone walls and serried colonnades been taken to build local houses and walls? He knew the English had taken some stone pieces from Leptis Magna in previous centuries, because they'd ended up in a folly at Great Windsor Park, knew too that the French had gone wildly overboard in their looting, taking vast numbers of worked stones and many, many hundreds of columns for Versailles. Perhaps the temples and other buildings here on the east side had suffered most at the hands of European foragers due to their proximity to the sea and, without a thought, had simply been broken up and transported away as the raw materials for other projects. He shook his head at the selfish acquisitive nature that had fed Europe's imperial vanity for centuries.

Then he slowly climbed the steps. With each step, he imagined the thoughts and dreams of those who had taken the same steps two thousand years and more before. At the top, he paused. Ahead of him was a flat foundation space, wider than the stair he had just climbed and deeper. He was unsure how far the foundation stretched away as, perhaps benefiting from a patch of natural earth where once there had been an open inner courtyard, a vigorous outcrop of shrubs twenty paces ahead of him cut off his view.

He knew from his map that not far beyond the temple was the coast road that ran through hundreds of miles of desert, linking each of the coastal towns on its unbroken route to the border with Egypt.

Sam turned and looked out to sea, then closed his eyes and breathed deeply, smelling the clear, herb-tinged air of another age. Below him had once been the bustle of the quayside. He saw the Roman galleys tied up alongside in the harbour, loading up with grain and olive oil, and heard the roaring protests of lions, caged for transport. Heard, too, the wails rising from a line of frightened prisoners as they were whipped aboard the waiting galleys and into slavery. All cargoes destined to serve the demands of distant Rome – the mega city at the heart of the empire.

A little reluctantly, Sam opened his eyes. Time to start work. He began to inspect the top step. It was plain stone, well cut but now weathered and tired. Following Professor Bertram's instructions, he walked to the extreme right of the top step. There, he knelt and, with the back of his hand, swept away the light covering of sand that had accumulated. Nothing, just plain stone. How could this be?

He descended to the next step and swept another skim of sand away and, at once, he felt a weight lift from his shoulders. There was the promised tile: ornate, decorative, its abstract pattern mysterious but familiar. Seeing the artefact for real, he knew exactly what it was – a representation of one side panel of one of Helen's mystery boxes. He cleared away the sand from the next step down, this was plain stone. Descending a further step, he uncovered another patterned tile, this varied in appearance slightly from the first tile but was of the same design. Sam swept sand from the step below, nothing, but the step below that one had a tile. The tiles were fixed on alternate steps.

Straightening up, Sam hurried across the stairway to the left-hand side.

He swept away sand from the top step, nothing. Clearing the step below immediately exposed a tile. Switching his attention to the next step down, he was not surprised to find it unadorned. The step below had a tile, and so the pattern repeated.

Sam paused. Taking a water bottle from his rucksack, he drank, dropped the bottle back into the bag and pulled out his camera. Now, at last, he could create his own visual record of the tile sequence – what he believed, somehow, represented the boxes' opening code. Looming over the top tile of the left-hand side, he carefully photographed it then zoomed in for a close-up. Next, he moved down two steps and photographed the second tile twice. Working his way down the left side, he cleared sand from each alternate step to reveal a tile and photographed it.

It took only a short time to photograph six tiles, representing the six patterned sides of one box. Each tile triggered the same sense of familiarity. They were on the right track, wherever it led.

Crossing to the right-hand side, Sam repeated the process. Again, there were only six tiled images; below the thirteenth step, every stone was plain. Sam had what he wanted. Whatever the images would prove to mean, they were here, just as Professor Bertram had said. His journey had not been a fool's errand.

Sam sat on the steps of the Temple of Jupiter and reviewed the pictures. They were all good, and he took the time to give each picture a sequence and position name. He wished he could email them away at once, but from bitter experience, he knew that Cassiter and his team had extensive monitoring capabilities. Much as he would have loved to send a copy to Edinburgh right now, he had no intention of risking their being intercepted nor of providing anyone with an opportunity to fix his current position. He'd just have to get the camera home safe.

The job had been laughably easy. A glance at his watch showed it was still only mid-morning. Now he had a long wait until the RIB returned for him. With time on his hands, Sam decided he'd have a quick scout around the area and find a quiet spot out of the sun to eat and wait out the afternoon.

A dirt track ran off from behind the Temple's raised foundations before dropping down to where it crossed the wadi. At present, there was just a trickle of water moving along the bed of the watercourse, so he could step through it without any trouble. Much of the plant growth to the wadi sides was bent over towards the sea. There must have been a strong flow in recent days. He was aware that any rain here or inland would cause the wadi to swell into an impassable torrent almost at once. The flooding could subside and vanish as quickly as it first emerged.

Looking up at the blue sky, he guessed today was going to be a dry one. Across the wadi, the path rose to enter Leptis Magna proper. He set off.

***

Helen reached across the table and squeezed Julie's forearm. They had both heard Grace's voice echoing down the hall from the manse's front door as she welcomed DI Brogan and his cheerless sergeant.

'They're both in the kitchen, come along in,' said Grace.

A moment later, Brogan and Price followed Grace into the room. Helen, Julie and Davy were all sat around the table.

'Would you like tea or coffee?' said Grace.

'Not for us, thank you,' said Brogan. 'We're on a tight schedule. I want to get along to the hospital to question those two we picked up last night.'

'I hope you throw the book at them, inspector,' said Helen.

'Well, let's see. First, I want to clear up a couple of points.'

Price had her notebook out and stood ready to take notes.

'What can we tell you?' said Helen.

'It's not you I want to speak with. It's these two who I need to question.' He gestured towards Davy and Julie. 'Perhaps in private?'

'I've nothing to say that Helen can't hear,' said Davy.

'I won't say anything without her being here,' said Julie.

'You can come with us down to the station, and we'll continue the interviews there, if you won't cooperate.' Price's hand pointed away over her shoulder in an abstract direction to the police station.

'Thank you, sergeant. I'm sure we can work this through without recourse to that.' Brogan approached the table. 'Do you mind?' he said, pointing at one of the chairs.

'Please sit, inspector. I'm sure Davy and Julie will want to help you. We have enough problems without wanting to fall foul of the police too.'

'Oh. What problems are they?' said Price.

'Life. Just life,' said Helen, waving the sergeant towards the chair next to Brogan. 'What's to become of the two intruders?'

'They've been kept in hospital for observation overnight. We're going to speak with them now. But it's all a bit tricky, I'm afraid.'

'How so? They were caught in the act,' said Helen.

'That's the problem, isn't it? The attending officers took Davy and Julie's statements once the two men had been hauled off to hospital with head injuries.'

'And? What's the problem?'

'Helen, in the UK you have a right to use reasonable force in self-defence. But there is no general property owner's right to shoot intruders or attack transgressors.' Brogan turned his gaze towards Julie. 'Nor is there a right to beat people about the head with a wooden stave.'

'But they were trespassing, and they were going to hit Davy on the head. I only hit one of them to stop that.'

'Perhaps. But it's not clear how the second man got his head injury.'

'What are you getting at inspector?' said Helen.

'The inspector means your friends are in the frame for a violent assault that put two men in hosp—'

'Thank you, sergeant, I can manage to explain this. The problem you two face is that it's not clear what crime the intruders committed that could stand up in court.'

'Inspector, your officers saw the two men being removed from our trench. They were looting. One was going to cosh Davy. Aren't they crimes enough?'

'I'll need to speak with the men shortly, but I'm not hopeful.'

'Oh, come on!'

'Listen, they have a very expensive lawyer. It appears they claim to be extreme-weather hikers, whatever that means. They were in Edinburgh for the New Year celebrations and stayed on for a few days to enjoy the snow. They were out enjoying themselves on a night-time hike, and one of them apparently fell into your trench. While trying to help his friend, the other was attacked and knocked into the trench by Julie.'

'That's rubbish!' said Davy, rising to his feet. 'Total lies—'

'Just sit down, sir,' said Price, also rising from her seat. She fixed Davy with a steely stare.

'What about my collar bone? They broke that.'

'Everyone just calm down,' said Brogan. 'Sit. Let's talk this through.'

'I did push one of them into the trench,' Julie admitted hesitantly, 'but the other was already down there digging about. The man I pushed pulled me down with him when he fell, and we landed on top of the other one; he got hit on the head with my stick during the fall.'

'And how did the other one hurt his head?' said Price.

'I hit him,' said Davy. 'It was an accident,' he squeezed Julie's hand tight, silencing her.

Price made a point of referring to her notes. 'You weren't in the trench, sir, how could you have hit him?'

'I don't know. It all happened so fast and in the dark.'

'You don't know how you hit him?'

'Inspector, please let's not lose sight of the fact that these two men were the intruders, looting our archaeological site. Julie and Davy have just been caught up in something not of their making.'

'I know. But let's be clear, there is no evidence of these men having looted anything; they had no artefacts in their possession. Crossing another person's land is not against the law in Scotland. Their excuse is not very believable, I grant you, but it is an excuse, and without other evidence to corroborate Davy and Julie's version, no sheriff court is going to convict these men. In fact, I can tell you now, no procurator fiscal would bring the charges in the first place.

'I'm more concerned that any counter-complaint will almost certainly stick against Julie. It's even possible that there are Health and Safety charges to be brought against you as the landowner for knowingly leaving that trench without proper guardrails around it.'

Davy was about to speak again when Price raised a single cautionary finger and glared over it into his eyes. He remained silent, turning his attention to Julie who was being hugged by Helen.

'We're going over to the hospital now. I'm sorry, but it doesn't look good. Julie, you've told us you hit one man on the head with your stick. You hit the other man's head by accident or design when you fell into the trench. The evidence points to them as the victims.' He stood and Price shadowed his moves. 'Does your family have a solicitor? If so, I'd give them a call.'

'I don't have any family; I don't know any solicitors.' Julie had gone white and was trembling.

Helen's hand squeezed her arm just a little tighter. 'Don't worry; we're your family now. I know a very good lawyer. I'll call him right away.'

Brogan nodded an acknowledgement and gave a sheepish smile. 'I'm sorry, but we must follow process.'

'Must you? Really?' said Helen.

'The law is the law,' said Price.

'I am sorry, truly. I don't doubt Julie, really I don't. Let's see what these men have to say, then take it from there, okay?' Brogan turned and led Price out.

***

Within the enclosed spaces of Leptis Magna, Sam felt less exposed. Moving quietly and with caution to avoid any unexpected encounters, he spent a couple of hours weaving to and fro through excavated parts of the city to take in some truly spectacular sights. All the while, his observations told him he was alone, yet a sixth sense kept flagging something, some nebulous concern he could not quite pin down.

He had made a point of seeking out the ancient theatre. Its soaring semicircle of tiered stone seating looked down onto the stage, which was itself backed by a stone wall topped with columns whose high lintels would once have supported an awning to shade the stage beneath. Behind the stage, the columns and internal divisions continued, reaching back to outline what would once have been a honeycomb of spaces and apartments, providing everything necessary to support a great theatrical event.

His appreciation of Leptis Magna grew at every turn. After falling to the invading Muslims, the city of perhaps fifty thousand people had been abandoned. Perfectly positioned to export Africa's produce to Roman Europe in the north, it was of no value, had no purpose, to its east-facing Muslim conquerors. As such, it had been abandoned, left to the encroaching desert sands. Sands that had both obscured and protected the buildings and statues, burying them for centuries.

Leaving the theatre, Sam continued through the ancient streets. He really wanted to visit the Septimius Arch, the triumphal arch built to honour Septimius Severus. The Roman emperor had been born an African Roman in Leptis Magna and had risen to the very top of the empire.

As he approached the arch, he hesitated. Even from a distance, he could tell it was a huge and imposing structure yet, in contrast, adorned with the most intricate stonework. It was frustrating, but the arch's position spanning the straight road into the ancient city was just too exposed for him to get close.

Beyond the arch, at the far end of the road leading into the ancient city, was a visitor centre. Peering carefully from cover, he could see it was guarded by armed men. Probably some of the men he had seen that morning. Keen as he was to visit the arch, it would not do to tempt fate. The guards may be choosing to ignore him for now, but they would have to react if he walked into their line of sight. And that would be unavoidable thanks to the excavations having cleared the main roads and larger public buildings by removing as much as twenty feet of sand while leaving the surroundings buried and untouched. Unintentionally, the excavators had created the perfect shooting range along the road from visitor centre to arch.

Sam moved on. He took time to explore the Hadrianic baths. Surrounded by the walled remains of their labyrinthine buildings, the baths were shaped just like a modern swimming pool but with tiered steps leading into the water that could double as seating for socialising bathers. They were currently half-full of rainwater, perhaps waist height he thought.

Choosing a spot beside the walls of the bathhouse where nobody could approach unexpectedly from behind, Sam sat and ate the lunch he had prepared for himself in the fishing boat's galley. Afterwards, he moved back through the city, northwards, directly up to the coast. There, he dropped to the waterline, and concealed from the view of any prying eyes, he continued along the coast, returning to his starting point of the morning at the harbour's protective promontory and its tumbled lighthouse. Slipping in among the fallen blocks of stone, he found a quiet spot deep amid the jumble. It offered shelter from the sun and concealment from any unexpected visitors.

Sam frequently looked along the gaps between the fallen stones. In one direction, he could see out to sea where the RIB would come from, and looking in the other direction, he could see the silt beach where he was to be collected. That was not a suitable spot to wait out the afternoon, far too open; he was happier with his current position and would make the five-minute walk across the little silt beach to the pickup point at the due time. Even so, an instinctive uneasiness, born of military training, refused to leave him. Maybe it was just the eerie silence. There had been no sign of any other presence, no one had offered any threat, but any unknown party was a risk, and something was keeping him on high alert.

Chapter 14

FRIDAY JANUARY 17TH - p.m.

Davy put down the telephone handset and turned to the others.

'Well?' said Helen as Julie looked on anxiously.

He broke into a smile, which told them the answer.

'It's going to be alright. DI Brogan says the two men have gone. They slipped away this morning, a while after their solicitor had been to see them. Apparently, there was some sort of commotion in the corridor outside their ward, which distracted the policeman guarding them. By the time he'd sorted it out and got back, the two had skipped. Brogan didn't get a chance to speak with them, so there is no complaint for Julie to face.'

Tears appeared in Julie's eyes as the emotional turmoil finally found release. She leant into Davy's good shoulder. Helen and Grace both closed on Julie to offer congratulations and support.

'DI Brogan did say to tell you to get the trench properly fenced off, just in case.'

Helen nodded absently. The private security contractors were taking over today, they would certainly have that covered already. More worryingly, if the intruders had slipped away, unwanted by the law, where had they gone, and where would they show up next?

***

In mid-afternoon, a patrol boat had sailed westward along the coast heading in the direction of Misrata. Later, as the sun nudged closer to the western horizon, a black dot appeared to the north. It grew bit by bit into an oil tanker. Oil tanks empty and riding high in the water, it had come slowly in, making for the Khoms oil terminal, just a couple of miles along the coast. Otherwise, the sea had been as quiet as the land.

The sun had set with no sign of Captain Blue and his fishing boat. Sam had not worried. From his position on the promontory, just a few feet above sea level, he doubted he would be able to see for much more than eight or ten miles at best. From what Captain Blue had indicated, his vessel could cover that distance in less than half an hour. The captain was probably hanging off the coast until dark to avoid any prying eyes. Yes, shore radars at the tanker terminal and at the Khoms and Misrata pilot stations would pick him up far offshore, but a fishing vessel going about its business would be of no concern to anyone. Sam guessed the patrol ship he'd seen earlier in the day would be another of Captain Blue's friends.

The darkness that followed on the heels of sunset was modified a little by a shining crescent moon. About twenty minutes before pickup time he felt a sense of satisfaction as a vessel's lights appeared in the north. It came on quickly. As it neared the shore, it began a slow turn. Sam was just about to head to the rendezvous when he paused, there was something different about the RIB being swung out from the fishing boat's side.

He pulled out his binoculars and studied it as it hung above the water. Blue was launching his larger RIB. Sam could think of no obvious reason why, unless Blue was landing more contraband or planning to pick up something, some people, to smuggle north. Sam was not happy and hurried across the beach to the ancient eastern quayside from where he could watch the RIB's approach.

Having chosen a spot where he was screened from the beach by a thicket of bushes, Sam had barely settled down when the RIB swung round the little promontory and ran towards the beach. The coxswain eased back the engine at the last moment and spun the helm, slowing the RIB and turning it sideways to the beach, where it bobbed gently in the waves a few yards offshore. The crewman at the front of the RIB stood and peered into the darkness ashore.

Sam checked his watch; it was exactly an hour after sunset. With a deep breath, he hitched his rucksack up and stepped out from behind the bushes. He was spotted and the crewman shouted, pointing in Sam's direction. At once, the coxswain got the RIB moving forwards, nudging its prow against the beach just ahead of Sam's approach. The crewman jumped out at the water's edge and hurried onto the beach, he carried one end of the RIB's bow line, pulling taught to hold the RIB on the beach. He waved towards Sam.

Sam was uneasy. He had to board the RIB, to stay ashore would have condemned him to certain capture by one Libyan faction or another. Yet, there was no obvious reason for Blue switching the RIBs. No reason not to either. Hanging off a few paces along the beach, Sam glanced about, peering away into the darkness. There was no sign of the armed guards coming for more contraband nor of anyone bringing more passengers for the outward trip.

The crewman on the beach called towards Sam, beckoning him on. In frustration, the man turned and shouted something at the coxswain, and Sam saw a look of anxiety flash across his face. It was a trap.

Sam turned to move off the beach into the backing scrub, but the crewman, realising what was happening, shouted an alarm and ran towards Sam. Launching a desperate rugby tackle, he took Sam at the knees, receiving a heavy boot in the face while bringing Sam down to the sand with him. Sam kicked out again, driving his heel hard into the crewman's stomach. The gasp and curse told Sam the blow had done its work. He bent his knee, drawing his boot up and pushed down hard. The contact with the crewman's face caused a cry of pain and put the man out of action. Sam scrambled to his feet then stopped dead before raising his hands in surrender.

He was looking directly at the barrel of a weapon – an assault rifle's muzzle thrust forwards, only inches from his chest. The muzzle of a second weapon, a pistol, was pressed against his temple. Beyond the gunmen, he could see the RIB. The coxswain using the engine to keep the bow against the sand while his crewmate remained out of action. The reason behind the use of the big RIB was clear now. It had carried four extra men, all concealed low as it came in to the beach. Two of them were on the beach pointing weapons at Sam. Two more had risen from below the line of the gunwale and were also moving forwards. One man limping, the other assisting him.

Sam recognised the smaller of the two approaching men. Cassiter. He cursed his luck, cursed Captain Blue and his treachery. Now Sam understood the real reason he had been so constrained on the journey here. Captain Blue had other passengers on his vessel – it had been a trap all along.

As Cassiter approached, the crewman Sam had injured climbed to his feet. The man snarled and pulled his seaman's knife from its sheath. He glared at Sam then took a step towards him, drawing back his knife hand ready to strike.

'Stop!' Cassiter commanded.

The crewman glanced towards Cassiter than turned back towards Sam, swinging his arm to strike the blow. The blade never reached Sam's chest. The report of a pistol sounded and the man stopped. An expression of surprise on his face, his legs buckled, and he dropped to his knees. A second shot, at closer range, punched through the man's back and into his heart. He fell forwards with a little sigh. Cassiter prodded the body with his stick then turned his attention to Sam.

'Mr Cameron, we meet again, and this time there are some things we need to talk about, without any unwanted interruptions.'

'I can't say it's a pleasure,' said Sam. He rolled his eyes to the side. 'This is a bit of overkill though. Don't you think one gun's enough?'

'Cameron, I'm not stupid. You have a reputation, and I've seen you in action. I think two guns pointing at you are just enough. Now tell me what you found.'

'Found? Where?'

'Don't be cute with me, Cameron. I haven't followed you halfway around the world to this God forsaken corner for fun. What did you find?'

'Nothing, I'm here as a tourist.'

'We know you are here to find a code. I enjoyed my time in Malta, though your African priest friend didn't. He did tell me everything before he died though. Where have you put it?' Cassiter waved his pistol towards Sam. 'Get his rucksack; let's see what's inside.' His third man hustled behind Sam and pulled the rucksack straps free of his shoulders. Returning to Cassiter's side, he pulled open the bag for his boss to check.

'We know you have the boxes. That Ethiopian priest couldn't stop talking once I'd got him started. We know you need to open the boxes, know the key is somehow hidden here at Leptis Magna. Why not make it easy on yourself and just tell me? You know how persuasive I can be.'

Sam shook his head. 'I have no idea what you're talking about.'

'Come, come, Mr Cameron. One chance only, tell me what I need to know,' said Cassiter while rifling through the rucksack. He stopped and turned his attention back to Sam. 'There's nothing in here. Where is it?'

'Where is what?'

'This is becoming tiresome now, Cameron. Just answer my questions.'

Sam remained tight-lipped.

Cassiter struck Sam on the side of the face with his walking stick. 'Search him,' he said.

Sam was jostled, patted and prodded. Then his phone was pulled from his pocket and the camera wrenched from its neck lanyard.

'Ah, what's this?' said Cassiter. 'Your phone. No doubt, you'll have that female minister of yours on speed dial. Shall I call her for you?' Cassiter moved closer and looked intently at Sam. Then he shook his head and put the phone away in his own pocket. 'No, I don't think so. I'd rather give her the news of your passing face-to-face.' He laughed and gripped Sam by the throat – squeezed. 'She'd like to hear the news from me, don't you think?'

He loosed Sam's throat and inspected the camera. 'Why would you want a fancy camera with you? Your phone includes a good quality camera. Perhaps you were photographing something special. Something that demanded best quality tools? An archaeological artefact?' Cassiter lifted his head to meet Sam's eye. 'A key perhaps?' Cassiter tabbed through the camera's stored photos.

'What are these pictures? What do they mean?'

'Just a tourist's holiday snaps.'

'Don't take me for a fool, Cameron. Just tell me while you still have breath. You're going to die tonight, no matter what. I promise, if you help me, I'll leave your American girlfriend alone.'

Beyond the wadi, in the western part of the city, Sam spotted torchlights flickering. The sound of Cassiter's gunshots must have finally dragged the site guards back into play.

'I can tell you nothing now. Those pictures are meaningless to me, I've nothing to tell until I analyse them. Your only hope is to let me live, so I can solve the problem. And if we're going, we need to go now. Look over there; your shots have alerted the local guards, they're combing the site.' He nodded to the west.

Cassiter slipped Sam's camera into his pocket as he looked towards the flashlights then back at Sam.

'Agreed, it's time to go, but not for you. I'm quite sure we have experts who will be able to decipher the clues now you've found them for us, thank you. You are officially retired. Much as I'd like the pleasure of killing you, I can think of nothing more exquisite than your lady friend's angst and suffering while you are in the hands of one of the local extremist groups, which will, of course, be inevitable. Once they've done with you, I'll visit her. You can just imagine what's going to happen then.'

Sam glared defiantly at Cassiter as the man behind him slung his weapon and applied wrist ties. He slapped the side of Sam's head, banging it against the other captor's pistol muzzle. The two men laughed and repeated the action. A little trickle of blood ran down from Sam's temple as his ankles were tied together.

'What's this all for?' said Sam. 'What can be worth so much killing?'

Cassiter leant in close to Sam's face. 'Power. Something you wouldn't understand. It's all about power.'

'People don't need to die for it.'

'Power, true power, comes from fear. Fear grows through death. Death and suffering brings perfect obedience. Now, enough chat; you need a few moments to prepare yourself for a meeting with the site guards. They will certainly have to hand you over to the local militia. And believe me, the militia will fall over themselves to sell you to the extremists. You'll be worth a lot of money. You've got a very difficult ending ahead of you, Cameron. Best enjoy these quiet moments while you can.'

Cassiter waved his pistol muzzle, and Sam was forced to his knees.

The coxswain's voice from the RIB urged them to hurry. Sam could hear the voices of the site guards more distinctly now. He chanced a glance and saw the torch lights were closer, spread in an open line along the west bank of the wadi, searching methodically. These guards were trained to deter site looters, probably had a standard search pattern to follow; now they were applying it to a different end. The lights disappeared as the guards dropped into the wadi. They would emerge on the eastern half of the site in moments.

Cassiter struck Sam a blow on the head with the butt of his pistol, leaving him swaying on his knees. A guard kicked him in the back, sending him flat onto the sand.

The guard stooped. 'Get ready to suffer, English.'

'I'm Scottish.' Groggy, he could only provide the conditioned response.

'No. You're dead. Right now, you're the living dead, believe me.' The guard swung his shoulder allowing his assault rifle to slew down and bang into Sam's temple. 'Dead. They're going to fry you, man. And I mean fry.'

'Okay, let's go now,' said Cassiter, turning to step towards the RIB. Involuntarily, the anxious coxswain revved the engine. The sound reached out across the evening and was echoed by the shouts of the site guards who now knew where to focus their attention.

Cassiter's stick and feet tangled in the bow line abandoned by the dead crewman, and as he stooped to pull the bow line clear, a spurt of controlled gunfire burst out of the shadowed undergrowth close behind the beach. Three rounds cut through the guard who loomed over Sam; he gasped and dropped dead. The second guard dropped, a neat bullet hole drilled through his forehead. The third ran for the RIB while simultaneously attempting to unsling his assault rifle to return fire. A round in the leg sent him sprawling into Cassiter, knocking his boss into the water. Cassiter wrapped the bow line tight around his wrists and gripped hard.

'Go! Go!' Cassiter ordered the coxswain who had, in any event, decided it was time to leave. The RIB was already moving away from the beach, picking up speed with every moment and dragging Cassiter out into deeper water. There, in the wet darkness, the coxswain paused to pull Cassiter back on board.

On the beach, the wounded guard looked out to sea, calling on the RIB to wait. He took a step into the waves, and his leg gave out, dropping him into the water.

From out of the darkness, a darker shadow hurried onto the beach, stooped and lifted Sam.

Sam offered no resistance. Semi-conscious, he thought he saw a man in a dark robe loom over him. He didn't really care, couldn't care, as he lapsed into unconsciousness.

The shadow swung Sam onto his shoulder and retreated from the beach, melting back into the black of the undergrowth.

The wounded man at the water's edge had seen none of the abduction. Once he had dragged his eyes from the receding RIB, he had focused on the shouts and moving torchlights of the approaching site guards. He dropped onto the sand, overcoming the pain in his leg to let off two rounds at the nearest torch beam. It dropped and the cry confirmed a hit. He turned his attention to the second torch, fired and again made a kill.

The torches went out. The wounded man's muzzle flashes had confirmed his position on the beach. Knowing that, he tried to move his position, crawling along the water's edge, but it bought him no time. A thunderous torrent of unidentified fire poured from the beachside bushes into which Sam had been carried. Hit once, twice, he raised himself in an involuntary reaction to the pain and his body was immediately riddled with more shots.

A few moments later, the site guards hurried onto the beach. They raised their guns and fired forlorn and frustrated shots after the retreating RIB then turned their attention to the bodies on the beach.

Chapter 15

SATURDAY JANUARY 18TH

Sam regained consciousness in a dark space. It took a few moments for him to assess his situation. He was alive, his hands were still tied behind his back, his ankles bound, and he was in the rear of a moving vehicle. The itching on his face told him he was covered by some rough material or rags. Was he being hidden? From whom? He stayed quiet, waited; it was all he could do.

The motion of the vehicle suddenly changed. It was going over much rougher terrain, and Sam braced his legs to steady himself and prevent his head from rocking against the metalled sides. He didn't know how long the bumping lasted, five minutes, perhaps fifteen. At one point, he must have lost consciousness again. When he next stirred, there was silence, and the motion had stopped.

Suddenly, he heard a hatch pop up, and the sacking cover was pulled away. He blinked in the early morning sunlight as thick arms reached in and pulled him out. Semi-conscious, he could only groan a protest as he was hoisted on to the man's shoulders, and they set off at a run. While the fog in his mind began to clear, Sam realised there were three other men, all armed, all running with him. Their flowing, black robes and head coverings had been perfect cover at night. Now, in the light of day, they were more conspicuous.

Hoisted over the big man's shoulders, he could not see where they were going, other than it was along a sandy track that sloped downwards. He could see that the big black 4x4 they had travelled in had simply been abandoned at the point where the track had narrowed to block its progress.

One man ran behind them, constantly turning to check they were not followed; the other two ran ahead. Whoever his abductors were, they were not part of the Leptis Magna security team. Yet, their anxious behaviour told Sam they were not of the militia who would have moved with more confidence within their own areas.

The sound of the men's running feet changed. The sand-cushioned thuds were replaced by the thundering of boots on wood; they were running out along a little pier. The man's voice behind called out a warning, and Sam lifted his head to see two gunmen had appeared beside the abandoned black 4x4, pointing and shouting an alarm.

The man trailing behind Sam and his carrier paused, raised his weapon and fired. One of their distant pursuers dropped, hit, the second raised his weapon and fired. His uncontrolled firing was ineffectual. Sam's tail man fired again, and the second pursuer was dead.

The running stopped; urgent orders were exchanged. Sam was bumped down onto the pier's wooden boards then rolled to the edge where other hands took him and dragged him down. He banged onto the deck of a motor launch, and the black-clad men jumped down after him. Engines roared, powering the launch away from the pier. Then the thunderous clatter of a deck-mounted heavy machine gun obliterated every other sound as it laid down suppressing fire along the route they had just run. Once the launch pulled out of range, the gunfire ceased, and Sam could get his bearings at last.

He looked about the launch; it had a crew of four: the machine-gunner, the coxswain and two hands. There were four other men, all clothed completely in black. One of them, the big man who had carried Sam from the vehicle to the launch, now approached him, combat knife in hand.

'No!' Sam braced himself for the blow; it didn't come. Instead, the big man rolled Sam over onto his stomach and sliced the ties from his wrists and ankles. Then Sam was sat up, propped against the launch's gunwale, and one of the others came forwards and offered him bottled water. Sam had no idea who his rescuers were, was just happy that there was a chance they were what they appeared to be. He took the water and emptied the bottle in one go, before rubbing the cable-tie burns on his wrists. The big man laughed, slumped down beside him and offered Sam a biscuit.

Sam took it, ate. 'Thank you. Now, who are you?' he said.

The man smiled at him. 'My name is not so important. You may not remember me, but my team and I saw you once before.'

Sam looked at the man and shook his head. 'Sorry, I really don't recall. Where?'

'In Nairobi. We escorted Bishop Ignatius and whatever the treasure was that he gave to your lady friend. We had left the Thorn Tree Café and were entering our vehicle at the entrance to the Stanley Hotel when you went in to meet her.'

'Yes, of course; the bishop was leaving as I arrived. I'm sorry I didn't recognise you.'

'No matter, we were only background then, and today, you have had other things to think of.'

'I'll second that,' said Sam. 'So you work for Bishop Ignatius and his Church?'

'No. We, all four, are believers, but we don't work for the Church. We are part of the Ethiopian Army. You know, I trained at Sandhurst, an exchange training programme.'

'I know Sandhurst. That's where I did my officer training.'

'So, we are brothers in arms, my friend.'

Yes, so it seems, and thank you. I really thought my time was up.'

'It is our pleasure. Perhaps we will all have a drink together when we get ashore?'

'Great, I'm up for that.' Sam slapped his hand on the launch. 'But look, Ethiopia doesn't have a coastline, much less a navy. What exactly is happening?'

Sam's rescuer laughed again and produced another bottle of water which he shared with Sam. 'Our Church wanted to ensure you got out of Libya alive, so Bishop Ignatius does what he does, and my government supplied us and arranged with the Egyptian government for logistical support. This launch is from an Egyptian patrol ship lying offshore. It will ferry us back into Egypt where an Ethiopian military plane is waiting to take us to Addis Ababa.'

'Really? The Egyptian government will help like that?'

'I know – we are mostly Christian, they are mostly Muslim'—he shrugged and pursed his lips—'but Ethiopia can be a good and strong friend. Behind the scenes, we help them, and they help us.'

Sam leant his head back against the gunwale, closed his eyes. 'Well, thank God. Thank everyone's God.'

***

A message from Sam had reached Helen mid-morning and lifted a weight of worry that had been building in his absence. Shortly after she had learnt of Sam's departure from Libya, Elaine and Grace had arrived, quickly followed by Francis, then Xavier and Angelo.

'I see Sam's vehicle is back in the drive. They've done a good repair job; there's no sign of damage,' said Francis.

'Yes, the garage returned it this morning. I haven't been out to inspect it yet, but Sam will be pleased to have it back.'

Julie and Davy had been invited for lunch too. As people took their seats around the big kitchen table, Davy, his arm in a sling to support his broken collarbone, attempted to supervise proceedings. Meanwhile, Julie assisted Grace in bustling around the kitchen and disregarding him, while putting the final touches to the meal.

At the table, Helen shared what details she had of Sam's escape from Libya. It was a comfort that Sam was being evacuated to Addis Ababa. Helen knew their friends there would ensure his safety. On the other hand, it took him further away from where he needed to be.

With just a shrug and a pursing of his lips, Xavier addressed the problem. Before lunch was served, his private aircraft was readying for take-off, destination Addis Ababa. It would collect Sam and return him directly to Edinburgh sometime on Sunday.

Over lunch, it was agreed that Davy, Julie and Grace would return to the trench that afternoon to take advantage of the afternoon daylight in a search for clues as to exactly what the night-time intruders had been seeking. Helen phoned the security company to ensure the site guards were expecting the visitors.

They all agreed, any further progress would depend on Sam's return.

***

Eugene Jr looked at the two men. The lawyer's advice had been that there would be little prospect of a prosecution. Once the police had the facts, they would let the issue slip away. To accelerate the process, on Friday morning, Eugene Jr had given the lawyer instructions to pass to his men. They obeyed them to the letter. Just before Friday lunchtime, a commotion had arisen in the hospital corridor, and by the time it was over, the two men were in a car and heading away into the city.

'My father is not happy with either of you. How you could allow yourselves to be overpowered by a girl? It is unbelievable. He intends to discuss it with you personally.' Pausing for theatrical effect, he felt a little tingle inside when he saw the two men visibly blanche at the news that they had attracted Eugene Parsol's attention. The power his father wielded was immense, and one day it would be his.

'I suggest you pick up your game and don't do anything else to cause upset before he arrives.' He waved them away, and the men left his hotel suite as quickly as possible. He crossed to the window and looked out. It faced west and, between the snow showers, afforded him a view along the length of Princes Street. A full mile away, at the far end of the street, was another imposing stone-built hotel; together, they bookended the thoroughfare.

Directly beneath his window, he could see the canopy that covered Waverley Station, the city's main rail hub. To his right, he traced the line of buildings that fringed the full north side of Princes Street; somewhere among them was a top-floor suite that had been Cassiter's base before things had gone so badly wrong for him in the city. The street itself was quiet amid the intermittent snow showers. Buses and trams rolled back and forth, and a few pedestrians dotted between shops or hoisted umbrellas before hurrying across the road for the temporary sanctuary of the bus shelters that punctuated its length.

His father and Cassiter were already on their way. Apparently, Cassiter had made a breakthrough in Libya. Imperfect, but enough to draw the big guns to Edinburgh.

He turned and glowered at the closed door of his suite. He could not afford to be embarrassed by any more schoolboy errors and would need to up his own game too. Knowing his father, the two men would be punished for their failing. Parsol Jr determined to watch the process carefully. One day, he would take over. If the punishments meted out now were not what he judged to be sufficient, when his time came, they would be punished again.

***

Davy stood at the edge of the trench where he divided his time between chatting to two security guards about the merits of a football winter shutdown and directing Julie and Grace who had clambered down into the trench and were blissfully disregarding him.

'Watch your step down there, Grace; the stones can be slippery.'

'And what about me? They're slippery for me too,' said Julie, throwing a stone up towards Davy, aiming to miss.

He reached out his good hand and caught the passing stone. 'You be careful too, Julie.' He laughed and inspected the stone. 'Hey, well done, this has a piece of pattern on it.'

'Really? What's it like?' said Julie.

'Not sure, it's only a fragment. Here, take a look,' he said, tossing the stone back into the trench.

Julie caught the stone and inspected it. 'You're right. We'll see if we can find any more.'

Chapter 16

MONDAY JANUARY 20TH

In the manse's study, Xavier and Elaine were settled comfortably to either end of a settee. Opposite them, in another two-seater, Helen had positioned herself close to Sam. Grace had put the afternoon tea tray on the study desk and sat there to pour cups of tea for Angelo to distribute.

'Well, we're all happy you got out alive, thank God,' said Helen to a round of nods and murmured agreement.

'Yes, I'm pleased myself, but that doesn't deflect from the big problem. Cassiter took my camera with the pictures of the steps at the Temple of Jupiter. My whole trip was a waste of time.'

'Not a complete waste of time,' said Xavier. 'We now know for certain that it's the same organisation from last year that is involved. And like before, we know they are unable to proceed without our contribution. They always seem to need us to solve the problem.'

'So they can sneak in and snatch whatever it is at the last minute? I don't think so,' said Grace.

'I think you're right. Try as they might to steal a march on us, it seems they cannot proceed far without us,' said Helen.

'That certainly was the case last time; it may still be. But for sure, once Cassiter had the photographs, which he must have assumed were the key, he did not seem to worry about my living any longer. That we are searching for the key to open our boxes is known. They now have the photographs, which might help them, but it definitely seems to block us off again. Yet, we have the boxes, so they cannot make any progress in opening them. Short of my going back to Leptis Magna for a second round of photograph taking, it's an impasse.'

'Well, you can forget Libya,' said Helen.

'Don't worry; I have no intention of going back. There were several bodies left on the ground over there; I'm thinking everyone is going to be on high alert now. There's no chance of getting in and out in one piece again.'

'So, my friend, where are we?' Xavier's eyebrows furrowed slightly, and his palms opened out in a tandem display with a hunching of shoulders.

'Tell you the truth, Xavier; I was hoping you might be able to shed some light on it for us. Are you sure there is nothing you can add?' said Sam.

Xavier's eyebrows arched yet higher, and his next shrug was more pronounced. 'I have no idea how to open your boxes. Yes, they are part of our heritage. But they are not a part of the daggers' story that I know of. This is something different. My people have never had a knowledge of this.'

'So, we're stuck,' said Grace.

'What do you think we should do, Sam?' said Helen.

'I don't know. I really don't. But we have to come up with something, fast. Cassiter and his people are on the move; they certainly won't wait. I expect they may just come for the boxes now and that means more deaths.'

Sam stood and crossed to the desk to get more tea. Grace leant across the desk, taking his cup from him.

'What are these?' said Sam, an ingrained professional interest kicking in as he ran his fingers over the shards of splintered stone on the desk.

'Oh, don't worry about them. They're the bits I found with Julie and Davy out at the trench over the weekend. I was going to show them to you when you had a quiet moment.' Grace handed him his refilled teacup with a smile. 'You can see them another time.'

'Thanks,' said Sam, taking the teacup and nodding an agreement that he would look another day. He returned to his place, putting the teacup on the occasional table between the settees. Then he walked back to the desk. Grace raised the biscuit plate, but Sam waved it away. He began sifting through Grace's little pile of splintered stones.

'Is this everything you found?'

'Yes,' said Grace.

'Are you sure? Was there more that you didn't bring back?'

'Maybe … I don't know. It gets dark early; we were only there for an hour. It seemed to me most of the smaller bits of stone had been crushed under the remains of the roof – there wasn't a lot left. Is it important?'

'Perhaps. I'll need to speak with Davy or Julie. I'm sure they will be able to give me a formal site appraisal.'

'What is it Sam? What's going on?' said Helen.

'I don't know. See this?' Sam lifted a piece of stone the size of a matchbox. 'It's a splinter off something larger. I'd guess the whole was originally cricket-ball-sized.'

'How big is that?' said Helen.

'Think baseball.' Sam held the stone up to the natural light of the window. 'The worked surface has a pattern that seems just a little familiar. I feel I know it.'

Helen joined him at the window, took the stone from Sam and looked at it. 'Oh yes, I know this,' she said.

'You do?'

'Yes, I found one at the site, the day I was run off the road. You're right; it's about baseball size but actually a cuboid not a sphere. It had a pattern on it too, I think like on this little piece.'

'Where is it?'

'I don't know, Sam. I was run off the road and ended up in hospital, remember?'

Sam leant in and kissed Helen's cheek. 'Sorry, professional interest, I can't help it.'

Helen pushed Sam's shoulder before handing him back the shard. 'Help it! Remember, girlfriends always come first.'

'Sorry,' said Sam, with a grin.

Helen thought for a moment as Sam showed Xavier and Elaine the ornate shard of stone. He traced out the engraved patch on one surface.

'I thought it would be of interest to you, so I put it in my shoulder bag. I guess it's still in your car.'

'I'll go out and have a look for you,' said Grace.

'Thanks.' Helen dipped her hand into Sam's sports jacket pocket and pulled out the fob. 'It should be on the floor somewhere. Maybe look under the driver's seat too, in case it got shoved under there during the crash.'

Grace was quickly back with the shoulder bag.

Helen rummaged inside. The stone was still there. In the comfort of the study, the stone suddenly seemed more elaborately worked than she had thought in the trench. With a smile of triumph, she passed it to Sam.

'Whoa, what is this?' said Sam. Taking the stone, he turned it in his hand. As Helen had said, the stone was cuboid. Five faces intricately worked, one rough. He held it out for them all to see. 'Look, this is a cusp, very complex stone working. You take a larger stone, which is one of a series that combine to form an archway. One end of each bigger stone is whittled away to eventually leave a regular-sized section as part of the arch, with this much smaller appendage or cusp sprouting out beneath it like a fruit from a tree.'

'Amazing,' said Helen, inspecting the stone properly.

Elaine took it, inspected it carefully and gave a curt nod before passing it to Xavier.

'There is much work in this stone. I do not recognise the images, but they feel familiar, they seem … they seem attractive yet not … uh … how do you say, not normal?' Xavier held the stone out to Helen again and looked to her for a response. She reached out to take the stone from Xavier.

'I'll take that if you don't mind,' said Sam, reaching over to nudge Helen's hand aside, lifting the stone from Xavier's palm himself.

'Sam!' said Helen.

'Wait a minute,' said Sam and hurried off to the kitchen where he rinsed away the roof-fall dirt. He looked at the rinsed stone then rubbed it against his sports jacket sleeve. Looking again, he returned to the study to present it back to Helen.

'There, just look at that. Beautiful, perfect.'

He dropped into Helen's hand a perfectly worked stone, its crisp edges and flowing patterned surfaces revealed. Everyone gasped.

'What is it, Sam?'

'Like I said, it's a cusp. A carefully patterned cusp.'

'It looks new,' said Grace.

'I don't know how old it is. It could be ten years old, a hundred years old; it could be a thousand years old. As old as the chamber it was part of. Inside the chamber, the stone's never been exposed to any weather. It might as well have been stored in your cupboard.'

'Wow.'

'Yes, wow. But here's the real wow. I know the pattern. As Xavier said, it's familiar. Look at it – you'll all know it too. It's the same as on our boxes.' He looked around the group as they tried to understand the implications. 'It's the same as on our boxes!'

Sam hurried off and returned a couple of minutes later with the two wooden boxes. He placed them on the desk and brought the stone cusp close by. The style was the same, but it took a few moments of twisting and turning to establish that the patterns on five of the six faces of one box were exactly reproduced in the five worked faces of the stone cusp.

'What does it mean, Sam?' said Helen.

'Well, it's all conjecture. But let's accept the tiles set into the steps at Leptis held the original Roman code to open the boxes, and let's accept the Templars somehow found or acquired the boxes and knew the code that was hidden in plain sight in Leptis Magna. Then we should assume they did what any sane person would do, that is make a copy of the tiles from the steps, make a copy of the opening code.'

'We don't need the Leptis Magna photographs to open the boxes then,' said Grace. For just a moment, a murmur of excitement flurried round the group.

'I'm afraid it's not that simple. It would appear all the other stones in the trench are splintered or crushed to useless fragments. There were twelve images at Leptis. Six set into either side of the temple steps. I'm guessing that with six sides to a cuboid cusp we would need two cusps to represent all twelve images, if that's even how it would work, and we don't know that. We have one; it appears only this one survived the roof fall. A great find, but it's only half of what we need. We're back to square one again.' He left the shards on the desk and walked back across the room. Pausing to place the intact cusp on the occasional table between the settees, he took his place on the settee.

'Is that it? Are we done?' said Helen, lifting the cusp and balancing it in her palm.

'We're never done,' said Sam, trying to be positive. 'Right now, I need a little while to think through the implications. Hell. Sorry, but hell! We almost had it. So close.'

He lapsed into silence and a pall of gloom settled across the party.

Suddenly, a face appeared at the study window. Francis was staring in and waving.

Grace jumped up. 'I'll let him in.'

Francis entered the room, buoyant and full of good cheer. He came to a halt inside the study doorway, Grace close in behind.

'My goodness, I'd thought to find a party not a wake! Come on everyone, Sam's back safe and sound—'

Grace tapped his shoulder and shook her head as Francis turned an enquiring eye in her direction.

'Sam lost the pictures, then we thought Davy and Julie had found an alternative solution up at the trench.'

'Well, that's good isn't it?'

'Not really, I'm afraid,' said Sam, crossing the room to shake Francis' hand. He waved a hand over the shards of broken stone from the trench. 'It's all crushed to useless crumbs thanks to the roof fall.'

Francis' face dropped as he surveyed the crushed stone. He didn't understand what the stones represented but could tell the damage was serious. 'Oh no, I'm sorry. What next?'

Sam gave a little shrug of his shoulders and returned to his spot on the settee. 'I don't know. I can't go back to Leptis Magna, that's for sure. There will be a workaround, there has to be.' He projected a positive tone but nobody was fooled. The key to the boxes was destroyed – they were stumped.

Francis sat in the cosy chair positioned beyond the occasional table. 'And what's this?' he reached over and tapped Helen's hand.

'It's the stone I found up at the trench. It's been stuck in the car while it was away being repaired.'

'Oh really?' said Francis, taking the stone from Helen's hand. He looked at it carefully and, glancing over the stone, caught Helen's eye and raised an eyebrow. 'Well, that's your story, Helen. Best stick to it.' There was a twinkle in his eye.

'What do you mean?'

Francis held the stone up. 'Come on, surely you recognise it?' He turned to Sam. 'You must, I'm sure.'

Sam and Helen both shook their heads.

'If I didn't know better, I'd say this has been taken from the cusped arches at Rosslyn.'

'Cusped arches?' said Helen.

'Rosslyn?' said Sam.

'Rosslyn Chapel. You must have been there. Surely.'

'Of course,' said Sam, while frantically trying to think himself back into the building.

'I've certainly been there. We went together, Sam, last spring,' said Helen.

'Yes, we did. I've been two or three times over the years. But I have no recollection of what Francis is talking about.'

Francis lifted the little block of stone above his head and squinted up at it as though it were in situ. 'Well, the whole inside of that building is so ornate it's possible to miss just about anything.' He lowered his arm and turned to look at Sam. 'But trust me, I know exactly where to look. Though it's an Episcopal church, there have been a number of events I've attended over the years, and it's of particular interest to me. Behind the altar is the most famous stonework, the Apprentice Pillar; you've all heard of that?'

A round of dutiful nods followed.

'Well,' said Francis, 'forget the pillar for now. As a Catholic, you'll all understand why finding a sub-chapel actually within Rosslyn called the Lady Chapel fascinated me. With such a name, it should be Catholic, so of course, I had to notice it! I've always made a point of saying a little prayer there when I've visited.'

Xavier turned to look at Angelo, gave a little smile then turned his head back to the group. 'Of course, you would. I would if I was there. Angelo too, yes?'

Angelo nodded.

'Go on,' said Sam. 'What about the Lady Chapel?'

'It's just a little place, behind the main altar, three or four paces deep. Like all of Rosslyn, it has the most wonderful stonework, but the cusped archways of the Lady Chapel are quite magnificent. Of course, nobody talks about the Lady Chapel; it's tucked away behind the Apprentice Pillar which gets all the focus and star treatment.'

'And how does this link to us and my stone?' said Helen.

Francis held up Helen's stone. 'Imagine the arches in the Lady Chapel are the petrified boughs of fruit trees in an orchard. Each of these carved stone cusps is like an apple hanging down from its bough. Protruding beneath every arch in the Lady Chapel is an intricately worked series of paired cusps like this.' He shook the solitary cusp.

'How alike?' said Sam.

'Exactly.'

'Francis is right; I remember now, I've seen them myself,' said Elaine.

'What does this mean, Sam?' said Helen.

'I don't know. But if Francis and Elaine say they're the same then I do think it's worth investigating.' Sam took the stone from Francis, looked at it carefully then passed it across to Xavier who had reached out a requesting hand.

Xavier compared the patterns on the boxes with the faces of the engraved cusp stone. He pursed his lips, nodded thoughtfully and finally passed the stone to Angelo.

'I agree with your view that the stone has the same pattern as one of the boxes. What this means, I do not know.' Xavier gave an emphatic shrug.

'Well it must mean something, but what?' said Francis.

All eyes turned to Sam, hoping for insight. He remained silent for a long thoughtful pause. At last, he stood, retrieved the stone cusp from Angelo and looked at it again.

'I think we need to understand the context. Let's accept that the boxes and the cusp are linked. What is the link? It's the patterned surfaces. The patterns that Bishop Ignatius' scholars think represent the key to opening the boxes. By the way, I have no idea how that works. The key was included in a tile sequence at Leptis Magna, probably set there by the person who made the boxes.'

'So, what's the same sequence doing engraved on stone cusps in a Scottish chapel?' said Helen. 'It makes no sense.'

'On the surface, I agree. Though, as soon as you scratch the surface, the link to the Templars appears, and they are never predictable, but their actions always have purpose.'

'And the purpose is?' said Grace.

'Timing, or rather the sequence of events, is everything here. We know the boxes predate the Templars and are probably a product of classical Rome, perhaps even relating to the worship of Jupiter. We'll never know for sure. That's why the original code is embedded in the stairway to the Temple of Jupiter in Leptis Magana.'

'Why? I really don't understand,' said Francis as he took a seat, his brow deeply furrowed.

'I don't think any of us do. This is just conjecture. But think about it. Somehow, the engraved faces we see on Helen's boxes, our cusp from the trench, the patterns in the tiled steps at Leptis, and now, thanks to Francis, cusps in the Rosslyn Chapel, all represent the same imagery. Why?'

'If you have an insight my friend, this is the time to share it with us all,' said Xavier.

'As I said, the sequence is key. First, the Romans, like all the ancient civilisations, needed places to store secrets. There was no Fort Knox then, no unbreakable vault. Building a container or vessel that would hold a secret and protect it from others depended on guile and craftsmanship. Trusting an individual human memory with the code was a vulnerability – anyone here ever forgotten a PIN number or a telephone number?'

Helen and Francis nodded and were quickly copied by the others.

'So the code had to be written down somewhere. Somewhere permanent like the steps to the Temple of Jupiter. But written in a way that only those in the know would realise they were looking at anything more than a series of patterned tiles. Just like some people might hide their PIN number as part of a phone number in their diary.'

'What doesn't make sense to me, Sam, is what use is a secret box that can only be opened at the Temple of Jupiter. It seems so ... so ... elaborate,' Francis glanced round the group seeking support.

'Francis, I don't know. Perhaps there were originally three boxes. One stayed at the Temple of Jupiter, one stayed elsewhere, perhaps in a temple in Rome, and a third box shuttled between them with secrets inside.'

'But Sam, Leptis Magna ... it's the back of beyond. Why have such an elaborate code there?' said Francis.

Sam perched himself on the edge of the desk. 'To us, Leptis Magna does seem remote, but during the Roman period, it was anything but. And a whole dynasty of Roman emperors came from the city. Septimius Severus was a big name and Leptis Magna a big city. Perhaps, he or one of his sons relied on the priests of the Temple of Jupiter to keep secrets and pass messages. Who knows? We do think that's where the boxes were used before the Templars' involvement.'

'And the Templars would have gathered them up as they did so many other artefacts,' said Xavier.

'Yes, and back to our sequence, I'm thinking that takes us to the trench in the woods. Or rather to the Templar base and refuge in the village of Temple. Helen inherited the woods along with the surrounding farmland, just across the fields from the remains of the Templars' original chapel and preceptory. We learnt last year that the original farm lease documents made a big point of ensuring the woods were kept and preserved by the farm's tenants. I'm thinking, when the Templars had to give up their place in the village of Temple, they had already created an underground chamber in the woods. In it, they had set a copy of the Temple of Jupiter tiles in a series of cusps. Like that,' he pointed to the solitary stone cusp.

'But they're all broken and ruined,' said Helen.

'Yes, and now, thanks to Francis, we learn that it appears our Templar friends have made a replica in Rosslyn Chapel.'

'But why there, and how? I thought they were forced to disband,' said Helen.

'Do you remember when we went to visit Rosslyn Chapel last year, before you and I had any inkling of any links to the Templars?'

'I do. You took me, doing the tourist visit. It was beautiful.'

'Yes. And remember the nearby castle, Rosslyn Castle. I told you how the chapel and castle were linked.'

'You did. It was the earl of someplace, yes?'

'Almost. The castle was the Baron of Rosslyn's family seat, the Sinclairs. The baron inherited the earldom of Orkney.'

'That was it, the Earl of Orkney.'

'Yes, and the Earl of Orkney, also titled the Baron of Rosslyn, built Rosslyn Chapel some years after the Templars were disenfranchised and lost their preceptory in the nearby village of Temple.'

'There's always been local lore that the Sinclair family had some connection with the Templars. That the chapel may have been built for their purposes,' said Francis, more comfortable as the topic moved into territory that he was familiar with.

'You're right, Francis; we've all heard the rumours. They were definitely meant to have a connection with the Templars in the past,' said Elaine.

'Oh yes, I've heard all that before,' said Helen. 'The Grail myths and so on.'

'Bearing in mind what you've unearthed in the past year, I don't think we should write anything off as myth,' said Francis.

Helen gave him a smile. 'Sorry, Francis, you're right.'

'So, where does that leave us, Sam?' said Elaine.

'I don't know what connection there really is with the Sinclair family, but let's bear in mind how careful the Templars have been, so far, in ensuring their secrets would be hard to find, but could be found, when the time and the people were right. We've also previously seen they did duplicate some sensitive secrets. Perhaps whatever code they engraved into the stones of their subterranean grotto, if that's what they actually did, was later reproduced in the chapel at Rosslyn.'

'You think we've found a solution to the code?' said Helen.

'I don't know. All we have is a single unbroken cusp from the trench and Francis' assurances that the same thing can be seen in Rosslyn. I trust Francis' observation skills, but we need to go to Rosslyn and establish the facts.'

Elaine looked at her watch. 'I think it's too late this afternoon. It will be shut before we can get there. I know the priest there, Peter, the Reverend Dr Peter McEwan. He's very accommodating. Perhaps, we can arrange to call in first thing? So we can have a look before any tourists turn up.'

'Will there be tourists in mid-winter?' said Helen.

'I would think so. Perhaps fewer with the snow but there are always tours calling in. Though I doubt first thing in the morning, the tour coaches have to travel first,' said Elaine.

'Okay, if you can set that up, Elaine, it would be much appreciated. Now, if you don't mind, everyone, I think I need a bit of time alone to think through all these loose ends, see if I can draw something together.'

***

A tall man, smartly dressed in a plain dark suit pulled open the door. In the hotel corridor were two similarly dressed men. All three nodded curtly to one another in recognition, and the visitors entered the suite. They scanned round, politely acknowledging Eugene Jr where he sat at the suite's desk. Then they turned back to the entrance and signalled.

Parsol's wheelchair rolled silently into his son's hotel suite followed by two further men in plain dark suits. He ignored the tall windows and their view across the city, steering directly to the broad table on which Eugene Jr had placed a computer. Cassiter followed in behind Parsol; he paused briefly at the window and looked wistfully out over the scene that had once been his own office vista. His expressionless face concealed the anger he felt at his loss. It was a loss entirely attributable to Cameron and Johnson.

'Ah, my son,' said Parsol, stretching out a hand in greeting. They shook, then the young man stooped and kissed his father's cheeks.

'Father, it is good to see you,' he said as he straightened up and nodded towards Cassiter, who nodded in response.

'Well, how goes things?' said Parsol.

'It is confirmed that Cameron has returned to Edinburgh. Somehow, he escaped from Libya. I have cars detailed to follow anyone who moves. Other than that, I have followed your instructions and caused no further disruption while waiting for your arrival.'

'Good, I am glad *somebody* can follow my instructions.' He threw a glance towards Cassiter. 'Are you certain it is Cameron?'

Cassiter bristled. He almost never made mistakes. Events were showing he should not have left Cameron to die in Leptis. Happily, they now showed too that Cameron had survived.

Once Cassiter had been dragged into deep water, it had been a struggle to scramble onto the RIB and safety, but at least Cameron's waterproof camera had protected the pictures, which Cassiter had channelled to his office in Paris. However, it had proven not to be just a simple key after all. His instruction to run image recognition software, to find some link, anything, had yet to bear fruit, and it had become clear Cameron was still needed.

As in the past, the archaeologist was proving to be their best chance of unpicking the problem. Leaving him to die on the beach had been a potentially costly error. Parsol had not been pleased with him. So, though Cassiter did not understand how Cameron had survived the attack on the beach, at least his survival had taken the sting out of what had been the first falling out with his paymaster.

Cassiter walked over to stand beside Eugene Jr. 'We are running blind and depending entirely on your men; they must remain alert. Your father and I have personal scores to settle with Cameron and the Johnson girl. When the time is right, we will make then suffer to atone for the trouble they have caused us. I believed I had taken the key from Cameron at Leptis Magna. That seems not to be the case. The pictures secured mean something, but Cameron may be required to unravel them. For now, they need to stay alive to solve the puzzle. Make sure your people understand that.'

Chapter 17

TUESDAY JANUARY 21ˢᵀ

'You just can't predict winter weather in the Lothians,' said Francis, from behind the wheel of his parish minibus. He had insisted they wait until the morning rush hour had subsided before driving out of the city and heading southwest towards Rosslyn Chapel. Edinburgh was behind them, and he waved a hand towards the white covered fields that flanked the road. 'Last year was wet and windy, the year before quite mild.'

'It must be four or five years since we've had a winter as snowy as this,' said Elaine from a seat in the rear.

Francis nodded. 'That's right. The children love it but give me mild and dry every time.'

The minibus suddenly jolted, rocking everyone inside as it bumped out of a pothole. 'Sorry! I missed that one.' Francis returned his attention to the road.

Ten minutes later, he cautiously nudged the minibus along the little road that led to Rosslyn Chapel. The chapel was partly obscured by the visitor centre that cast a protective shield around it from the roadside, ensuring access was properly controlled. The car park was empty. Having eyed its pristine covering of snow, Francis had decided to stick to the road and drove on to the visitor centre entrance. He stopped and put his church's blue disabled parking permit on the dashboard in front of the steering wheel. He turned and winked at Helen. 'Can't have Xavier walking across that snowy car park – it's not safe. Here we are everyone; let's go.'

They entered the visitor centre, and as the automatic doors closed, a middle-aged woman stepped forwards to greet them with a warm smile.

'Hello, everyone, I'm Silvia, the visitor centre manager. Welcome, I'm not psychic, but on a morning like this, it's a fair bet you are the group Reverend McEwan asked me to help.' She beamed another smile. 'Now, he mentioned Elaine. Did I get that right?'

Elaine stepped forwards. 'Aye, I spoke with him yesterday. Thank you for sparing the time for us. I think it's Sam who should explain what we're looking for though.' She pointed to Sam and fell silent.

The visitor centre manager turned her attention to him, reaching out a hand, which he shook. He introduced the rest of the party. It was clear that Silvia had been briefed by the Reverend McEwan, and she had as many questions to ask Helen as Sam had for her. She tried to contain herself, with only limited success.

'Helen, yes, I was told it was you from St Bernard's. Such an awful business at your church last year. I followed it on the news. Very frightening, I'm sure I wouldn't have coped at all. I'll be happy to help today; just let me say first how much I feel for you, all of you. It was an awful business.

'Now what I've got in mind for today is to hand you over to our chief guide, Oliver; he knows everything there is to know, and when you've seen what you want, he'll bring you back for a hot drink and a bun on me. How does that sound?'

It had been springtime when Helen last visited Rosslyn Chapel. The courtyard had been filled with warm air and welcoming sunlight, birds swooping and chirping. Individual tourists had strolled leisurely around while various tour groups were hustled into order by their respective guides.

Today was very different. A low, grey sky, cold wind and flurries of snow combined to add to the visitors' discomfort. A black tarmac track had been cleared and salted between visitor centre and chapel entrance. Off to their left, a member of the catering staff had cleared snow from a small patch of the courtyard behind the centre's kitchen door. The clearing had been scattered with crumbs and scraps for the birds who had now gathered to eat, busily hopping this way and that, the pecking order changing with each arriving bird.

Ahead of them, fiercely protective gargoyles overlooked the chapel door. It cracked open, and an elderly man appeared, dressed in warm and sensibly thick corduroys and a roll-neck sweater. 'Welcome. I'm Oliver.' He ushered the group in and pushed the door shut behind Angelo who had brought up the rear.

Oliver's local accent was soft, though still discernible. 'Silvia has said you are to be given every assistance. She mentioned Elaine, I think. He looked around and caught Elaine's eye as she stepped forwards.

'Hello, Oliver,' said Elaine.

'Have we met?' said Oliver, shaking her hand.

'I've been out here for several ecumenical events and exchange meetings, that sort of thing.'

'Yes, yes, you do look familiar now you mention it. Sorry for not picking that up at once.' He raised his hands and glanced about the chapel. 'We have so many visitors.' Oliver remembered Elaine now – few words, retiring, but ultimately the one who knew how best to address a church problem or unpick an issue. And of course, he had heard and read about Helen Johnson and St Bernard's.

'So what can I do for you today?'

Elaine nodded towards Sam.

Sam stepped forwards. 'I'm afraid we are pressed for time. Could we focus on some specifics please?'

'Of course. What exactly?'

'We're interested in the Lady Chapel mostly.'

Oliver nodded then waved a hand towards the altar and to the open space behind. 'This way then. The Lady Chapel is set behind the altar. Its stonework is, of course, excellent, but it's mostly an empty space.' He started to walk along the side aisle leading the group towards the altar. After only a few steps, he paused and pointed up towards one especially distinctive carving.

'I recognise your accent's American,' he said to Helen. 'This is one for you; what do you think that is?'

Helen looked up at the image engraved into the stone. 'A plant?' she said, with a shrug.

'Yes, a plant, but we have a little bit of a debate running over it at present.'

'How so?'

'Look at it closely. You see the plant's leaves? What plant do you think it is?'

'I have no idea.'

'Some think it's a palm. On the other hand, some are quite convinced it's a tobacco leaf.'

'And?'

'This church was built in the 1450s and Columbus didn't discover the Americas until 1492, nearly fifty years later.'

'So, it must be a palm leaf then,' said Helen.

'Perhaps,' said Oliver as he walked past the altar and led them towards the eastern end of the church. 'Certainly, if that were the only mystery here there would be no debate. As I said, the chapel was built fifty years before Columbus reached the New World. I'll show you another unusual stone engraving in a little while and that one will really get you thinking.'

Stopping at a neat arch formed between two pillars, he spread his hands out to left and right. 'The Lady Chapel. You can see it's not much more than a man's length, six or seven feet, but it spreads almost the width of the church.'

Oliver paused in his explanation as Francis, Xavier and Angelo all stepped through the arch and stopped to issue a silent prayer. Helen joined them, and Sam hung back slightly, staring up at the arch before wandering away along the width of the Lady Chapel. Other than the solid stone of the eastern wall, the small chapel had no internal walls. It was divided into sections that were defined by a series of thick pillars and elaborately decorated arches. Looking between the serried pillars, it was possible to see through all sections at once, across the whole width of the chapel.

However, Sam was not focusing on the beauty of the whole. Only one thing had grabbed his attention, and he could not look away. Francis had been right about the Lady Chapel. There were stone cusps everywhere – it was like walking into an orchard laden with fruit! Set opposite each other, at the base of the first arch was a facing pair of cusps. Further facing pairs sprouted like fruit from beneath the archway as it rose to meet at the apex. Sam looked through the arches that separated the sections of the chapel. Along its whole length, each archway was adorned with paired cusps, the successive pairs coming closer together as their arch closed towards its apex.

Sam wandered under the arches studying them all. Stopping in one section, he smiled to himself. One of the cusps was missing. Broken off by some accident in antiquity. He did not dare to think what punishment would have been meted out to the clumsy curate who had broken it. He thought of Francis' suggestion that Helen had looted her cusp from Rosslyn and smiled again.

Eyes only on the array of cusps, it seemed to Sam there were hundreds sprouting from beneath the arches. Each one was a neat cuboid whose volume – just like the one Helen had found out at Temple – would equal no more than a cricket ball. Each cusp had five decorated sides and one side plain save for a protruding stem that linked the cusp back to the arch stone from which it had been carved. The scale of the work made him pause. It would have taken years, perhaps decades, to carve all the cusps in the Lady Chapel. He continued on his way through the sections. For size and shape, any one of the cusps could have been switched for Helen's trench stone.

Sam's brow creased slightly as he studied the carved patterns on the face of the cusps. Some were of clearly recognisable biblical scenes, others seemed less godly, and yet more were so obscure as to defy recognition. He kept moving from section to section, studying all the cusps but not finding any that matched the symmetrical swirl design on Helen's boxes.

'Ah, you're interested in the cusps,' said Oliver, catching up with Sam.

'Yes, I'm searching for a pattern.'

'Oh, why's that?'

'Just some research, a theory, that's all.'

'Well, you've got plenty to search through. Some of the cusps have meanings that we've deciphered; others remain a bit of a mystery. Just call out if there's anything I can help you with.'

'Thanks, I will,' said Sam.

Oliver glanced towards Helen. 'If you follow me, I've something else to show you.'

'Okay, what is it?' she said.

'This way,' said Oliver, walking past Sam into the final section of the Lady Chapel. 'See, here's the famous Apprentice Pillar. It makes up one outer corner of the Lady Chapel. Look through this last arch at the south wall.' He pointed through the arch towards the outer wall. 'There, do you see it?'

'What am I looking at?'

'Look at the stone around the window, the carving. It's heads of maize, your corn. Again, carved and set into the church's design fifty years before any Europeans were meant to have reached the Americas. It's a puzzle.'

'Wow, you're not kidding. How is that possible?'

'No idea. The image shouldn't be there, can't be there, but there it is. If you accept this, and very few argue against it now, it moves the tobacco leaf or palm leaf debate into a different context.'

Linking her arm through Oliver's, she tilted her head, gaining a different perspective on the carving. 'Oliver, I can see it, corn. That is a puzzle.'

'Yes, it is.'

Helen glanced back to Sam who was oblivious to her conversation, his head, also tilted up, methodically working through the series of arches all laden with their outcropping pairs of cusps.

Oliver turned too and immediately tensed. 'I'm sorry, Sam, you'll have to stop that,' he said. 'The Chapel rules are inviolate. No photographs inside the building.'

'Sorry, what did you say?' said Sam switching his attention away from the decorative arches.

'No photographs, please.'

For just a moment, Sam appeared confused. Then he glanced at the phone in his hand. 'Oh, don't worry. I'm not taking pictures. I'm comparing my photograph from elsewhere with your cusps. I'd thought there would be a match but you have so many, it's like searching for a needle in a haystack.'

'Can I see?' said Oliver, crossing to see Sam's phone. He looked at the picture of Helen's trench stone. 'Where did you take this?'

'Just away on a dig elsewhere. Helen found it. I'd thought there might be some linkage with yours, but it seems not.'

Oliver looked up from the phone screen and smiled at Helen. 'I didn't realise you were interested in archaeology too.'

Helen laughed. 'It was all a bit of an accident really.'

'And coming here was a long shot,' said Sam. 'I'm sorry; it seems we may have been taking up your time unnecessarily.'

Oliver looked back at the screen. 'Well, perhaps, perhaps not. I really would like to know where you found your cusp.'

'On some land I inherited on the other side of the river Esk,' said Helen.

Oliver nodded. 'That was a lucky thing. How far off?' He returned his attention to the phone, flicking the screen, changing the displayed pictures so he could see the other faces of Helen's cusp. Oliver moved two or three steps away and didn't wait for Helen to answer. 'I've been here a long time. And I've studied every stone in the place.' Now he was looking up at the ceiling arches. Muttering to himself, his eyes scanned the ceiling area, searching for something.

'There we are,' he said triumphantly, pointing at an arch that spurred out and away from the side of the Apprentice Pillar. 'I knew I had seen your picture before. It looks very similar to some of the cusps on this arch. What do you think?'

Sam joined Oliver, looked up, and his face immediately broke into a smile. Oliver was right. The pairs of cusps on this arch seemed very similar to the photograph, in fact pretty much identical. 'It looks like a match.'

'Yes, it looks like a good match to me too,' said Oliver. 'You were on the right track. If you'd kept going another few minutes, you'd have spotted it without me.' He waved his arm back through the arches beneath which they had already come. 'You started your search from the wrong end of the Lady Chapel, that's all. If you'd begun from this end, the search would have been over almost before it had begun.'

Sam studied the series of cusps set into the archway rising above his head. He looked about, comparing this arch with all the other arches' cusp pairings. As each arch rose towards its apex, successive pairs of sprouting cusps were necessarily closer together than the pairs beneath. In almost every instance, an arch's highest cusp pairing emerged around a foot below the arch's apex allowing some distance between the facing cusps so their engravings could be admired.

He fell silent for a little while evaluating what he saw.

'Our arch is different,' he said.

'Yes, the cusps of each arch have different sets of images.'

'No … well, yes to that. But no. You see the cusps in all the other arches have a generally consistent spacing and positioning.' Sam's hands rose up to describe an archway. 'But look at our arch; see the difference.'

'I see it,' said Helen. 'On all the other arches, there is a clear gap between the top pair of cusps—'

'That's right, two stone cusps jutting out from either side of the rising archway can't occupy the same place in space, so the highest pair emerge a little below the peak of the arch, leaving a clear space between the facing cusps.'

'But not on this arch,' said Helen, pointing up.

'Right, the cusps on this arch emerge differently. On this arch, the top two cusps emerge closer to the apex or peak, and their leading faces are almost touching one another.'

'You're right,' said Oliver. 'I'd always wondered about that. Assumed some mason in antiquity must have got his angles wrong.'

'I don't think so,' said Sam. 'If it's as I think, those boys didn't make mistakes.'

Francis and Xavier joined them with Grace and Angelo following behind. Everybody compared the photo with the cusps on the archway and unanimously agreed the patterns were the same.

'Do you see how the front faces on each successive pair of cusps changes? As though each successive pair has been rotated,' said Francis. 'Like a series of dice throws, each time turning to present a different face.'

'I do, why would that be?' said Helen.

'No idea. This arch contains a sequence of cusp images that we have not yet made much progress in interpreting,' said Oliver.

'Perhaps, because they are not to be interpreted,' said Sam. Helen could see the look come across his face that showed he'd made a breakthrough.

'What is it, Sam?'

Sam gave her a little smile and turned his attention to Oliver. 'Oliver, I know you said no photographs, but I really need to take pictures of each of the cusps on this arch. Just this arch, that's all.'

Oliver shook his head. 'Sorry, Sam, it's out of the question. If I let you take pictures, I'd be frogmarched off the premises in no time.'

'Come on, Oliver, there must be a way, an exception?'

'Sorry, nothing I can do at all. But look, speak with Silvia. She's your lady. The office has photographs of everything, all the stonework. She'll have good quality pictures. They are available to researchers and for press and PR. Speak to her. I'm certain she will sort out what you need.'

Content with what they had found, Sam was impatient to speak with Silvia and headed off. The rest of the group hung back to admire the Apprentice Pillar, before moving on to follow Helen's instruction and wonder at the line of engraved corncobs that decorated the stone window frame. A little way off, just beyond the altar, another early-bird tourist had braved the weather to make a visit. Still wrapped up against the elements, the man had taken a seat and was offering a prayer as Sam hurried for the exit.

Between the Reverend McEwan's exhortations, Elaine's occasional church connection with the chapel and Sam's own academic reputation, Silvia had been happy to allow him access to the photograph archive. She had expressed surprise at the specificity of his request and commented on his interest being unusual. Nobody had ever asked for the pictures he wanted, but she quickly transferred them to a memory stick and passed it over before guiding Sam to her office door.

'I'm afraid something unexpected has come up. I've got to attend to it now. But please still stop for a coffee. It will warm you before heading back to Edinburgh. The coffees are on me, remember.'

Sam looked across the visitor centre to the café where Helen and the others had gathered. Joining them, Sam waved the memory stick. 'Exactly what we want; Silvia really delivered the goods.'

'And what exactly do we want?' said Helen. 'I saw that look on your face in the chapel – you worked something out. Come on, spill the beans.'

Instinctively, Sam lowered his voice. 'I was stumped at first by all the archways with their pairs of cusps. So many, and I couldn't think why. When Oliver showed me the archway featuring our cusp, I was still puzzled. Again, why so many cusps?'

'It's a decorative style, surely,' said Francis.

'Well, that seems logical, and I can't argue with that, but I do think there's an altogether more Templar explanation.'

'Oh?' said Francis.

'Yes. A great way to hide a secret is to place it in plain sight so nobody even imagines it is a secret. The Templars have got form in that department. Remember, we've seen it before – last year, when we managed to solve the puzzle of the church window? The message contained in the stained glass was there for all to see but only made sense to the initiated.'

'That is so. It is the way, I know it,' said Xavier. He was pale, and in spite of the heating, his hands shook even while clasping his coffee mug.

Grace reached her arm around Xavier's shoulder, pulling him in close to her. 'Xavier, you're shivering,' she said.

'Xavier, we'd better get you home; it's far too cold for you out here,' said Helen.

'No, no, no. I am fine. Let us hear Sam's thoughts. Then we go, yes?'

'Okay then, if you are sure. But let's hurry it up a little, Sam.'

'Fine. So, I grant you the rash of cusps sprouting from beneath every arch is attractive, but I think it's actually been created to hide one set of cusps in particular. Ones that carry the same imagery as the tiles at Leptis Magna. Hidden in plain sight.'

'But Sam, why here? It's not a Templar chapel. And anyway, it was built a hundred years and more after the Templars were disbanded; we know that. It can't be a Templar church, so it can't be a Templar secret,' said Helen.

'That's a little problem, I grant you. But thanks to the cusp you found in the trench up in your Templar woods, we do know there was a stone reproduction of the Leptis imagery there. And that was Templar land. There, in the underground chamber, probably a little chapel, they placed the imagery that is the code to safely open the boxes.'

'But they're not in the trench, they're in Rosslyn Chapel,' said Francis, a pained look on his face.

'Yes, they are. And I'm sorry, Francis, but there's a leap of faith required here.'

'Well, we're used to those, aren't we?' said Helen, gently joggling her shoulder against Francis'.

'Oh yes, we can do leaps of faith,' he said.

'Come on, Sam, put us out of our misery,' said Helen.

'Two simple steps. First, we've seen before that the Templars always left a workaround in case their first clue was lost. Like an insurance policy. I think the underground chamber would have been built to hide the code as a series of decorative cusps. Davy and the others could find no moveable artefacts in the trench or any signs of an alternative use.

'Second, Helen is right that Rosslyn Chapel was built years after the Templar Order was dissolved. There is no clear and direct link between the two. But we do know from Helen's link with the St Bernard's church tradition and through Xavier that the Order still continued along a secret strand even after it was dissolved. At some point, a surviving Templar, perhaps, no, quite certainly, one of Helen's predecessors, decided a backup code was needed.'

'Francis told us about the Sinclair connection—'

'And the Sinclairs own the land and built the chapel. I would imagine if there really were a link between the Sinclairs and the Templars, it would be a simple step for any surviving influential Templar to have the chapel's design incorporate the required elements. Especially, if he were footing the bill,' said Sam.

'With all the other ornate stonework simply a means of hiding the one set of information that they really needed to be certain would survive,' said Helen.

'Exactly. I'm guessing that information will be the cusps.'

'So, back to the beginning, how will you use them to open the box?' said Helen with a sideways glance towards Francis. She could tell he was pleased she had asked the question.

'That will have to wait until we get back to the manse. I have an idea and now's the time to test it out.'

'And now's the time to get Xavier back too,' said Grace, taking his hands in hers and gently rubbing them. Angelo nodded and stood, placing a protective hand on Xavier's shoulder.

***

'I don't understand why this chapel has suddenly become so important. Is there something I have not been told?' said Cassiter.

In silence, Parsol motored his chair over to the window and looked out across the city. His son had surrendered the suite as the most appropriate work base for his father. Junior's bags had been moved along the corridor to another room, equally luxuriously appointed though lacking the extra reception room that was now doubling as his father's control centre.

Parsol did not enjoy the public domain, and although his interests spread far, he rarely left the security of his chateau base. He had employed Cassiter as a confidential contractor for the past several years, and he trusted him to deliver. It suddenly seemed a long time ago, but only a few months had passed since he had met Cassiter in Princes Street Gardens, a location which now formed part of his view.

In the months since that meeting, Cassiter's rise within the organisation had been meteoric. He was remarkable for being absolutely unremarkable; he could fade unnoticed into the shade of any group. Parsol was not fooled; he knew that Cassiter could punch out of that greyness with the strength and speed of a great white taking its prey. He looked up at him.

'For once, we are dealing with something that is beyond my

knowledge. This Rosslyn Chapel has never featured in our understanding. It is something that either my ancestors were not privy to, or it must have acquired relevance after the original dispersal of the task bearers and dissolution of the Templar Order. Whatever took Cameron and the Johnson woman out to the chapel this morning must have been important,' said Parsol.

'And the Sardinian priests were there too,' Said Cassiter.

'Yes, no doubt scavengers, gathering for their scraps! I am aware of the links between the family that owns the chapel and the Templars. Indeed you investigated them for us a year or two ago.'

'That's right; I remember reporting on it to you. It all seemed more fable than fact.'

'And yet, they are drawn there. Why?'

'I intend to go out myself to find out exactly what the link is,' said Cassiter.

'Good. There must be something, some connection. We need to know what it is. Now, tell me, Cassiter, what of the camera? What links have your people made?'

'They are searching every possible archive to get image matches, but there's nothing, nothing at all. Have your own people come up with any historical link?'

Parsol shook his head. Then he turned his chair back to the window. 'Keep me informed and keep a tight watch on them all. Cameron is the one who will unwrap the final puzzle. It seems it was set apart from the earlier elements, the daggers that you helped us retrieve last year. For now, we still need him and the Johnson girl alive so they can show us the things we don't know. But we cannot risk them stealing a march on us. We are very close now; I can feel it.'

***

Sam had printed out the photographs from Silvia's memory stick. There was a wider angled picture taken from the altar that showed the complete archway. It featured the whole series of protruding cusps, like stone fruits hanging forever from the boughs of some ancient petrified tree. The cusps were set in facing pairs protruding from beneath either side of the arch, each successive pair closer together than its lower neighbour as the arch's sides neared its apex. He placed this picture at the centre of the kitchen table.

On the right side of the arch, each cusp had the same set of patterned faces, but as the mason had progressed up the arch, each successive cusp was rotated to present a different face forwards. This presentation style was repeated with the cusps on the left side of the arch.

To the left end of the table, he laid out six pictures. They represented the front facing sides of those cusps protruding from beneath the left side of the arch, ordered just as they appeared in the wide-angled photo. To the right end of the table, he laid out six pictures. These represented the front faces found on the cusps of the right side of the arch.

Xavier and Francis sat in silence at one side of the table, watching Sam.

'Here they are,' said Grace, delivering the two ornate boxes from their hiding place in the tunnel that linked the manse to St Bernard's church.

'Thanks,' said Sam, taking the boxes and placing them in the middle of the table beside the photograph of the full archway. He stepped back to regard the whole display, Grace stood beside him, and a studious silence settled for a little while.

'Sam, I see a problem here,' said Francis.

'Go on,' said Sam.

Francis waved his hand to the right. 'You have six photographs over there of the faces of the right-hand cusps. But within the archway, each cusp displays only five faces, one face is missing where a cusp's stem attaches to the stone beneath the arch. Where does the picture of the sixth face come from? And it's the same at the left-hand side,' Francis pointed to the left-hand end of the table.

'Yes, you're right but try thinking of a cusp being like a dice. Its sides are marked one to six. At any time, you can see the one number facing upwards and if you look around the dice's sides, you can see four other numbers. One number you can never see, because it's facing down.'

Sam lifted one of the boxes from the table. He turned it in his hand before placing it carefully on the table again. 'Now, instead of dice think of our box. The cusp is a representation of the box's pattern. One face is always invisible whether that be the box face down on the table or the stone face attaching the cusp to the arch. And like the dice, we can predict the face we don't see based entirely on the remaining faces we can see.'

'And what does that mean?' said Xavier.

Sam shrugged. 'It's a pattern, but I'm not sure yet.'

Xavier stood, nudging Francis as he rose. 'Perhaps we should leave Sam alone for a little while.'

Francis rose too, and the pair left the kitchen, heading for the living room. Grace followed them out, and Sam settled down to think through what the image sequences meant.

He looked at the wide-angle photograph of the whole arch then focused on the cusp faces displayed to the left-hand side. Gathering the six pictures from the left side of the table he sifted through them. Nothing was obvious. Was there a pattern to be found in the order of the cusps? But if there *was* a pattern there, what did it mean? As he mulled the problem over, almost without thinking, he began checking the photos of single cusp faces on the desk, referring back to the image of the complete arch and ordering the photos as if re-creating exactly the two sides of the arch here on the kitchen table.

Now he had a sequence, so what to do with it? He speculated that the pairing together of the cusp-face images meant he should be pairing the corresponding box faces. He brought the actual box faces side by side to mirror the picture arch he had created. Turning them this way and that. Nothing happened.

Sometime later, Helen shuffled into the room. 'What's happening, Sam? Any progress?'

Sam shook his head. 'I think I have reproduced the required sequence here.' He pointed to the photos, now laid out to describe a neat arch. 'But when I align the faces of the actual boxes in that order nothing happens. In fact, I've no idea of what should happen. Even if I am aligning them correctly, if that's what we are supposed to do, I'm wondering if there's another component, something else I've overlooked. I don't see how shuffling the boxes around will open them. I've tried that often enough already.'

Helen stood beside him and looked down at the table. 'How do you know you have the correct faces in order?'

'I've taken it directly from the main archway photograph,' he leant across the table and tapped the image.

'Yes, but is that how you are meant to look at the cusp faces? Did the architect intend you to view the cusp pairs from the direction of the altar?'

Sam looked back at the main photograph. 'You know, I think you may have something, Helen. You know, I could have made a schoolboy error here.'

'Really? That's not like you.' Helen pressed her shoulder against his. 'Are you slipping, Mr Cameron?'

'Let's see. The main photograph has been taken from the direction of the altar, so all the cusp faces we see are captured from that angle only, and that's the order of our cusp photographs. We identified this arch was slightly different from all the others. Remember how the top pair of cusps actually touch one another just beneath the apex of the archway? Unlike our archway, all the other archways had their top cusp pairs positioned a little lower from the apex so the top pair of cusps did not touch. They all had a sufficient gap so you could see the imagery on the facing cusps.'

'Yes, that's right,' Helen agreed. 'The guy at the chapel thought it had been a simple architectural mistake.'

'We don't. And now I think about it more, the two faces touching could be indicating our starting point. Instead of looking at the face of the arch side-on – as photographed from the altar – see?' Sam lifted up the wide-angle photo for Helen to see more clearly. 'In fact, it's the cusp faces facing each other under the arch that are the paired images, just as you suggested.'

'But you can't see the top two images, because they are too close together.'

'No problem. Seeing as we know where the other sides are, in relation to one another, we can work that out by a process of elimination to predict exactly what the unseen sides of the top pair are, just like with dice. Give me a couple of minutes, and I'll have my pictures rearranged into the right order.'

Between references to the main archway photograph and the order of the faces as they appeared on the actual boxes, Sam reordered the sequence of photographs in his pictorial arch. Then he straightened up, looked down at his new arrangement and put an arm round Helen's shoulder. 'Now we have a new order. Shall we see what happens?'

Helen watched Sam in silence as he brought the boxes close together, aligning the two faces that matched those hidden by their close proximity at the apex of the arch. 'Just like the top pair of cusps beneath the arch in the chapel, we'll start with these two faces touching, so we can't see those faces. Now change the positions so the next two faces are touching ...' Sam brought the box faces together as he spoke then moved the boxes around so the photographic image sequence was followed as he continued through all six positions. Nothing happened. He looked at Helen, disappointed. 'Well, that didn't work! I must have done something wrong.'

Helen began to say something then hesitated.

'Go on; what are you thinking?' Sam encouraged her.

Helen pursed her lips for a moment. 'Well ... what if the boxes must remain touching while going through the sequence?'

'Worth a try,' said Sam. He moved the boxes back to the starting position, two faces touching. Referring again to the pictures, he slid one box up and over the other to bring the second pair of cusp faces together while always keeping the boxes in contact with one another.

Suddenly, he froze. 'Did you hear that?' he asked, his hands still.

Helen shook her head. 'No. What happened?'

'The box just clicked.'

'How? I didn't hear it.' She leant closer to the boxes.

'I have no idea.' Sam held his breath as he slid the top box across so its bottom face rested on top of the lower box. He felt another click from the lower box.

'I heard that one,' said Helen, excited. 'You're on to something. Keep going.'

Sam carefully continued the sliding sequence bringing twinned faces together as prescribed in the cusps' photograph sequence. With each movement, there was a further click. With one more move to make, he paused and turned to look at Helen. 'Nearly there.'

'Do it.'

Sam slid the boxes. The final move brought them, once more, to rest side by side on the table. There was a sixth click and nothing happened.

'What now?' said Helen.

'I don't know,' said Sam, pulling his hands away. He looked at Helen again who was trying hard to hide her disappointment.

'I thought that was it, that you'd opened them.'

'I did too. There were definite clicks.'

'Yes, I heard some of them.'

They were suddenly both aware of a little group behind them. Their small exclamations – the tension in their voices – had alerted the others that something special was happening. Their friends had gravitated to the kitchen and watched with growing excitement, only to now share the disappointment.

Amid dejected mutterings, Sam reached out for the boxes. 'Well, it's back to the drawing board. With those clicks, I really believed we'd done it. We must have done something wrong.'

'What was making the clicks, Sam?' said Helen.

'I'm not sure; some force must have come into play. Gravity, perhaps? I'm guessing, but that would only enable things inside to move downwards when the box was tilted. From the scan, we know there is nothing loose inside to do that. Magnets maybe; there is a little gap or void between the two layers of gold, and in that space, there are some little strips or bars of metal, but I don't know, I'm not convinced the Romans had a sufficient grip on magnetism.'

He began to lift one box, then sensing some motion beneath his hand, he stopped, lowered the box gently back onto the table and let go. He studied it carefully. 'Well, look at this!'

His friends closed in behind and around him.

'What is it, Sam?' said Helen.

With one finger, he gently pried at a side. 'This side has moved a little. Can you see the thin black line that's appeared along this edge? I think it will open.' He tapped the box and tried to work a fingernail into the slimmest of cracks, to no avail.

'Here, let me have a go,' said Grace, leaning over Sam's shoulder and wiggling the fingers of her right hand in front of him.

He ran a finger across the edges of her nail-bar engineered talons before pulling it back with a wince. 'Oh, those are lethal weapons. Careful, Grace, you could have someone's eye out with them!'

'There's a college party tonight. Got to look my best. Now, let me at your box.'

'Okay, but be careful, don't use any force, just try to ease the edges apart.' He slid onto the adjoining chair and allowed Grace to sit in his. 'Be very careful.'

Grace settled into the chair and drew the box closer to her while Elaine looked disapprovingly at her daughter's new nails. Grace could feel the tension with everybody's eyes on her. The glittering nail of her index finger ran along the edge of the box, tracing the slightly darkened line where the sides had parted.

'Whatever you do, Grace, do it slowly and gently. Don't force anything,' said Helen.

'Okay, okay, everyone back up a little. You'll be joggling my shoulders if you aren't careful. Back up.'

There was a shuffling of feet as the crowd obliged, then Grace traced the black line of the box edge for a second time.

She pressed her fingernail forwards just a little, worked at the gap and felt a tiny amount of give. Pressing again, her fingernail slipped in further. Then she was able to use the nail as a lever to work the edges apart.

'If this breaks my nail, you'll be paying for a replacement.'

'Concentrate on the task at hand.' Elaine's gruff voice reached Grace from the crowd behind.

'It's okay, Mum, I've got this.'

Grace returned her focus to the box. She could feel the lid's resistance weakening. With just another wriggle of the fingernail, the edges parted. Escorted by Grace's guiding fingers, one side panel hinged smoothly down to rest flat on the table.

It was open. At last, they'd opened a box.

And yet, the box was just as Sam's scan had indicated – empty. Everyone stared, lost for words, and the sense of anticipation that had pervaded the group evaporated.

Finally, Grace broke the silence. 'Oh, that's no good.'

'Let me see,' said Sam, reaching across and sliding the box towards him. There was nothing inside. The side that hinged down had a sheet of glass fixed flat to its surface; it glimmered up at him. He twisted the box and bent down closer to the tabletop, so he could look carefully inside the box without raising it from the table.

'Is there anything inside?' said Francis.

'No, nothing,' said Sam. 'But I can now clearly see how it's constructed. The ornately patterned surface layer is, as we know, wood. That is lined inside with a thin layer of gold, defining the shape of the box. Within that is fixed the inner layer of gold, as though lining the box. Between the two layers of gold is a narrow void space. The box has a wafer-like or sandwich construction. All perfectly engineered, then inside, just a big empty space.'

'So what's it all for?' said Helen. 'A box full of nothing is no use at all.'

'Sam, I don't understand,' said Francis. 'If there is nothing in the box, what makes it so vulnerable? Couldn't we have just forced the lid off at any time?' Murmurs of agreement confirmed nobody else could understand the vulnerability.

'I know it seems quite innocent but look. Now the box is open, we can see the inside of the lid is faced with glass. And see here, between the two layers of gold, you can just make out some little shapes lurking in the shadows of the void space; they are a whole series of magnets. When the two boxes are moved in the correct sequence, the various magnets are pulled and pushed into a series of positions that combine to release the locking grip on the opening side. I'm guessing, any false move or violence against a box's structure will propel these magnets down to break the glass.

'I think it's the glass that is important. The glass holds a message. Use force against the box, and you change the magnets from intricate locking mechanism to mini battering rams that propel themselves into the glass, splintering it and destroying the message before it can be read.'

Everyone focused on the open box side that lay face up, its glass surface glinting beneath the electric ceiling light.

'There's nothing there,' said Grace. 'Nothing's written on it at all.'

'No,' said Sam, 'nothing's written on it. But look …' He pulled out a pocket magnifying glass and leant closer to the lid, inspecting it closely. 'What I had thought were blemishes in the glass are not. I think they are shapes etched in. Very finely. If you didn't know to look, you'd probably never notice them.'

'What do they say?' said Helen.

'Nothing. They appear to be geometric shapes, six circles etched into the glass in two ragged rows of three, that's all.' Sam looked around the group. 'I'm afraid they mean nothing to me. Nothing at all.'

'Wait, Sam, what about the other box? Perhaps there are more in there? Yes? No?' said Xavier, raising his hands a little. 'Maybe that one will open too.'

Grace did not wait to be invited. She reached out and drew the second box closer to her. Turning it, she quickly found a side that now revealed a black line, signing a fractional gap that had opened. 'There's a crack in this one too. I could open it,' she said, allowing her fingernail to trace the breach. Again, she worked at it, and in only moments, she was carefully guiding the box's opening side down onto the tabletop.

'Good work, Grace, next time you want your nails done, I'll pick up the tab,' said Sam.

'I'll hold you to that,' said Grace as she released the second box into Sam's control.

'Nothing inside,' he said to a chorus of disappointed sighs from behind him. 'Identical wafer construction. See, its hinge-down side also has a glass layer that could be broken by the little bars housed within the void. So it's both locked and protected by the same method.'

Sam raised his magnifying glass and inspected the glass surface. 'Same here too. Geometric patterns etched into the glass. But no meaning.'

'Why didn't you see the shapes in the glass during the scan?' said Francis.

'For all their skills, ancient craftsmen could not produce the perfectly smooth glass we expect today. Until you know they're there, the shapes appear as just natural variation in the glass.'

'What are the shapes?' said Elaine.

'They're different to those in the first box. Look, pass me some paper and I'll sketch them out. See what we think.'

Helen's kitchen notepad worked its way through the group of onlookers, and Sam made a sketch of the shapes formed in the glass of the first box. He passed over the finished picture and it quickly did the rounds. Everyone looked at the six circles he had drawn. Two rows, each containing three unevenly spaced circles, everyone remained silent.

'I've tried to draw the circles to scale. They are uniform in shape, just regular circles, but each varies in size a little, from an inch and a half up to two and a half inches.'

Sam sketched the shapes in the glass of the second box. These were different. Only four shapes, each an ovoid and each a slightly different size. The first three shapes were positioned in an angled group. The fourth oval was set apart from, but close beside, the lower of the group of three. Again, these shapes were all of a similar size but not exact, ranging a little above or below three inches in length and none more than one and a half inches at its widest part.

'And you went to Libya, of all places, to find a code to open these boxes? That has to rank as one of the most dangerous wild goose chases ever,' said Helen. Her disappointment undisguised.

'Yes, but there must be something. Think about the investment and effort we know the Templars expended in keeping the boxes both safe and apart so nobody could open them. There absolutely must be something. We just don't know what it is,' said Sam.

'Well, I'm stumped,' said Francis, looking around the group. 'What next?'

'Do the shapes have any special meaning? Mathematical perhaps,' said Xavier.

'Not that I can see. The question is what do we use shapes for?' said Sam.

No one had an answer, and everyone watched in despairing silence as Sam drew both boxes to himself and studied them carefully. He pulled his car keys from his jacket pocket and shone the little key light on the glass. Then gently drew his finger across the shapes, feeling the edges – obvious now that they knew to look.

He drummed his fingers on the table. 'What am I missing? What is missing from this scene?'

No one replied. Seconds turned into minutes while everyone waited for Sam.

'Coffee, anyone?' said Grace. There was a concert of affirmative responses, people eager to break the tension. She hurried across the kitchen to get things organised.

Returning to the table, Grace placed a stack of side plates and a plastic container on the table. 'I got us cupcakes earlier. Only six, I'm afraid, someone will have to miss out.'

'I'll share one with you,' said Helen.

'Okay, that'll be great. I'll bring the coffee over now.' She left the table as Angelo began passing the plates around. He pulled open the cake-box lid and proffered it towards Elaine. She carefully lifted out a cupcake then slid the box to Helen who took one to share with Grace and passed the box back to Angelo who placed cakes on both Xavier's and his own plates. Francis took one and slid the box to Sam who had been absently watching the process.

Grace returned with coffees as Sam sat staring at the cake box. He reached out, twisted it one way then the other.

'Sam, take your cake,' said Helen. 'Otherwise, Grace and I might just have to take it from you.'

'Oh yes, we love our cupcakes,' said Grace, sitting again.

Sam leapt up. 'I've got it!' he said, lifting the remaining cupcake from the plastic box then returning it. He lifted it out again, placing it in front of Grace before displaying the empty box turning so everyone could see it.'

'It's a cupcake box,' he said.

'Yes, we know,' said Helen.

'No, no. Grace, you're a genius. That's a cupcake box.' He prodded at one of the ancient boxes urgently. 'Well, not exactly cupcakes, but see – the cupcake box is indented to hold the cupcakes in place. The glass in the boxes is indented very slightly, just enough to align or position something, though obviously not cupcakes. I'm thinking the indentations are to place and align things, probably tokens or some such. Tokens shaped just like those I've drawn.'

'This sounds good, Sam. But what tokens? Do we know these shapes?' said Xavier. His hands folded in towards his chest. 'Not me. I know nothing of these shapes. Nothing.'

'Well, let's look again at what I've drawn. I've sketched them down roughly and can do it again more accurately. Between the two boxes – in one, there are six circles'—he placed the end of a pencil across the shapes, estimating their diameters—'almost the same but each one just a slightly different size. And in the other, there are four roughly oval shapes. Again, they're similar in size but not exact.'

Sam looked about the group. Francis looked down at the table and Xavier shrugged.

'Could the circles be six moons or maybe planets?' asked Grace.

'Perhaps, but we only have one moon. And the ancients only recognised five planets: Mercury, Venus, Mars, Jupiter and Saturn.'

'Moon and planets combined then? That might represent six circles,' said Francis.

'True, that could work,' said Sam. 'But we'd need to find the moon and planet tokens from somewhere, and I don't have the slightest idea where to start looking. Never mind the four ovals, that's a whole other—'

'Sam!' Helen's voice silenced him. Her eyes were bright with excitement. 'You don't need to find anything.' She clutched his arm, squeezing it hard. 'I know exactly what fits in the spaces, and it's not planets and moons, believe me.'

'You do? How? What is it?'

Even as Helen had spoken up, a sense of self-doubt crept into her voice. 'If I'm right, I have the tokens already. I'm not sure, but it seems too much of a coincidence.'

'Where?' said Sam. 'What's the coincidence?'

Helen glanced about; everyone was looking at her. 'Last year, when I first went to the bank in Switzerland, I spent a little time going through John Dearly's safe-deposit box. You all know about it and have seen some of the things I brought from it. Not least that.' She pointed to where her original box rested on the table. 'That's from Switzerland, and it wasn't alone. There was another box there with some coins and medallions. Six and four, I think.'

'Okay, were the medallions oval shaped?'

'Yes, I think.'

'Are you sure?'

'I can show you.' Helen pulled her phone from her pocket and began scouring the picture archive.

It was during the previous summer that Helen had first visited Zurich and Swiss banker Franz Brenner's private bank. There, she had learnt of the true extent of her inheritance from John Dearly and his predecessors. They had maintained a private account to keep their business secret. In the bank's vault, she had accessed a safe-deposit box; it contained a whole range of artefacts. Some things they had already used to solve early parts of the puzzle; some, like her ornate box sitting on the table, were live. And there were yet more things to be evaluated.

She had photographed everything and was now flicking through her photos. She paused.

'Here they are.' She flicked on to the next image then back again. 'Yes, spot on. I'm sorry they aren't so clear; I didn't bother taking them out of the box. They're overlapping a bit, but you can just about make out there are six round coins and four oval medallions, see.' She handed the phone to

Sam.

Sam studied the picture then turned to look at her. He grinned. 'Helen, you've come up trumps again, I'm sure of it. Can you remember anything remarkable about the artefacts?'

'Not really. But back then, I had my mind on other things, remember?'

'I remember.' Sam passed the phone to Grace who looked, then passed it on.

'You know what this means, don't you?' said Sam.

'I guess I'm going to Switzerland again?'

Sam smiled at her. 'I guess you are. Thank you. It beats going back to Libya! Oh, and as soon as possible, please.'

Helen rolled her eyes. Then she turned to Xavier. 'I don't suppose you'd mind if I used your plane? Sam seems in a hurry.'

Xavier smiled at her, waving a hand up and over his shoulder. 'For you, of course. You don't need to ask. Now go, get ready, go! Angelo will call ahead to have the plane on standby.'

'I'll come with you,' said Grace.

'Don't you have a party tonight?'

'This sounds more fun. Anyway, you're recovering from a bullet wound; somebody needs to look after you.'

'Sam, there is something I just don't understand,' said Xavier.

'Go on,' said Sam.

'The boxes are Roman artefacts, but you didn't think the Romans were good with magnets. How can this be?'

'Yes, tricky. I've been thinking about that. It might be that the boxes are not true Roman artefacts at all. The ancient library at Alexandria, just along the coast from Leptis Magna, was a repository for ancient knowledge. Some of that is reputed to have been well ahead of Roman thinking. Perhaps, knowledge of such things existed there … maybe even the boxes themselves.

'It is possible that the Romans looted the boxes from Alexandria. They were good at looting. Perhaps they took them before the library was burnt down, which did happen during a period of Roman influence. I don't know, but it would certainly explain the confusing artistic style. But it's just a guess; we can never know for sure.'

Chapter 18

WEDNESDAY JANUARY 22ND

Cassiter strolled along the aisle towards the altar. His man beside him was quick to point out the guide who had advised Cameron. Oliver was standing beside the altar, watching their approach. Cassiter could just make out the heads of a couple beyond the altar where they were busy considering the merits of the Apprentice Pillar. Otherwise, the place was empty. The persistent snow and bad weather continued to deter visitors.

'Gentlemen, welcome to Rosslyn Chapel. My name's Oliver, and I'm here to help. Just ask, and I'll be happy to address any questions you may have.'

'Well, there is something you can do, thanks. My colleague, Dr Cameron, was here with a party yesterday. They were very interested in the archway over there. Sam said you had been very informative; he's asked me to come in and give a second opinion. He mentioned I should speak with you.'

'I'd be delighted to help you, of course. Mostly, he was interested in the arches of the Lady Chapel. Come on, I'll show you.'

'Please do. Sam has a theory he wants me to examine thoroughly, to see if I can pick any holes in it. He's deliberately not told me the details of his visit, so I can approach it with a fresh eye. If you would be good enough to talk me through things from scratch, we would much appreciate it. Then he and I can compare notes to see if we come to a similar conclusion or if there's more investigation to be done.'

'It's my pleasure,' said Oliver. With so few visitors on-site, he was only too happy to fill his time with something constructive. He quickly guided Cassiter to the archway at the centre of Sam's interest.

A while later, Oliver slipped out of the chapel and hurried across to the visitor centre where he explained the situation to Silvia who prepared a second memory stick for Sam's colleague. She told Oliver to send the visitor across as soon as he was finished; she'd be more than happy to speak with him.

***

Grace helped Helen up the steps into the manse. They pushed off their shoes and brushed away the light dusting of snow that had caught them in the walk from taxi to front door. 'We're back,' called Grace. 'Anyone in?'

'I'm in the study with Francis and Xavier.' Sam's voice reached them as they slipped off their coats. His head appeared around the study doorway. 'Welcome home. A successful trip, I hope?'

Helen laughed. 'Oh yes, we've got the goods.' She moved as quickly as she could to the study, greeted everyone, and with a little groan of comfort, settled into her chair behind the desk. 'Oh, that's better,' she said, closing her eyes, sighing. She eased her leg out, straightening it and stretching.

'Well?' said Sam.

'Franz was away on a skiing trip, so I saw his chief cashier instead. He's so nice.' She opened her eyes. 'I have what you want; let's hope it's what we need.'

Sam sat in the chair beside the desk as Helen opened her bag and pulled out a small but sturdy little box. Sam turned the box, inspecting each side carefully. He looked up at Helen. 'No mysteries with this one?'

'None. It's a simple box. The lid just comes off.'

Sam lifted the lid and peered inside.

'Everything is just as I first found it last year. Six old coins and, beneath them, four medallions.'

Sam took out the artefacts and spread them across the desk. He inspected each one carefully then turned them over and examined the reverse sides.

'What do you think?' said Helen.

'Hmmm,' said Sam. 'Hmm.' He pulled out his pocket magnifying glass and did a more detailed inspection of each artefact then measured their sizes before finally ordering them by size on the desk. He looked up. 'I think it's time to make sure these are the right things.'

'Do you think they are?'

'I think they are, but let's just make sure. These round ones are not coins. I see why you might have thought they were, right sort of size and shape. But they are something else. Tokens of some sort.

'These are quite special. One side is marked, the other is absolutely smooth, no monarch's head, no text, no image, nothing. I think having an image on only one side avoids confusion as there is only one logical way to place the discs into the glass indents – image up, so the worked face can be seen. You can't get it wrong. I'm guessing, if you have got the box open and have the tokens in your hand, you've passed the security tests and can just place your tokens in the indents to access the message. And look at this, on five of the discs, there's an identical design style: an ornately worked border, the centre filled by a simple line engraving.

'Then the sixth. Had you noticed that already?' Sam gently touched the disc where it rested on the table.

'Not really. I glanced at them on the flight over, but they were meaningless to me.'

'Well, you should have recognised this one.' He slid the disc across the desk towards her.

It had the same ornate border as the others, but as she studied the central section Helen realised what she was looking at. 'It's the Templar seal. Two knights on a single horse.'

'Spot on.'

'Great, so what's it for?'

'I don't know. But the Templar seal tells us the contents are their secret; we are on the right track.' He drummed his fingers on the desktop. 'I might take the lot off to my place and spend some time alone to think it all over. I need peace and quiet to concentrate for a while.'

Grace entered the study carrying a tray with teapot and cup, and a plate with bacon rolls. 'Right, you lot, this is for Sam. Remember, Helen, you said on the plane the best bet was to leave it with Sam to think through. Mum and I have bacon rolls and tea ready for everyone else in the kitchen.' She put the tray on the desk and looked about. 'Come on then, let's go.' She took Helen's arm and shooed the unresisting priests out of the study.

Sam moved round the desk and sat in Helen's chair. He decided to focus on the two rows of golden tokens first. Lifting the smallest, he attempted to place it in the smallest indentation. It slipped into place and Sam smiled. 'Looking good,' he said to himself as he reached for the second token.

One by one, he fitted tokens into their appropriate places. But as he searched for meanings and patterns, nothing came. Only the token to the top right, the Templar seal, was recognisable. The other five tokens were without apparent meaning. He gently spun the discs in their grooves, steadying his breathing. The quiet stretched out.

Looking across at the second box, Sam wondered if it might help to turn his attention to that one and the oval medallions for a little while.

Even as he reached out for the box, he saw what he needed, and his hand kept going, past the second box, settling instead on a neat little desk calendar that Helen had recently received from the management at the late Archie Buchan's sheltered housing complex in Dunbar, East Lothian. A small offering of thanks for Helen's cash bequest to restore the fire-damaged cottages where poor Archie had been so cruelly killed last summer. His had been the first death of many.

The calendar's January picture had caught his attention. One glance at the engraving on the bottom right token confirmed his impression. It was the Bass Rock, a prominent rocky outcrop located just off the coast, opposite the town of North Berwick, only a few miles from Dunbar.

He picked up the token and looked more carefully. No doubt at all; it carried an engraving of the Bass Rock's distinctive outline of high cliffs and domed summit. But why? What was the Bass Rock doing on this ancient token?

What makes the Bass Rock special? Sam wondered. It's permanent. Distinctive, for sure. But they're not enough to work with on their own. There must be something else.

Not a Templar base. There were Templar settlements dotted across East Lothian, but he'd never heard of a connection with the Bass Rock.

He turned his attention to the other tokens. Now he had a geographical theme to play with, almost at once he recognised another.

'That's Arthur's Seat and Salisbury Crags,' he muttered, touching the bottom left disc. Once identified, the engraved pattern on the disc was obvious. The craftsman's skills faithfully reproduced an image of the ancient volcano that had worn down through the ages to form a distinctive hunchbacked hill, the centrepiece of Edinburgh's royal park, its lower slopes defended by a fringing line of cliffs or crags.

Sam's adrenalin was rising. He lifted out the middle bottom disc to get a closer look. Its central feature was just a bump.

A geographical feature? A hill, perhaps? Certainly unremarkable.

Bottom right, the Bass Rock in East Lothian. Bottom middle, unknown bump or maybe hill. Bottom left Arthur's Seat in Edinburgh. He swivelled the tokens in their places. 'What are you hiding from us?' he muttered to the box. 'What is it? What am I missing? What feature is there between the Bass Rock and Arthur's Seat? Dirleton Castle, perhaps?'

He crossed to a bookcase, selected a map of southeast Scotland and spread it out across the desk. His finger tapped on Arthur's Seat before tracing a line eastwards towards North Berwick and the Bass Rock. There were few distinctive hills to consider as his hand continued to track back and forth across East Lothian's mostly gently rolling farmland.

He paused at Dirleton Castle for a moment then shook his head. It's certainly built on a hill. But the engraving doesn't feature a castle or any building for that matter, just a plain mound or hill. If it were Dirleton, wouldn't the engraving feature the castle? His hand continued on.

His search ended back at North Berwick with no further distinctive hill features. And there it was, under his finger, North Berwick Law! Actually at the town of North Berwick. His initial enthusiasm waned as he considered its proximity to the Bass Rock. Were they too close together?

He reached again for the desk calendar and began flicking over the monthly pages. He stopped at August. The photograph of North Berwick Law was a near perfect match for the engraving on the middle token.

Sam was content that he knew what the engravings on the bottom three tokens represented, but he still had no idea what their purpose was.

He sipped his tea, then leant forwards and again studied the tokens carefully. His magnifying glass flicked from one to another and back again.

'Ah ha. What have we got here?' He leant still closer, peering through the magnifier at the left-hand disc, Arthur's Seat. Now he saw the tiniest little dot punched into the rim of the token, completely concealed within the border decoration, unless somebody was searching or knew to look. He scanned the token again; further round the rim, he found another mark, a tiny cross.

Switching his attention to the disc featuring North Berwick Law, he found a single dot, just like on the first disc. And checking further round the rim, found another concealed mark, two dots. He moved on immediately to the right-hand token, and there, buried in the border pattern of the Bass Rock token, he found two dots and yet further round, he found three more.

After a little thought, Same rotated the tokens so one dot and one dot aligned, two dots and two dots aligned – so that all three tokens in the bottom row were aligned by their dot marks, one to the next.

Returning his attention to the left-hand token, the one featuring Arthur's Seat, he considered what the purpose of the tiny cross mark was. He scanned the left-hand token in the upper row and felt satisfied to discover, buried within its border pattern, a single cross and a double cross. He rotated that token in its indentation until the single cross lined up with the single cross on the token in the line below.

The rotation had brought the token's double cross mark round to a three o'clock position – pointing along the top row of tokens.

Sam started working more quickly. The middle upper disc had both a two cross and a three cross sign within its border. He lined up the two crosses with those on the left-hand token. This positioned the three crosses at about two o'clock on a clock face.

The Templar token set in the upper right indent had both a three cross and a three dot marking. Sam rotated the token within its indent and aligned the three cross mark with the same mark on the upper middle token. He checked at once to see if the Templar disc's three dot mark aligned with the three dot mark on the lower right Bass Rock token. It did. It worked. This, surely, was how the tokens had to sit.

Bottom left, Arthur's Seat. Bottom middle, North Berwick Law. Bottom right, the Bass Rock. Each with a dot pattern on the rim that could be used to align them neatly.

The bottom left and right tokens also had a little cross sign and a three dot sign respectively. The position of these two signs were locked in by the alignment of the other dot patterns. The two signs also aligned with identical marks in the top row to lock those tokens in position too. Perfect.

So, in that case, what did the top row of discs represent? More geography?

Following a logical process, Sam tried to isolate the geographical feature, if that's what it was, of the top left token. The position of the bottom left token's single cross at ten o'clock suggested whatever it was lay to the north and west of Arthur's Seat. He pulled the map across the desk and started to trace a line, then stopped. His heart suddenly sank.

Sam knew exactly where the line was taking him. He looked again at the token and recognised its shape – Cramond Island. A place familiar to him from innumerable coastal walks, but that was not what had thrown his thoughts into turmoil.

His mind had once again returned to the previous summer, to a time when they had not yet understood the violence and depths of brutality their opponents would sink to. He thought about poor Suzie Dignan, the museum worker who had so willingly offered to help, had found Sam the clues he needed and had died for her troubles. Murdered, drowned by

Cassiter and his men who then abandoned her body into the tidal flow at Cramond Island in a failed attempt to conceal the true cause of death. Sam blamed himself for her death. The weight of her loss was a burden he would carry, always.

He forced his attention back to the upper row of tokens. The Cramond Island token had two crosses at nearly three o'clock, roughly east, that lined up with the middle token in the upper row. He looked at the shape displayed on the middle token. It was odd. Logically, heading east from Cramond Island was heading out to sea, so it must be an island, but even knowing it was an island, he did not recognise the engraved shape on the middle upper row token at all.

He ruled out Inchcolm at once. It was more north than east. Only a few months earlier, he had made the trip out to Inchcolm to visit his friend Pete Summers, the resident archaeologist. If it were Inchcolm, it would have to have included Inchcolm Abbey in the engraving. The ruin of the abbey was the dominant feature on the island today just as it had been back in its heyday when the Templars had laid their plans. There was no building on the middle token, just an unfamiliar shape.

Casting back to his early school days, he began to recite a list of the islands. 'Inchgarvie, Inchcolm, Inchmickery, Cramond, Inchkeith …' Inchkeith was certainly east of Cramond Island, but it was completely the wrong shape. But what if …?

He turned to the computer and opened a photograph search site. It took a minute or two, but he found confirmation of what he wanted.

Throughout his life, he had seen Inchkeith Island hundreds of times from the shore. But what if you were looking at it from Cramond Island? That was it! Problem solved. All the engravings were true line of sight representations from one to the next. Like most locals, he was familiar only with the view of Inchkeith seen from the shore. But seen from Cramond

Island, Inchkeith had a completely different profile, a profile that matched the one on the token.

There was only one thing left to identify – the Templar token. Where could it be? Was it even a place? What did the Templar image itself represent?

Sam leant across the desk to look again at the map and began tracing lines across it with his finger.

He pulled open a drawer and rummaged for a ruler and pencil. Positioning the ruler on the map, he slowly drew a line, while talking himself through his thinking process.

'So, the three tokens in the bottom row are each identified by the location engraving. Now draw a line to link the three locations on the map … it's straight. Hmm …

'Two locations linked by line of sight is fine, easy. Three locations linked by line of sight that actually form a straight line is extraordinarily unlikely, unless that was the choice being made from the outset; the straight line is the reason for the choices. And what does that mean for our top row of tokens?'

Using the ruler, Sam began to draw another line on the map, this one linking Cramond Island to Inchkeith Island. Then he kept going. He hoped it would take him to the place designated with the Templar sign.

The pencil kept moving, crossing the blue of the estuary, leaving a black line in its wake as it progressed steadily out towards deeper water. At the point on the map where the firth finally merged into the North Sea, the pencil crossed a dot of isolated land. Sam pulled back. Now he was talking out loud. The excitement was back in his voice.

'Join the dots by line of sight. Three in a row and there you are. The Isle of May!' He drew a circle round the little island.

Sam closed his eyes and thought through the steps he had just followed. Then, content, a smile played across his lips.

***

'Knock, knock,' said Helen, pushing open the study door. 'Any progress yet?'

Opening his eyes, Sam smiled, nodded. Helen knew right away. She disappeared back into the hall. 'Breakthrough, everyone!' She entered the study, and everyone else was there in a moment.

It did not take long for Sam to explain his reasoning and its product.

'So, it's the Isle of May then,' said Helen.

'So it seems. I'm guessing that whatever the Templars hid is out there. The concealment is so complex, it must be very important.'

'You know what I think is there,' said Xavier.

Francis nodded. 'I do, and I think the same. It is the real treasures of the Templars, not their bars of gold and boxes of coin.'

'Do you really think it might be the Grail?' said Grace.

'It would be a wonderful day if it was, truly wonderful,' said Francis.

Xavier stood up, rested his hands on the side of the desk and glanced about the group, finally locking eyes with Helen. 'Henri de Bello started all this from here so long ago, sending his ring bearers away to the ends of the earth. Now perhaps, it falls to us, to you, Helen, to complete the circle and restore what was.'

'Yes. And the Isle of May … it's so close. Who'd have thought? Who'd ever look there? Henri de Bello, you clever, clever man. He'd the whole world to choose from, and he hid it in his own backyard!' said Helen. 'Well done, Sam; this is great. When are we going out there?' Helen fixed Sam with an expectant look.

'As soon as possible. Though perhaps, it's not a journey for you with that leg wound. I've never been to the May, but I've heard it's pretty wild, especially in winter. I want to speak with Pete Summers at Historic

Scotland. He knows all these islands like the back of his hand. If we're going out there, we need his advice for certain.'

There was a collective lifting of the mood as progress was recognised and a plan started to form. Grace stood. 'Well, I don't know about all of you, but I'm putting the kettle on again.'

Angelo stood to help, lifting Sam's mug and plate, but Grace intervened. 'Thanks, Angelo, but I'll take that stuff.' She eyed an uneaten roll crust and some bacon fat. 'The birds will welcome the extra food in this bad weather.' Taking the few steps towards the window, she passed behind the desk and froze.

'Sam! Sam, there's someone out there. Outside the window!' Grace rushed to the window. 'He's going, running down the drive.'

Sam and Helen joined her at the window, quickly followed by the others. Angelo had sprinted to the door. They watched him rush past the window and hurry down the drive before vanishing into the road.

'What did you see, Grace?' said Sam.

'There was somebody crouched beneath the window. As I approached, he jumped up and ran. Sorry, I didn't really get a good look at him.'

'Don't worry about that. I think we know who it was, don't we?'

Xavier gave a slow nod. Elaine remained impassive.

'Hell, look at that.' Sam tapped on the window. There was a small cleared circle amid the snow that had built up on the window frame.

'What is it?' said Helen.

'Microphone, held against the glass.' He peered out and down to the ground. 'Looking at the way the snow's been crushed down out there, I'd guess whoever was listening in was there for a good while. Oh hell – sorry.'

'That's okay, Sam. But what does this mean?'

'It means they know what we know. I can't believe I let this happen.

How stupid.'

'Sam we have the manse and the church buildings swept for bugs regularly. Nobody could anticipate that they'd actually risk sending somebody in like that.'

'I should have done. I should. I'm going outside to get a closer look. I'll tell you what this does mean – there's a race on to be the first to get to the Isle of May.'

Angelo reappeared at the entrance to the drive. He shook his head and raised his hands. The spy had got away.

***

Parsol's chair was pulled in tight against the edge of the suite's dining table. He was leaning forwards, looking at the map Cassiter had just marked up. The red circle surrounding the Isle of May signed their destination.

'There it is. After all these years, generations of searching, we're here.' Parsol smiled. He reached out a hand and gripped his son's arm. 'Go now; inform everyone that we are close. They have shared the long wait. Let them enjoy this moment. Then hurry back.'

Eugene Jr left, and for a few moments, the room lapsed into a silence broken only by Parsol's forced steady breathing.

'Cassiter. Your man has done well. Make sure he is rewarded.'

'He did his job. It's only what I expect of my people.'

'Nonetheless, he should receive something.'

'Okay, I'll see to it. I've got a team on standby and transport will be in place shortly. The Isle of May. Quite a surprise.'

'We have scoured half the world for this, half the world! It seems that old trickster de Bello was cunning up to the very end. Hiding the treasury so far away in Crete, the perfect decoy, the finest false trail. And yet, here we are, back where it all began. He hid our greatest treasure right where it all started. The fox!'

Chapter 19

THURSDAY JANUARY 23RD

The roads of North Berwick had been thoroughly salted and they glistened a wet silver-black. Squinting against the road dazzle and the low risen sun, Sam concentrated on driving safely and complying with the one-way traffic system while Helen looked out for their destination.

To their right, Forth Street was lined with a mix of two, three and four storey residential buildings, one or two restaurants and public houses and a couple of service buildings. To their left, on the coast side, the houses were lower, one and two storey homes. Over the years, many had been expanded, linked together to form a solid terrace with only the occasional gap left to give pedestrians a glimpse of the coast beyond.

Helen counted off the house numbers as they passed. 'This is it, just ahead on the left. Look, there's a space right outside where you can pull in.'

Sam parked his car outside the two storey home. 'Well, I'm pleased to say nobody tailed us,' he said. They got out and, following a cautious glance around, Sam stepped to the door and gave a short rap on the knocker.

Pete Summers pulled open his front door. 'Come in, come in. Good to see you, Sam. A happy New Year to you. And you must be Helen. Happy New Year to you too. I've heard a lot about you, pleasure to meet you at last. Come in.'

A little further along the road, a works van rocked slightly for just a moment as an occupant, concealed behind the smoked glass of the rear-door windows, stretched his legs to reach his phone and send a message. Whatever the reason Cameron had expressed a desire to visit this Pete Summers, he had wasted no time in doing so.

***

Pete led Helen and Sam along the hallway and into a living room.

'Wow, you have one special view here,' said Helen, crossing to the windows and looking out over the Forth. 'And your house just seems bigger on the inside than it does from the street.'

'Well, I like it. Suits me to a T. This room is big, but I think it seems even bigger because of the open aspect.'

'And what an aspect. Look, Sam, Pete's garden wall has a gate that leads right down to the beach – heaven!'

'Take a seat, both of you. I've had coffee on in anticipation of your arrival; I'll bring it through now, okay?'

'Fine by me,' said Helen, settling in a seat with a view out across the Forth.

Pete returned with a tray and served coffees and biscuits.

'I just love your location,' said Helen.

'Yes, if you like the Forth, it's perfect. Just over there, at the end of the beach, is the town's harbour. I keep my own boat there, only a minute's walk along the sand.'

'And which island it that?'

'Straight out is Craigleith. Way over to the left is the Lamb, beyond that is Fidra, but you'd need to go upstairs to see that from the bedroom window.'

'What about the Bass Rock, can you see that from here?'

'No, that's off to the right, beyond the harbour, it's very close by, but all the town's buildings obstruct the view. Still, I know it's there. Now what can I do for you both?'

Sam lifted the briefcase he'd brought in with him and opened it. 'Pete, thanks for seeing us. I know you like your privacy, so I appreciate it. I've got a problem and was hoping you might be able to help.'

'Go on, I'm listening,' said Pete.

'I'm interested in the Isle of May.'

'Ah, the May. What can I tell you?'

'I think I need to go there, discreetly. I know there are pleasure cruise visits, but we're out of season right now. Tell me, who'd be on the island at this time of year, and who should I speak to about getting access?'

'Hmm, Scottish Natural Heritage is the responsible authority, but the RSPB'—Pete glanced towards Helen—'that's the Royal Society for the Protection of Birds, has an interest too. The island's a bit of a conservation and research hotspot. At this time of year, there are no tourists or visitors, but there is a conservation and observation team there all year, except for the Christmas and New Year weeks.

'I was in the office yesterday and, just by chance, was speaking with one of the Isle of May coordinators. She wants to do some cross-island bird tracking this summer to see what the mix is between the May and Inchcolm.' Pete turned to Helen. 'I'm based on Inchcolm during the summer months.'

'Sam told me.'

'Oh, right then, you know. Anyway, she was telling me, with all the bad weather since Christmas, her team has not got back to the island yet.

She's planning to get them out early next week.'

'So the May's unoccupied at present?' said Sam.

'Exactly.'

'Great. Pete, I want to get out to the island before the observer team returns. How can I do that?'

'I'm not sure you can. You'd need permission, certainly a good reason, and a boat of course, but you won't get one. Those boats that know the waters are chartered all year round to service the observer teams. They get to ferry the tourists through the summer as a bonus, with the permission of the authorities. The captains won't risk their service contracts for a one-off journey that breaches the rules.'

'There must be a way, Pete. We're desperate.'

Pete frowned. 'Sam, you're a good friend. I'd love to help, but can't you just wait a few days until the team are back on the island? Who knows, you might even get to go out with them.'

'We can't wait. Look, Pete, I'll be straight with you. There's no secret that Helen and I have been in the wars this past while. Remember, you even got me out to Inchcolm last year because of that Templar find you made. Your original clue set us on a course halfway round the world and back to here. To the Isle of May. You also know what that has led to, some of the people who have died. It's been on the news, in every paper ...'

Pete nodded. 'I've followed it all. Believe me, Sam, you've been at the root of more than one bout of gossip I've overheard in staff canteens. Is it still dangerous, even now?'

'I'm afraid so. Look, Pete, I know you hate all the social mishmash, but please can you speak to the people, get me permission to land? I really need it.'

A long pause followed, during which Pete subconsciously sucked air through a gap between his front teeth. It generated a little whistling hiss, the sound jolting him back so that he focused on Sam again. He let out a long sigh.

'Okay, I'll speak to her. But only because it's you asking. And you know I'm going to have to host a bunch of ornithologists on Inchcolm next summer because of this. You're going to owe me.'

'Thanks, Pete. I can't tell you how grateful we are.'

'Well, you're a friend.' Pete looked at Helen, and his face broke into a smile. 'I don't have many, so I suppose I'd better look out for the few I have.'

'I haven't quite finished yet, Pete. What do you know about the history of the May? Is there a Templar connection?'

'Nothing that I know of. Though bearing in mind how we found that Templar's gravestone on Inchcolm last year, I suppose anything's possible. The Isle of May was certainly a place of pilgrimage in ancient times, and various religious buildings were erected there in the past. I think there was some toing and froing over control; it seemed to bounce around a bit. It even rested with one of the English churches way down south for a while. At some point, I'm not sure of dates offhand, certainly by around the early fifteenth century, the bishop of St Andrews had control. Sometime after that, it was abandoned.'

'Inchcolm appeared to have no connection with the Templars either—' said Sam.

'And look where that took us,' said Helen, with the slightest of shudders.

'I remember you telling me last year that Inchcolm was under the control of the bishop of St Andrews back then too. Could that be a link?' said Sam.

'Could be. St Andrews certainly profited from all the pilgrims who travelled to the May's sanctuary site. But Sam, what's the big hurry? Why do you need to get to the May so quickly?'

'It's better you don't know, Pete, for your own safety. What else can you tell me about the island?'

Pete stood and gazed northwards through his living-room window. To his right, at the beach's end, the harbour wall and a line of sturdy low-slung buildings showed blurry grey through the snow shower that had just blown in. Out to sea, the island of Craigleith had vanished, lost behind the falling snow. 'On a good day in summer, you can just see the May from here. It's nearer the Fife coast than the Lothian side but remote and hard to get to from either side of the Forth. Any further out, and it would be in the North Sea.

'For all its remoteness, there is evidence of human occupation almost since man first followed the retreating ice sheets north at the end of the Ice Age.'

'What's the shoreline like?' said Sam.

'Rugged, rocky, cliffs. Only a few landing spots. To the west is a little shingle cove, Pilgrim's Haven. That was used in the days of sail and oar. Near high tide, sailors would just beach on the shingle, then they could float off with the next tide. But it's exposed when the wind blows down the Forth from the west. If the wind was to blow the wrong way, you'd either never get in or would be trapped ashore. There's Altarstanes, that's another possible landing spot further around the coast, but it has the same problem with a westerly wind.'

'Not very inviting. Any other option?'

'Not much better, I'm afraid. There is a newer concrete jetty built on the east side at Kirkhaven; it's the one most used today. There's a natural inlet fixing a clear line of approach from the sea, but it's rocky to either side. Let your boat's head drift for a moment, and you'll be on the rocks. Once you're in though, it's a secure enough berth. It's difficult when the wind and sea are up in the east or north. In the current weather, I wouldn't fancy trying either option for a first visit to the May. My advice is wait a few days.'

Sam exchanged glances with Helen. Both knew it couldn't wait. If their reference to the Isle of May had been picked up by the eavesdropper, Cassiter could already be en route to the island.

'Point noted. But I'm not sure we have the time. Is there anything else you can tell us?'

Pete gave a resigned shrug and sat again. While his own life was all about avoiding the glare of public engagement, he knew Sam well enough to know he would not shrink back under any circumstances.

'Well, it's long and thin. A little over a mile long, less than half a mile wide at its widest, much narrower for some of its length, and lies roughly north–south, shaped a bit like an uncut cigar. Archaeological finds show the May has always had a mystic or religious function. I recall it was Saint Adrian who first established a Christian settlement and chapel there. Later, King David commissioned the Benedictines in England to establish a monastery on the May. They expanded the original chapel. As I say, at some point, possession passed to the bishop of St Andrews.'

'There's definitely a Christian building on the island then?'

'A ruin. Nothing of any substance, some stone flooring and partial walls. I suspect that much of the stonework was taken and recycled into housing by the small group of fishermen who set up home there later.'

'Okay, I guess I'll have to work with what I can find. But first, I need a boat.' Sam glanced meaningfully at the framed photograph featuring Pete beside his pride and joy. A sturdy looking RIB.

'Oh, Sam, not my baby.'

Sam gave the slightest of nods. 'If you could, Pete, It would be much appreciated. I'd owe you one.'

'Owe me one? More than one, I'm thinking.' Pete stood and looked out through the window. 'It's over at the harbour, in the yacht club. I've got it out of the water for the winter.' He glanced back towards Sam whose face betrayed no emotion.

'We can cover the cost of it for you, if you are worried about that,' said Helen.

'It's really not the money. It's taken me ten years of horse-trading to work up to that beauty. In fact, I hardly ever get to take it out at all. Just a couple of weeks running around in the spring and again before the onset of autumn. I'm working on Inchcolm Island all summer.'

Sam joined Pete at the window. 'I'd appreciate it if you'd help, old friend.'

After a long pause, Pete sighed. 'Okay. I'll have to get it ready and into the water. When do you want it?'

'Tomorrow morning, please,' said Sam, putting an arm round Pete's shoulder.

Pete blew out a long slow breath of air and shook his head in resignation. 'Are you okay with the boat out on the water? I guess I could pilot it for you. At least I've been to the May a few times; I'll know better what to expect.'

'Thanks for the offer, but I've got somebody in mind for this trip, and to tell you the truth, things might get a bit hairy. You've done enough; I'd rather keep you at arm's length from all this, for your own good.'

Pete didn't object. His was a world of books and trowels.

Sam excused himself for a moment and stepped out into the hall. From there, he made a phone call. It was answered promptly.

'Hello, Bill? Sam here, Sam Cameron. How's Bristol at this time of year? Kept busy?' Sam fell silent as his old friend greeted him and moaned about the state of the world.

'Bill, I'm in a bit of trouble here and could do with your expertise.'

'Cameron, I'm beginning to think I only hear from you when you're in trouble.'

'I'm embarrassed to admit it's certainly starting to look that way.'

'Well, what can I do for you?'

'I need the best boatman I can find.'

'Okay. Where are you going?'

'The Isle of May.'

'Oh, I know that one; it can be hell if the weather's coming from the wrong direction. A couple of the guys and I were on a short MoD dive contract a couple of years ago near the Bass Rock. Took our boat over to the May on a down day. What do you want to do over there?'

'All I want you to do is pilot my RIB; I'll be doing the rest.'

'Hmmm. When?'

'We sail tomorrow morning.'

'That's quick. What's the weather like?'

'Rubbish. Snow showers, plenty of wind, sea's pretty heavy.'

'Sounds fun, not. Let me check flights, and I'll get back to you to confirm my ETA.'

Sam trusted Bill completely. They had served together on several occasions during his military days. Their paths had crossed again at a Bristol diving club, when Sam was teaching at a local university and Bill had retired from military service to work at the club. In the past year, Bill had responded to help Sam escape when he was being pursued by Cassiter's men in Bristol docks.

***

Back in the manse, Xavier sat beside Sam at the kitchen table. He reached out a hand and pressed it gently on Sam's forearm. 'My friend, you are going into danger.'

'Well, that seems to be the way of things. I'm hoping to have a head start on Cassiter's boys. Get finished and off the island before they even know we've set off.'

'That would be good.'

'What would be better is if I was going too,' said Helen.

'You're in no fit state to be going to any islands right now. You've got a bullet wound in your leg,' said Elaine.

Sam smiled a thank you towards her. 'That's right. At least Elaine is speaking sense. You couldn't manage the physical pressures in your current condition.'

'So, I've to just sit and twiddle my fingers while you're off doing heaven knows what.'

'Bluntly, yes. I know you're mobile, more than you ought to be, but the Isle of May in winter is tough. With this weather, I doubt you'd even manage to get out of the RIB, much less get about the island. Anyway, let's be clear, this is your show. You need to be here at the centre ready to respond if anything goes wrong. It's no good us both being isolated on a small storm-locked island.'

Helen tutted and took a mouthful of rosé. She put the empty glass on the table. 'See what you're doing to me, Sam Cameron – driving me to drink!'

Xavier arched his eyebrow, tilted his head slightly to look Helen in the eye and smiled at her indulgently. 'I think Sam is not the cause here, no?' He picked up the wine bottle and refilled her glass.

'Thanks. I know it's not Sam's fault. It's just so frustrating to be an invalid, Xavier. So frustrating.' She lifted the glass and cradled it in her hands.

'My friend, I think you should not travel alone. Like Helen, I cannot manage such an expedition, but please take Angelo. He is strong and more than capable. I will stay here with Helen. If, as we think, you uncover some of our Church's most holy relics then there must be a priest on hand for validation and to ensure the proper care is taken.'

Sam was about to object but stopped himself. Angelo was indeed fit and capable, and Sam knew him to be courageous. 'That's good of you, Xavier, thank you.' Sam leant round Xavier. 'If you're up for it, Angelo?'

Angelo's nod and confident grin combined to assure Sam he was making a sound choice. 'That's settled then. Thank you. Now there's one thing left to do. I need to work out what the four oval medallions from box number two tell us. I've got a good idea. If you'll all excuse me, this is one where some peace and quiet is called for.'

Xavier raised a restraining hand. 'Sam, before you go, please, another point I don't understand. How can a glass sheet contain a message of the Templars when its box was made hundreds of years before they existed?'

'Good point, Xavier. I wondered about that. I think the boxes were used differently. Probably the original use of the boxes involved painting or waxing a message directly onto the glass. Shatter the glass and the message is gone. To reuse the box, just wash away the former message.

'I'm thinking that the Templars either ground their required indents into the original glass or just replaced that original glass with fresh sheets.'

Xavier half raised a hand in acknowledgement as Sam stood and took the second box and four medallions.

***

Cassiter stepped out of the car and crossed to the harbour side. The working day was not over but northern darkness had already settled. The enclosed waters of the little haven shimmered golden under the harbourside lights, complimented from one corner by the floodlight of a small shrimper whose owner busied himself prepping for the next trip out.

A man emerged from a nearby van and hurried over to join Cassiter.

'It's over there,' said the man, nodding discreetly towards a RIB that bobbed gently as it strained between its mooring line and the pull of the ebbing tide. 'He put it into the water after lunch and spent some time working on it before driving off to his office in Granton. I don't know what he did there.'

Cassiter looked out across the harbour towards the sturdy RIB.

'It's a nice one,' said the man.

'Okay, once that fisherman leaves and the harbour is quiet, I want you to fix a tracker on it. Be sure to check back to base to ensure it's working properly. Then standby here. We have a vessel coming up from the south. It won't get into the Forth until the day after tomorrow. Meanwhile, I want to know as soon as there's any action brewing. Be careful; for the time being, we must not intervene. I just need to know what they are doing.'

Cassiter turned and walked back to his car, satisfied he had a clear understanding of what was happening, and there was nothing more he could do. The high tide was going to be just after seven the next morning. Cameron would want to move around then.

***

A tapping sound on the study door had Sam lift his head as Helen entered, wine in hand.

'How's it going?' she said.

'I think we're making progress. Come see.'

Helen stood next to the desk. She rested a hand on his shoulder and rubbed gently. 'Are you sure going out there tomorrow is a good idea?'

'I've checked the weather. The wind will be dropping a bit overnight, and with Bill at the helm, I'd be pretty confident anywhere. He knows his stuff.'

'So you said earlier. He's another one of the mysteries from your past.'

'No mystery. Bill's ex-SBS, Special Boat Service. That's the webbed feet version of the SAS. If it weren't for him, I'd never have got out of Bristol last year. I can trust him completely.'

'I sometimes wish just one of your old buddies was a chess player.'

'You know, I've probably got one somewhere. But right now, Bill's the man, trust me.'

'I do, Sam, I do. Now, where have you got too?' She put her glass on the desk and pulled a chair close.

Sam arranged the four medallions on the desk. 'These are the approximate positions they occupy when placed in the glass. See, together these three form a shape a bit like a beech leaf.'

'Or a bay leaf maybe?'

'Perhaps. Certainly a slender ovoid, a very rough ovoid, with some jaggy edges.'

'Holly even. What does it mean?'

Sam turned the computer screen so Helen could see. 'Look here. It came to me after a little while. We know this is all leading us to the Isle of May. What shape is the island? It's long and slim, a bit like a leaf. There are plenty of pictures and maps of the island but only one or two with a decent range of its features or geographical names. See, there's Altarstanes, in modern English you might call that Altar Stones, and there's Pilgrim's Haven.'

'Okay, where do these take us?'

'Remember, Pete told us that Pilgrim's Haven was an old pre-power boat landing place. Beaching on the shingle.'

'Yes.'

'I'm thinking three of the four medallions combine together to form the rough shape of the island. The shape could never be formed exactly – back then they didn't have modern-day plotting devices or bird's-eye views. Now, look carefully at the bottom medallion of the three. Down here, at what would be our south end of the island … see the medallion's pattern around the edge and look closely at that tiny mark. It's actually a Templar cross.' He passed his pocket magnifying glass over the medallion, so she could see clearly.

'It marks the indent on the map where Pilgrim's Haven is!' said Helen.

'Exactly my thought. I really can't tell what these other patterning elements represent until I'm there. But I think we need to start off at Pilgrim's Haven.'

'What about the fourth medallion?'

'I don't know yet. It must have a purpose; there's a place for it in the glass adjacent to the southern end of the island, beside Pilgrim's Haven. But it seems to be placed separately from the other three that form the island's shape. Right now, its engraving just seems to be a series of lines. But see here … it has a tiny Templar cross to one side and another here too. Perhaps they link with the other little cross marked at the spot that may represent Pilgrim's Haven. We just don't know yet.'

'Another one for field research then?'

Sam nodded. 'Yes, we'll be quick though. I need to get there, sort it and be off the island before any of the heritage people are ferried out or Cassiter shows up. I'm guessing that will be Monday at the latest, so at best, we've got the weekend to wrap this up.'

Chapter 20

FRIDAY JANUARY 24TH - a.m.

Pete Summers stood on the harbourside breakwater, his face writ with a raft of anxieties. He worried for the wellbeing of his friends, had concerns over the safety of his RIB and was as uncomfortable as ever with having to meet yet more new people.

Sam wrapped an arm round Pete's shoulder. 'Don't worry; we'll take care of her.'

In spite of a nod of acknowledgement, Pete was far from reassured. In the water beneath them, Bill was at the helm and had the RIB nuzzling gently against the harbour side, close beside a column of iron rungs set into the stonework. He was large-framed and unshaven with a long, grey-streaked ponytail flowing from beneath his woolly hat to trail down his back. To any uninformed observer, Bill was just an earring short of a pirate.

Angelo embraced Xavier and Francis then climbed down and stood on the deck waiting for Sam to load their kit.

Having lowered rucksacks and tool bags, Sam let the line drop into the

RIB. He shook Pete's hand. 'Thank you, Pete. You've been a great help. I'll keep in touch.' He let go of Pete's hand, bid farewell to Xavier and Francis before turning to Helen. They exchanged hugs and kissed briefly.

'You be careful out there,' she said.

'Don't worry, we'll be back almost before you know we're gone. I'd be more concerned about *you* right now. Why not give Brogan a call. He's sympathetic and, one way or another, things are coming to a head now. Any protection would be useful.'

'I'll see how things play out. Maybe call later today.'

'Do that. Now, I have to go,' he said as a slightly impatient revving of the engine reached up to them from the water below. A final hug and kiss, then Sam clambered down the iron rungs into the RIB. Even as he steadied himself and looked up, Bill had the RIB underway. First a gentle manoeuvre, lining up on the little harbour's mouth, then he opened up, firing the RIB ahead, out into the still black of pre-dawn open water.

A van parked on the quayside at the end of the breakwater betrayed no sign of life to Helen, Pete and the two priests as they passed by. Inside, an observer made an urgent phone call to his boss. The game was on.

***

Nearly an hour had passed. The sun had risen above the horizon to light another grey day. The journey north across the firth had been uneventful though uncomfortable. Fortunately, the wind had dropped overnight and the waves had followed it down, but a persistent swell that had built over several days continued to roll in from the northeast.

'Let's do a circuit of the island,' said Sam.

Bill nodded and altered course slightly to allow them to run north along the island's western edge. As they moved into the protective lee of the island, the rolling swell vanished, and the endless motion dropped. The going was suddenly much easier.

A rugged expanse of low-lying rocks provided a protective fringe to the southern tip of the island. They pushed on and the coastline quickly rose, becoming sheer black cliffs.

The island's rock was ancient volcanic stone, hard and durable. Nonetheless, the efforts of the seas had, over thousands of years, punched through lines of weakness to create a wicked and unwelcoming spectacle for seafarers, inaccessible sea caves and jagged, arched recesses punctuated the unforgiving façade.

'I don't fancy this shoreline much,' said Bill.

Sam pulled out a clear plastic bag containing a chart featuring the island and showed it to him.

'I know it's pretty inhospitable, but there are a couple of spots that might work. I'm reckoning that just beyond that next outcrop we should see Pilgrim's Haven. That was the traditional landing spot in previous generations. We could nudge in a bit and have a look as we pass. What do you think?'

'No problem.' Bill turned the helm slightly to starboard and had the RIB edging in. As they moved ahead, Pilgrim's Haven came into sight.

The haven was a narrow inlet ending in a shingle beach. Bill guessed the inlet might be little more than a hundred paces wide and narrowed to twenty or so at the shingle beach. Set well back in a recess between high cliffs, the beach was completely sheltered from the eastern weather, but any wind blowing down the Forth from the west would make for a hazardous landing.

Bill did not go right into the cove. Attempting to beach and missing the little line of shingle would almost certainly have fatal consequences, ending the expedition before it had properly begun. They would make a decision on where to berth once the options had been appraised. He turned the RIB's head and continued on round the island.

'Look up there … it's the lighthouse,' said Sam. Pointing across the rocky skyline to where the dull grey-brown stone of the island's main building appeared briefly in a break in the cliffs, Bill kept them moving on.

***

'Patch it through,' said Cassiter. He kept the line open and began selecting a feed on his computer.

'What is it?' said Parsol, driving his wheelchair across the floor of the hotel suite to join Cassiter.

'We've got a visual. Here it comes now. See.' He pointed at the computer screen.

'What's this?'

'The North Berwick Seabird Centre has live camera feeds from the Isle of May, focusing on certain spots. My team in Paris have taken control of the cameras. They're monitoring Cameron's progress wherever possible.'

'Good, your tracking device already confirmed where he was heading. But I like pictures. They can be very informative. Who are the two men with him?'

'Near the bow is one of the Sardinian priests, the younger one. There's Cameron, and I don't yet know who the third man is.'

'Find out what you can.'

'We're already on it. Nothing yet. He's a bit of a mystery, just appeared for the first time at the harbour this morning.'

'Well, keep on it. I don't want any surprises. How's my yacht doing?'

'En route. It will reach the Forth tomorrow morning. Then I'll join it at once with a team and get out to the island.'

'Okay. I would have liked my son to travel in your party. He should be there to represent me, but he has other business to deal with. I am not happy that I cannot come.'

Cassiter knew what Eugene Jr's role was to be and understood the older man's frustration at not being able to lead on this final leg of their quest.

'I know but landing on the island can be tricky, all but impossible in your circumstances, if the weather is bad.'

Parsol moved his chair to look out of the window. 'It does not seem so bad today.'

'No, but the forecast is bad again. Best stick with our original plan. Come out by helicopter, once we have secured the site.'

'Agreed. But you must make sure Cameron is still alive then, I want to see his end, personally. Then we can go on to deal with the Johnson girl, together.'

Cassiter smiled. Most of his killings were dispassionate. Who the victim was did not matter to him, although their suffering was always a pleasure. But in Helen Johnson's case, there was history; her killing mattered to him. It mattered to him a lot.

***

They had devoted much of the morning to doing a double circuit of the island, making sure every possible feature was appreciated before landing. Other than two or three little inlets, it was as unwelcoming a shore as could be imagined. Where the sheer cliffs and crags did drop away, ranges of coastal rock filled the sea to form an impenetrable barrier.

'You see the line of sea-level rocks ahead?' said Sam.

Bill looked to where Sam was pointing. 'Yes, I see. It was immediately behind them that we saw the sheltered channel, first time around. You said it led into Kirkhaven. Fancy giving it a go?'

'Yes, I reckon it's our best bet for landing today. It's got a proper little concrete jetty, and the rocks create a lee for the channel.' Sam thrust the plastic-wrapped chart under Bill's nose.

'Looks good to me too. Let's line it up and go see.'

Bill turned the RIB hard to starboard and eased back on the engines as he assessed the little channel ahead. It was a tight opening and seemed to get narrower further in. The power of the sea broke against the great beds of sea-level rock to either side, allowing a relatively clear run-in for a powered craft.

'What do you think?' said Sam.

'No problem; we'll give it a go.' Bill pushed the engine a little harder, and the RIB moved steadily ahead. Slipping into the channel formed between the two rock beds, the RIB moved into protected waters. Two grey seals had pulled themselves out onto the rocks, and they watched the RIB go by. A little beyond, another seal's head bobbed up, and it watched the passers-by too.

Sam jumped off the RIB onto the cement jetty, pulling a bow line with him. He tied it to a steel cleat to secure the RIB then went to help Angelo unload the kit. Three rucksacks, two tool bags.

Bill hopped up onto the jetty and bent to check Sam's bow line was secure. He had the loose end of a second line in his hand and stepped ahead, securing it to a further set of cleats. Straightening, he assessed the RIB, watching as the now ebbing tide had it straining gently against the two bow lines. He peered into the water beneath then looked back to Sam with a grin.

'She's safe enough here, it'll do nicely. Another hour or so and she'll ground on the sand as the tide goes out. That'll be fine, but I'm reckoning we won't be able to float her again until the middle of the afternoon.' He stepped along the jetty and secured a stern line, allowing just enough slack so the RIB could settle evenly on the sandy bottom.

'Okay, we've got to survey the island first, so I don't think we'll need the RIB for a while,' said Sam.

'Fine, you're the boss. Where to now?' said Bill.

'Step one, let's get our kit under cover in case the weather turns again. Look, the visitor centre's only about four hundred paces north. See, over there, up the slope. We'll take everything there now, collect our thoughts and then get on.'

The three men each shouldered their own bag and, between them, shared the burden of the tool kits on their journey up the track that rose quickly away from the sea. At some point in the past, the track had been surfaced with tarmac but time and steady use had worn away much of the original top layer. Now they walked on a rough and rutted surface of broken stone. The island was devoid of trees. The year-round winds and thin earth prevented any from gaining a hold.

Nonetheless, most of the island was green. A peat surface had built up through thousands of years of mosses and rough grasses growing and dying. The current generation's growth knitted together to protect the underlying peat whose continuity was frequently interrupted by exposed outcrops of black–grey volcanic bedrock.

Nature's constructions were supplemented by the works of long-dead hands; their efforts using the same stone to create the boundary walls that spread out across the southern end of the island. Walls built thick enough to withstand the harsh weather and high enough to provide permanent shelter from the wind for the island inhabitants as they went about their daily business.

The visitor centre itself was a low-slung modern structure, built of wood. A central core of locked storerooms and toilets had an all-round overhanging roof, reminiscent of some great broad mushroom cap sprouting up from the island's rock core. The public space was open sided and open plan, but the solid central core ensured visitors could always be certain of finding at least one side where they could shelter from the wind. The construction's design perfectly met its role of offering a sheltered rallying point for summer visitors while they waited to board a departing ferry.

'Pete visited the island's coordinator yesterday afternoon. He got us a key for one of the old lighthouse keepers' cottages; it's the accommodation used by the duty heritage staff. They won't be out here until next week, so we can use it for now. He said we should leave the key in the front door when we're finished.'

'Sounds good. Where is it?'

'Just up the hill. According to my map, the track runs up from the jetty, past this visitor centre and continues to some cottages, the pump station and a reservoir. It's called Fluke Street. And at the top of the hill, beyond all that, is the lighthouse.'

'A pumping station. What's that for?' said Bill.

Sam glanced at some notes he'd made. 'It seems there is a run of thick cast-iron pipes that carried compressed air to the fog horns at either end of the island. Not needed any more.'

'Fair enough,' said Bill. 'Shall we have a quick cuppa here? Get some warmth into our bones before we start the search?' Bill pulled a thermos flask from his rucksack. 'I had them fill this when I arrived at Edinburgh Airport this morning. Expensive but good.' He sat down at a sheltered wooden bench and table with a wonderful open view across the jetty below. 'Only these plastic mugs I lifted from the servery counter, I'm afraid. But it's still hot.'

'Oh, that's got a kick,' said Sam.

'It should have, I added a good measure of whisky,' said Bill as Angelo, quiet but reassuringly attentive, grinned in appreciation.

***

Helen stood on the steps of St Bernard's. She felt proud of the changes that were taking place. Under Elaine's guidance, the renovations and alterations in the nave continued apace. It would soon be a true community centre; right now, the social and support activities were focused in the former church hall next door. As soon as the works were complete in the church, the hall's activities would decant across, and the hall would then receive its upgrade.

A dark blue car drew to a halt outside the church, and Helen stepped down to greet the occupants. A wince flashed across her face, signalling the pain she felt in her leg wound, but that was quickly masked when Brogan and Price got out of the car. Brogan shook Helen's hand; Price gave a tight smile of acknowledgement.

'There's a lot going on here,' said Brogan, raising his voice above a burst of machine noise that sounded from within the church. He gestured towards the skip, full of rubble, outside the church.

'Yes, we're keeping busy. I think it's going to be great once everything is finished. Though it's Elaine who is managing the work. Seems I'm only needed now to sign cheques from time to time. Thank you for coming inspector; let's go to the office. Best we go round the outside. As you can hear, it's a building site in there.' She led the way along the side of the church and in through the new solid, wooden back door.

'Hey, this is great,' said Brogan as he settled into one of the comfortable office chairs arranged in an informal meeting cluster to one side of the room. What had been the vestry was now a welcoming open office.

'Yes, I like it. Elaine made sure this back area was finished first. Coffee?' She stepped to the window wall where a new worktop supported a freshly installed coffee machine.

'Thanks, I will.'

'Not for me, thank you,' said Price, settling in the chair next to her boss.

Helen joined them. Passing Brogan his coffee, she gently lowered herself into the chair opposite him.

'That looks sore. Are you sure you should be out and about?'

'I'll be fine, thanks, got to keep it moving.'

So, what can I do for you?' he said.

'Well, I'm afraid I've something of a confession to make.'

Price leant forwards very slightly.

'Go on,' said Brogan.

'Our old trouble is back.'

'What exactly do you mean?'

'The killers have resurfaced. I ... we hoped it was all resolved after the incident in Crete last year but apparently not.' Helen noticed that Price had produced her notebook.

'Where are they? What have they done?'

'Everywhere, everything. Running me off the road here, a priest was killed in Malta recently—'

'Were they responsible for your gunshot wound?' said Price.

'Yes.'

'Why didn't you report this at once? You realise withholding information is an offence. It's especially serious where firearms are—'

'Thank you, sergeant. You're quite right, but there are extenuating considerations here.' Brogan gave his sergeant a cautionary glance and she fell silent.

'It's all coming to a head now,' said Helen.

'What about the old Italian priest who's been around recently ... Xavier, isn't it? Where does he fit in?' Price could not contain her curiosity.

'Sergeant, I said, enough.' Brogan turned to look at Helen. 'What about you and Sam, don't you need protection? In fact, where is he?'

'He's gone out to the Isle of May, something he needs to investigate there.'

'I see, and who's he gone with?'

'Angelo and an old friend from his service days.'

'Angelo?' said Price.

'The young priest from Sardinia, Xavier's assistant.'

Brogan was silent while he considered what Helen was telling him. Finally, he spoke. 'Bearing in mind your reluctance to share information with us in the past, what's triggered this sudden revelation?'

'As I said, it's all coming to a head. I can look after myself, but there are innocents involved. We saw what they did to Elaine last year, how they killed John Dearly. I can't risk any more innocent bystanders suffering over this.'

Price was bristling with a score of questions, but Brogan used a cautionary glance to restrain her. He cleared his throat, hesitating.

'Tell me, Helen, does the name Rupert Peterson mean anything to you?'

'Of course, I know him. Why do you ask?' Helen was suddenly doubly on her guard. She had mixed feelings about Rupert Peterson. Yes, the British Secret Service officer who Sam had said was from MI6 had helped them out in Africa, but she was acutely aware that he had been instrumental in putting them in trouble's way to start with.

'A little while back, I had a visit from him. He expressed a particular interest in you and Sam, wondered if I'd keep him in the loop if anything brewed up here. In fact, I'd go further, he required I keep him closely informed.'

'I see.'

'Sir, who is this Peterson? I've never heard of him.'

'No, sergeant, you won't have done. He's MI6. And please, don't write his name in your notes. As far as the likes of you and I are concerned, he doesn't exist.'

Price pursed her lips in frustration. Then she sat in silence while Helen recounted the events of the past few days.

'Helen, I'll lay on security for your people at once. Under the circumstances and knowing the history that won't be a problem. But you understand, I must inform Peterson. He will do whatever his people deem appropriate, and that will be out of my hands.'

'Sir, why are the security services so interested in all this? It's not terrorism. It seems more like gang crime, not a mainstream security concern.'

'I don't know why; they move in a different world to ours. Do *you* know, Helen?'

She shook her head and Brogan stood up. 'Right, I'm going to need to make some calls. In the meantime, please make sure you and your connections don't do anything to put yourselves in danger. Oh, and Helen, please, once I've made arrangements, don't go off the grid or do anything provocative.'

Chapter 21

FRIDAY JANUARY 24TH - p.m.

They left their tools and the heavier bags on the visitor centre's table. Sam hoisted a small rucksack onto his shoulders and set off with Angelo and Bill. Initially, they retraced their steps towards the jetty. Then Sam opted for the higher-level path from where they would be able to look down on their RIB as they passed above it. Sam pointed them to the right.

'Up this way. The priory isn't far.'

'And there's a tourist information sign,' said Bill.

'Sorry, guys, I should have mentioned this already. Pete passed a warning on to us that we should not leave the designated paths under any circumstances. The island supports a huge breeding population of puffins. They nest underground, so the earth is one big honeycomb. If you manage to miss the puffins, you'll catch a rabbit burrow. So be careful.'

The three turned off the main track and followed a path up a steep incline. It was little more than four feet wide but was sheltered by head-height stone walls built to either side. The walls appeared designed to protect weary travellers from the weather while channelling them up to the priory. Each was bookended by sturdy pillars of dressed stone, and between the pillars, Sam could see ahead to St Adrian's Priory. His heart sank immediately. The ancient buildings were in a worse state than suggested by the pictures he had tracked down, mostly gone. The roof, beams and walls of the support buildings had been stripped away to foundation level, he guessed to provide building materials for subsequent generations of island inhabitants. The main building had lost its roof and parts of the walls too. It stood forlorn. Scanning about, he spotted the stumps of a couple of columns. The last remains of something grand.

The three men stepped out from the sheltered path onto the tight-cropped green turf that surrounded the buildings. They all stopped abruptly in response to a flurry of movement. Then they relaxed, realising it signed only the exit of a group of rabbits whose daily grazing routine had been rudely disturbed by the unexpected arrivals. The bowling-green-short grass beneath their feet seemed to be emitting crackling sounds. Sam knelt and smiled to himself – snails, rather empty snail shells, thousands of them. Standing again, he began an inspection of the priory grounds. His every step signed by the cracking of shells.

Angelo and Bill sensed Sam's disappointment and hung back while he quickly traversed the priory site. It was all bare and broken stone walls, flagstones and, in places, only foundations. However, the whole priory site was still bounded by a functional stone-wall perimeter. What remained of the priory itself had clearly been gutted hundreds of years before. The shell offered no clues as to what hiding place the Templars intended them to find.

'It's not looking good,' said Bill.

'No, it's not. I think we should push on. Just over the crest of the hill behind the priory, we should drop down into Pilgrim's Haven.'

'It's a narrow island,' said Angelo.

'Certainly is here at the south end. It gets broader in the middle, nearer the lighthouse, but this is the area we need to focus on. In the Middle Ages, the landing at Pilgrim's Haven was an access point for the priory. I'm not sure what we're looking for. Everything leads us to this part of the island, either here at the priory or over there at Pilgrim's Haven. Let's see what the haven offers. We discovered previously that the Templars concealed everything really well but, if you have the clues and can figure them out, things can be found.'

'You have any more clues?' asked Bill.

'Well, I've got the medallions – they seem to represent the island. Three of them form the shape of the island, so there's just one left to understand.'

'Let's go then,' said Bill, heading up the slope past the priory in the direction Sam had indicated. Higher up, set into the boundary wall behind the priory were two further sturdy pillars marking an exit point. They headed for the pillars. Bill passed through first. 'Hello, look what I've found,' he said.

'What's up?' said Sam as he and Angelo caught up.

'Nothing bad. See, it's the air pipe you were talking about.' With his boot, Bill prodded a brown, rusted and flaking pipe. Perhaps eight inches in diameter and suspended about a foot off the ground on a long series of brackets, the pipe stretched away towards the unseen south horn.

'I do not understand this. If the pipe is not needed now, why is it here?' said Angelo.

'Money,' said Bill. 'It's always money. Probably cheaper just to leave the scrap in place.'

'Perhaps, or it might have been left to minimise disturbance to the bird colonies. Maybe a bit of both. Anyway, watch you don't trip over it; we don't need any broken legs right now. Let's keep moving,' said Sam, taking the lead and following the line of the air pipe. A short distance on, he turned, making his way along the crest.

Sam stopped and pointed downwards to where rock outcrops and freestanding boulders lined the drop to a stony shingle beach. The sound of the waves rolling in and out of the inlet carried up the slope to mix with the whistle of the wind and the cries of passing gulls.

'I need to be down there. I want to see what the Templars saw when they came here. Coming?'

He set off cautiously, scrabbling down the steep slope. Bill and Angelo held back to give him a clear passage before following him one after the other.

Reaching the rocky beach, Sam stepped away from the slope towards the water's edge. The rough rocks began to give way to more rounded stones then shingle which crunched as it shifted under foot. Sam looked out to sea and traced the progress of a wave running into the inlet. To either side of him, sheer walls of rock soared above. Behind him, the steep green bank closed the exit. Ahead, the wave continued remorselessly on into the inlet. It seemed to swell, rising then rolling up the shingle in a hissing rush and crash before drawing away only to be replaced by the next in line.

'This is a haven?' said Angelo.

'Get it wrong, and you'll be smashed against the rocky cliffs. Get it right, and you'll come straight in with the waves and end up beached on the shingle. No problem,' said Bill.

Sam had been studying the rock formations. 'I'm not sure what I'm looking for exactly, but I'm certain the clue must be here.' He swung his bag down to the ground, unfastened it and fished inside to pull out a sturdy waterproof storage box.

'What's that you've got?' said Bill.

'The medallions. I've mounted the three that represent the island, and here's the fourth, which ultimately must be linked to either here or the priory, I guess. If it's the priory, we're stuffed. So let's hope it's Pilgrim's Haven.' He carefully flicked open the box and withdrew the fourth medallion.

Bill looked at it and shrugged. 'Over to you, mate. I haven't a clue.'

Concentrating on the engraving on the fourth medallion, Sam tried to find a pattern. Nothing. Yes, the pattern could represent a cove, but it could be any cove. He had to trust that its position on the glass sheet reflected actuality. It was set at the lower end of the other medallions, so placing it here, where they now stood at this end of the island. Surely, it must represent a larger scale plan of this little part of the island.

The fourth medallion's engraving seemed to split into two halves. To one side, an engraving of a three-sided shape, like a coastal opening or cove. Yet its shape bore only a partial resemblance to the shape of Pilgrim's Haven. One side of the cove's cliff walls did just about match, as did the steep slope behind him, but the shape of the other cliff wall showed no likeness to the engraving at all.

He had no idea what the simple Y shape engraved on the other half of the medallion meant. It was clear, bold and, on a map, might have represented two tributary streams flowing together to form a single river. The tail end of one tributary stream reached across the centre line of the medallion to touch the cove engraving, assuming he was correct about that. Could it mark an entrance? He stepped further out onto the wet shingle, seeking a new angle but still finding nothing.

The tide had turned, just on the flood. The water level was near its lowest point, revealing a flat bed of rock off to one side of the inlet that had been submerged and quite invisible when they had inspected the inlet from the boat earlier in the day.

'Watch your step, Sam. There are some sharp rock splinters among the shingle, and they look pretty lethal,' said Bill, following him out.

'Right, thanks,' said Sam, re-focusing, trying to find the pattern that wasn't there. He knew the Templars had used coastal profiling to map the hiding place of their treasury in Crete. Surely, they could have done the same here. It was logical, but he could not find the profile in the engraved medallion.

'Ahh!' said Sam, stumbling then lifting his foot in pain.

'Steady, man,' said Bill, grabbing Sam's arm. 'I told you to watch out.'

They both looked down at the jutting spear point of rock.

'Nasty. Any more weight on your leg, and that would have gone right thorough your boot.'

'It would have. Thanks, Bill.' Sam glared down at the stone then allowed Bill to help him hobble back to the dry pebbles above the high waterline. He sat and pulled his boot round to inspect its sole.

Bill knelt down. 'No problem, it didn't get through the sole. Just going to hurt for a while, that's all.'

'Where did that rock come from? Between the tidelines you'd think the sharp edges would be worn off,' said Angelo.

'I'm thinking there's been a rockfall. This stuff is hard, very hard. It can stand, unflinching, for a thousand years easy, probably more, much more. But eventually, everything falls. A lot of these coastlines are being constantly eroded underwater too. When they go, they go big,' said Bill.

'Yes, atrophy. Eventually, everything breaks down,' said Sam, nodding and stretching out his leg gingerly.

'I think you just stood on a shard from a rockfall. You have rotten weather out here; it's bound to have a wearing effect on the rocks.'

'Could be,' said Sam. Something stirred in his subconscious. 'Could be.'

Bill pointed out across the inlet. 'Look over there. See that mass of black rock that's just been exposed now by the tide? Maybe it's come down recently. In fact, if you look up the side wall, some of that rock face is mighty fresh. I think that whole face of rock has come down. What do you think?'

Sam struggled to rise, and Angelo, ever watchful was there, reaching out to support him.

'Let me have a look,' said Sam. He lifted the fourth medallion again. 'You might have something there, Bill. If we assume that the side of the inlet which suffered a rockfall is this section of the medallion's cove engraving, that would explain why the profile engraved on the medallion is so different to reality – the geography has changed. If you ignore that section, the other parts of the pattern just about match with the other sides of the inlet. Well done, Bill. Well spotted.'

'Anything for a mate. I'm thinking you'll probably be wanting to buy me a bottle of whisky though.'

'A bottle? I'll buy you a barrel!'

'Deal.'

Sam turned his focus back to the medallion. 'There's a problem though.'

'Oh, there goes my whisky.'

'Look here.' The three men leaned in close to the medallion in Sam's hand. 'If I'm interpreting this properly, perhaps the Y represents the layout of a tunnel. In which case, we would have expected a concealed entrance in that rock face where a branch of this Y touches the edge of the cove outline. But the entrance must have fallen into the sea with the rockfall. The entrance is gone.'

'Ah hell,' said Bill.

'Perhaps, this is not so bad,' said Angelo. 'Maybe, the door is gone, but the corridor behind is still there. No? Yes?'

Sam slipped his arm round Angelo's shoulder. 'You might be right, Angelo, you just might. The rock's so hard – what didn't fall is not going to crumble. If there was anything behind, it'll still be there.'

All three focused hard on the inlet's side wall. Sam took binoculars from his bag and began to search in detail. 'It's no good, the light's too poor. Where's summer sun when you need it?'

'What can we do?' said Angelo.

Sam lowered the binoculars and handed them to Bill who, in turn, scanned the fresh cliff face.

'I think we need to get much closer to those rocks. We'll need the RIB for that.'

'By the time the tide's in and she's afloat, there won't be time to bring her round before sunset.'

'Yes, I think we need to go back to pick up our kit, find the cottage and get sorted out for the night. We can take the RIB round to the inlet in the morning.'

***

'There's something odd going on,' said Cassiter, ending the phone call he had just taken and hurrying for the table. He waved away one of Parsol's men who had been using the computer.

'What do you mean odd?' said Parsol as he steered his wheelchair to join him. 'What's happening?'

'My team have got a fix on Cameron and his friends. This morning we saw them sail past the island's bird cameras. Now they have appeared in shot on the island. The live footage has been captured and forwarded to us. Here it comes ...'

Both men waited for the link to open.

'Here it comes. Yes, see, there's Cameron struggling down the slope and his two men following behind,' said Cassiter.

'What's he up to?'

'I'm not sure.'

Sam's image grew large on the screen as the camera zoomed in.

'What's he looking at? I need to know.' Parsol's hand slapped down on the table edge. 'I need to know!'

'It seems they're surveying something … the cliff face?' said Cassiter. 'I'll have them use the cameras to try and see what he was looking at or for.'

Chapter 22

SATURDAY JANUARY 25TH - a.m.

They were up well before dawn. Bottled gas to the cottage stove had provided the power for Bill to rustle up porridge and tea for breakfast. As the sun broke over the island, they left the key in the front door of the little terraced cottage and headed back down the hill towards the visitor centre.

'Bill, we'll put our bags in the RIB now, and Angelo and I will walk across the island to the haven if you can take the RIB round. I'd like to have a good look at Pilgrim's Haven from the ridge above before we start. We'll meet you down on the shingle.'

'No problem, boss. I'll get away now. See you both over there. Hey, this busying about is just like old times. It's great.'

'Let's hope it's not too much like old times,' said Sam. 'I recall a couple of quite dodgy moments.'

'Yes, but we got through okay, didn't we?'

They carried the kit down to the jetty where the RIB bobbed gently against its lines. Bill immediately got the engine running, and Sam and

Angelo set off back across the island to Pilgrim's Haven.

***

Bigger than many coastal cargo ships, Parsol's well-appointed luxury yacht was holding its position in the Firth of Forth a little distance off Dunbar. It was waiting for the arrival of an important passenger. Here, the estuary had already widened so much that the boat could happily stand off the town all day without disrupting the steady flow of shipping in and out of the various port destinations along the Forth. Equally important, it was beyond the attention of the Forth Ports' authorities whose writ ended a few miles further up the coast near North Berwick.

***

'Any news?' said Grace as she settled into the chair next to Helen.

'Nothing, but we agreed no phone calls, just in case Cassiter's lot can listen in somehow. He'll only call in an emergency.'

'So, no news really is good news.'

Helen smiled at Grace and reached out her hand.

Grace took it and squeezed. 'It'll work out for sure.'

'Well, I pray it does. I should be there with him.'

'You'd only be a hindrance with that leg. Right now, he's better able to work out there without you.'

'I know, but I still want to be there. Sam shouldn't be doing this alone.'

'He's got Angelo with him and his mystery friend Bill. He's not alone.'

'But they're not me.'

'Okay, what do you want to do?'

'Sam reckoned it would take about thirty-six hours to follow the clues and reach a conclusion or not. I'd like to go down to North Berwick and wait for him there. His friend, Pete Summers, said I could wait at his home for the RIB's return, if I wanted, but I'm not sure I can drive that distance yet.'

'I'm not sure you can drive at all yet. I'll take you. When do you want to go?'

'I guess we could go down this evening. I'll call Pete and confirm a plan.'

***

In the open water beyond the inlet, Bill lined the RIB up for a run-in on Pilgrim's Haven and its sheltered beach. He held the RIB's position for a few moments, weighing up his options before moving ahead. Constantly scanning the sea around him and checking ahead to the shingle, he powered in then cut down his speed and prepared to synchronise his approach with the regular run of the waves. He held position a dozen yards off the shoreline and shouted across to Sam and Angelo who were standing ready to join him on the RIB.

'I'll come in closer on the next wave, but I don't want to beach the RIB in case it comes down on some more of those shards like you stood on yesterday.'

'Looks like we're getting wet feet then,' said Sam to Angelo.

The RIB nosed in behind a beaching wave, and they both stepped forwards to meet it.

'Jump on quick!' called Bill.

Sam and Angelo scrambled over the bow, even as Bill had the RIB powering hard astern.

'Well, that cleared the cobwebs away,' said Sam, working his way along the RIB's deck towards Bill.

'Welcome aboard,' said Bill. 'I'm thinking you're both going to need to change your clothes and footwear.'

'Too right we will. It's suddenly bitterly cold.' Sam gave a shiver. He eyed Bill. 'I see you're dressed for the part though.'

'I've learnt that whenever somebody tells me I've got a job *on* the water, it'll eventually mean me being *in* the water.' Bill's clothes and boots were in a plastic bag on deck, while he presented proud and practical in his wetsuit.

'Good thinking. I won't get changed yet, just in case. Best we suffer a little while longer.'

'You're going to get wet again?'

'Probably. Let's go over and check out this cliff face.' He turned his attention to Angelo. 'We'll have to stay wet a little longer, I'm afraid.'

Angelo gave a resigned nod.

Bill kept the RIB running astern before executing a tight turn to bring them face-to-face with the inlet's sheer rock wall. He pointed straight ahead at the mass of black rock that was now just breaking above the water's surface between them and the cliff. 'That lot was not on the chart you showed me yesterday. There should have been a straight drop from the cliff to the seabed. Those rocks can only have come from one place – the cliff face.'

'Can you take us a little further round, Bill? I want to get a better look at the cliff face above.'

'No problem. When do you think the cliff face fell?' Bill began carefully edging the RIB round the flat bed of rock that filled the sea beneath the cliff face where once there had been clear water to navigate.

'No idea. Could have been five years ago, maybe just five days. The cliffs on the other side of the inlet are covered in guano. This side isn't. Mind you, there's a bit of an overhang, so birds can't roost so easily. It could be the birds have never been able to mess up over here. On the other hand ...' Sam fell quiet, concentrating on the cliff face while Bill manoeuvred the RIB. 'Right, Bill. Try to hold your position here for a moment will you?'

Sam was intently scanning the rock face. He frequently raised his binoculars to look at half-promising features, trying to work out what the implications of any rockfall were and, if it were the case, how the Templar concealment would appear now.

'What are you looking for?' said Angelo.

'Last year in Crete, we found the Templars were able to take an ancient tunnel system and modify it, so they could load their secrets in unnoticed, concealing the entrance when they were done. I'm thinking there would be no reason for them to change a winning plan. Problem is, if this is the right place, the tunnel entrance has dropped down into the sea.'

Sam returned his focus to the rock face. 'Can you head back to where we started please?'

As the RIB manoeuvred round, he kept his gaze locked on the cliff face. He thought about the shape of the island as formed by the three medallions; he considered the discreet cross on the medallion that he now believed should have corresponded to this side of the inlet and its rock face. The entrance would have been there – once.

'I can't get any closer, or we'll run into that bed of fallen rock. In fact, I'm thinking with the tide ebbing, give it another half-hour, and you'll be able to stand on it. It's formed a platform.'

Sam looked down at the water. 'I see what you mean.' The rock face appeared to have come down in great blocks that had settled on the bottom and now rested together, shoulder to shoulder – immovable objects that partially filled one side of the inlet, creating something of a tidal flat.

He turned his attention back to the cliff just as a screeching gull flew between them and the rock face. He caught his breath. There it was, just for a moment, then gone again. He stared hard, keeping his focus on the spot. Slowly, slowly, it reappeared. Sam raised his hand pointing at the cliff. 'There! Look. Right there.'

The flashing white distraction of the passing gull had brought a contrast to his view, highlighting a black hole in black stone, all cast in shadow from the overhang. The tunnel. It was there, open and exposed to the elements. No clues to interpret, no puzzle to solve. A black hole in a black wall, just waiting for them.

'I see it,' said Bill.

Angelo grinned and wrapped an arm round Sam's shoulders.

'Mark that spot, Bill! I need to get up there.'

'Got it. This won't be easy, Sam. That hole is a good fifteen feet above the water, and the tide's on the ebb still.'

'Could we wait for high tide; float underneath it?'

'I wouldn't fancy it. That bed of rock could rip the RIB to bits if the waves get up. Hell, even in calm waters, it would be a risk.'

'Okay. Any suggestions?'

'What kit have we got?'

'Ropes, torches, water, emergency rations, sacking, some tools — spades, hammer, a crowbar, trowels and so on.'

'Trowels? What use are they?'

'Bill, I'm an archaeologist. Of course I've brought trowels.'

'Let me see the rope you've got,' said Bill.

Sam opened one of the kit bags and pulled out a sturdy rope.

'Too thick. Anything slimmer, lighter?'

'There's this one,' said Sam. He pulled out a slender rope.

'That might do, and we could use that trowel of yours too. You were always a good climber, Sam. I'm thinking I might have got a bit too heavy for this one. Look, up above the tunnel mouth, there are a few jaggy outcrops. If we get onto the rocks when they're dry and weight the thin line with your trowel, we might be able to throw it up and over the outcrop. Catch the line on its way down, and you can climb up it to the entrance.'

Sam laughed. 'How come it's me doing the climbing?'

'You're lighter than I am and fitter. Whoever goes up needs to be quick, I doubt that line will hold for long.'

With a plan at last, they floated off the bed of fallen rock for a little while as the sea level dropped enough so the waves did not break across the whole surface.

'Come on then, let's go,' said Sam.

Bill cautiously edged the RIB in towards the rock bed while Sam leant over the bow and talked him in. 'You're clear to go right alongside the edge of the rock bed. It simply drops away sheer to the bottom. I'm telling you, boys, these are big blocks of stone.'

Just as the bow of the RIB was about to bump up against the rock, Sam lowered a fender over the side. It squeezed and emitted a squeal of tortured rubber when it absorbed the shock.

'Everyone out, quick,' shouted Bill, struggling to keep the RIB in position. Sam jumped onto the wet rock surface, steadied himself and turned to take the bags from Angelo who then followed him onto the rock.

Bill pulled away, taking the RIB out to the middle of the inlet. Once happy with the position, he threw the anchor overboard. He waited a little while to be sure the anchor was holding then pulled on flippers, a mask and snorkel. Without any splash, he slipped over the side. Sam and Angelo watched Bill disappear from view. They waited anxiously for him to resurface.

Beneath the waves, Bill worked his flippers, powering down to check how the anchor was set in the seabed. Content, he returned to the surface and swam to the rocks, where Sam and Angelo pulled him up and out of the water.

After Bill had collected himself, Sam led them all across the rocks to the point immediately beneath the tunnel mouth.

Trowel tied to the thin line, Sam tried several times to heave it up over the outcrop above the tunnel. On each occasion, he got closer but never quite there. Eventually, with a despairing lunge, he launched the trowel and its trail of line. It flew up and over the outcrop and dangled from the other side.

Sam fed more of the line out, jerking and shaking it to encourage its movement over the outcrop, where, gradually, the weight of the trowel began to take over and pull down, descending towards the waiting men.

Removing the trowel, Sam tied both ends of the line together, doubling its thickness.

'Are you sure you fancy this?' said Bill.

'Got to be done, and I'm the lightest. It has to be me.'

'Okay, I know. But look, Angelo and I will stand together, form a frame. Climb on our shoulders, and that will give you a head start. If that rope holds your weight for more than a minute, you will be very lucky. You want to avoid a nasty fall onto these rocks.'

'Agreed, and thanks for the pep talk, Bill. Now let's get on with it, shall we?'

Angelo and Bill braced themselves as Sam clambered up onto their shoulders, a torch in one pocket and the shorter, thicker rope tied to his waistband. He took the strain on the dangling line, gradually applying more and more weight until his boots left the shoulders of his supporters and he was hanging free. He started to swing in the breeze. Bill grabbed the trailing end, holding it steady while Sam began to climb.

'Quick as you can, man, quick as you can!' said Bill, straining to keep the slender line steady. Angelo, calm, prepared, stood arms outstretched, gazing up towards Sam. He was ready to break the fall if it came.

Sam moved steadily up the line, hand over hand, a constant pull, never jerking. Expecting the line to snap or cut on the jagged rock supporting it above at any moment, he finally made it to the lip of the tunnel mouth. Feeling the stress building in the rope, he instinctively reached out a hand and found the tunnel's edge just as the line snapped. The broken ends dropped from above, trailing around him as he swung by one hand from the tunnel's lip.

He gripped his fingertips against the hard stone, determined it wasn't all going to end here, then swung his dangling hand up, managing to get a second hand holding on to the lip. His shoulder and arm muscles were strained to the limit from the effort it took to pull himself up, scramble over the lip and roll into the tunnel. He lay for a minute on his back, breathing deeply, happy to be alive.

Then he crawled back to the edge and looked down. Bill and Angelo were looking up. Their faces broke into broad grins, and all three cheered, punching the air. 'You've still got what it takes, Sam Cameron!' Bill shouted.

Sam took a moment to inspect the tunnel mouth. He caught his breath. This was weird. Not man-made at all. He flashed his torch down the tunnel, flicking the beam across the floor, the walls and the roof. The stone was rough, not smooth, but nonetheless quite constant, forming a tunnel about eight feet in height and twelve feet in width. The tunnel swept down and away beyond the reach of his beam. Amazed, he took an involuntary step forwards. This was an entirely natural construct. He'd been in such phenomena before, in America and Iceland, but he couldn't recall hearing of one in the UK. A lava tube. He flicked off his torch and turned back towards the daylight.

'Let's get the bags up first,' shouted Sam, waving the end of the stout rope he had brought up with him. He wrapped it around his waist as a precaution and began hauling up the bags.

With their kit stacked behind him in the tunnel, he took a moment to tie some foothold knots in the rope and lowered it again. Fixing it tightly around his arms and hands, he backed a little way into the tunnel and braced himself. 'Okay, first man, come on up.'

***

Cassiter looked intently at the computer screen. The camera feed from Pilgrim's Haven could not have been clearer. Things were working out perfectly. Cameron and his team had shown the way, now he could move in, take over, gather what Parsol wanted and commence exacting revenge on Cameron and the churchwoman. At last.

'I want you to take us there, now,' he said.

The captain had been watching the screen too. 'No problem, sir. I'll have you there in no time.'

Cassiter put in a call to Parsol. Things were moving at last. He had Cameron in his sights.

Chapter 23

SATURDAY JANUARY 25TH - p.m.

Sam, Angelo and Bill sat together, just inside the mouth of the tunnel. Bill had peeled off his wetsuit and all three had towelled dry. They were now dressed in fresh clothes, laughing and passing round the whisky flask that Bill had produced.

'That's the first obstacle crossed. Now, Sam, tell me what we're expecting to find at the end of this tunnel,' said Bill.

'I'm not sure. For all we know, somebody else already spotted the opening and found whatever's meant to be in there.'

'You think?' said Bill.

'I don't think so. We knew to look and still only saw it by luck,' said Angelo.

'I hope you're right,' said Sam. He produced the fourth medallion and looked again. He now knew for certain the engraved lines to one side of the medallion represented the inlet. He knew also that the tunnel mouth should have emerged at a place which, following the rockfall, no longer existed.

Now he knew why the line leading away from the engraving of the cliff face ran so straight – it represented the straight run of a lava tunnel.

From the lines engraved on the medallion, it was clear that the tunnel they now stood in would eventually join with another. They were in one branch of a Y-shaped tunnel complex. And halfway up the other short branch, another cross was marked. Sam guessed that *this* was their goal. The stem from which the two branches sprouted seemed to only be there for positional context.

It was an easy to follow plan. Walk along their branch to the Y-junction, ignore the stem, turn and walk back along the other branch. 'I don't know what we'll find ahead, but there's only one way to find out.'

'Let's get going then,' said Bill, and they all stood.

Angelo hesitated, glancing towards the daylight.

'Are you alright with tunnels?' said Sam.

'Yes. Yes, of course. But when we come back, how will the last man get down?'

They all peered over the lip to the now dry rock below.

'Good question,' said Bill. 'How?'

'I don't know yet. Let's worry about it later. Come on, time to go.'

They coiled the rope and stowed it back among their kit. Each hefted a load on their shoulders and they set off down the tunnel. Sam led, his torch playing across the rock floor. Immediately behind him, Bill and Angelo kept their beams focused on the walls and roof to ensure any obstacles were spotted in good time. There were none. The tunnel continued in a straight, though steadily descending, line beneath the island.

'What made this, Sam?' said Angelo.

'Looks like it's been burnt through by some giant laser,' said Bill.

'You're not a million miles from the truth there,' said Sam.

'What do you mean?'

'I believe this is what's known as a lava tunnel.' He stretched out and slapped the wall. 'All this is volcanic rock. Sometime in the past, a long, long time ago, there was a lot of volcanic activity in this area. Quite a few of the islands on the Forth trace their origins back to that. Now they're all worn down to what we see today.'

'So where's my laser?'

'Heat, not laser. Basically, a lava tunnel can form when a crust of rock cools over the flowing lava, enclosing it like an underground river. Eventually, when the lava flow stops, the molten lava in the tube drains back down, leaving a hollowed out space behind it called a lava tunnel. The primal forces of nature could and did construct things that are still well beyond the capacities of modern man.'

They walked on in silence for only a couple more minutes, following the tunnel on its downwards incline.

'Stop! The tunnel junction is just ahead. This might be tricky.'

'What's up?' said Bill as Sam edged cautiously forwards.

'We're in one branch of a Y-shaped tunnel and need to turn into the other branch. But the stem of the Y drops away quite steeply. I wouldn't fancy tumbling down that slope. In fact, let's rope ourselves together and get round one at a time. One long stretch step will get you round into the other branch. If anyone does lose their footing, we'll have them securely tied in.'

Bill and Angelo joined Sam and studied the junction. 'Yep, I agree. We should make that turn without any problem, but no harm in taking precautions. What do you say? Same as before? One man moves, swing the kit after him then the others follow.'

'That'll work.'

Bill shone his torch down into the Y's stem and whistled. 'I tell you what, Sam, you say, slope; I say, sheer drop.'

'Well, let's be careful.'

The three men roped up. Sam led and made it round safely. The kit was swung round then Angelo followed. Finally, Bill came round and they were all together again.

'Looks like it's up this time,' said Sam, flashing his torch along the tunnel, the beam tracing a rising floor level. It was narrower than the branch they had just left, the roof slightly lower. 'Single file for you two, behind me. Watch your heads too!'

***

Cassiter pointed a finger at the display screen. 'Okay, captain. You've seen where they went and how they got up to that tunnel mouth. I need you to put me and my team there with the right equipment to do the job.'

The captain was silent for a long moment before turning to look Cassiter in the eye. 'The forecast has turned again; there is bad weather on the way.'

Cassiter tapped the screen and looked dispassionately at the captain. 'I told you what I needed.'

Suddenly unnerved, the captain glanced away. 'We can do this. I'll get everything organised now.' He looked at Cassiter's stick. 'I think we'll need to rig some sort of hoist for you. Forgive me, sir, but I doubt you'll manage even a rope ladder.'

'Do as you think fit. I've put this task on your shoulders. But get it right.'

The captain turned away, unsettled by the emptiness in Cassiter's eyes and the unspoken threat in his words. He reached for the intercom and called for his first officer.

***

After about two hundred paces, Sam had paused his group and referred again to the medallion, confirming that its design work included a tiny

---

Templar cross, marked halfway along the engraved line that represented the branch tunnel they were following. He knew in his heart what the mark signified and was excited to see what lay ahead. 'There'll be something up ahead. I want you both to keep a look out for any kind of anomaly. We've dealt with Templar concealment before, and they have always been incredibly ingenious. I don't know how far ahead it will be; there is no scale guide. Just be alert, otherwise we'll overshoot.'

They resumed their upward march at a slow pace all eyes searching for something unknown.

'Hello, what's this?' said Sam, coming to a halt. To the right was an opening, apparently as natural as the tunnel itself. He shone his torch into the space. It was another tunnel branch, much narrower, less than four feet across and six feet high. An arm's length into the branch tunnel, his torch beam stopped. Sam whistled.

'Somebody's been busy; I don't know how they got that here,' said Bill.

'Hard work for sure. Thing is, can we get past it?' said Sam. He stepped forwards and looked closely. His hand traced across a heavy iron door that was set into an iron frame, sealing the branch tunnel completely. The door was further reinforced with crossbars.

'No problem. If we had some explosives, I'd get it down in a minute,' said Bill.

'Thankfully, we haven't,' said Sam, continuing his inspection. He couldn't see any hinges; they must be set behind the equally heavy iron doorframe. 'It must hinge inwards. It's got bolts and padlocks, and that main lock is the size of a Christmas cake. Short of Bill's explosives, any suggestions on how we open it? In fact, let's get some proper light on this now.'

Angelo rummaged in one of the bags and pulled out two lantern

282

torches. He positioned one in the tunnel, the other close against the base of the iron door. He straightened up and looked more closely at the door and frame. 'We have a doorframe like this in the original part of our church in Sardinia. I have never seen the door for it; it's been missing for as long as I know. But the frame is the same as this. Thick iron and bolted to the walls. You will never move the frame.'

'Okay, that's useful. Thanks, Angelo. But I don't do, never. Why was the door missing in your church? Where did it lead?' said Sam.

'I don't know where the door went; I've never seen it. Inside was an empty room, a storeroom. I always thought, maybe it was once a strong room. Xavier would know.'

'Yes, but we will never get a phone signal through all this rock. Can you remember where the hinges were?'

'I have seen the hinge points in the frame many times. There were three hinges. I remember, because they were not how we place them today. One was at the middle but that was small. The other two were very near the top and bottom and much longer hinges, they each reached almost to the middle hinge.'

'So, pretty well the whole door is supported by the hinges. No weak spot.'

Angelo gave a shrug and made a little tutting sound. 'No weak spot.'

Sam returned his attention to the door, tracing his hand across its surface. He trailed it up, following the line where the door bedded against the thick frame. Then he traced it across the top and down the other side.

'I hate to say this, it's against every rule in the archaeology book, but we need to get through this door today, and it seems to me only violence will do the job.'

'I'm all for a bit of violence, Sam, but that thing's solid. You heard, Angelo. Even the frame will be bolted solidly to the walls. We don't have the kit to break through,' said Bill.

'Maybe, maybe not. Look, here … see the metal of the door? See how it is pressing out against the doorframe. That's the metal thickening as it rusts. Even the doorframe has expanded outwards. This iron door's been standing in a tunnel for seven hundred years. The conditions are perfect for rust. The door and frame will have effectively bonded into one solid piece of iron.'

'But that is no good for us,' said Angelo.

'Don't you believe it,' said Bill, scrabbling in the kit bags. 'Ever seen a hulk? An old ship, abandoned, its metal left unpainted, unprotected from the sea and weather?'

Angelo shook his head.

'Well, stand back; I'll show you what happens.' Bill approached the door with a crowbar and hammer. He looked to Sam. 'Can I?'

Sam stepped back. 'Okay. But, Bill, slowly. We don't know what's behind the door.'

With a throaty chuckle, Bill moved into the branch tunnel's mouth. He looked closely at the door and selected a point close to the frame, a foot or so above the middle line of the door. Placing the short-toothed end of the crowbar against it, he tapped the door lightly with the hammer, getting his eye and hand in. He turned to look at Sam, received a nod of assent, and hammered hard on the bar. Nothing happened. He hit again and a third time.

On the fourth stroke, the teeth of the crowbar punched through the iron rust and kept going as Bill hit it again. A further blow, and the bar was through the door.

'Perfect, the whole thing's corroded. It's just a barrier of rust. There's going to be a bit of hard work, but we can cold chisel our way through in no time.' Bill began to work the crowbar free to repeat the process.

Sam, Bill and Angelo took turns attacking the rust sheet. Up, across, down, back and up again. Bit by bit, they cut through the door as though it were the lid of a giant tin can. Sam called a halt when they were left with only a foot-long strip of uncut door beside the middle hinge. He tried to peek through the cut gap, but it was too narrow to allow any sort of view.

The three men looked at one another – Bill, pleased he had been able to help out his old friend and comrade, Angelo, wishing his mentor Xavier could be there, and Sam, desperately hoping that whatever was on the other side of the door would bring an end to Cassiter's mad run of killings, assaults and schemes. Please, let this be the endgame.

Sam rested a hand on the door, level with, but on the far side from, the uncut section. He applied a little weight. Nothing happened.

'Put your back into it, Sam. Push!' said Bill.

Sam pushed. Still, nothing happened. From behind him, Bill and Angelo leant forwards, each placing hands on the door, adding their weight. With a crinkling sound, the section of uncut rust bent a fraction.

'It's going,' said Bill. 'It's going now!'

They pressed harder, and the uncut section of the rust door began to move slowly, creasing then folding back along its remaining uncut length like a tin can's lid being levered open.

As the door continued its opening swing, small shafts of light from the lantern torches picked out glimpses of the interior, any more of a view was constantly blocked by the moving bodies of the three men.

With the door finally folded back on itself, Sam called out. 'Okay, guys; now let's be careful not to touch this door again. It seems to be holding, but rust is quite weak. Don't bump against the door, or it may well come down on you.'

Sam switched on his little torch and swung the beam through the doorway. He flicked it all around, and from every direction, lights flickered back at him.

'What's going on?' said Bill.

Crossing himself, Angelo intoned a prayer.

'Aladdin's cave,' said Sam. Any guilt he had felt over brutalising the iron door melted away in the dazzling rainbow reflections that responded to his torch beam. 'Come on, let's check this out.'

Sam carefully stepped over the doorframe's rough-cut and rusty bottom edge. Bill and Angelo followed, each bringing a lantern torch that threw light up and around the chamber, a circular space, perhaps thirty feet across. Its walls rose dome-like towards a central point, rough, yet uniform in appearance, just like the tunnel outside.

It's a lava cave,' said Sam.

'Great, only an archaeologist could think about the structure at a moment like this. What have we found, Sam?' said Bill.

Sam looked around the room. The floor of the chamber was lined with rows of glittering piles. He stooped and looked at the nearest one. A neat heap of shimmering light glinted before him. There were gold and silver necklaces of linked gem chains. Yellow, red and green stones flashed and blacked in the changing light only to flash again. Each pile was corralled by a rusty collection of rectangular iron strips – iron strongbox bindings whose wood had vanished, disintegrated over many centuries of exposure to the moist, enclosed, subterranean environment.

He moved on along the row of more neat piles: bejewelled rings, signet rings, broaches, tiaras, pearls and pendants. The next row had more piles of similar bounty. The third row of piles had a different mix. Here were ornately worked gold and silver beakers and goblets, trays and platters, the gold colours still clear and full of lustre, the silvers darkened with tarnish, waiting patiently for a kind hand to burnish them back into life. There were knives, spoons and trinket boxes. In the rows beyond were fabulous ornaments of ships, birds and animals, all mingled with statuettes of warriors and naked girls, of gods and terrors. Sam struggled to take it all in.

'How much is this lot worth?' said Bill in a hushed tone that had previously only ever been heard during covert actions with the SBS. 'I don't believe it, Sam. You could buy the world with this lot.'

Angelo had gravitated towards the rows of crucifixes and religious iconography and was busy touching and blessing. Sam could see tears in the priest's eyes as he knelt and lifted items, kissed them and blessed them again.

Forcing himself to detach from the minutia of every discovery, Sam tried to focus on the larger picture. What had they really found here? He looked beyond Angelo to see ornately worked daggers and swords, all gold and silver. These were definitely weapons for the ceremonial, not the fight. They seemed to come from a number of cultures and eras: Greek, Roman, Persian, North African, European, Indian, pre-Christian, Christian, Islamic.

There were extravagantly decorated arrowheads and spear points, the heads too exquisitely worked ever to warrant firing and their shafts long turned to dust. A pair of fabulous gold-headed spears stood proud against the wall, their silver shafts making them impossibly heavy for throwing but perfect for royal display.

Angelo remained on his knees; Bill wandered back and forth, just enjoying the moment. For all the excitement, Sam was puzzled. Yes, this represented a hundred and more kings' ransoms. But he could not see any one thing that might be the motivation for all the fanaticism and cruelty. What did Cassiter and the others really want? Could it just be jewels? Or was there something more here? He took the time to review the cave and its contents properly, slowly turning a full circle.

Beyond the pair of silver-shafted spears, the glittering spoils faded slightly. In this area was a copper plinth, dull-greened over time. It rose around six inches from the floor of the cave, was three feet wide and about eight feet long. Sam had no idea what its original purpose would have been. It was big and heavy, and once, somewhere, must have fulfilled an important function. Perhaps it was an altar base, or maybe it had had some ceremonial role.

In any other context, such an artefact would have been the centrepiece of a discovery, the peak of many an archaeologist's career. Here, it was swamped by the richness of its surroundings. Still, Sam wondered. Its plainness seemed to make it special. Lonely, placed in isolation at the centre of the great plinth was a small piece of gold, flat and only half the size of a playing card.

He stooped to pick it up, looked at the engraving. It featured the Templar seal of two Templar knights on a single horse. Here, they rode away from the sunrise and towards what may have been a tree or plant topped with a few dotted holes, beneath the Templar seal was engraved a ship carrying a box. He knew he'd seen it elsewhere recently and quite innocently slipped it into his pocket for later consideration.

Immediately beyond the low plinth, he noticed another. Again, greened copper, but with a much smaller footprint than the first and taller, like a nightstand. Resting on the top was a small gold casket. Instinctively, he moved towards it and lifted the lid.

'What have you got there?' said Bill, momentarily pulling his attention away from a golden throwing knife, part of a duo, that he was balancing in his palm.

'I'm not sure,' said Sam. 'I'm really not sure.'

Angelo joined Sam, and his reading of the artefact within the casket was altogether more definite. With a gasp, Angelo reached out his hand, then stopped himself, unsure he was worthy. He knelt, rested his hands on the edge of the plinth and began to pray with a fervour that drew Bill over to the plinth.

'It's a metal cup, not even gold, look at everything around us. What's the big fuss over this simple thing?'

'It's blackened silver. I think Angelo believes it to be the Grail.'

'Nah, he's got that wrong. I saw a documentary on the Grail. Jesus and the disciples weren't rich. They only had cheap drinking beakers. Pottery and the like. That can't be the Grail.'

'That's certainly the modern thinking. But there are counter views,' said Sam.

'Huh?'

'Yes, the disciples were poor, rejected personal wealth, extolling the virtues of giving away wealth—'

'There you are then.'

'Well, not quite. Sure, Jesus is reputed to have saved the poor people. But he also cured and saved merchants and administrators, and they weren't so poor. Jesus, his disciples and their followers needed financial support to feed and sustain them on their travels. That had to come from grateful gift-givers. And wealth was not just coin, it was found in a whole range of artefacts, including, I guess, silver chalices.'

Bill nodded, unimpressed, while Angelo reached out a hand to grip Sam's, seeking some comfort, some assurance he was not dreaming.

'Wouldn't they need to have sold it for food?'

'Probably, I imagine they would have sold everything, eventually. But the Last Supper was a big set-piece meal. Why wouldn't you use your best silver? Of course you would, even if it was only passing through your hands for a few days.'

Angelo rose to his feet. Still gripping Sam's hand, he reached out his free hand to gingerly touch the Grail.

The sound of a cocking weapon reached them from the doorway behind.

'Mr Cameron, hands up, please. Then do not move a muscle, or you are all dead. It does seem as though this is becoming something of a habit,' said Cassiter, carefully stepping through the doorway. Four guards followed him. A fifth remained at the door.

Sheltered by Angelo's body, Sam's hand discreetly closed the gold casket and all three men turned as one, raising their hands in the face of an array of pointing weapons.

Cassiter waved two men forwards. 'Cable tie their hands. Then we can see exactly what they've found for us.'

CHAPTER 24

SATURDAY JANUARY 25TH - evening

Their evening meal finished, Grace had worked her way round the manse. The ground floor windows and kitchen door were all locked and bolted. She had just done the rear bedrooms and was securing the last of the upstairs windows. In a little while, they would be setting off for North Berwick.

'I'm not happy about this,' said Price, standing in the hall. She had taken first watch as an overtime shift. After a long day, she had not planned to include a journey down the coast to North Berwick. Nor could she allow Helen to go without her – DI Brogan would never forgive her.

'I just think we need to be there when Sam gets back,' said Helen.

'I can understand that. But really, wouldn't it be easier just to let him come here? You still haven't told me why he went to the May. What exactly is going on? What's he up to?'

The hallway was thronged. Xavier and Francis stood to either side of Helen, Elaine behind, all facing off to DS Price.

'Look, based on what's happened to you recently, I'm going to have to call in a second escort vehicle. It's Saturday evening. That's going to put a huge pressure on staffing. Why not wait until Sunday morning? Things are always quieter then.'

'There's something going on outside!' Grace's voice came down the stairs. A moment later, her running feet crossed the upstairs landing, and she appeared at the top of the stairs. 'Something's happening.' She started down the stairs.

'What is it? What did you see?' said Price.

'A dark van just parked out front, behind the garden wall, right beside the driveway entrance. I saw men getting out.'

'Stay calm, that doesn't mean there's a problem. It could be perfectly innocent. I'll go out and—'

The sound of splintering glass reached them from the study. More came from the kitchen. A percussive detonation in the study rattled its door. The sound of another blast came from the kitchen.

'Stun grenades,' shouted Price. As the explosive sounds faded, more breaking glass could be heard then a faint hissing sound. 'Gas, we need to get away. Is there another exit?' She looked about, drew her telescopic baton and moved close to Helen. 'Whatever happens, stay close to me. They'll need to get through me to get to you.'

'There is a way out,' said Helen.

'Which way?' said Price, pulling out her radio and calling in her distress alert.

Grace reached the bottom of the stairs. 'This way, follow me,' she said, brushing past them and hurrying towards the rear of the hallway where she pushed open the access door to the basement stairs. 'This way.'

The sound of boots landing on the study floor was echoed by a similar sound from the kitchen. Price looked towards Grace. 'The basement will be a deathtrap.'

'No, Grace is right; there is a way,' said Helen.

With a doubtful sigh, Price nodded. 'Okay, let's go.'

Elaine had already shepherded Xavier and Francis to the doorway.

Grace guided them through. She smiled bravely at her mother. 'You get them down, Mum. I'll help Helen.'

'No, you go. You can open the passage doorway easily; it's hard for me now with my damaged hand.'

Grace hesitated for just a moment, worry for her mother writ across her face.

'Just go,' ordered Elaine. 'Hurry now. Get the passage open.' She pushed her daughter towards the steps.

'I'll be back to help as soon as I've opened the passage,' said Grace as she turned and hurried down the steps past Xavier and Francis. Reaching the far end of the basement passageway, she stretched out her arms and legs, forming a saltire shape with her body, seeking out the concealed trigger points that would open the hidden doorway into the tunnel that linked the manse and St Bernard's church.

Elaine took the key from the door and entered it into the stair side of the lock just as Helen hobbled through the doorway followed by Price.

'Get her down the stairs, I've got this,' said Price, putting her hand on the door's edge.

'No, Elaine, you see to Francis and Xavier, I'll manage down myself,' said Helen, pushing Elaine towards the steps. Elaine hurried down to help the older men.

To the sound of boots running down the hall, DS Price slammed the door shut and turned the key. She pressed her shoulder to the door and braced herself. 'Hurry! I really hope there's an exit down there, or we're sunk.'

A hard kick against the door turned her attention back towards the attackers.

'Stand back. I'm a police officer. Stand back!'

There was a moment's silence; she heard a muttering then a laugh. The boot returned, and the door reverberated against her shoulder. Helen leant her shoulder against the door in support.

Grace appeared at the foot of the steps. 'Come on you two, we're all set.'

'I can't leave the door, or it'll cave. Go now, Helen, make sure the others are away.'

Helen shook her head and grimaced as a reverberation from the door pained her wounded leg.

'What are you doing? Jesus Christ, get away or we're both done,' hissed Price, her back now fully braced against the door while the attackers continued to beat on it.

Reaching beyond the sergeant, into the narrow space behind the door, Helen grabbed two brooms from a cleaning alcove set into the wall.

'You absolute beauty,' said Price, wincing as two boots hit the door at the same time.

Helen wedged the broom handles between the door and wall and gave Price a slightly manic grin. 'I'm going to put the lights out then go down. There'll still be enough light coming from the exit at the end of the basement passageway for you to see. Follow me down; we'll make it. Don't stop for anything, just run for the end of the passageway. When you get there, Grace will close it; then we'll be safe.'

'Just like that,' said Price, though she did feel that the brooms were now taking most of the pressure.

'Just like that. Welcome to our world! Now, time to go.' Helen hobbled down the steps and disappeared from view into the basement corridor as Price readied herself to follow. The brooms were holding the door but the assailants must have felt a change in the resistance. Sensing something was afoot, the team leader fired a shot at the door just as Price moved away from it. The bullet passed through the wood panelling and entered her shoulder, throwing her off balance against the wall. She cried out in pain then struggled down the steps while the attackers redoubled their efforts.

Just when Helen reached the far end of the passageway, there was a cracking sound from the stairway above – the door was in. Elaine caught her as she stumbled through the secret entrance. Grace stood poised, ready to activate the closing mechanism. The moment Price followed Helen through the passage entrance, the secret access door slid firmly closed.

Inside the tunnel, everyone stood still for a moment, safe but stunned. Price took in her surroundings, looking around the long, stone-built tunnel, dry with an even flagstoned floor and steady electric lighting.

The first of the attackers was halfway down the stairway when the light in the passageway below cut off with the closing of the secret door.

'Lights! Lights!' he shouted. Somebody at the top of the stairs found the switch and suddenly everything was brightly lit again. The team swept the basement and found nothing.

Puzzled, the team leader headed off to report to Eugene Jr who was waiting in the vehicle outside. The team leader paused in the drive; their vehicle was gone.

'Armed police! Armed police! Put your weapon down and lie flat on the ground.'

'Armed police! Put down your weapon, now!'

The team leader threw his pistol onto the ground and knelt, before slumping forwards, prostrate.

Boots crunched on the snow-coated gravel as armed police squads hurried for the front door.

Even as Brogan knelt to demand information from the now cuffed team leader, he could hear more police warning shouts coming from the manse.

'Where's my sergeant? Do you have Helen Johnson in there? Where are they?'

The team leader was quite stunned by the rapid turn of events. 'They vanished, just vanished.'

Brogan gripped the man's collar and jerked. 'Don't play me for the fool. We heard the distress call. They were here. What have you done with them?'

A shout of 'all clear' reached him from inside the house. Brogan stood and hurried for the front door even as four cuffed men were led out.

'Is my sergeant in there? Any sign of the property owner?'

His sense of foreboding grew with a succession of shaken heads. He pushed past and into the manse. 'There's nobody else here,' said the leader of the armed response team. 'The house is clear.'

'Hello? Hello, is anyone there?' A voice reached the two men from beyond the broken basement door.

'What the hell?' The armed response leader brought his weapon up to the ready and advanced towards the broken door while calling into his radio for backup. Even as more of his men returned to the hall, Brogan was intervening.

'It's okay, officer. It's okay. That's my DS. I'd know her nippy voice anywhere.'

Price emerged from the stairway, her arms up and hands linked together, one supporting the other, blood dripping from the bullet wound. 'Police, I'm police,' she called out. Stepping fully into the hall, she kept her hands raised while her boss calmed the situation.

'You're hit,' said Brogan, reaching his sergeant and gently guiding her arms down.

'I'll be fine sir. I hope … and "nippy", really?'

'Get a medic in here now,' he shouted. 'Come on, let's get you sorted out.'

Leaning on her stick, Helen emerged. 'Inspector Brogan, she saved us, saved us all.'

***

Parsol snapped at the men who were using their body weight to steady the ramp they had positioned next to the helicopter's sliding door. 'Come closer, there's still a gap. Move it closer!'

The men responded and Parsol was able to drive his chair out of the helicopter, down the ramp and onto his yacht's helideck. He was immediately followed by his personal guards. He stopped, and as his normally luxuriant and coiffured raft of silvered hair was tugged and blown in the gusting wind, he barked at the pilot. 'Be ready to leave at a moment's notice.' Then he rolled straight ahead, directly towards where the helideck joined the rear of the bridge deck, leaving his pilot and the crew to ensure everything was secured.

'Captain, give me an update,' he said, rolling in through the bridge's wing door.

'Cassiter and the shore party are away, sir. They have located the tunnel and entered. Communication's difficult; they're underground. But one man's been left on their RIB, and we're in touch with him. I understand another is acting as a runner inside the tunnels, ferrying messages back and forth. So we are getting updates sporadically.'

'Good. What progress?'

'They have located and taken control of the assets. There are three prisoners. I am to tell you one is called Cameron.'

'Excellent. At last, things are going our way. Has Cassiter identified our specific requirements?'

'I can't say, sir. No message has come through mentioning requirements or anything specific being found.'

'Get a message to your man on the RIB; I want to know exactly what Cassiter has found. Exactly!'

'Yes, sir.' The captain hurried over to his first officer and issued instructions then returned to Parsol.

'There is something else, sir.'

'Yes?'

'From your son.'

'Ah, good. Another success.'

The captain hesitated and was immediately caught in Parsol's steely gaze.

'No, sir. I'm afraid something has not gone to plan. Your son is fine. He had to withdraw, but his team has been taken by the police. He has asked me to inform you that they have not yet taken Helen Johnson.'

'Hell! What happened? *Merde*! That was the easy part. Get him on the line for me.'

'I can't, sir. He has gone silent, to avoid any risk of being tracked down by the authorities.'

Grim-faced, Parsol powered his chair across the bridge. He paused to look out at the Isle of May, a dark shadow set betwixt a dark sky and sea. He banged his fist against the toughened glass of the bridge's side window. 'I wanted it all finished tonight. Finished! … Well, as long as the boy's safe; she will have to wait.'

'There is another problem, sir.'

Parsol turned his chair. 'What else? Captain, all that matters is Cassiter has secured my goals. And that he now ferries them back here along with

Cameron. Tell him he can dispose of the other two prisoners; they are of no significance.'

'We can't do that, sir.'

'What? Get it done.'

'I'm sorry, sir, really, it can't be done. With the changing tide, the RIB can't get access to the tunnel mouth. We'll have to wait for the tide.'

'How long?'

'I think four or five hours, perhaps a little longer.'

'Impossible. I must retrieve the assets now. Can't you send in my helicopter to collect them?'

'It can't lift directly from the tunnel mouth; I understand there's a cliff overhang above it. It's quite inaccessible by hoist from above. We'll need to get whatever you want into the RIB before we do anything, either ferry it out or airlift it from there. And never mind the tides, the wind is getting up and the forecast is bad for the next twelve hours. High winds, possibly more snow. I need to stand off the island now. Get into open waters and ride it out. Then go back in when the weather eases.'

Parsol motored his chair back across the bridge, stopping directly in front of the captain. 'You will maintain your position here. Under no circumstances may you go off station. We must be here, ready to move as soon as we hear from Cassiter.'

'But, sir—'

'Captain, I insist you maintain this position, no matter what.'

'I must advise against this course of action, sir.'

'Captain, your advice is noted. Now, either you follow my orders and keep us here, ready to take Cassiter and my assets off the island at the first possible instance, or I will have my men remove you from your command, permanently.' He waved to his bodyguards who flexed and bristled. 'I'm sure that young man is more than competent enough to follow my instructions in your stead.' He pointed to the first officer.

'I will do as you instruct, sir. You can rely on me, always,' the captain said, backing down.

'Thank you. Now, I am going to my cabin. Ensure I am kept up to date with any changes.'

***

DI Brogan drew his car to a halt just up from Pete Summer's house. He looked carefully around. All was quiet, though there was a light on in the hallway. He recognised the unmarked police car that was parked immediately outside the door and knew it contained two specialist firearms officers. Things were as he had instructed.

'Are you sure this is where you want to be?' he said.

'Yes, I've arranged with Pete that we can stay here tonight.'

'Well, okay, if you insist.' He turned to look into the rear. 'And you two ladies, wouldn't you be happier in Edinburgh?'

'No,' said Elaine.

'We're with Helen, thanks,' said Grace.

Brogan gave a sigh. 'Okay, I need to get back to Edinburgh now. Those two officers in the car over there will be on duty all night. I'll be back in the morning to speak about what happened.'

'Would you thank her for me please?' said Helen.

'Thank who?'

'DS Price. I know she's seen us as a bit difficult, but when push came to shove, that didn't matter. We're all in her debt.'

'No debts here, Helen. We're all just doing our duty. But I will tell her, and thank you. She'll appreciate it.'

***

Sam, Bill and Angelo were propped against the wall, their hands cable tied behind them. One of Cassiter's guards stood watch over them. The other guards, having taken the prisoners' rucksacks, had emptied out the contents and were now filling them with treasures.

Cassiter had carefully inspected each treasure pile before the guards were allowed to touch them. Following his instructions, they were working systematically, putting the first pile from the first row into the first rucksack, the second pile into the second rucksack and so on. Once the three rucksacks were full, they filled Sam's tool bags with the next two piles.

'Right, we're off,' said the lead guard as he hoisted the rucksack onto his shoulders.

'Be careful at the tunnel junction. I don't want anything dropped down into that pit. Once you get to the tunnel mouth, empty the bags in the same order as you loaded them. I want to see an orderly row of piles when I get down there. Then hurry back here with the bags for more. Shifting all this is going to take some time. Oh, and have the RIB send a message to the ship's captain: when the weather lifts, they will need to send a lot of strong bags across, so we can package this lot for transport out.'

Sam watched the four men leave through the doorway and heard their steps receding down the tunnel. He looked at the remaining guard, then to Cassiter.

'I can see you, Cameron. Don't get any ideas. I've told the guard to shoot first, and I won't ask any questions later.'

'You've got these wrist ties so tight my hands are going to sleep.'

'Good, that'll keep you out of trouble. But believe me, you won't need them for much longer.' Cassiter continued to prowl among the neatly piled rows of treasure; he checked every pile with meticulous attention.

'What exactly are you looking for?' said Sam.

Cassiter did not answer, just kept looking. A little later, his four guards returned and confirmed the weather was worsening. Then they loaded up the next piles into the bags and set off again.

Time passed while Cassiter continued with his methodical inspection; meanwhile his guards had made several more round trips to the tunnel mouth. Cassiter had reached the copper plinths. Ignoring the larger flat but empty one, he focused on the taller one that supported the gold casket. He opened the lid of the gold box.

'Now, what have we got here?'

Angelo leant forwards, straining against the ties that bound his wrists. 'Don't touch that. You are not fit. Do not—'

The guard kicked Angelo's face then struck his head with the butt of his pistol. 'Shut up, you. Another sound, and I'll put a bullet in you.'

'There we are then,' said Cassiter while nodding approvingly to the guard. 'The priest tells the story. This is clearly what I thought it was. Number one on the shopping list. Now, what's next?'

CHAPTER 25

SUNDAY JANUARY 26TH

It was just before one in the morning, and the poor weather had continued unabated. The captain exchanged glances with his first officer. Both knew holding their current position was dangerous. There was no margin for error, a failed engine or loss of steering would have them against the cliffs in a matter of minutes. Even an exceptional wave or gust of wind could present a problem.

The yacht's second officer emerged from the radio shack at the back of the bridge. It was equipped with all the latest communication technology, ensuring that, wherever they were in the world, Eugene Parsol was kept at the centre of everything. Tonight, though, only one thing mattered to him and the other officers. He had been tuned into BBC Radio 4's regular 00.48 broadcast of the Met Office Shipping Forecast. Leaning against the roll of the ship, he lurched across the bridge.

'Well?' said the captain.

'Looking better, sir. The depression should be passing us about now, moving out into the North Sea.'

'And?'

'We should see the wind ease and shift to an easterly as it passes.'

'Thank God for that,' said the captain.

'No sign of any change yet,' said the first officer, who was monitoring the direction that the spray was moving across the ship's bow. Still from the west.'

'Let me know as soon as you detect a shift. Once it's in the east, we'll at least be in the lee of the island. I'd better go and let him know. I'm guessing, as soon as we get any shelter from the wind, he's going to want us to attempt some sort of transfer from the island.'

'Surely, he'll at least wait until daylight,' said the second officer.

The captain gave him a wry look. Then glanced towards the first officer. 'You've got the con now.' He caught the yacht's next roll to launch himself away across the bridge deck.

***

A cry reached up from the depths of the tunnel and into the cave. Cassiter and the guard looked up at once. The faintest sound of a splash followed.

Cassiter cursed then pointed at the guard. 'Stay alert. Those idiots have dropped something at the junction. I'd better see what's going on. Whoever did it is going to pay.' Leaning on his stick, he carefully crossed the rough metal lip of the doorway and stepped into the tunnel beyond. Raised voices made clear that blame was being apportioned ahead of Cassiter's involvement.

The remaining guard watched him go then glared at his prisoners. He approached them, kicked Angelo hard in the leg. 'Stay still, all of you, or I'll shoot. Remember Cassiter's warning.'

The three prisoners averted their gaze. Content with his dominance, the guard took the opportunity he had been patiently waiting for. He hurried across to the remaining piles of treasures, holstered his pistol and stooped to browse, seeking out a few choice jewels that he could hide away.

From the depths of the tunnel, Cassiter's voice rolled up and into the lava cave, echoing and bouncing around as he raged. The guard smiled to himself, content to be free of any blame.

'Sam, can you move your hands towards me?' said Bill in a barely audible whisper.

Sam threw him a questioning look.

'Bit like your man over there, I've been naughty. Those throwing daggers I was admiring? I've got one down my trousers.'

Sam grinned and began to twist round as far as the constraints would allow.

'Down the front.'

'Of course it is,' muttered Sam.

He glanced up at the guard who was absorbed on the far side of the cave, busy trawling through a neat pile of gem-laden rings. Sam and Bill shuffled their bodies round towards each other, and Bill arched his legs towards Sam. 'Go for it.'

Sam delved in, his hand immediately settling on the knife handle. He pulled it out, the blade still securely tucked in its sheath.

Bill swung his body round to present his hands towards Sam and gripped the blade's sheath. 'Pull it out now,' he said.

Sam pulled back and the knife slid free from its sheath. 'Here goes. Hold your hands steady; I'm having to guess,' said Sam.

'I'll position it first,' said Bill. Using his fingers, he guided the blade between his hands and got it resting on the tie that bound him. 'Right, slice now.'

Sam applied pressure through the blade as he shifted his body position to draw the blade across Bill's ties. He felt the bite of the slicing blade, felt the cut and the release of pressure as the tie gave. Sam's hands were tied so tightly that they objected to any further efforts and the blade fell onto the ground between him and Bill.

'Hell,' muttered Sam.

The heavy gold blade landed with a dull metallic clatter, and the guard looked up. He dropped the rings he'd been appraising and hurried across the cave while unholstering his weapon.

'He's mine,' said Bill. He wrapped his fingers round the knife handle and, swinging his arm forwards, launched the blade in a single motion. Even as the guard freed his pistol and lined up for a shot, the blade was flying towards him. He saw something moving, had no idea what it was and never found out. The perfectly balanced and heavy-weighted gold blade plunged into his chest. His finger instinctively contracted, firing off a shot that ricocheted twice before falling spent, harmless and unseen.

Bill hurried to pick up the throwing dagger's twin and used it to free Sam and Angelo's hands.

'Great throw, Bill,' said Sam.

'Knife throwing champion in the SBS, three years running. You don't forget your core skills in a hurry. What now, Sam?'

'We need to get away from here,' he said, stooping to pick up the dead guard's pistol. 'One handgun won't hold that lot off for long.'

'Where to?'

'We can't go down so the only way is up.' Sam paused for a moment, handed Bill the pistol and crossed the cave to the golden casket. He lifted out the tarnished silver goblet and stuck it inside his jacket before lifting one of the lantern torches and pointing Angelo towards the second one. 'Right, let's go.' He stepped out into the tunnel and turned upwards. They set off quickly.

They could already hear a man coming up the tunnel to find out what was happening in the cave.

The tunnel began to take a slight turn.

'You guys go on. I'll delay them a bit then catch you up. For God's sake, find an exit, or we're all done,' said Bill.

'Right,' said Sam. He knew if they were to have any chance, time to find an exit was essential, if one even existed. He put his hand on Bill's shoulder. 'Thank you. If they come up this way, you buying us even a couple of minutes could be crucial. Don't wait any longer than that; there's either an exit or there isn't.'

'Clear off the pair of you,' said Bill, with a grin. He lay down on the tunnel floor waiting for all comers.

Angelo put one of the lanterns down for Bill.

'No, take it with you. Dark's better for me now.'

The priest nodded and followed Sam up the tunnel.

After a little more than a hundred paces, the tunnel came to an abrupt halt.

'What now?' said Angelo.

'We hope for a break.' Sam inspected the tunnel's end face; it was solid natural rock. Knowing the Templars' skill at concealment, he tapped the surface firmly with his knuckle, winced at the pain and recognised it was truly solid. Reaching up, he continued his inspection, the higher part of the end wall was equally solid as were the sidewalls.

'What do you think?' said Angelo.

Sam tilted his head up. Here, the roof height had raised slightly, though he could still reach up and touch it. In the light of his lantern, it seemed consistent with the walls and floor. He did a circle, taking in the whole of the tunnel roof. 'Looks solid to me.'

'There's no way out then,' said Angelo.

'Seems that way.' After lowering his head and allowing his neck to rest a few moments, Sam felt motivated to check one more time. He looked up and turned another circle. This time, he saw something that raised his suspicions. Stepping back down the tunnel a few paces, he looked at the roof then returned to the tunnel's end.

'Angelo, would you give me a boost up? I need to check again. It's just a suspicion, but a section of the roof here appears just too consistent. I need to check more closely.'

Angelo bent, gripped Sam round the thighs and lifted him up. Sam bent his head to avoid butting the roof.

'That's great; just hold me steady for a moment.' Sam moved his hand across the roof, rapping his knuckles on the stone. He was beginning to write off his suspicion, when in one corner of the tunnel roof, the reverberation changed. He rapped again, checking the extent of the anomaly.

'Let me down, Angelo; we've got something here.'

Back on two feet, Sam looked up at the inconspicuous corner of roof. He raised his lantern high. 'There's something up there. That bit of roof is artificial.'

'Can you open it?'

'There's no sign of any controls or latches, so the answer is no. Only, let me try something, it's a long shot, but what the hell. It's all we've got right now.'

Dropping to his hands and knees, Sam directed the full light of his lantern into the corners. 'Interesting,' he said, then stood and focused the light and his attention on the junction of wall and roof. 'Very interesting.'

Sam handed Angelo his lantern then positioned himself in the corner close beneath the false roof. 'Stay well back, Angelo; I have no idea what will happen here.'

He spread his legs, positioning his feet against inconspicuous spots at the junction of wall and floor. Raising his arms, he reached for the spots he had identified high in the walls, his body describing a saltire. 'Here goes nothing,' he said and twisted his ankles to apply pressure against the chosen spots where wall met floor; simultaneously, he pressed hard with his hands.

Nothing happened. Sam tried again. 'Come on, move. Open, damn you. Open!' He pressed a third time and heard a momentary grinding sound above. He immediately moved away and looked up to the corner, nothing had shifted.

'What were you trying to do?'

'I thought they may have employed an early forerunner of the opening mechanism used in the tunnel between St Bernard's and the manse. Maybe I'm wrong, or maybe it's just that it hasn't been opened in seven hundred years. It's bound to be a bit sticky; even *their* engineering wasn't infallible.'

Suddenly, they heard the report of a weapon being discharged, four shots in rapid succession, a cry of pain then a roar as an automatic weapon emptied its entire magazine in an uncontrolled frenzy.

'They're here.'

'Sounds like it,' said Sam. He returned his attention to the roof. 'It's a panel, I know it. Just stuck.' Moving underneath, he jumped up and thumped the roof, then repeated the action with all his effort. Turning his attention back to the wall, he repeated the opening trigger procedure. With a grind and groan, the stone panel started to hinge down.

'Keep back!' Sam shouted and threw himself to one side.

A panel, only twelve inches wide and thirty-six deep, had hinged down. Sam raised his lantern to look more closely. 'The reverse of the panel is a flagstone. It must be the floor of a building. Get ready, I'll go up and check it's safe, you just follow me up.'

More gunshots echoed up from the tunnel, another cry then running feet. Bill appeared. As he entered the lantern's light, Sam saw Bill was soaked in blood. It looked like it was coming from a head graze.

'Okay?' said Sam.

'Fine, I've had worse,' said Bill, touching his head then pointing to a hole in the arm of his jacket. 'Two hits, but I've put two of them down. Ran out of ammo, or I'd have taken the lot out. If that's the exit, get up there now; they'll be here any moment.'

'We'd better get you out first. Come on we'll lift you.'

Bill patted his chest and waved a hand around his wounds. 'Thanks, Sam, but I'll never manage through that hole in the time we've got. Just go, check it's all clear up there, and I'll try to boost Angelo up.'

The men hugged one another.

'Now get away.'

Standing beneath the opening, Sam jumped up. Catching the edge of the hatch, he pulled himself up then stopped. 'Hell, I don't fit.' He dropped back to the floor, reached inside his jacket and pulled out the tarnished silver chalice. Without any ceremony and before Angelo could stop him, he tossed it up through the opening. They heard it land with a thin clang on the flagstone floor above.

Sam jumped again, pulled himself up and levered his head and chest through the hatch. Above, everything was in darkness, cold and fresh. The only place it could be was within the ruin of St Adrian's Priory. Just for a moment, as he sought to push himself up and out, he heard a strange crackling noise in the cold night air, quite distinct, then it was gone. In that instant, he felt hands grip his legs then pull hard. He resisted, but more hands gripped him, and suddenly, he was falling back into the tunnel.

Lying prone on the tunnel floor, he looked up. A guard loomed over him, his pistol pointing directly at Sam's head. A second guard held Angelo and Bill at gunpoint.

A walking stick struck across Sam's face, instantly raising a wheal.

'Cameron, you have plagued me for long enough. Consider that your last hurrah.' Cassiter prodded Sam in the chest with his stick. 'Understand, the only reason you and your friends aren't dead right now after this little trick of yours, is I'm three men down.'

He directed his remaining guards. 'You men, get him up, and get them all back down the tunnel. They can start carrying the bags for us.'

Sam looked up at Cassiter. 'Bill's in no condition to carry anything, he's been shot twice.'

'If he can't carry, he's no good to me. Let's have him shot a third time, and get it over with.'

'Whoa there. Steady on, man. I've got one good arm; I can still carry.'

Cassiter looked down at Sam. 'You see, Cameron, learn. As long as you can carry, you can breathe. Stop carrying; stop breathing. Now, tell me, where does that hatch lead?'

'Outside somewhere, I don't know. You pulled me back in before I could check it out.'

'No matter then. Let's go. Hurry.'

'At least let's bind up the man's wounds; he'll work all the better for that.'

'No, he'll manage as he is, or he'll die.'

Under the cautious watch of the armed guards, Sam got to his feet, and they set off down the tunnel.

They passed the entrance to the cave and kept walking. When they stepped past a dead guard, Cassiter stooped to retrieve the dropped machine gun. He picked up a second weapon from another body further on. At the Y-junction, they all stopped.

'The remaining bags are already on the other side of the junction. Guards, you two go round first and get ready for the prisoners to follow you. I will guard them until they are back with you in the other tunnel branch. Then I'll follow. Let's move quickly now.'

The two guards slipped round the sharp tunnel junction and called out that they were ready for Cassiter to send the prisoners round. Sam went first and was quickly followed by Angelo.

'You next,' said Cassiter.

'Sorry, mate. I don't think I can make it. I've lost too much blood,' said Bill from where he had slumped, propped up against the tunnel wall, his legs outstretched.

'Your choice and your loss,' said Cassiter, raising his weapon and aiming directly at Bill's chest. 'Get up and carry your bag or die right now.' He firmed his grip on the machine gun and gently squeezed the trigger. Nothing happened. Cassiter looked at the weapon in disgust, then, as Bill laughed, he threw it down and produced his own pistol, steadied and aimed.

'Hold hard there! Do not fire your weapon. We have you covered.'

Cassiter spun round, arcing his pistol to aim up into the tunnel.

'Put your weapon down now, or you are dead.'

Defiant, Cassiter strained to see who was challenging him from what, moments before, had seemed a deserted dead end. All he became aware of was two red dots dancing gently back and forth from the outstretched sleeves of his jacket to his chest and back again.

Cassiter took an involuntary step back, away from the red dots, and tripped on Bill's outstretched legs. With a gasp, Cassiter tumbled backwards. He dropped his weapon and fell towards the abyss.

Cassiter's desperate grasping hands, powered by the cruel grip of his fingers, managed to catch and clasp Bill's hand as he fell.

His plunge was stopped before it could start when Bill instinctively gripped the falling man's hand. Cassiter dangled over the edge, legs waving, his weight dragging on Bill, quickly pulling him flat to the floor of the tunnel, his head lying over the lip, giving him an unwelcome view beyond

Cassiter and down into the chasm.

'Pull me up, man. Pull me up!'

'My shoulder's too weak.'

Cassiter's fingers locked tighter against Bill's in an unbreakable vice-like grip. He twisted his head up and round, and could just see Sam leaning out over the lip of the other branch tunnel, kneeling and reaching his hand out.

'Here, take my hand,' said Sam.

Cassiter stretched up and over but couldn't quite reach. Fingertips just touching. He looked towards Bill again. 'Take the weight, man; get me up a bit more. Pull!'

Fighting the pain of his wounds, Bill strained to lift Cassiter higher. His face was pulled hard against the tunnel's rock floor. Locked in position, Bill saw Cassiter reach up again for Sam's hand. He could see Sam leaning out and down in a desperate bid to reach the man.

For the first time, there was fear in Cassiter's eyes, then desperation as he turned his gaze to where his hand gripped Bill's. There, blood had started to flow more vigorously from Bill's untended wounds. It was flowing down his arm, over his hand and now seeped between their interlocked fingers.

Cassiter's grip was slipping. 'Please, please save me,' he shrieked, their fingers beginning to slide apart.

Sam made a desperate lunge and was himself grabbed by Angelo just in time to stop him falling headfirst.

There was no safety net for Cassiter. His hand parted from Bill's. He screamed in fear and fell, twisting and bumping into the black. The screams ended before a distant splash recorded his end.

Heads hanging over the lips of their respective tunnels, Sam and Bill eyed one another. They lay still for a long moment. Killing in action was something they both understood and had done whenever necessity demanded. But failing to save a life, any life, was always hard to take.

The sound of rapidly receding footfalls signed the exit of the two remaining guards. Clearly, they did not fancy slugging it out with a new force, particularly now Cassiter was gone.

A new sound emerged from behind Bill to replace the retiring footsteps. A slow handclap. 'Well, that was very moving. Very poignant. And I have to say, Sam, it's exactly why you were never invited to make the leap from the military to our service. Too much heart. Far too much.'

Sam rose to his feet at the sound of the familiar, languid tones. He paused for a long moment, composing his thoughts. Then he slipped round the tunnel edge to rejoin Bill who was sitting on the floor, somebody in black combat fatigues crouched beside him, applying first aid. Beyond was a group of figures in identical black, mostly armed with automatic weapons, and at their head was a very familiar face.

'Rupert! Where in God's name did you spring from?' demanded Sam.

A squad of men began to move forwards, and Sam put up a hand to halt them. Reaching back round, he beckoned to Angelo who quickly joined him. They stepped aside, and the squad of men advanced to the tunnel junction where, one by one, they slipped round and began the pursuit of Cassiter's remaining men.

'Sam Cameron, don't we always meet in the most interesting places?' The rolling female voice, with its rich American accent, shifted Sam's attention. He strained to see the black-dressed figure now standing next to Rupert.

'What on earth are you two doing here?'

'Well, Sam, that's not the most effusive thank you I've ever received, but I'll put that down to stress.' Rupert Peterson stepped forwards, offering his hand. 'Glad you all made it; Tracy and I thought it was a bit touch-and-go for a while.'

'How did you get here?'

'Why, you opened the entrance into the priory for us, honey. Just as well you did, otherwise you were on your own,' said Tracy, smiling. Sam marvelled that the CIA agent always contrived to look glamorous, no matter what the circumstances.

'Are these people our friends? I don't understand,' said Angelo.

'That depends how you classify your friends. I think we're on the same side, mostly.'

'Come, come, Sam; you can do better than that. Now, it's time to get you all out of here, don't you think?'

'There are things, important things, they must not be left,' said Angelo.

'I understand, sir. Don't you worry; we've got it all under control.'

'No, Angelo is right. This is an archaeological superstore – everything needs to be logged and recorded. There's so much here.'

A foldout stretcher had been produced and men were already carrying Bill away. Suddenly, Sam and Angelo were being hurried up the tunnel.

'Follow me, boys. Plenty of time to talk once we are in the fresh air,' Tracy's voice reached back to them as she led the upward march.

More armed men were on guard at the treasure cave's entrance. Angelo made a lunge for it, determined to return to the artefacts that had so entranced his before. He had no chance.

'Come along, Angelo. Sam, please keep Angelo on track, would you be so good?' Rupert's voice was languid, so relaxed it almost seemed disinterested, yet the squad of black-clad men around him took every word as a hard order. Sam and Angelo were allowed no further opportunities to delay the procession.

Just as Sam took his turn to scale the rope ladder now rigged from the opening in the tunnel's roof, the sound of distant gunfire rolled up the tunnel towards them. He looked up to see Rupert's face peering down.

'Sounds like our boys have caught up with the remnant. That won't take long to tidy up. Come on up, Sam, plenty to talk about.'

Emerging through the open hatch in the flagstoned floor, Sam took in the scene. Rupert was not short on manpower, and torch-lit shadows moved everywhere. He saw Bill being carried away. Under the supervision of two black-clad men, Angelo was reluctantly following the stretcher.

In the organised confusion, and as electric torches flashed this way and that, Sam started to look about the flagstoned remains of the priory floor.

'Looking for something, old man?' said Rupert, coming to stand beside Sam.

'No,' said Sam.

'Oh, it seemed that you were.'

'No. Other than an explanation for all this.' He swept his arms out. 'Where did you come from? Why?'

'Sam, honey, you don't think I'd leave you in trouble, do you?' said Tracy, appearing from the shadows to stand at Rupert's side.

'I'm afraid I'm going to have to search you. Nothing personal, you understand. Just protocol,' said Rupert.

Sam didn't bother resisting. He knew Rupert would simply have pulled in sufficient muscle to facilitate his request.

'What's this?' said Rupert, pulling a slim gold plaque from Sam's jacket. He held it up and Tracy shone her torch on it. 'Very heavy, I think it might be gold.' The pair peered more closely at the artefact.

Sam had forgotten all about the piece that he had pocketed earlier. 'Just a memento I picked up. Actually, I thought it might make a nice gift for Helen. She's been having a hard time of it.'

Tracy shone the light into Sam's face. 'That's sweet. How is my special friend?'

'Not so good; she was shot recently.'

Tracy nodded. She knew all about the incident. She played the torch back over the gold piece, taking it from Rupert's hand. 'You know, Rupert, that's sure as hell not what we're looking for. What say we let it go? Our little thank you for all their trouble.'

Rupert looked again at the small gold tablet. 'Certainly. As long as we are all clear it didn't come from here.'

Tracy slipped the gold plaque back into Sam's jacket pocket. 'Remember, we've never seen it. Okay?'

'Fine by me—'

'We've got a movement on the yacht. Over.' Rupert's radio crackled and spat out its message.

'What's happening? Over,' said Rupert.

'The helicopter is preparing for take-off. A man in a wheelchair has just embarked. Over.'

Rupert looked towards Tracy. 'Parsol. He's making a run for it.'

'This one's for me, I think,' she said. Reaching up to the side of her face, she pivoted down a discreet little mic and began issuing instructions.

Rupert gave a shrug of his shoulders and leant in towards Sam. 'I sometimes think she overcomplicates matters. I'd have just waited for it to land. In weather like this, it won't go for much more than three hours without refuelling.' He straightened up as Tracy ended her call.

'Come on, you should see this,' she said, leading them out from the shelter of the ruined priory and up towards the crest of the hill behind.

As soon as she stepped onto the rabbit-cropped grass outside the ruin, the sound of snail shells crackling underfoot began. *That* was the sound I heard earlier, thought Sam.

At the top, they stood braced against the buffeting wind, waiting.

'I think you might have been looking for this, old man.' Rupert produced the goblet from inside his jacket. Sam reached for it, and Rupert pulled it back. 'Sorry, this is confiscated.'

'How did you know?'

'Well, Sam, we are HM's Secret Service. It's our job to know. And let's face it; if you're involved in a great big explosives and gunfire incident in Edinburgh, of all places, we're going to notice.'

'And let me tell you, honey, blowing up half a mountainside in Crete and suddenly your friends at the Vatican Bank are solvent and restored as big international banking players again … it's something we needed to know about.'

Rupert stepped closer to Sam. 'Once one of our people in the Vatican had looked into it all and reported back, it was clear that the really big prize had not been found yet. Whoever managed to get their hands on the relics would command enormous power and influence. Some national governments might have been marginalised, even swept away. So we had to watch over you to ensure no harm came to you.'

'Or to the Templar relics,' said Tracy.

'I'm sure I don't know what you're talking about. The finds in these tunnels are an archaeological treasure trove. It's our history; you can't just take it.'

'I'm afraid we can, and we are. Your finds represent a threat to national security,' said Rupert.

'Both our national securities,' said Tracy.

'Nonsense.'

'You think? I don't know if that silver cup in Rupert's jacket is the Holy Grail or just some junk pot. And you know what? I don't care one way or the other. I do know a quarter of the world's population venerate its concept and a fair proportion of them would go to war to protect it or liberate it.'

'And another quarter of the world would reject it. And plenty of them would be happy to fight to destroy it,' said Rupert.

'That little cup, real or otherwise, has the power to trigger conflicts and bloodshed like we haven't seen since the world wars. And believe me,' Tracy's voice suddenly took on a hard edge, 'that ain't happening on our watch.'

Sam saw Rupert's nod of agreement. Then all three switched their attention as Rupert's radio crackled into life again.

'It's taking off now, sir. Helicopter is clear of the deck. Over.'

Tracy walked a few yards along the hillcrest and stooped to shake the shoulder of a kneeling figure who Sam had not previously noticed. Then she hurried back to join them.

'Okay, now let's nail this problem my way. Here comes the show.' She linked one arm with Rupert's, flicked her mic back down beside her lips and turned to look over the hillcrest.

Nothing happened for a moment, then a helicopter appeared, rising slowly, fighting for its position against the still gusty wind. It started to turn, setting up to run south across the Forth.

'Now!' Tracy shouted into her mic. 'Now!'

Her operative fired the shoulder-launched missile, sending it off with a roar and a bright flash. That initial light had scarcely diminished before the missile met its target, converting the aircraft into a yet brighter ball of flame. It dropped from the sky a short distance from the yacht.

There was a gleam of triumph in Tracy's eye. 'That's how you fix a problem, yes, sir!' she shouted to the wind. 'That's how you fix it.' She turned to accept Rupert's congratulations.

A minute or two later, the three turned to head back towards the priory.

'Is that it?' said Sam.

'Hell, no. Rupert's got a press release to issue about the tragic loss of reclusive billionaire industrialist Eugene Parsol in a helicopter crash. And he's got to establish an exclusion zone while the rescue services clean up. Just so happens there's an American navy ship on a courtesy visit to Scotland. It's at anchor in the Forth right now. I believe it's getting ready to come right over to lend a hand.'

'We've jointly agreed on a safe home for the treasures, where nobody will find them in a thousand years,' said Rupert.

Sam scowled at them both. 'You think? The previous owners thought the same thing. You can't hide history forever.'

'I think we can, honey.' Tracy gave Sam a long sweet smile. 'Now, I've got things to do. Rupert, can you move Sam along?'

'Come on, old man; let's get you home.'

Daylight was coming. The unseen sun, having started its rise behind the clouds, was forcing just enough light through to signal the dawn.

It took less than ten minutes to cross to the other side of the island, pass the visitor centre and climb the slope beyond. There, on the higher ground, was one of the few level spots sufficiently wide to form a helipad. Designed only for medical emergency evacuations, this morning it was hosting a black Wildcat helicopter. Sam could see Angelo inside. He guessed Bill was there too.

'Go on, man, that'll get you home in no time. Oh and remember the Official Secrets Act,' said Rupert.

Sam gave him a wry look. 'That might work on me. But I don't think that trick will silence a priest like Angelo; he's not British.'

'No, of course not. But there are people in the Vatican who think like us. They'll make sure he stays quiet.'

Rupert thrust out his hand. 'Sam, I'm sorry, truly. One day, I hope we can work together on something that doesn't exploit you, or Helen.'

Sam shook his hand. 'Somehow, I don't see that happening.'

***

Pete Summers opened his front door and beckoned his visitors inside. He glanced towards the two policemen who sat in their car, watchful and alert. The clerical visitors might not normally have raised much interest, but Brogan had warned them to trust nothing and that there may be a religious element involved. Two priests appearing in the early hours sporting long black winter cloaks was not normal for North Berwick. A discreet sign from Pete confirmed things were in order, and they settled back down.

'Come in, please. You're both most welcome,' said Pete.

'Any word?' asked Francis, hurrying in and stamping his feet against the cold.

'We've not heard from Sam. Anything from Angelo yet?'

'No, Xavier has had no word either,' said Francis.

'Come into the living room, quietly though. Everyone's been up all night – Grace and Elaine have just dropped off.' Pete led the two priests through into the living room and as far from the two sleeping women as possible.

'Where's Helen?' said Francis.

Pete pointed into the garden, where they could see Helen looking out across the beach towards the northern sky. There, the darkness had not quite surrendered to the rising sun.

'My goodness, she must be cold,' said Francis.

'I think so, but when I went out to her, she sent me away.'

'Look, she's shivering.'

'Why is she out there?'

'I'm not sure. Watching, I think. I thought I'd persuaded her to come in a little while ago but then something odd happened.'

'Odd?'

'Yes, there was an explosion to the north ... roughly where you would expect to find the Isle of May.'

'Good Lord. Come on, Xavier,' said Francis.

In silence, the two old priests stepped out through the glass doors. Pete quietly closed the doors and watched from behind the glass.

Helen sensed their presence but did not acknowledge them, continuing to maintain her vigil across the water. The wind had shifted direction and had begun to ease a little, but the high waves and strong tide were still a risk. It would be very dangerous to try to cross the Forth in a RIB under such conditions. She prayed the explosion was unrelated to Sam's party, but how could it be?

The snow flurries rallied again into a steady fall and reduced visibility further. Now she could not see much further than the waterline at the end of the beach. She shivered and drew her jacket tight around her, but the wind cut through it, and the landing snowflakes quickly melted to soak into her skin.

Francis nudged Xavier and waved him further forwards. The two old priests stepped up, one to either side of Helen, and each raised a hand to envelop her in a sweep of their cloaks. She did not push her friends away and silently welcomed the blocking of wind and wet. They could feel her shivering as she continued to stare out into the snow.

A movement amid the falling snow caught Helen's attention. She stiffened; the old priests felt it and saw her straining to see. They looked but could see nothing.

'There's something out there,' she said.

'I see nothing,' said Xavier.

'Something is coming, look.' Helen forced a hand out from beneath the protective layers of cloak and pointed straight ahead.

'That's too high, Helen; that's the sky,' said Francis.

'Listen, what's that?'

A moving shadow showed blurry through the falling snow, followed by the snow-muffled thunder of engines.

'It's a helicopter,' said Helen, a note of disappointment tinging her voice.

'Yes, and it's coming our way,' said Francis.

The black-bodied helicopter suddenly burst clear of the snow and paused, hovering over the beach. No amount of snow could muffle the roaring power of the engines now. Grace and Elaine hurried out into the garden.

'What's happening? What is it?' said Grace.

Faces appeared at the window of the hovering Wildcat's side-panel door and hands waved.

Helen pointed up at the helicopter. 'It's Sam! He's waving to us.' She stepped clear of the protective cloaks and waved her arms enthusiastically.

'Angelo! Xavier, I see Angelo; he's fine.'

Then the helicopter advanced and passed overhead with a deafening roar. As it disappeared behind the house, the noise quickly faded. They all hugged and talked at once while moving back into the warmth of the house.

As Pete pressed shut the glass doors, Helen's phone signalled receipt of a message.

"Landing East Fortune Airfield shortly. Ready for collection. xx"

'How long to get to East Fortune Airfield?' said Helen.

'Ten minutes, with a police escort,' said Pete.

Helen smiled. 'Time to go then.'

ABOUT THE AUTHOR

D. C. Macey is an author and lecturer based in the United Kingdom.

A first career in the Merchant Navy saw Macey's early working life devoted to travelling the globe. In the process, it gave an introduction to the mad mix of beauty, kindness, cruelty and inequality that is the human experience everywhere. Between every frantic costal encounter was a trip across the ocean, which brought the contrast of tranquil moments and offered time for reading, writing and reflection. Those roving days came to a close, however, with Macey serving as a ship's officer in the North Sea oil industry.

Several years working in business made it apparent that Macey's greatest commercial skill was the ability to convert tenners into fivers, effortlessly and unerringly - a skill that ensured Macey had the unwelcome experience of encountering those darker aspects of life that lie beneath the veneer of our developed world and brought fleeting glimpses into the shadows where bad things lurk.

Eventually, life's turbulence, domestic tragedy and impending poverty demanded a change of course. As a result, the past decade and more has been spent in lecturing and producing predominantly corporate media resources, so allowing Macey the opportunity to return to the written word.

Throughout it all Macey is certain that a happy home and laughter have proven time and again to be the best protection against life's trials.

• • •

For more information: **contact@dcmacey.com** and visit: **www.dcmacey.com**

Printed in Poland
by Amazon Fulfillment
Poland Sp. z o.o., Wrocław

53792710R00195